The Chalice of Death by Robert Silverberg—The promise of eternal life for some, of instant death for others; could anyone, even an Earthman, master its amazing secret?

Down to the Worlds of Men by Alexei Panshin—It was their time of final testing, and, taken from the safety of the Ships, set down on a hostile, primitive world, each of the chosen must find a separate path to survival. . . .

Blind Alley by Isaac Asimov—It was a unique moment in Galactic History, the first and only encounter with an intelligent race of non-Humans. But now that they'd been found, what was the Empire going to do with them?

Honorable Enemies by Poul Anderson—Could Dominic Flandry turn the diplomatic tables on an opponent with the power to anticipate his every thought?

Here are the stories of rulers fighting to preserve their power, of rebels fighting to seize it, fascinating tales from—

ISAAC ASIMOV'S WONDERFUL WORLDS OF SCIENCE FICTION #1
INTERGALACTIC EMPIRES

Great Science Fiction from SIGNET

INTERGALACTIC EMPIRES

Isaac Asimov's Wonderful Worlds of Science Fiction #1

Edited by
ISAAC ASIMOV, MARTIN H. GREENBERG,
AND CHARLES G. WAUGH

A SIGNET BOOK

NEW AMERICAN LIBRARY

Copyright © 1983 by Isaac Asimov, Martin H. Greenberg, and Charles G. Waugh

ACKNOWLEDGMENTS

"Chalice of Death" by Robert Silverberg. Copyright © 1957 by Royal Publications Inc.
Reprinted by permission of the author.

"Orphan of the Void" by Lloyd Biggle, Jr. Copyright © 1960 by Ziff-Davis Publishing
Company. From FANTASTIC SCIENCE FICTION STORIES. Included in the author's
collection, THE METALLIC MUSE (Doubleday, 1972). Reprinted by permission of
Kirby McCauley, Ltd.

"Down to the Worlds of Men" by Alexei Panshin. Copyright © 1963 by Galaxy
Publishing Corporation. Reprinted by permission of the author.

"Ministry of Disturbance" by H. Beam Piper. Copyright © 1958 by Street & Smith
Publications. Reprinted by permission of the agents for the author's estate, the Scott
Meredith Literary Agency, Inc., 845 Third Ave., New York, NY 10022.

"Blind Alley" by Isaac Asimov. Copyright © 1945 by Street & Smith Publications;
Copyright renewed © 1973 by Isaac Asimov. Reprinted by permission of the author.

"A Planet Named Shayol" by Cordwainer Smith. Copyright © 1961 by Galaxy Publishing Corporation. Reprinted by permission of the agents for the author's estate, the
Scott Meredith Literary Agency, Inc., 845 Third Ave., New York, NY 10022.

"Diabologic" by Eric Frank Russell. Copyright © 1955 by Street & Smith Publications.
Reprinted by permission of the agents for the author's estate, the Scott Meredith
Literary Agency, Inc., 845 Third Ave., New York, NY 10022.

"Fighting Philosopher" by E. B. Cole. Copyright © 1954 by Street & Smith Publications.
Reprinted by permission of the author.

"Honorable Enemies" by Poul Anderson. Copyright © 1951 by Columbia Publications;
copyright renewed. Reprinted by permission of the Scott Meredith Literary Agency
Inc., 845 Third Avenue, New York, NY 10022.

CONTENTS

INTRODUCTION: EMPIRES

The Latin term *imperator* was used by the Romans as a title for the leader of an army. It is roughly equivalent to our "general." Eventually, it came to be applied, in particular, to the supreme leader of all the armies of Rome; to the "generalissimo," so to speak.

By the first century B.C., the Roman realm was coming, more and more, under the influence of a single man, with the Senate and the other government officials little better than puppets. The single ruler held his power from the fact that the army was loyal to him and would obey his commands. Therefore the most important and realistic title he held was *imperator*, and from Augustus Caesar on, we no longer speak of the Roman Republic, but of the Roman Imperium; or, to use the English distortion of the term, the Roman "Empire." What's more, the *imperator*, by the same distortion, became emperor."

The Roman Empire arose from the gradual conquest of the entire Mediterranean world by the Romans, who originally ruled a small section of central Italy. Because of this, the term "empire" came to refer to any group of different peoples (or cultures, or nations) ruled by a people (or culture, or nation) that has conquered or absorbed them all. Such an empire is usually ruled by a single person who is a member of the conquering unit, and in the empire the conquerors usually have special privileges.

The term has been extended to all such realms, both before and after Roman times.

The first empire in history is usually considered to be the Akkadian Empire, established by Sargon of Agade about 2320 B.C. The smallest realm commonly given the name is perhaps the Athenian Empire, which, for about fifty years, ruled the shores of the Aegean Sea.

On the whole, empires cannot extend their rule without limit, since problems of communication and administration increase rapidly with increasing area. The Roman Empire itself reached its maximum extent about A.D. 125, at which time it was rather overextended. It moved to the defense and contracted very slowly over a period of thirteen centuries before the last scrap of it (the city of Trebizond in Asia Minor) was submerged.

Still, as we move forward through history, from the time of Sargon of Agade onward, we find that technology slowly (but rather steadily) advances. With technological advance, the ability to conquer, defend, and administer an empire increases, so that, on the whole, the size and power of empires has increased with time.

Prior to modern times, the largest and most spectacular empire was that of the Mongols. Starting from almost nothing, Genghis Khan and his generals conquered a tract of land that is roughly marked out by the modern lands of the Soviet Union, China, Afghanistan, Iran, and Iraq. What's more, the colossal task was all done in fifty years. (However, the Mongol Empire broke apart, and most of it vanished, in another fifty years.)

In modern times, empires have grown larger still, especially since advances in the science of navigation have made it possible for a nation to control the coasts of distant continents, and to work its way inward wherever weakness exists. The first noncontiguous empire (a realm connected by sealanes rather than by a continuous stretch of land) was that of Portugal, established about A.D. 1500.

The largest, most populous, and most powerful empire of all time was of this kind. It was the British Empire, which reached its maximum extent after World War I, at which time it controlled roughly one-quarter of the land area and the population of the entire planet. The British Empire was still at its maximum extent in 1945 at the end of World War II, and in the most amazing reversal in history, that empire vanished completely by twenty years after that date. The British, without military defeat, simply gave it up, as something they could no longer reasonably retain.

Nowadays, the age of old-fashioned empires is over. The large nations of today are either more or less homogeneous in culture (China, India, Indonesia) or they are "federations"—that is, unions of equal parts (at least in theory). Thus, the United States is a federation of states; Canada of provinces; the Soviet Union of socialist republics; and so on. Similarly, the League of Nations and the United Nations are examples of (very weak) federations of nations.

And where, in all this, does science fiction come in? Well, it is inevitable that science fiction writers look forward to a world in which the human species continues to increase its range.

Starting from a small patch of land in east-central Africa, the various hominids, culminating in *Homo sapiens sapiens*, have spread out over all the Earth's surface. It seems inevitable to the ever-romantic mind of the science fiction writer that we must now spread first to the Moon, then to the remainder of the Solar system, and finally to the stars.

And with that expansion, there is bound to be the notion of expanding political systems.

What kind? It would be pleasant if, along with the various advances of technology that *must* accompany (and, indeed, precede) expansion through space, there should be an equivalent evolution of political systems, administrative techniques, societal and economic devices.

Easier said than done. The empire remains the favorite symbol of the large state, and it has taken over the imagination of the science fiction world. Nor is it the most recent empires, after the fashion of the British, that are used as models. Rather, the mood, the atmosphere, the paraphernalia is that of ancient and medieval times.

For this, I myself am largely responsible. There were, before my time, stories about Earthmen meeting other intelligences, or living on other worlds as well as Earth, of conquering or being conquered, but the first attempt to write a series of such stories with a rational historical background, and to achieve considerable popularity as a result, was mine. It was my foundation series, which began appearing in 1942, that set the fashion.

In 1942, to be sure, the European empires, particularly the British, were still in existence, and seemed likely to be eternal, but they didn't influence me. I modeled my "Galactic Empire" (a phrase I think I was the first to use) quite consciously on the Roman Empire.

Ever since then, other science fiction writers have been following the fashion, and have written series of their own after the fashion of the foundation series. In fact, in the late 1970s the

Galactic Empire reached the movies in the enormously popular *Star Wars*, which, here and there, offered rather more than a whiff of the Foundation. (No, I don't mind. Imitation is the sincerest form of flattery, and I certainly imitated Edward Gibbon, so I can scarcely object if someone imitates me.)

In this book, then, we have nine stories by nine authors illustrating nine different versions of Galactic Imperial history, since each is part of a series of at least three stories. One story included is, inevitably, one of mine, and it happens to be one that is the least typical of my empire stories.

I hope that in reading the stories in this anthology, you will enjoy comparing and contrasting the manner in which top-notch writers use the imperial theme to consider problems that, in sheer size at least, transcend those that would have involved merely planetary empires.

Isaac Asimov

CYCLES

The idea of Galactic Empires appears in science fiction at least as early as Robert William Cole's *The Struggle for Empire* (1900). But it was not until 1942 that Isaac Asimov introduced the idea of imperial cycles in the first of a series of stories now known as the Foundation Trilogy. Since then his conception has become part of a widely accepted framework for the successful future history of humanity.

Donald A. Wollheim (*The Universe Makers*, 1971) sees this cosmogony as having eight steps: expansion throughout the solar system, followed by first flights to the stars, the rise of Galactic Empire, the golden age, the decline and fall of empire, the interregnum, the rise of another more permanent empire, and the ultimate challenge to God. Of course, everything doesn't fit into this sequence and everyone doesn't use, or agree with, all of the steps. Yet many writers continue to employ imperial cycles, and it is with that concept that this section is concerned.

For "The Chalice of Death," the first of three "Calvin M. Knox" stories eventually collected as *Lest We Forget Thee Earth* (1958), Robert Silverberg constructs a variation of the hidden "second foundation" theme. But he also adds on Barsoomian-like aliens and a Wellsian-like portrayal of a degenerate future earth.

"Orphan of the Void," by Lloyd Biggle, Jr., deals with the odd little things that can sometimes bring an empire crashing down. It is the first of three novellas ("Monument," *Analog Science Fiction*, June 1961, and "Still, Small Voice," ibid., April 1961, are the others) that depict the transformation and humanization of a self-serving Terran Federation into a nurturant force for the development and democratization of primitive peoples throughout the galaxy. The original series has never been published as a book because the last of the stories was expanded into *The Still, Small Voice of Trumpets* in 1968. However, that novel was followed by a sequel (*The World Menders*) in 1974.

Later expanded into a Nebula Award-winning novel (*Rite of Passage*, 1968), "Down to the Worlds of Men" is part of Alexei Panshin's Great Ships/Colonies series. Earth's attempt at creating a Terran Empire has collapsed and the few remaining transport ships represent the last vestiges of civilization. Their complex relationships with the colonies are partly altruistic, partly utilitarian, and, as this story suggests, partly self-serving.

Chalice of Death

by *Robert Silverberg*

CHAPTER 1

It was mid-day on Jorus, and Hallam Navarre, Earthman to the Court, had overslept. It had been a long night for the courtier, the night before: a night much filled with strange out-system wines and less strange women.

But duty was duty. And, as the Overlord's Earthman, Navarre was due at the throne room by the hour when the blue rays of the sun lit the dial in Central Plaza. Wearily, he sprang from bed, washed, dabbed depilator on his gleaming head to assure it the hairlessness that was the mark of his station, and caught the ramp heading downstairs.

A jetcab lurked hopefully in the street. Navarre sprang in and snapped, "To the Palace!"

"Yessir." The driver was a Dergonian, his coarse skin a gentle green. He jabbed down on the control stud and the cab sprang forward.

The Dergonian took a twisting, winding route through Jorus City—past the multitudinous stinks of the Street of the Fish-mongers, where the warm blue sunlight filtered in everywhere, where racks of drying finfish lay spreadwinged in the sun, then down past the Temple, through swarms of mid-day worshippers, then a sharp right that brought the cab careening into Central Plaza.

The micronite dial in the heart of the plaza was blazing gold. Navarre cursed softly. He belonged at the Overlord's side, and he was late.

Earthmen were *never* late. Earthmen had a special reputation to uphold in the universe. Navarre's fertile mind set to work concocting a story to place before the Overlord when the inevitable query came.

"You seek an audience with the Overlord?" the cabbie asked.

"Not quite," Navarre said wryly. He slipped back his hood, revealing his bald dome. "Look."

The driver squinted at the rear-view mirror and nodded at the sight of Navarre's shaven scalp. "Oh. The Earthman. Sorry I didn't recognize you, sir."

"Quite all right. But get this crate moving; I'm due at court."

"I'll do my best."

The Dergonian's best wasn't quite good enough. He rounded the Plaza, turned down into the Street of the Lords, charged full throttle ahead—

Smack into a parade.

The Legions of Jorus were marching. The jetcab came to a screeching halt no more than ten paces from a regiment of tusked Daborians marching stiffly along, carrying their blue-and-red flag mounted just beneath the bright purple of Jorus, tootling on their thin, whining electronic bagpipes. There were thousands of them.

"Guess it's tough luck, Sir Earthman," the cabbie said philosophically. "The parade's going around the Palace. It may take hours."

Navarre sat perfectly still, meditating on the precarious position of an Earthman in a court of the Cluster. Here he was, remnant of a wise race shrouded in antiquity, relict of the warrior-kings of old—and he sat sweating in a taxi while a legion of tusked barbarians delayed his passage. Once again he cursed the rule that forced him to live at such a distance from the Palace, knowing as he did so that the arrangement was deliberately designed to serve as a constant reminder of the precariousness of his position.

The cabbie opaqued his windows.

"What's that for?"

"We might as well be cool while we wait. This can take hours. I'll be patient if you will."

"The hell you will," Navarre snapped, gesturing at the still-running meter. "At two demi-units per minute I could be renting a fine seat on the reviewing stand. Let me out of here."

"But—"

"Out." Navarre leaned forward, slammed down the meter, cutting it short at thirty-six demi-units. He handed the driver a newly minted semi-unit piece.

"Keep the change. And thanks for the service."

"A pleasure." The driver made the formal farewell salute. "May I serve you again, Sir Earthman, and—"

"Sure," Navarre said, and slipped out of the cab. A moment later he had to jump to one side as the driver activated his side blowers, clearing debris from the turbojets and incidentally spraying the Earthman with a cloud of fine particles of filth.

Navarre turned, clapping a hand to his blaster, but the grinning cabbie was already scooting away in reverse. Navarre scowled. Behind the usual mask of respect for Earthmen, there was always a lack of civility that irked him. It was another reminder of his ambiguous position in the galaxy, as an emissary from nowhere, a native of a world long forgotten and which he himself had never seen.

Earth. It was not a planet any longer, but a frame of mind, a way of thinking. He was an Earthman, and thus valuable to the Overlord. But he could be replaced; there were other advisers nearly as shrewd.

Navarre fingered his bald scalp ruefully and flicked off his hood again. He started across the wide street.

The regiment of Daborians still stalked on—the seven-foot humanoids with their jutting tusks polished brightly, their fierce beards combed, marching in an unbreakable phalanx round and round the Palace.

Damn parades anyway, he thought. Foolish display, calculated to impress barbarians.

He reached the Daborian ranks. "Excuse me, please."

He started to force his way between two towering artillery men. Without breaking step, a Daborian grabbed him by the scruff of his neck and threw him back toward the street. An appreciative ripple of laughter went up from the onlookers as Navarre landed unsteadily on one leg, started to topple, and had to skip three or four times to stay upright.

"Let me through," he snapped again, as a corps of tusked musicians came by. The Daborians merely ignored him. Navarre waited until a bagpiper came by, one long valved chaunter thrust between his tusks and hands flying over the electronic keyboard. Navarre grabbed the base of the instrument with both hands and rammed upward.

The Daborian let out a howl of pain and took a step backward as the mouthpiece cracked against his palate. Navarre grinned and slipped through the gap in formation, and kept on running. Behind him, the bagpiping rose to an angry wail, but none of the Daborians dared break formation to pursue the insolent Earthman.

He reached the steps of the Palace. Fifty-two of them, each a little wider and higher than the next. He was better than an hour late at court. The Overlord would be close to a tantrum—and in all probability Kausirn, the sly Vegan adviser, had taken ample opportunity to work mischief.

Navarre only hoped the order for his execution had not yet been signed. There was no telling what the Overlord would do under Kausirn's influence.

He reached the long black-walled corridor leading to the throne room somewhat out of breath. The pair of unemotional Trizian monoptics guarding access to the corridor recognized him and nodded disapprovingly as he went toward the throne room.

Arriving at the penultimate turn in the hall, he ducked into a convenience at the left and slammed the door. He was so late that a few moments more wouldn't aggravate the offense, and he wanted to look his best.

A couple of seconds later, the brisk molecular flow of the vibron had him refreshed and back in breath; he splashed water on his face, dried it, straightened his tunic, tied back his hood. Then, stiffly, walking with a dignity he had not displayed a moment before, he stalked out and headed for the throne room.

The annunciator said: "Hallam Navarre, Earthman to the Overlord."

Joroiran VII was on his throne, looking, as always, like a rather nervous butcher's apprentice elevated quite suddenly to galactic rank. He muttered a few words, and the micro-amplifier surgically implanted in his throat picked them up and tossed them at the kneeling Navarre.

"Enter, Earthman. You're late."

The throne room was filled. For this was Threeday—audience-day—and all sizes and shapes of commoners thronged before the Overlord, each hoping that the finger of fate would light on him and bring him forward to plead his cause. It was Navarre's customary job to select those who were to address the Overlord, but he saw coldly that Kausirn, the Vegan, had taken over the task in his absence.

He advanced toward the throne and abased himself before the purple carpet. A sudden sensation of heat told him that Lagard, the slave who operated the spotlight from the balcony, was having a field day with the Earthman's glitteringly bald head.

"You may rise," Joroiran said casually. "The audience began more than an hour ago. You have been missed, Navarre."

"I have been employed in your Majesty's service all the while," Navarre said. "I was pursuing that which may be of great value to your Majesty and to all of Jorus."

Joroiran looked amused. "And what may that be?"

Navarre paused, drawing in breath, and prepared himself for the plunge. "I have discovered information that may lead to the Chalice of Life, my Overlord."

To his surprise Joroiran did not react at all; his mousy face showed not the slightest sign of animation. Navarre blinked; the whopper was not going over.

But it was the Vegan who saved him, in a way. Leaning over, Kausirn whispered harshly, "He means the Chalice of *Death*, Majesty."

"Death . . . ?"

"Eternal life for Joroiran II," Navarre said ringingly. As long as he was going to make excuses for having overslept, he might as well make them good ones. "The Chalice holds death for some—life for thee."

"Indeed," the Overlord said. "You must talk to me of this in my chambers. But now, the audience."

Navarre mounted the steps and took his customary position at the monarch's right; Kausirn had at least not appropriated *that*. But the Earthman saw that the Vegan's nest of tapering fingers played idly over the short-beam generator which controlled the way the hand of fate fell upon commoners. That meant Kausirn, not Navarre, would be selecting those whose cases were to be pled this day.

Looking into the crowd, Navarre picked out the bleak, heavily-bearded face of Domrik Carso. Carso was staring reproachfully at him, and Navarre felt a sudden burst of guilt. He had promised Carso a hearing today; the halfbreed lay under a sentence of banishment, but Navarre had lightly assured him that revokement would be a simple matter.

But not now. Not with Kausirn wielding the blue beam. Kausirn had no desire to have an Earthman's kith and kin plaguing him on Jorus; Carso would rot in the crowd before the Vegan chose *his* case to be pled.

Navarre met Carso's eyes. *Sorry,* he tried to say. But Carso stared stiffly through him. Navarre had failed him.

"Proceed with your tale," Joroiran said.

Navarre looked down and saw a pale Joran in the pleader's square below, bathed in the blue light of chance. The man looked up at the command and said, "Shall I continue or begin over, Highness?"

"Begin over. The Earthman may be interested."

"May it please the Overlord and his advisers, my name is Drusu of the Loaves; I am a baker from Dombril Street who was taken with overmuch wine on yesternight, and did find myself in another man's wife's arms by the hour of midnight, all unconscious of what I was doing. The girl had given me to understand she was a woman of the streets; not only was I befuddled by the wine but by the woman's lies. The man himself arrived at his home late, and did fly into a mighty rage from which he could hardly be dissuaded."

The story went on and on—a rambling account of the negotiations between the outraged husband and the besotted baker. Navarre's attention wandered; he glanced around the court, spying here and there a person whom he had pledged to assist this day. Of all days to oversleep! Kausirn held the reins, now.

" . . . and finally we came before your Nobility for adjudgment, Sire. The man desires a night with my wife as fee simple for the insult, plus payment of one hundred units; my wife refuses to grant this, while his will have naught to do with either of us."

On his throne, Joroiran scowled and twisted fretfully. Such petty matters embarrassed and annoyed him, but he kept up the pretense of the public audience at Navarre's advice. Even in a galactic society, a monarch must keep touch with his subjects.

The Overlord turned to Navarre. "What say you in this matter, Earthman?"

Navarre thought for a moment. "All four must be punished—Drusu for straying from his wife, his wife for not being loving enough to keep her husband's undivided affections, the other woman for seducing Drusu, her husband for taking so little care of his wife as to allow a stranger to enter his home of a night. Therefore—Drusu is sentenced to supply the offended husband with bread, free of charge, for the period of a fortnight; the erring wife is condemned to cut short her hair. But all four are sentenced to unbreaking rectitude of behavior for one year, and should any of you be taken with a person not your spouse the sentence will be death *for all four.*"

"Excellent, excellent," Joroiran murmured. Drusu nodded and backed away from the royal presence. Navarre grinned; he enjoyed delivering such decisions on the moment's spur.

Joroiran intoned, "Fate will decide who is next to be heard."

Fate—surreptitiously controlled by the generator hidden in the Vegan's twenty fingers—materialized as a ball of blue light high in the vaulted throne room. The ball lowered. For a moment it flickered above the head of Domrik Carso, and Navarre wondered if the Vegan would choose the halfbreed's case unknowingly.

But Kausirn was too sly for that. The beam swung tantalizingly over Carso's head and settled on a pudgy grocer at his side. The man did a little dance of delight, and stepped forward.

"Your Majesty, I am Lugfor of Zaigla Street, grocer and purveyor of food. I have been accused falsely of thinning my measure, but—"

Navarre sat back while the man droned on. The time of audience was coming to its end; Carso would go unheard, and at twenty-fourth hour the halfbreed would be banished. Well, there was no helping it, Navarre thought glumly. He knotted his hands together and tried to follow Lugfor's plea of innocence.

At the end of the session, Navarre turned to the Overlord—but Kausirn was already speaking. "Majesty, may I talk to you alone?"

"And I?" Navarre said.

"I'll hear Kausirn first," Joroiran decided. "To my chambers; Navarre, attend me there later."

"Certainly, Sire." He slipped from the dais and headed down into the dispersing throng. Carso was shuffling morosely toward the exit when Navarre reached him.

"Domrik! Wait!"

The halfbreed turned. "It looks like you'll be the only Earthman on Jorus by nightfall, Hallam."

"I'm sorry. Believe me, I'm sorry. I just couldn't get here in time—and that damned Vegan got control of the selections."

Carso shrugged moodily. "I understand." He tugged at his thick beard. "I am only half of Earth, anyway. You'll not miss me."

"Nonsense!" Navarre whispered harshly. "I—oh, forget it, Domrik. Will you forgive me?"

The halfbreed nodded gravely. "My writ commands me to leave the cluster. I'll be heading for Kariad tonight, and then outward. You'll be able to reach me there if you can—I mean—I'll be there a week."

"Kariad? All right. I'll get in touch with you there if I can influence Joroiran to revoke the sentence. Damn it, Carso, you shouldn't have hit that innkeeper so hard."

"He made remarks," Carso said. "I had to." The halfbreed bowed and turned away to leave.

The throne room was nearly empty; only a few stragglers were left, staring at the grandeur of the room and probably comparing it with their own squalid huts. Joroiran enjoyed living on a large scale, certainly.

Navarre sprawled down broodingly on the edge of the royal purple carpet and stared at his jeweled fingers. Things were looking bad. His sway as Joroiran's adviser was definitely weakening, and the Vegan's star seemed in the ascendant. Navarre's one foothold was the claim of tradition: all seven of the Joroiran Overlords had had an Earthman as adviser. The Overlord, weak man that he was, would scarcely care to break with tradition.

Yet Kausirn had wormed himself securely into the monarch's graces. The situation was definitely not promising.

Gloomily, Navarre wondered if there were any other local monarchs in the market for advisers. His stay on Jorus did not look to be long continuing.

CHAPTER II

After a while a solemn Trizian glided toward him, stared down out of its one eye, and said, "The Overlord will see you now."

"Thanks." He allowed the monoptic to guide him through the swinging panel that led to Joroiran's private chambers, and entered.

The Overlord was alone, but the scent of the waxy-fleshed Vegan still lingered. Navarre took the indicated seat.

"Sire?"

"That was a fine decision you rendered in the case of the

baker today, Navarre. I often wonder how I should endure the throne without two such ministers as you and Kausirn.''

"Thank you, Sire.''

Perspiration beaded Joroiran's upper lip; the monarch seemed dwarfed by the stiff strutwork that held his uniform out from his scrawny body. He glanced nervously at the Earthman, then said, "You spoke of a Chalice today, as your reason for being late to the audience. The Chalice of Death, is it? Or of Life?''

"It is known under both names, Sire.''

"Of course. Its details slipped my mind for the instant. It is said to hold the secret of eternal life, not so? Its possessor need never die?''

Navarre nodded.

"And,'' Joroiran continued, "you tell me you have some knowledge of its whereabouts, eh?''

"I think I do,'' said Navarre hoarsely. "My informant claimed to know someone whose father had led an earlier expedition in search of it, and who had nearly located it.'' The statement was strictly from whole cloth, but Navarre reeled it off smoothly.

"Indeed? Who is this man?''

Sudden inspiration struck Navarre. "His name is Domrik Carso. His mother was an Earthman—and you know of course that the Chalice is connected in some legend-shrouded way with Earth.''

"Of course. Produce this Carso.''

"He was here today, Sire. He searched for pardon from an unfair sentence of banishment over some silly barroom squabble. Alas, the finger of fate did not fall on him, and he leaves for Kariad tonight. But perhaps if the sentence were revoked I could get further information from him concerning the Chalice, which I would most dearly love to win for your Majesty—''

Joroiran's fingers drummed the desktop. "Ah, yes—revokement. It would be possible, perhaps. Can you reach the man?''

"I think so.''

"Good. Tell him not to pay for his passage tickets, that the Public Treasury will cover the cost of his travels from now on.''

"But—''

"The same applies to you, of course.''

Taken aback, Navarre lost a little of his composure. "Sire?''

"I have spoken to Kausirn. Navarre, I don't know if I can spare you, and Kausirn is uncertain as to whether he can bear the double load in your absence. But he will try it, noble fellow that he is.''

"I don't understand," Navarre stammered.

"You say you have a lead on the Chalice, no? Kausirn has refreshed my overburdened memory with some information on this Chalice, and I find myself longing for its promise of eternal life, Navarre. You say you have a lead; very well. I have arranged for an indefinite leave of absence for you. Find this man Carso; together, you can search the galaxies at my expense. I don't care how long it takes, nor what it costs. *But bring me the Chalice, Navarre!''*

The Earthman nearly fell backward in astonishment. The Chalice? Why, it was just a myth, an old wives' tale he had resorted to as an excuse for oversleeping—

Greed shone in the Overlord's eyes: greed for eternal life. Dizzily Navarre realized that this was the work of the clever Kausirn: he would send the annoying Earthman all over space on a fool's mission while consolidating his own position at the side of the Overlord.

Navarre forced himself to meet Joroiran's eyes. "I will not fail you, my lord," he said in a strangled voice.

He had been weaving twisted strands, and now he had spun himself a noose. Talk of tradition! Nothing could melt it faster than a king's desire to keep his throne.

For seven generations there had been an Earthman at the Overlord's side. Now, in a flash, the patient work of years was undone. Dejectedly Navarre reviewed his mistakes.

One: he had allowed Kausirn to worm his way into a position of eminence on the Council. Allow a Vegan an inch, he'll grab a parsec. Navarre now saw he should have had the many-fingered one quietly put away while he had the chance.

Two: he had caroused the night before an audience-day. Inexcusable. By hereditary right and by his own wits he had always chosen the cases to be heard, and in the space of a single hour the Vegan had done him out of *that.*

Three: he had lied too well. This was something he should have foreseen. He had aroused weak Joroiran's desire to such a pitch that Kausirn was easily able to plant the suggestion that the Overlord send the faithful Earthman out to find the Chalice.

Three mistakes. Now, he was on the outside and Kausirn in control. Navarre tipped his glass and drained it. "You're a disgrace to your genes," he told the oddly distorted reflection on the wall of the glass. "A hundred thousand years of Earthmen labor to produce—what? *You?* Fumblewit!"

Still, there was nothing to be done for it now. Joroiran had given the word, and here he was, assigned to chase a phantom, to pursue a will-o'-the-wisp that was half fancy, half lie. The Chalice! Chalice, indeed! There was no such thing.

And even if there were, the sky was full of stars. Navarre could search the heavens for a billion decades and not touch each world twice. And he dared not return to Joroiran empty-handed. That was what Kausirn was counting on. Navarre was a prisoner of his own reputation, of the reputation of Earthmen's ability to achieve anything they set out to do.

Navarre chuckled hollowly and wondered what would happen if they knew the truth—if they knew just how feeble the much-feared Earthmen really were.

Here we are, he thought. *A couple of million of us, scattered one or two to a world throughout the galaxies. We dictate policies, we are sought as advisers—and yet we were unable to hold our own empire. We don't even remember where our home world is.*

He tossed his empty glass aside and reached for the communicator. He punched the stud, quickly fed in four numbers and a letter.

A blank radiance filled the screen, and an impersonal voice said, "Citizen Carso is not at home. Citizen Carso is not at home. Citizen Car—"

Navarre cut the contact and dialed again. This time the screen lit, glowed, and showed a tired-looking man in a white smock. "Jublain Street Bar," the man said. "Do you want to see the manager?"

"No. Is there a man named Domrik Carso there—a heavyset fellow, with a thick beard?"

"I'll look around," the barkeep grunted. A moment later, Carso came to the screen. His thick-nostriled face looked puffy and bloated; as Navarre had suspected, he was having a few last swills of Joran beer before taking off for the outworlds.

"Navarre? What do you want?"

"Have you bought your ticket for Kariad yet?"

Carso blinked. "Not yet. What's it to you?"

"If you haven't bought it yet, *don't.* How soon can you get over here?"

"Couple of centuries, maybe. What's going on?"

"You've been pardoned."

"*What?* I'm not banished?"

"Not exactly," Navarre said. "Look, I don't want to talk about it at long range. How soon can you get over here?"

"I'm due at the spaceport at twenty-one to pick up my tick—"

"*Damn* your ticket," Navarre snapped. "You don't have to leave yet. Come on over, will you?"

Navarre peered across the table at the heavy-shouldered figure of Domrik Carso. "That's the whole story," the Earthman said. "Joroiran wants the Chalice—and he wants it real hard."

Carso shook his head and exhaled a beery breath. "Your oversleeping has ruined us both, Hallam. With but half an Earthman's mind I could have done better."

"It's done, and Kausirn has me in a cleft stick. If nothing else, I've saved you a banishment."

"Only under condition that I help you find this damnable Chalice," Carso grunted. "Some improvement that is. Well, at least Joroiran will foot the bill. We can both see the universe at his expense, and when we come back—"

"We come back when we've found the Chalice," said Navarre. "This isn't going to be a pleasure-jaunt."

Carso glared at him sourly. "Hallam, are you mad? There *is* no Chalice!"

"How do you know? Joroiran says there is. The least we can do is look for it."

"We'll wander space forever," Carso said, sighing. "As no doubt the Vegan intends for you to do. Well, there's nothing but to accept. I'm no poorer for it than if I were banished. Chalice! *Pah!*"

"Have another drink," Navarre suggested. "It may make it easier for you to swallow the idea."

"I doubt it," the halfbreed said, but accepted the drink anyway. He drained it, then said, "You told the Overlord you had a lead. What was it?"

"*You* were my lead," Navarre said. "I had to invent something."

"Fine, fine. This leaves us less than nowhere. Well, tell me of this Chalice. What is known of it?"

Navarre frowned. "The legend is connected with ancient Earth. They say the Chalice holds the key to eternal life, if the proper people find it—and instant death for the wrong ones. Hence the ambiguous name, Chalice of Life and Chalice of Death.''

''A chalice is a drinking-cup,'' Carso observed. ''Does this mean a potion of immortality, or something of the like?''

''Your guess is equal to mine. I've given you all I know on the subject.''

''Excellent. Where is this Chalice supposedly located, now?''

Navarre shrugged. ''Legend is incomplete. The thing might be anywhere. Our job is to find a particular drinking-cup on a particular world in a nearly infinite universe. Unfortunately we have only a finite length of time to do the job.''

''The typical shortsightedness of kings,'' Carso muttered. ''A sensible monarch would have sent a couple of immortals out in search of the Chalice.''

''A sensible monarch would know when he'd had enough, and not ask to rule his system forever. But Joroiran's not sensible.''

They were silent for a moment, while the candle between them flickered. Then Carso grinned.

''What's so funny?''

''Listen, Hallam. We don't know where the Chalice is, right? It might be anywhere at all. And so we can begin our search at random.''

''So?''

''Why don't we assume a location for the Chalice? At least it'll give us a first goal to crack at. And it ought to be easier to find a planet than a drinking-cup, shouldn't it?''

Navarre's eyes narrowed. ''Just where are you assuming the Chalice is? Where are we going to look for it?''

There was a mischievous twinkle in the halfbreed's eyes. He gulped another drink, grinned broadly, and belched.

''Where? Why—Earth, of course.''

CHAPTER III

On more-or-less sober reflection the next morning, it seemed to Navarre that Carso's idea was right: finding Earth promised to be easier than finding the Chalice (if it were proper to talk about degrees of ease in locating myths). It seemed a good deal more probable that there had been an Earth than that there had been a Chalice, and, if they directed their aims Earthward, their quest would have a more solid footing.

Earth. Navarre knew the stories that each Earthman told to his children, that few non-Earthmen knew. As a halfbreed Carso would be aware of them too.

Years ago—a hundred thousand, the legend said—man had sprung from Earth, an inconsequential world revolving around a small sun in an obscure galaxy. He had leaped forward to the stars, and carved out a mighty empire. The glory of Earth was carried to the far galaxies, to the wide-flung nebulas of deepest space.

But no race, no matter how strong, could hold sway over an empire that spanned a billion parsecs. The centuries passed; Earth's grasp grew weaker. And, finally, the stars rebelled.

Navarre remembered his father's vivid description. Earth had been outnumbered a billion to one, yet they had kept the defensive screens up, and kept the home world untouched, had beaten back the invaders. But still the invaders came, sweeping down on the small planet like angry beetles.

Earth drew back from the stars; its military forces came to the aid of the mother world, and the empire crumbled.

It was to no avail. The hordes from the stars won the war of attrition, sacrificing men ten thousand to one and still not showing signs of defeat. The mother world yielded; the proud name of Earth was humbled.

What became of the armies of Earth no one knew. Those who survived were scattered through the galaxies. But fiercely the Earthmen clung to their name. They shaved their heads to distinguish themselves from humanoids of a million star-systems—and death it was to the alien who tried to counterfeit himself as an Earthman!

The centuries rolled by in their never-ending sweep, and Earth itself was forgotten. Yet the Earthmen remained, a thin band scattered through the heavens, proud of their heritage, jealous of their genetic traits. Carso was rare; it was but infrequently that an Earthwoman could be persuaded to mate with an alien. Yet Carso regarded himself as an Earther, and never spoke of his father.

Where was Earth? No one could name the sector of space— but Earth was in the hearts of the men who lived among the stars. Earthmen were sought out by kings; the baldheads could not rule themselves, but they could advise those less fitted than they to command.

Then would come a fool like Joroiran, who held his throne because his father seven times removed had hewed an empire for him—and Joroiran would succumb to a Vegan's wiles and order his Earthman off on a madman's quest.

Navarre's fists stiffened. *Send me for the Chalice, eh? I'll find something for him!*

The Chalice was an idiot's dream; immortal life was a filmy bubble. But Earth was real, Earth merely awaited finding. Somewhere it bobbed in the heavens, forgotten symbol of an empire that had been.

Smiling, Navarre thought, *I'll find Earth for him.*

Unlimited funds were at his disposal. He would bring Joroiran a potion too powerful to swallow at a gulp.

Later that day he and Carso were aboard a liner of the Royal fleet, bearing tickets paid for by Royal frank, and feeling against their thighs the thick bulge of Imperial scrip received with glee from the Royal treasury.

A stewardess moved up and down the aisle of the liner, making sure everyone was prepared for blastoff. Navarre studied her impartially. She was a Joran native, pink-skinned, high-breasted, with only the flickering nictitating lid filming her eyes to indicate that she did not come from the direct line of Earth.

"A fine wench," Carso murmured as she passed.

"For you, perhaps. Give me an Earthwoman of the full blood."

Carso chuckled. "As a mate, perhaps; you fullbloods are ever anxious to keep your lines pure. But as for that one—if I judge you on past practice, you would not toss her from your couch if she sought a night's sport."

"Possibly not," Navarre admitted wryly. "But sport and bloodlines are separate affairs to me. Obviously this is not the rule in your family."

Carso stiffened in his seat. "My mother was forced by a drunken Joran, else I would be full-blooded like the rest."

"Oh," Navarre said softly. Carso had never spoken of this before. "I'm sorry. I didn't know."

"You didn't think she'd seek a Joran bed willingly, did you?"

"Of course not. I—wasn't thinking."

"Ready for blasting," came the stewardess's voice. "We depart for Kariad in fifteen seconds. Relax and prepare to enjoy your trip."

Navarre slumped back in the acceleration cradle and closed his eyes. His heart ticked the seconds off impatiently. *Twelve. Eleven. Nine. Six.*

Two. One. Acceleration took him, thrust him downward as the liner left ground. Within seconds, they were above the afternoon sky, thrusting outward into the brightly dotted blackness speckled with the sharp points of a billion suns.

One of those suns was Sol, Navarre thought. And one of the planets of Sol was Earth.

Chalice of Life, he thought scornfully. As Jorus dwindled behind him, Navarre wondered how long it would be before he would see the simpering face of Joroiran VII again.

Kariad, the planet nearest the Joran Empire's cluster, was the lone world of a double sun. This arrangement, uneconomical as it was, provided some spectacular views and made the planet a much-visited pleasure place.

As Navarre and Carso alighted from the liner, Primus, the massive red giant that was the heart of the system, hung high overhead, intersecting a huge arc of the sky, while Secundus, the smaller main-sequence yellow sun, flickered palely near the horizon. Kariad was moving between the two stars on its complex and eccentric orbit, and, in the light of the two suns, all objects in sight had acquired a purple shimmer.

Those who had disembarked from the liner were standing in a tight knot on the field while Kariadi customs officials moved among them. Navarre folded his arms and waited for his turn to come.

The official wore a gilt-encrusted surplice and a bright red sash that seemed almost brown in the strange light. He yanked forth a notebook and started to scribble.

"Name and planet of origin?"

"Hallam Navarre. Planet of origin is Earth."

The customs man glared impatiently at Navarre's shaven scalp and said, "You know what I mean. Where are you from?"

"Jorus," Navarre said.

"Purpose of visiting Kariad?"

"Special emissary from Overlord Joroiran VII; intent peaceful, mission confidential."

"Are you the Earthman to the Court?"

Navarre nodded.

"And this man?"

"Domrik Carso," the halfbreed growled. "Planet of origin Jorus."

The official indicated Carso's stubbly scalp. "I wish you

Earthmen would be consistent. Or are you merely prematurely bald?''

"I'm of Earth descent," Carso said stolidly. "But I'm from Jorus, and you can put it down. I'm Navarre's traveling companion.''

"Very well; you may both pass."

Navarre and Carso moved off the field and into the spaceport itself. "I could use a beer," Carso said.

"I guess you've never been on Kariad, then. They must brew their beer from sewer-flushings.''

"I'll drink sewer-flushings when I must," Carso said. He pointed to a glowing sign. "There's a bar. Shall we go in?''

As Navarre had expected, the beer was vile. He stared unhappily at the big mug of green, brackish liquid, stirring it with a quiver of his wrist and watching the oily patterns forming and re-forming on its surface.

Across the table, Carso was showing no such qualms. The halfbreed tilted the bottle into his mug, raised the mug to his lips, drank. Navarre shuddered.

Grinning, Carso crashed the mug down and wiped his beard clean. "It's not the best I've ever had," he commented finally. "But it'll do, in a pinch." He filled his mug again cheerfully.

Very quietly Navarre said, "Do you see those men sitting at the far table?''

Carso squinted without seeming to do so. "Aye. They were on board the ship with us."

"Exactly."

"But so were five others in this bar! Surely you don't think—"

"I don't intend to take any chances," Navarre said. "Finish your drink and let's make a tour of the spaceport.''

"Well enough, if so you say." Carso drained the drink and left one of Overlord Joroiran's bills on the table to pay for it. Casually, the pair left the bar.

Their first stop was a tape-shop, where Navarre made a great business over ordering a symphony.

The effusive, apologetic proprietor did his best. *"The Anvils of Juno?* I don't think I have that number in stock. In fact, I'm not sure I've ever heard of it. Could it be *The Hammer of Drolon* you seek?''

"I'm fairly sure it was the *Juno,*" said Navarre, who had invented the work a moment before. "But perhaps I'm wrong. Is there any place I can listen to *Drolon?''*

"Surely; we have a booth back here where you'll experience full audiovisual effect. If you'd step this way—"

They spent fifteen minutes sampling the tape, Carso with an expression of utter boredom, Navarre with a scowl for the work's total insipidity. At the end of that time he snapped off the playback and rose.

The proprietor came bustling up. "Well?"

"Sorry," Navarre said. "It's not the one."

Gathering his cloak around him, he swept out of the shop, followed by Carso. As they re-entered the arcade, Navarre saw two figures glide swiftly into the shadows—but not swiftly enough.

"I do believe you're right," Carso muttered. "We're being followed."

"Kausirn's men, no doubt. The Vegan's curious to see where we're heading. Possibly he's ordered me assassinated now that I'm away from the Court. But let's give it one more test before we take steps."

"No more music!" Carso said hastily.

"No. The next stop will be more practical."

He led the way down the arcade until they reached a shop whose front display said simply, WEAPONS. They went in.

The proprietor here was of a different stamp from the man in the music shop; he was a rangy Kariadi, his light blue skin glowing in harmony with the electroluminescents in the shop's walls. "Can I help you?"

"Possibly you can," Navarre said. He swept back his hood, revealing his Earthman's scalp. "We're from Jorus. There are assassins on our trail, and we want to shake them. Have you a back exit?"

"Over there," the armorer said. "Are you armed?"

"Yes, but we could do with some spare charges. Say, five apiece." Navarre placed a bill on the counter and slid the wrapped-up packages into his tunic pocket.

"Are those the men?" the proprietor said.

Two shadowy figures were visible through the one-way glass of the window. They peered toward it uneasily.

"I think they're coming in here," Navarre said.

"All right. You two go out the back way; I'll chat with them for a while."

Navarre flashed the man an appreciative smile and then he and Carso slipped through the indicated door, just as their pursuers entered the weapons shop.

"Double around the arcade and wait at the end of the corridor, eh?" Carso said.

"Right. We'll catch 'em as they come out."

Some very fast running brought them to a strategic position. "Keep your eyes open," Navarre said. "That shopkeeper may have told them where we are."

"I doubt it. He looked honest."

"You never can tell," Navarre said. "Hush, now!"

The door of the gunshop was opening.

CHAPTER IV

The followers edged out into the corridor again, squeezing themselves against the wall and peering in all directions. They looked acutely uncomfortable, having lost sight of their quarry.

Navarre drew his blaster and hefted it thoughtfully. Then he shouted, "Stand and raise your hands," and squirted a bolt of energy almost at their feet.

One of the two yelled in fear, but the other, responding instantly, drew and fired. His bolt, deliberately aimed high, brought a section of the arcade roofing down; the drifting dust and plaster obscured sight.

"They're getting away!" Carso snapped. "Let's go after them!"

They leaped from hiding and raced through the rubble; dimly they could see the retreating pair heading for the main waiting-room. Navarre cursed; if they got in there, there'd be no chance of bringing them down.

As he ran, he leveled his blaster and emitted a short burst. One of the two toppled and fell; the other continued running, and vanished abruptly into the crowded waiting-room.

"I'll go in after him," Navarre said. "You look at the dead one and see if there's any identification on him."

Navarre pushed through the photon-beam and into the spaceport's crowded waiting-room. He saw his man up ahead, jostling desperately toward the cabstand. Navarre holstered his blaster; he would never be able to use it in here.

"Stop that man!" he roared. "Stop him!"

Perhaps it was the authority in his tone, perhaps it was his baldness, but to his surprise a foot stretched out and sent the fleeing spy sprawling. Navarre caught him in an instant, and knocked the useless blaster from his hand. He tugged the quivering man to his feet.

"All right, who are you?"

He concluded the question with a slap. The man sputtered and turned his face away without replying, and Navarre hit him again.

This time the man cursed and tried to break away. "Did Kausirn send you?" Navarre demanded.

"I don't know anything. Leave me alone."

"You'd better start knowing," Navarre said. He drew his blaster. "I'll give you five to tell me why you were following us, and then I'll burn you right here. One. Two."

On the count of three Navarre suddenly felt hands go round his waist. Other hands grabbed at his wrist and immobilized the blaster. He was pulled away from his prisoner and the blaster wrenched from his hand.

"Let go of him, Earthman," a rough voice said. "What's going on here, anyway?"

"This man's an assassin," Navarre said. "He and a companion were sent here to kill me. Luckily my friend and I detected the plot, and—"

"That's enough," the burly Kariadi said. "You'd all better come with me."

Navarre turned and saw several other officers approaching. One bore the body of the dead assassin; the other two pinioned the furiously struggling figure of Domrik Carso.

"Come along, now," the Kariadi said.

"A good beginning to our quest," Carso said wryly. "A noble start!"

"Quiet," Navarre told him. "I think someone's coming."

They were in a dungeon somewhere in the heart of Kariad City, having been taken there from the spaceport. They sat in unbroken darkness. The surviving assassin had been taken to another cell.

But someone *was* coming. The door of the cell was opening, and a yellow beam of light was crawling diagonally across the concrete floor.

A slim figure entered the cell. Light glinted off a bald skull; it was an Earthman, then.

"Hello. Which of you is Navarre?"

"I am."

"I'm Helna Winstin, Earthman to the Court of Lord Marhaill,

Oligocrat of Kariad. Sorry our men had to throw you in this dank cell, but they couldn't take any chances."

"We understand," Navarre said. He was still staring without believing. "No one told me that on Kariad the Earthman to the Court was a *woman*."

Helna Winstin smiled. "The appointment was recent. My father held the post till last month."

"And you succeeded him?"

"After a brief struggle. Milord was much taken by a Vegan who had served as Astronomer Royal, but I am happy to say he did not choose to break the tradition."

Navarre stared at the slim female Earthman with sharp respect. Evidently there had been a fierce battle for power—a battle in which she had bested a Vegan. *That was more than I managed to do*, he thought.

"Come," she said. "The order for your release has been signed, and I find cells unpleasant. Shall we go to my rooms?"

"I don't see why not," Navarre replied. He glanced at Carso, who looked utterly thunderstruck. "Come along, Domrik."

They were led through the corridor to a liftshaft and upward; it was evident now that the dungeon had been in the depths of the royal palace itself. Helna Winstin's rooms were warm and inviting-looking; the decor was brighter than Navarre was accustomed to, but beneath its obvious femininity lay a core of surprising toughness that seemed repeated in the girl herself. Considering the fact that her rooms, unlike his own on Jorus, were in the Palace itself, he reflected that there must be both advantages and disadvantages to being a woman.

"Now, then," she said, making herself comfortable and motioning for the men to do the same. "What have you two done to bring you to Kariad with a pair of assassins on your trail?"

"Has the man confessed?"

"He—ah—revealed all," Helna Winstin said. "He said he was sent here by one Kausirn, a Vegan attached to the Joran court, with orders to make away with you, specifically, and your companion if possible."

Navarre nodded. "I thought as much. Can I see the man?"

"Unfortunately, he died during interrogation. The job was clumsily handled."

She's tough, all right, Navarre thought in appreciation. She wore her head shaven, though it was not strictly required of female Earthmen; she wore a man's costume and did a man's job. In other ways, she was obviously feminine.

She leaned forward. "Now—may I ask what brings the Earthman of Joroiran's court here to Kariad?"

"We travel on a mission from Joroiran," Navarre said. "For him, we seek the Chalice of Death."

A tapering eyebrow rose. "How interesting. I have heard of this Chalice. If it really exists, its value is fabulous. I wonder . . ."

She paused, and seemed to come to a decision. "With such a prize at stake, you may still be in danger," she said. "It was on *my* authority that you were released; Lord Marhaill knows nothing of this affair as yet—as far as I know. But even now, he is closeted with another man who disembarked from the liner from Jorus. Could he, perhaps, seek to beat you to your goal?"

The news was shocking, but Navarre forced himself to consider it calmly. The wily Kausirn would in all likelihood have more than one string to his bow. The situation looked critical— but would Helna Winstin continue to help them if she knew the truth?

Casting caution aside, he told her the whole story of their search for Earth in terse, clipped sentences. A strange look crossed her face when he had finished.

"Lord Marhaill is all too likely to side in with your friend Kausirn in this matter," she said. "If I help you, it may mean the loss of my post here—if not all our lives. But we Earthmen must stick together! What is our course?"

CHAPTER V

The Main Library of Kariad City was a building fifty stories high and as many more deep below the ground—and even so, it could not begin to store the accumulated outpourings of a hundred thousand years of civilization on uncountable worlds.

"The open files go back only about five hundred years," Helna said, as she and Navarre entered the vast doorway, followed by Carso. "Everything else is stored away somewhere, and hardly anyone but antiquarians ever bothers with it. I imagine they ship twenty tons a month to various outworld libraries that can handle the early material."

Navarre frowned. "We may have some trouble, then."

An efficient-looking Dergonian met them at the door. "Good

day, Sir Earthman," he said to Helna. Catching sight of Navarre and Carso, he added, "And to you as well."

"We seek the main index," Helna said.

"Through that archway," said the librarian. "May I help you find what you seek?"

"We can manage by ourselves," Navarre said.

The main index occupied one enormous room from floor to ceiling. Navarre blinked dizzily at the immensity of it.

Coolly, Helna walked to a screen mounted on a table in the center of the index-room and punched out the letters E-A-R-T-H. She twisted a dial and the screen lit.

A card appeared in the screen. Navarre squinted to read its fine print:

EARTH, *legendary planet of Sol system (?) considered in myth as home of mankind*
SEE: D80009.1643, Smednal, *Creation Myths of the Galaxy*
D80009.1644 Snodgras, *Legends of the First Empire.*

Helna looked up doubtfully. "Shall I try the next card? Should I order these books?"

"I don't think there's any sense in it," said Navarre. "These works look fairly recent; they won't tell us anything we don't know. We'll have to dig a little deeper. How do we get to the closed files?"

"I'll have to pull rank, I guess."

"Let's go, then. The real location of Earth is somewhere in these libraries, I'm sure; you just can't *lose* a world completely. If we go back far enough we're sure to find out where Earth was."

"Unless such information was carefully deleted when Earth fell," Carso pointed out.

Navarre shook his head. "Impossible. The library system is too vast, too decentralized. There's bound to have been a slip-up somewhere—and we can find it!"

"I hope so," the halfbreed said moodily.

Track 57 of the closed shelves was as cold and as desolate as a sunless planet, Navarre thought bleakly, as he and his companions stepped out of the dropshaft.

A Genobonian serpent-man came slithering toward them, and the chittering echo of his body sliding across the dark floor went shivering down the long dust-laden aisles. At the sight of the reptile Carso went for his blaster; Genobonians entered this system but little, and they were fearsome sights to anyone not prepared for them.

"What's this worm coming from the books?" Carso asked. His voice rang loudly through the corridors.

"Peace, friends. I am but an old and desiccated librarian left to molder in these forgotten stacks." The Genobonian chuckled. "A book-worm in truth, Earthman. But you are the first to visit here in a year or more; what do you seek?"

"Books on Earth," Navarre said. "Is there a catalog down here?"

"There is. But it shan't be needed; I'll show you what we have, if you'll take care with it."

The serpent slithered away, leaving a foot-wide track in the dust on the floor. Hesitantly the three followed. He led them down to the end of a corridor, through a passageway dank-smelling with the odor of dying books, and into an even mustier alcove.

"Here we are," the dry voice croaked. The Genobonian extended a skinny arm and yanked a book from a shelf. It was a book indeed, not a mere tape.

"Handle it with care, friends. The budget does not allow for taping it, so we must preserve the original—until the day must come to clean this track. The library peels away its oldest layer like an onion shedding its skin; when the weight of new words is too great—*whisht!* and track 57 vanishes into the outworlds."

"And with it you?"

"No," said the serpent sadly. "I stay here, and endeavor to learn my way around the new volumes that descend from above. The time of changing is always sad."

"Enough talk," Navarre said. "Let's look at this book."

It was a history of the galaxy, arranged alphabetically. Navarre stared at the title page and felt a strange chill upon learning the book was more than thirty thousand years old.

Thirty thousand years. And yet Earth had fallen seventy millennia before this book was printed.

Navarre frowned. "This is but the volume from *Fenelon to Fenris*," he said. "Where is Earth?"

"Earth is in an earlier volume," the Genobonian said. "A volume which we no longer have in this library. But look, look at this book; perhaps it may give you some information."

Navarre stared at the librarian for a long moment, then said, "Have you read all these books?"

"Many of them. There is little for me to do down here."

"Very well, then. This is a question no Earthman has ever asked of an alien before—and if I suspect you're lying to me, I'll kill you here among your books."

"Go ahead, Earthman," the serpent said. He sounded unafraid.

Navarre moistened his lips. "Before we pursue our search further, tell me this: *did Earth ever exist?*"

There was silence, broken only by the echoes of Navarre's voice whispering the harsh question over and over down the aisles. The serpent's bright eyes glittered. "You do not know yourselves?"

"No, damn you," Carso growled. "Else why do we come to you?"

"Strange," the serpent mused. "But yes—yes, Earth existed. You may read of Earth, in this book I have given you. Soon they will send the book far away, and the truth of Earth will vanish from Kariad. But till then—yes, there was an Earth."

"Where?"

"I knew once, but I have forgotten. It is in that volume, that earlier volume that was sent away. But look, look, Earthmen. Read there, under *Fendobar.*"

Navarre opened the ancient History with trembling fingers and found his way through the graying pages to *Fendobar.* He read the faded text aloud:

FENDOBAR. The larger of a double-star system in Galaxy RGC18347, giving its name to the entire system. It is ringed by eight planets, only one inhabited and likewise known as Fendobar.

    Because of its strategic location just eleven light-years from the Earth system, Fendobar was of extreme importance in the attack on Earth (which see). Starships were customarily refueled on Fendobar before . . .

    Coordinates . . .

    The inhabitants of . . .

"Most of it's illegible," Navarre said, looking up. "But there's enough here to prove that there *was* an Earth—and it was just eleven light-years from Fendobar."

"Wherever Fendobar was," Helna said.

There was silence in the vault for a moment. Navarre said, "There's no way you can recall the volume dealing with Earth, is there? This book gives coordinates and everything else. We could get there if—"

He stopped. The Genobonian looked at him slyly. "Do you plan to visit your homeland, Earthman?"

"Possibly. It is none of your business."

"As you wish. But the answer is no; the volume cannot be recalled. It was shipped out with others of its era last year, some time before the great eclipse, I believe—or was it the year before? Well, no matter; I remember not where the book was sent. We scatter our excess over every eager library within a thousand light-years."

"And there's no way you could remember?" Carso demanded.

"Not even if we refreshed your memory?" The halfbreed's thick hands shot around the Genobonian's scaly neck, but Navarre slapped him away.

"He's probably telling the truth, Domrik. And even if he isn't, there's no way we can force him to find the volume for us."

Helna brightened suddenly. "Navarre, if we could find this Fendobar, do you think it would help us in the quest for Earth?"

"It would bring us within eleven light-years—a mighty stride toward success. But how? The coordinates are illegible."

"The Oligocrat's scientists are shrewd about restoring faded books. They may help us, if they have not yet been warned not to," the girl said. She turned to the Genobonian. "Librarian, may we borrow this book awhile?"

"Impossible! No book may be withdrawn from a closed track at any time!"

Helna scowled prettily. "But if they only rot here and eventually are shipped off at random, why make such to-do about them? Come; let us have this book."

"It is against all rules."

Helna shrugged and nodded to Navarre, who said, "Step on him, Carso. Here's a case where violence *is* justified."

The halfbreed advanced menacingly toward the Genobonian, who scuttled away. "Should I kill him?" Carso asked.

"Yes," said Helna instantly. "He's dangerous. He can report us to Marhaill."

"No," Navarre said. "The serpent is a gentle old creature who lives by his rules and loves his books. Merely pull his fangs, Carso: tie him up and hide him behind a pile of books. He won't be found till tonight—or next year, perhaps. By which time, we'll be safely on our way."

He handed the book to Helna. "Let's go. We'll see what the Oligocrat's scientists can do with these faded pages."

The little ship spiraled to a graceful landing on the large world.

"This might well be Kariad," Helna said. "I am used to the double stars in the skies."

Directly overhead, the massive orb that was Fenobar burned brightly; farther away, a dim dab of light indicated the huge star's companion.

"Even this far away," Navarre said, "the universe remains constant."

"And somewhere eleven light-years ahead of us lies Earth," grunted Carso.

They had traveled more than a billion light-years, an immensity so vast that even Helna's personal cruiser, a warp-ship which was virtually instantaneous on stellar distances of a few thousand light-years, had required a solid week to make the journey.

And now, where were they? Fenobar—a world left far behind by the universe, a world orbiting a bright star in a galaxy known only as RGC18347. A world eleven light-years from Earth.

The Oligocrat's scientists had restored the missing coordinates as Helna had anticipated. Helna had packed a few things, and the three had said an abrupt good-bye to Kariad. They were none too soon; Marhaill's police had been stopping all strangers on Kariad and questioning them. Luck had been with them and they had gotten to the cruiser safely.

And they had swept out into space, into the subwarp and across the tideless sea of a billion light-years. They were driving back, back into humanity's past, into Galaxy RGC18347—the obscure galaxy from which mankind had sprung.

They had narrowed the field. Navarre had never thought they would get this far. Pursuit was inevitable, and he was expecting signs of it at any moment.

"We seek Earth, friend," Navarre told the aged chieftain who came out supported by two young children to greet the arriving ship.

"Earth? Earth? What be this?"

The old man's accents were strange and barely understandable.

Navarre looked around; he saw primitive huts, a smoking fire, naked babes uneasily testing their legs. The wheel of life had come full; one of mankind's oldest worlds had evidently entered its second youth.

"Earth is a planet somewhere in this galaxy," Carso said impatiently.

"I see," the old man said. "Planets . . . galaxies . . . these are strange words."

Navarre fumed. "This is Fenobar, isn't it?"

"Fenobar? The name of this world is Mundahl. I know no Fenobar."

Carso looked worried. "You don't think we made some mistake, do you, Hallam?"

"No. Names change in thirty thousand years." He leaned close to the oldster. "Do you study the stars, old man?"

"Not I. But there is a man in our village who does. He knows many strange things."

"Take us to him," Navarre said.

The astronomer was a withered old man who might have been the twin of the chieftain. The Earthmen entered his hut, and were surprised to see shelves of books, tapes, and an efficient-looking telescope.

"Yes?"

"Bremoir, these people search for Earth. Know you the place?"

The astronomer frowned. "The name sounds familiar, but—let me search my charts." He unrolled a thin, terribly fragile-looking sheet of paper covered with tiny marks.

"Earth is the name of the planet," Navarre said. "It revolves around a sun called Sol. We know that the system is some eleven light-years from here."

The wrinkled astronomer pored over his charts, frowning and scratching his leathery neck. After a while he looked up. "There is indeed a sun-system at the distance you give. Nine planets revolve about a small yellow sun. But—those names—?"

"Earth was the planet. Sol was the sun."

"Earth? Sol? There are no such names on my charts. The star's name is Dubihsar."

"And the third planet?"

"Velidoon."

Dubihsar. Velidoon. In thirty thousand years, names change. But could Earth forget its own name—so soon?

CHAPTER VI

There was a yellow sun ahead. Navarre stared at it hungrily through the fore viewplate, letting its brightness burn into his eyes.

"There it is," he said. "Dubihsar. *Sol.*"

"And the planets?" Carso asked.

"There are nine." He peered at the crumbling book the astronomer had given him, after long hours of search and thought. The book with the old names. "Pluto, Neptune, Uranus, Jupiter, Saturn, Mars, Venus, Mercury. And *Earth.*"

"Earth," Helna said. "Soon we'll be on Earth."

Navarre frowned broodingly. "I'm not sure I actually want to land, now that we've found it. I know what Earth's going to be like: Fendobar. It's awful when a world forgets its name."

"Fendobar is called Procyon on these charts," Carso commented.

"It was the Earth name for it. But now all are forgotten—Procyon, Fendobar, Earth. These planets have new names; they have forgotten their past. And we'll be coming down out of that past. I don't like it."

"Nonsense, Hallam." Carso was jovial. "Earth is Earth, whether its people know it or not. We've come this far; let's land, at least, before turning back. Who knows—we may even find the Chalice!"

"The Chalice," Navarre repeated quietly. "I had almost forgotten the Chalice. Yes. Perhaps we'll find the Chalice." Chuckling, he said, "Poor Joroiran will never forgive me if I return without it."

Nine planets. One spun in an eccentric orbit billions of miles from the small yellow star; three others were giant worlds, unlivable; a fifth, ringed with cosmic debris, was not yet solidified. A sixth was virtually lost in the blazing heat of the sun.

There were three other worlds—according to the book, Mars, Earth, Venus. The small craft fixed its sights on the green world.

Navarre was first from the ship; he sprang down the catwalk and stood in the bright, warm sunlight, feet planted firmly in sprouting green shoots nudging up from brown soil. Carso and Helna followed a moment later.

"Earth," Navarre said. "We're probably the first from the galactic worlds to set foot here in thousands of years." He squinted off into the thicket of trees that ringed them. Creatures were appearing.

They looked like men—dwarfed, shrunken, twisted little men. They stood about four and a half feet tall, their feet bare, their middles swathed in hides. Yet in their faces could be seen the unmistakable light of intelligence.

"Behold our cousins," Navarre murmured. "While we in the stars scrupulously kept our genes intact, they have become *this*."

The little men filed toward them unafraid, and grouped themselves around the trio and their ship. "Where be you from, strangers?" asked a flaxen-haired dwarf, evidently the leader.

"We are from the stars," Carso said. "From the world of Jorus, he and I, and the girl from Kariad. But this is our homeland. Our remote ancestors were born here on Earth."

"Earth? You mistake, strangers. This world be Velidoon, and we be its people. You look naught like us, unless ye be in enchantment."

"No enchantment," Navarre said. "Our fathers lived on—Velidoon—when it was called Earth, many thousands of years past."

How can I tell them that we once ruled the universe? Navarre wondered. *How can it be that these dwarfs are the sons of Earth?*

The flaxen-haired little man grinned and said, "What would you do on Velidoon, then?"

"We came merely to visit. We wished to see the world of our long-gone ancestors."

"Strange, to cross the sky merely to see a world. But come; let us take you to the village."

"In a mere hundred thousand years," Helna murmured, as they walked through the forest's dark glades. "From rulers of the universe to scrubby little dwarfs living in thatched huts."

"And they don't even remember their planet's name," Carso added.

"Not surprising," said Navarre. "Don't forget that most of Earth's best men were killed defending the planet, and the rest—our ancestors—were scattered all over the universe. Evidently the conquerors left just the dregs on Earth itself, and this is what they've become."

They turned past a clear brook and emerged into an open dell, in which a group of huts not unlike those on Fendobar could be seen.

The yellow sun shone brightly and warmly; overhead, colorful birds sang, and the forest looked fertile and young.

"This is a pleasant world," Helna said.

"Yes. It has none of the strain and stress of our system. Possibly it's best to live on a forgotten planet."

"Look," Carso said. "Someone important is coming."

A procession advanced toward them, led by the little group who had found them in the forest. A wrinkled graybeard, more twisted and bent than the rest, strode gravely toward them.

"You be the men from the stars?"

"I am Hallam Navarre, and these are Helna Winstin and Domrik Carso. We trace our ancestry from this world, many thousands of years ago."

"Hmm. Could be. I'm Gluihn, in charge of this tribe." Gluihn stepped back and scrutinized the trio. "It might well be," he said, studying them. "Yes, could indeed. You say your remote fathers lived here?"

"When the planet was called Earth, and ruled all the worlds of the skies."

"I know nothing of that. But you look much like the Sleepers, and perhaps you be of that breed. They have lain here many a year themselves."

"What sleepers?" Navarre asked.

The old man shrugged. "They look to be of your size, though they lie down and are not easy to see behind their cloudy fluid. But they have slept for ages untold, and perhaps——"

Gluihn's voice trailed off. Navarre exchanged a sharp glance with his companions. "Tell us about these Sleepers," Carso growled threateningly.

Now the old man seemed frightened. "I know nothing more. Boys, playing, stumbled over them not long ago, buried in their place of rest. We think they be alive."

"Can you take us there?"

"I suppose so," Gluihn sighed. He gestured to the flaxen-haired one. "Llean, take these three to look at the Sleepers."

"Here we are," the dwarf said.

A stubby hill jutted up from the green-carpeted plain before them, and Navarre saw that a great rock had been rolled to one side, baring a cave-mouth.

"Will we need lights?"

"No," said Llean. "It is lit inside. Go ahead in—I'll wait here. I care little to see what lies in there a second time."

Helna touched Navarre's arm. "Should we trust him?"

"Not completely. Domrik, stay here with this Llean, and watch over him. Should you hear us cry out—come to us, and bring him with you."

Carso grinned. "Right."

Navarre took Helna's hand and hesitantly they stepped within the cave mouth. It was like entering the gateway to some other world.

The cave walls were bright with some form of electroluminescence, glowing lambently without any visible light-source. The path of the light continued straight for some twenty yards, then snaked away at a sharp angle beyond which nothing was visible.

There were small footprints in the soft sand covering the floor of the cave; evidently they had been made by the boys of the tribe who had discovered this place.

Navarre and Helna proceeded to the bend in the corridor, and turned. A metal plaque of some sort was the first object their eyes met.

"Can you read it?" she asked.

"It's in ancient language—no, it isn't at all. It's Galactic—but an archaic form." He blew away the dust and let his eyes skim the inscription. He whistled.

"What does it say?"

"Listen: *Within this crypt lie ten thousand men and women, placed here to sleep in the year 11423, the two thousandth year of Earth's galactic supremacy and the last year of that supremacy. Each of the ten thousand is a volunteer. Each has been chosen from the group of more than ten million volunteers for this project on a basis of physical condition, genetic background, intelligence, and adaptability to a varying environment.*

"Earth's empire has fallen, and within weeks Earth herself will go under. But, regardless of what fate befalls us, the ten thousand sealed in this crypt will slumber on into the years to come, until such time as it will be possible for them to be awakened.

"To the finder of this crypt: the chambers may be opened simply by pulling the lever at the left of each sleeper. None of the crypts will open before ten thousand years have elapsed. The

*sleepers will lie here in this tunnel until the time for their
release, and then will come spilling out as wine from a chalice,
to restore the ways of doomed Earth and bring glory to the sons
of tomorrow.''*

Navarre and Helna remained frozen for an instant or two after
he had read the final words. In a hushed whisper he said, "Do
you know what this is?"

She nodded. '' *'As wine from a chalice—'* ''

"Beneath all the legends, beneath the shroud of myth—there
was a Chalice," Navarre said fiercely. "A Chalice holding
immortal life—sleepers who would sleep for all eternity if no
one woke them. And when they were awakened—eternal life for
doomed Earth, death for her enemies!"

"Shall we wake them now?" Helna asked.

"Let's get Carso. Let him be with us."

The halfbreed responded to Navarre's call and appeared, dragging the protesting Llean with him.

"Let the dwarf go," Navarre said. "Then read this plaque."

Carso released the squealing Llean, who promptly dashed for
freedom. The halfbreed read the plaque, then turned gravely to
Navarre.

"It seems we've found the Chalice after all!"

"It seems that way." Navarre led the way and they penetrated
deeper into the crypt. After about a hundred yards he stopped.
"Look."

A wall had been cut in the side of the cave and a sheet of
some massively thick plastic inserted as a window. And behind
the window, floating easily in a cloudy solution of some gray-
blue liquid, was a sleeping woman. Her eyes were closed, but
her breasts rose and fell in a slow, even rhythm. Her hair was
long and flowing; otherwise, she was similar to any of the three.

A lever of some gleaming metal projected about half a foot
from the wall near her head. Carso reached for it, fingering the
smooth metal. "Should we wake her up?"

"Not yet. There are more down this way."

The next chamber was that of a man, strong and powerful, his
muscles swelling along his relaxed arms and his heavy thighs.
Beyond him, another woman; then another man, stiff and
determined-looking even in sleep.

"It goes on for miles," Helna murmured. "Ten thousand of
them."

"What an army!" Navarre said. He stared down the long bright corridor as if peering ahead into the years to come. "A legacy from our ancestors: the Chalice holds life indeed. Ten thousand Earthmen ready to spring to life." His eyes brightened. "They could be the nucleus of the Second Galactic Empire."

"A bold idea," Carso said. "But a good one."

"We could begin with Earth itself," Helna said. "Leave a few hundred couples here to repopulate the planet with warriors. We could conquer Kariad, Jorus—and that would be just the beginning!"

"We would have the experience of old to draw upon," said Navarre. "The Empire would be built painfully, slowly, instead of in a riotous mushroom of expansion." He grinned broadly. "Domrik, Joroiran would be proud of us! He sent us to find the Chalice—and we've succeeded."

"He'll be surprised when he finds out what was in the Chalice, though!"

Navarre shut his eyes for a moment, let his imagination dwell on a galaxy once more bright with an Empire of Earth, of cities again thronging with his people after millennia of obscurity.

Never again, he promised, would Earth be forgotten.

Smiling, he reached for the lever that would free the first of Earth's sleeping legion.

Orphan of the Void

by *Lloyd Biggle, Jr.*

PROLOGUE

Harg stooped low, pushed the skin aside, and stepped through the narrow opening into his smoke-filled hut. His wife, Onga, straightened up from the clay stove, pushed the stringy black hair back from her face, and looked at him anxiously.

"What'd the sky-man want?"

"He says Zerg must have a party."

She gazed at him blankly. "What's a party?"

"It's eating things, mostly."

She paled and walked toward him with small, frightened steps. "They think we don't give Zerg enough to eat? Is that why they take him?"

"No. It's—". He gestured helplessly. "I don't know what it is. Like a Star Festival, maybe, but with just us. And there are to be gifts, the sky-man said. We must make joy."

"Joy!" she moaned. She sank to the floor, and sobs shook her frail body. Finally she controlled her grief and stared up at him, eyes wide with horror. "They take Zerg, and we must make joy?"

He turned away and stood peering through a window slot. "The sky-man said he would send the things—the party things. We must make the party at the dawn, and then we must take Zerg to the River."

She did not answer. After a time he turned and bent over her and gently raised her to her feet. "At the dawn—" he began.

"We will make the party. I do not know how, but we will make it. We will take Zerg to the River because we must. But

47

we will not make joy." There was savage determination in her face, and Harg, who had no conception of beauty, thought her beautiful.

An ominous rumbling sounded in the distance, and Harg whirled and hurried to a window slot. One of the sky-men's strange things-that-crawl came rocking down the path from the River. He watched it with mouth agape as it swirled along, sending clouds of dust high into the air. It veered suddenly and roared straight toward the hut. Harg stood his ground fearsomely, but Onga fled moaning toward the mat where little Rirga lay sleeping. The thing-that-crawls slowed with a clanking of tracks and came to a halt by the hut.

There was only one of the sky-men riding in it, and he jumped down and looked about. Harg stooped through the door and approached him humbly.

"Harg?" the sky-man said, speaking so strangely that Harg almost failed to recognize his name.

"Yes. Harg."

The sky-man turned, picked up a box, and set it at Harg's feet. And another, and still a third. "Par-ty," he said, mouthing the word strangely. "For par-ty."

"I understand," Harg said. "We will make the party."

The sky-man nodded, vaulted aboard his thing-that-crawls, and thundered away toward the River. Dust whirled about Harg, choking him, but he stood his ground until the sky-man had vanished over a distant hill. Then he turned slowly and carried the boxes into the hut. He placed them in a corner, stacking them carefully, and neither he nor Onga touched them again. When Zerg came strutting in waving an ornt he had caught, radiant with the frank pride of his three summers, he approached the boxes curiously, and Onga shouted him away.

They arose in darkness, and when the first dim light of dawn touched the top of one-tree hill, they awoke Zerg and his sister and made the party.

One box, the heaviest, contained food—delicious smoked meats, and bread, and a cake with awesome patterns traced upon it in color. They superstitiously held back from the cake and might never have tasted it had not one of Zerg's greedy little hands snaked out and broken off a large piece. After that they devoured it, smacking their lips over the sweet, melting texture. They ate the meat and bread, but the other contents of the box were odd, circular objects that Harg's puzzled fingers found no way to open.

The other boxes contained gifts. For Onga there was cloth, lengths and lengths of it, so finely woven and brightly colored that she regarded it openmouthed and sat fingering it until they had finished making the party. There was a doll for Rirga, a life-sized sky-baby doll that frightened her, and she would do no more than toddle up to it and touch it quickly before she scurried away. There was a knife for Harg, long, glimmering and sharp, and a hatchet, and fish hooks of the kind that the sky-men used with such wonderful fortune. For Zerg there were clothes that made him a sad little miniature sky-man, and they would have laughed had they been making joy.

And there was a tiny thing-that-crawls, with a tiny sky-man riding in it, and when Zerg handled it with his curious, prodding fingers it suddenly emitted a loud, grinding noise. He dropped it, and they all stared in amazement as it crawled away across the packed dirt floor of the hut.

Satisfied that they had made the party, they put all except Zerg's gifts back into the boxes and started off on the long, faltering walk to the River, with Zerg wearing his sky-man clothes and clutching the still-grinding thing-that-crawls.

At the River they skirted the mud huts of the natives and went to the shining, round-roofed huts that the sky-men had made. There were other families there, all with a child of Zerg's summers, and they huddled together in a long, strange hut while the children were undressed and sky-men and sky-women in white looked at them and handled strange, glimmering objects. Then they were outside by a towering thing-from-the-sky, and a sky-man was telling them quietly that they must make their farewell with Zerg.

Zerg, seeing tears in his mother's eyes, wept frantically, and Onga proudly wiped away her tears, and Zerg's, and firmly pushed him away.

There was weeping in other families, and Buga, who had had three daughters born to her in a miraculous birth, fell to the ground and rolled hysterically in the dust because the sky-men were taking all three.

An anguish of fright shook little Zerg when he reached the thing-from-the-sky. He shrieked and kicked wildly as he was carried up the steep metal slope, and when he reached the top a sky-lady in white picked him up and lifted him kindly for a last look at his family. And when he continued to scream and kick she took his hand and moved it up and down in a final, pathetic gesture before she disappeared with him into the yawning opening.

When the last struggling child had made its sobbing, wailing trip up the slope, the opening was closed. The sky-men moved them back to the edge of the meadow. Fire flashed around the thing-from-the-sky, and thunder roared, and it lifted upward until it became a shining speck and disappeared.

Harg and Onga plodded slowly homeward. Onga walked with her eyes on the rippling dust, and Harg halted, now and then, to gaze futilely up into the sky. Onga clutched the sleeping Rirga tightly in her arms, and she knew that both Rirga and the child that stirred within her would make that frightening journey into the unknown.

And she sobbed soundlessly, "What do they do with them? *What do they do with them?*"

I

Thomas Jefferson Sandler III looked out of his window on the ninety-eighth floor of the Terra-Central Hotel and saw the planet Earth at close range for the first time in fifteen years. He'd had his feet on genuine terra firma the night before, at the space port, and he'd flown from the port to the hotel—but that was a different Earth. An artificial Earth. A planet or a woman, he thought, never looks the same by daylight.

He swept his gaze over the welter of towers and spires that glittered brightly in the early-morning sunlight, watched the precisely stratified air traffic, and leaned forward to peer at the scurrying microbes in the street below.

"Earth," he said softly, and strained his eyes at the horizon. The city stretched as far as he could see, and farther. Galaxia, the greatest city on Earth. The greatest city in the galaxy. Its site had once been a desert, the guidebooks said; and now it was a garden spot, a prime tourists' attraction and the holy city of cities for businessmen and politicians.

"Capital of the galaxy," he murmured, and turned his gaze to the glistening white government buildings and green parks that stretched across the heart of Galaxia in an unbroken chain. He'd heard violent protests in the most distant parts of the galaxy about having a capital planet in such an out-of-the-way sector, but that didn't concern him. They could move it four galaxies away, for all he cared.

"Home," he said, and repeated the word doubtfully. That was why he was here. That was the reason for his long trek across the light years, to see Earth again. To see his home. And he stood looking out at the snowy puffs of cloud and the delicate blue sky and felt an overwhelming surge of disillusionment. Why should this planet be home to him? He turned away from the window and sang softly, mouthing the words in disgust.

> "Home is that place
> In deepest space
> Where memories burn.
> Home is a sigh
> For a color of sky,
> And a will to return."

He ended by cheerfully damning the planet Earth and adding a few choice curses for little Marty Worrel.

He'd run into Marty on a dozen worlds, or fifty, or a hundred. It seemed that everywhere he went he met Marty Worrel—if he happened into a dive that was cheap enough, and dirty enough, and illegal enough. Worrel was a man Sandler's age, with a wrinkled, ageless face and an insatiable thirst for alcohol. Inveterate wanderer of the galaxy, man of superb, hopelessly squandered talents, brilliant exponent of disillusionment, disgustingly enslaved alcoholic—that was little Marty. He could have been a genius at almost anything he chose to work at, but all he ever worked at was a bottle.

Sandler had last encountered Worrel on Kranil, and the shabby little fellow had managed to stay sober long enough to write a song. Or perhaps he'd tossed it off in a state of exhilarated intoxication. The facts of Worrel's activities were always hard to come by.

But he had written the song, and Sandler had met Worrel in a tough spacers' hangout near the Kranil City port and heard a slatternly bar girl give the song its first public performance. "Homing Song," Worrel had called it, and like most of Worrel's conversation the words were sometimes immortal poetry and sometimes nonsense, but the melody was a haunting, soaring masterpiece of poignant emotion. It entwined itself into Sandler's consciousness and defied eviction. Even if it had not he couldn't have forgotten it, because it swept across the galaxy on hyperdrive, and everywhere Sandler went he heard it. Even on Earth—he'd heard it the night before, in the hotel's Martian Room, sung with enticing gestures by a tall, sedate-looking blonde.

It was the song that brought Sandler to Earth. Its words had pounded away at him, home . . . home . . . home, and its melody had tormented him, and finally he had signed on a run across half the galaxy to Earth. To home. And he had arrived only to learn that he had no home, and the bitter realization pained and frustrated him.

He was Pilot First Class T. Sandler, and his brightest memories were the blur of unidentified stars and the sweeping emptiness of space—meaning everywhere or nowhere—and he didn't give a spacer's damn where he went. Or as he'd heard another spacer put it, home was the nearest planet with a breathable atmosphere.

Sandler dropped into a chair and visiphoned the space port. He reported to Inter-galactic Transport and gave his name and code number. "I want the first assignment that'll get me off this damned planet," he said.

The dispatcher chuckled, did some checking, and said, "You're stuck here for forty-eight hours. That's the best I can do."

"I'll take it," Sandler said.

He walked back to the window and looked out at the soft blue sky of Earth. "And as long as I'm here," he told himself, "I might as well have a good look at it. I certainly won't be coming home again."

The hackie leaped in front of him as he came out of the hotel, gripped his lapel, and babbled with pathetic, well-rehearsed enthusiasm. "Ground tour? See everything you want to see. Stop anytime you want and look around. Can't do that on an air tour. I'm an expert, I am. I can show you anything in Galaxia worth seeing. Make a day of it and see all the sights. What d'ya say, mister? Reasonable rates. Three credits an hour and you get a personally guided tour."

"Let's go," Sandler said.

The hackie ceremoniously escorted him to a shabby ground car, got him seated, and took his place in front. He beamed with triumph. "Yes, sir. Where to first, sir?"

"Just drive around," Sandler said.

"Ever been in Galaxia before?"

"Can't remember. Probably was here when I was a kid."

"Then you come from Earth."

"Originally, yes."

The hackie seemed vaguely disappointed, as though he might have to curb his enthusiasm somewhat in describing Earth's wonders to a native Earthling. "Well, then," he said. They were gliding smoothly along Vega Boulevard toward Government Circle, where two dozen stellar boulevards converged. "Art Institute, Galactic Museum of Natural History—they got stuff there that gives you nightmares for weeks. Then there are all the government buildings. Congress isn't in session, but they take visitors through the House of Congress on tours. Then there's the Museum of Space Travel—"

"That might be interesting. Let's try that one."

The hackie nodded, and their speed picked up somewhat. Sandler leaned back against the worn cushions and idly watched the buildings flow past him: elegant shops, towering luxury hotels, the sprawling office buildings from which galaxy-wide businesses were directed, occasionally behind a high wall and park-like blur of greenery the Earth residence of a galactic multibillionaire or the official residence of a cabinet minister.

They made a three-quarter circuit of Government Circle, passed the vast House of Congress, and started up the spacious parkway called Government Mall.

"Shorter this way," the hackie said.

Sandler doubted it, but he made no protest. The mall was beautiful. Flowering trees from a hundred planets, or perhaps a thousand, dotted the sweep of sparkling green grass. The splendid government buildings stood at regular intervals, each in a style of architecture native to a planet of the Galactic Federation, each surrounded by a small park landscaped with such specimens of that planet's flora as lavish care could keep flourishing on Earth.

They drove down Government Mall for a mile and turned right onto Luna Avenue, and Sandler raised his eyes from a cluster of purple-leaved shrubs to glimpse briefly the facade of the government building they were passing. The shock of recognition jolted him.

"Stop!" he shouted.

The hackie glanced around at the traffic and wailed, *"Can't stop here!"*

"That building—back there, the one on the right. Can we stop anywhere close to it?"

"Should be able to."

They turned off, followed a curving drive, and entered a two-level parking pavilion—lower level, ground cars; upper level, air cars.

"What building is this?" Sandler asked.

The hackie consulted a map. "The Ministry of Public Welfare."

Puzzled, Sandler reached for the map. "Never knew there was such a thing," he said.

He wondered what memory he could have of this building. Could he have seen a similar structure on another world—its native world? If so, why should a passing glimpse of it startle him so?

"I want to look around," he said, opening the door. Uneasiness flickered in the hackie's face, and Sandler grinned and handed him a ten-credit note. "There's pay for two hours with a nice tip. We haven't been out half an hour. If I'm back any time during the next hour and a half, I'll expect to find you waiting."

The hackie's head bobbed. "Right." He took a newspaper from the storage compartment.

Sandler stepped onto an escalator and rode up to the air car level. The building was enormous, a three-quarter circle stretching its arms about the parking pavilion. It was undistinguished in every way except one. Its windows were the darnedest things Sandler had ever seen.

Only he had seen them—somewhere.

They were circular, but each circle was punched in at the top by a stabbing indentation. Sandler said aloud, "Like sticking your finger into an arnel cake." And then, startled, "What the hell is an arnel cake?"

A passer-by spun around and regarded him strangely, and Sandler strode away and rode the moving ramp into the building. It seemed to be nothing more or less than a vast office building. Clicking machines could be heard through open doors. To a spacer accustomed to a different mechanical breed, they were alien machines, and their functions of writing letters, making records, sorting and filing seemed strangely exotic. Occasionally a pretty junior secretary darted out of a room, stepped onto the ramp, and rode away purposefully. Closed doors were marked with a man's name, a fancy title, and the word "Private." Sandler rode from one end of the building to the other and back again. He left the ramp where a glowing sign and an arrow pointed at the auditorium.

He recognized the room as soon as he stepped through the doorway. He recognized the myriad of globes that hung from the ceiling, dark because the room was not in use, but with planetary markings of a myriad of worlds dimly visible on their exteriors. He recognized the curving plastic front on the control room above the stage. He recognized the plushy seats and the flecks of gold that ran through the rich brown tapestry. He recognized . . .

He moved down the aisle, sat down, and leaned forward. When had it happened? In this life, or in another?

A bloated, bald-headed man—Mr. Minister, they called him—with a loud, sonorous voice that rose and fell in endless gyrations. A nurse with kindly eyes, a warm smile, and a body that had a friendly roundness despite the white stiffness of her dress. A small boy who hid behind the nurse and clung frantically to her skirts. A tall, thin, haughty-looking woman with fur on her dress bending over and staring at the boy and saying, "Aren't his ears a little pointed?" A gruff-looking doctor in a white coat. Other people dashing in and out, a moving blur of faces.

Mr. Minister: "You're an important woman this morning, Mrs. Sandler. You're the five millionth mother to adopt a child through the Ministry of Public Welfare."

Mrs. Sandler: "I think his ears are pointed."

The doctor: "No more than yours are."

Mrs. Sandler: "Well, I suppose I'll have to take him. I've waited three years, and I expected to wait two or three years more. He'll have to do. But I hate getting one so old. They always have so many nasty habits that have to be broken—or so I've been told. If one could only get them when they're babies, then they could be brought up properly."

Mr. Minister (horrified): "What's that? You wanted a *baby?*"

Mrs. Sandler: "Of course I wanted a baby, but I knew I couldn't get one."

Mr. Minister: "If she wanted a baby, why didn't you get her a baby?"

The Doctor: "If she wanted a baby, why didn't she have one herself?"

Mrs. Sandler: "I didn't come here to be insulted!"

Mr. Minister: "Why didn't you get her a baby?"

The Doctor: "There aren't any within light-years of here—not for adoption. We tried babies once, and the mortality rate was horrifying. So now we don't take a child until it's two or three.''

Mr. Minister: ''Well, if that's the way it has to be—we've kept the visiscope men waiting long enough, I guess. These films will be run all over the galaxy, you know. Does the boy know his lines?''

Nurse: ''He knows them perfectly.''

Mr. Minister: ''Say your lines, boy.''

The boy: ''Won't!''

Mr. Minister (whispering): ''Now get this, brat. We're going in there in front of the cameras, and you're going to do exactly what the nurse has told you, or I'll bat your ears off! That better be clear!''

Eyes half-closed, Sandler stared vacantly at the stage. Had he really stood there as a boy and chanted his lines like a very small robot? Had he ridden the hall ramp beside the tall, unfriendly woman, cringing at the coldness of her hand on his? Had he stood in the parking pavilion beside the shining air car and looked back at the building's odd windows and thought, ''Like sticking your finger into an arnel cake''?

A song unwound itself slowly in his mind, a lament of sad-dened beauty that had brought him halfway across the galaxy, home to Earth where he had no home.

> Home is a sigh
> For a color of sky,
> And a will to return.

''For a color of sky,'' he mused. Not the pale blue sky of Earth, nor the infinite shades of blue and lavender and green and yellow and red that he had seen in his tireless treks across space. A blue sky that was not blue. A touch of green in the sunset, a touch of pink at the dawn and bright promise of the day to come.

He rode the ramp to the end of the hallway and stopped at an information desk. The young lady in charge smiled encouragingly, and Sandler said, ''I have a problem. I was an adopted child, and I'd like to find out who my real parents were and where I come from.''

Her smile faded. ''You were adopted through the Ministry of Public Welfare?''

''Yes. Right here in this building.''

"We only discuss these cases with the adopting parents."

"They're both dead."

"I see. Would you fill out this card, please?"

She dropped the card into a slot, and less than a minute later it flipped out of a delivery chute. Stamped across its face in bright red letters were the words, "File Negative."

"Evidently no such records were kept," the girl said. "Sorry."

II

The blonde had finished her song, and she was moving about the Martian Room, chatting with the guests and acting as an informal hostess. Sandler sat at an out-of-the-way table half concealed behind a bushy, fern-like plant, and the blonde walked past without seeing him, glanced back, and turned toward his table.

"You look lonely," she said, sliding into the opposite chair.

Sandler smiled. The music was playing softly in the background, some of the exotic plants gave off pleasing scents, and he had just finished a delicious terrestrial steak. But if the baffling emptiness he felt could be called loneliness, she was right.

"You're a spacer, aren't you?"

"Yep. Here today, light-years away tomorrow. A poor insurance risk, a poor matrimonial risk, and in the eyes of the politicians, a generally poor citizen."

"According to the politicians, you aren't a good citizen unless you vote the right way."

"Maybe that's it. I'm always in space on Election Day. Have some desert with me?"

"That's nice of you, but no, thank you. I'll have some coffee, though, if you don't mind."

Sandler touched a button and gave the order. Seconds later a server rolled across the room and gently attached itself to his table.

Sandler served the coffee. While they drank it he studied the girl, and she met his gaze effortlessly and without embarrassment. She was considerably older than he'd thought—thirty, at least. Her blond hair had darkish overtones that suggested it might be natural and a brilliant, almost bluish sheen that denied it. He tossed the problem aside. A man could go crazy speculating about a woman's hair.

"I heard you sing that song last night," he said. "Do you like it?"

"Everyone likes it. I sing it four or five times a night."

"It's an idiotic song," Sandler said. "Some of the words are nonsense."

"The words are beautiful."

Sandler chanted in a mocking singsong, "Home is a light across the night of love enshrined. Home is the smart of tears and a heart of faith left behind. Explain that, please."

"Feelings can't be explained. You've never had a home."

"You're right. I haven't. I can hardly remember my life before I was adopted—I was too young. I never got along with my foster parents, so I ran away to space when I was sixteen."

"That's odd," she said. She plucked a handkerchief from her bosom, blew her nose loudly, and added, "Dammit!"

"Something wrong?"

"I had a man. Government worker, fairly high up and doing well. We were going to get married and raise a big family. Then this song came along, and all of a sudden he had to go home. Only he didn't have any home. Like you, he was adopted, and he never knew where he came from. But he was determined to go, and off he went. I haven't heard from him since."

"If he was a government worker, maybe he was able to find out where he came from."

"I don't think he even tried. At least, when he left he didn't know where he was going."

"You should have gone with him."

"He wanted me to, but that song does things to me, too. I'm from Earth, from a small town on the other side of the planet, and do you know what I'm going to do? I'm leaving this place at the end of the month and going home. I'm going to buy a little restaurant and marry some local man if there are any available and make a home for as many children as I can have."

"The words are idiotic," Sandler said. "It must be the melody."

"Odd that it doesn't do anything to you. I thought it affected everyone."

"It brought me back to Earth. I thought I was coming home, but this planet isn't home. Not to me. At the Ministry of Public Welfare, today, I tried to find out where I came from. They say they have no record of it."

"They're lying, then. The government has records of everything."

"Are you certain about that?"

"Positive. I haven't lived in Galaxia for ten years without learning a thing or two about the government. Complain to your congressman."

"Congress isn't in session. Besides, spacers don't have congressmen."

"Complain to one of the congressmen-at-large. Tell him you're a traveling salesman, or something."

"I might do that," Sandler said. "Thanks. And good luck with the restaurant. And the large family."

She nodded and moved on to the next table. Sandler waited until he heard her sing the "Homing Song" one more time before he went up to his room.

As a spacer, Sandler considered the popular concepts of night and day to be awkward frames of reference. His living habits were adapted to duty time and free time, and during his free time he slept when he felt like it and generally conducted his life to suit his own convenience.

It irritated him to have his habits imposed upon by such an arbitrary thing as a planet's period of revolution. The dusters—as spacers referred to non-spacers—were always making appointments for times when Sandler preferred to sleep, and offices and stores were only too frequently closed when he felt like transacting business.

When he arrived at the Congressional Office Building he was mildly irked, but in no way surprised, to find no humans present except a score of weary custodians who were charting the routes of their robot cleaners by the flickering lights of control panels. He waited, got into conversation with the clerks as they arrived, and so charmed half a dozen young ladies that appointments with any of fifty congressmen were his for the asking.

Congressman Ringlow, a big, blustery, man-of-the-people type, inclined his shaggy head at Sandler and pointed at a chair. "Mr. Sandler? T. J. Sandler?"

"That's correct."

"Thomas Jefferson Sandler?"

"The third."

"I knew your father."

"My foster father," Sandler said. "I knew him, too—vaguely."

The congressman stiffened. "He was a close friend of mine,"

he announced haughtily. "I remember talking to him about you just after you ran away. He was very disappointed with you."

"We disappointed each other."

"Yes. Well, I suppose there are two sides to any disagreement. What can I do for you?"

"I was at the Ministry of Public Welfare, yesterday, trying to find out a few things. Such as where I came from originally and who my real parents are. I was told that no record was kept of this information."

"I can understand your wanting to know, but I can't very well help you if there's no record."

"I've been reliably informed—" He smiled, remembering the singer's confident assertion. "I've been reliably informed that the government always keeps records. I feel that I'm entitled to that information, and I resent being lied to."

The congressman stiffened again. "Here! That's rather strong language."

"I'm beginning to feel rather strongly about this."

The congressman got to his feet and strode to the window. "Your father—foster father—was a decent person," he said thoughtfully, speaking with his back to Sandler. "I think he'd have wanted you to have that information if you wanted it. I'll see what I can do."

"Thank you. You can reach me at the Terra-Central Hotel. Or leave a message there if I'm not in."

The message was waiting when Sandler got back to the hotel. Congressman Ringlow had checked with the Ministry of Public Welfare. No records had been kept on the background of a child placed for adoption by the ministry. This was a long-established governmental policy, pursued in the best interest of all concerned. The congressman expressed his regrets.

Sandler took an air cab out to the space port, reported at the offices of Interplanetary Transport, and presented his resignation. He collected his back pay and pay for accumulated leave time, and withdrew his retirement and savings funds. He converted most of this small fortune into Inter-galactic travelers' checks, which could be cashed anywhere in the galaxy with no identification other than a reasonable number of fingers to match the ten fingerprints on each check.

From the space port he flew directly to the Ministry of Public Welfare. He demanded a personal interview with the minister. After a series of awkward interviews with underlings, during which he became increasingly adamant, he obtained an appointment with the third assistant to the fourth sub-minister. He was shown into the office of a long-faced young man who squinted timidly at Sandler through bulging contact lenses. His pale countenance had a comical look of near-fright.

"It seems," he said shyly, examining a piece of paper, "that you made a certain inquiry at the information desk yesterday."

"I did."

"You did not accept the information that was furnished. You went to Congressman Ringlow and asked him to obtain further information for you."

"I did."

"And you still aren't convinced that we don't have the information you want."

"I am not. Until I am convinced, you're going to continue to hear from me."

"I have this for you," the official said. "It's a photograph of your record card. This card represents the ministry's complete record on any adoption case. You will find here all the information that is available with regard to your background. We've had so many queries of late—many quite as persistent as yours—that we've decided to supply similar photographs to any person requesting one."

Sandler took the photograph and glanced over it quickly: Medical report on the child, description, fingerprints, report on the foster parents, notes on follow-up investigations. A crisp notation on his running away at the age of (approximately) sixteen. End of record.

"Satisfied now?" the official asked hopefully.

"I'll be perfectly satisfied after I've compared this with the original."

"I'm afraid that's impossible. No unauthorized person can be permitted—"

Sandler's hand was in his pocket. He moved it slowly and revealed the bulging muzzle of a flame pistol. The official's eyes widened and his throat made gurgling noises.

Sandler spoke softly. "You have a master file screen on the wall. I'd hate to have to use this. At such close range there wouldn't be much left of you but your head and two legs. It would probably make me sick. Are you going to dial the file number, or shall I?"

"There's nothing there you don't already have."

"Then there can't be any harm in showing it to me. Photographs are very easily tampered with, and I don't like this blank space in the upper right corner. Dial."

The official dialed. In his nervousness he got the wrong card and had to dial again. Sandler made a quick comparison and turned, grinning triumphantly. "Just alike, you say? Look in the right-corner. 'Source One eighty-seven.' What does that mean?"

The official quickly darkened the screen. "I haven't the faintest idea."

"It refers to the world of my origin, doesn't it?"

"I don't know." He looked at the flame pistol and added, "It might."

"There'll be a list of planetary sources somewhere. Where is it?"

"I don't know. The ministry hasn't handled any adoptions for years, and I don't know anything about them."

Sandler decided to believe him. "Why all the secrecy about this?"

"I don't make policy. I just follow orders."

"A lucky thing for you." He pocketed the pistol. "Now listen—I'm not going to tell anyone where I got this information as long as you don't mention it. If you make a complaint, I'll say I bribed you for it. Is that clear?"

"Certainly."

"Get away from your desk."

Sandler found the recorder and erased their conversation. "If anyone asks you," he said, "you forgot to turn it on. I thank you for your cooperation."

He rode the ramp back to the parking lot. No alarm sounded. A few minutes later he was back at his hotel. He rented a private pool, floated lazily in the water staring at the brilliant designs in the tiled ceiling, and sang lustily. "From far I come, a drifting scum upon the void. No home have I, no world to cry, nor asteroid."

He wanted to go home. He was going home. The far-reaching, all-powerful, omniscient galactic government was stubbornly opposed to his so much as knowing where that home might be. He formulated several crucial questions, and he began to make plans to shake some satisfactory answers out of responsible officials. By the neck, if necessary.

III

The blonde sang a different song in the Martian Room that night, and afterward she stopped at Sandler's table and said glumly, "Heard the news?"

"What news is that?"

"Ministry of Public Welfare. Censorship Department. The 'Homing Song' is bad for public morale. Further performances prohibited."

"How could that song harm anyone?"

"It couldn't, unless it's bad to make people want to go home. And since it isn't, I figure there's something about it that might harm the government."

Sandler nodded thoughtfully. It was of a pattern, along with the ministry's refusal to give him the information he wanted. "What would happen if you sang the song?" he asked.

"It would cost me a month's pay, at least. I could even get into trouble for telling you this. The censorship is supposed to be kept confidential. The government seems to think the song will run off and hide if professional performers stop singing it."

"That's ridiculous. Everyone in the galaxy knows it by this time."

"Try that argument on a governmental edict."

"What would happen if the public demanded the song? I mean, supposing your audience started calling for it the next time you're on?"

"I still couldn't sing it. But it would be fun!"

"We'll try it and see what happens."

As she moved onto the stage for her next song, he called out, " 'Homing Song'!"

A murmur of approval rippled about the room. The blonde ignored it, and as she started her song, Sandler called out again. The other guests began to chant, " 'Homing Song'!" and drowned out the music.

Sandler sat back to enjoy the confusion, felt a firm hand on his shoulder, and found himself staring at the credentials of a government public investigator. He paid his check and followed along meekly.

Outside the door he faced the burly officer and demanded, "What's the charge?"

"Disturbing the peace. Endangering public morale."

"You'll have some fun proving that, fellow, with everyone in the place doing the same thing."

"I'll prove it." He patted his pocket. "I have a recording. You started the disturbance."

"If you can convince a judge that it was a disturbance."

At Police Central Sandler was registered and passed along to the night court. The white-haired judge listened to the charges, had the evidence played, and questioned the investigator incredulously.

"You say the Censorship Department has prohibited this song, but the public has not been informed. The defendant certainly could not have known that he was asking the singer to do something unlawful. There is no indication that the hotel guests or its management regarded his actions as a public disturbance. The evidence points to the contrary." He paused. "I doubt that the courts will uphold the censorship order against the 'Homing Song,' but I see no need to concern myself with that question now. Case dismissed."

"I intend to appeal the dismissal," the investigator said haughtily.

"The law states that you may make such an appeal at your discretion. I shall schedule a hearing for ten tomorrow morning before Judge Corming, and I recommend that in the meantime you give some consideration to the meaning of the word 'discretion.' "

As a final insult to the investigator, he fixed bond at ten credits. Sandler posted the bond, caught a ground cab, and then dismissed it two blocks from the station. He strolled slowly along Vega Boulevard and several times stopped to look cautiously behind him.

The investigator's presence in the Martian Room had been no accident. His arrest on the flimsiest of pretexts had been no accident. The government wanted him out of the way, and if Judge Corming refused to cooperate the case would be appealed further, or the police would fabricate new charges. If he didn't want to spend the next few years trying to break rocks with a light hammer on a low-gravity satellite, he'd have to move cautiously.

He heard strains of music, entered a small café, downed two drinks, and lost his newly acquired caution. He turned to the musicians and shouted, " 'Homing Song'!"

A near riot followed, but Sandler did not wait to see the

outcome. He hurried off into the night, taking his patronage to another café, and to a stylish restuarant, and to a smoke-filled tavern, and with identical results. By the time he got back to his hotel, two dozen eating and drinking places along Vega Boulevard were rocking to the chant " 'Homing Song'!," police cars were swooping down from all directions, and Sandler was in a mildly intoxicated condition.

From his hotel room window, he looked down at the clusters of police cars and tried to make out what was happening. Above him the sky was clear, the stars bright and coldly distant.

"Somewhere out there is where I belong," he told himself. "And I'm going there. It may be only a dump of a planet, but it's mine."

> A moonlet drear
> With atmosphere
> Is sacred ground.
> The barren loam
> Of any home
> Is flower-crowned.

An air car darted across the face of the hotel building, slowed abruptly, and dropped past his window. He threw himself to the floor as a heavy flame gun burned the air above him, wrecked his bed, and bored into the far wall. He dove for his baggage and came up with his own pistol, but the air car was already out of sight.

The hotel manager charged in a few minutes later, surveyed the damage, and stood fretfully wringing his hands.

"I think," Sandler said calmly, "that someone doesn't like me. It might be better for both the hotel and myself if I were to check out."

The manager agreed enthusiastically.

Traveling a tortuously meandering route, Sandler checked in at a shabby spacers' hotel near the port. He registered under an assumed name, paid for one night in advance, and settled into his cramped room to make plans.

He had no intention of placing himself in the hands of the police a second time, and when he failed to appear in court he would be a bona fide fugitive from justice. The government would begin searching for him openly. His photo would be circulated, transportation agencies would be notified, and port officials alerted. His situation would grow more perilous by the minute. Whatever he did had to be done quickly.

At dawn he carried his belongings to the port. He left them in a rented locker, descended to a lower level, and at a dispenser bought a handful of tokens for the only anonymous means of transportation in Galaxia—the overburdened pneumatic underground railroad. The masses facetiously referred to it as the air train.

Sandler changed trains five times and rode to the end of the line in a distant part of Galaxia. In a public visiphone booth, he hung his coat over the visual transmitter and made four calls.

A distinguished Galaxia attorney: "My dear sir, we might be able to establish your right to information about your parents and the planet of your origin, but what good would that do if government officials were to swear under oath that no record of this information exists? You'd win your point without gaining a thing."

The editor of a leading opposition newspaper: "We're always happy to embarrass the administration, but we don't want to embarrass it *that* much. The Department of Censorship would close us. I advise you to get away from Earth while you're still healthy."

A prominent visiscope commentator: "The less I know about this, the better I'll like it."

An opposition congressman: "Your case isn't the first I've heard about. Sure, we could stir things up a bit. But it wouldn't help you, and the Expansionist Party would spend a billion to defeat me next election. My advice: Forget it!"

Sandler checked both viviscope and the newspapers and found no mention of the disturbances over the "Homing Song." He wondered if the government would be satisfied if he quietly faded away. At a minimum there would be a galaxy-wide Confidential on him. Never again would he be able to use his own name or land openly on a planet without undergoing continuous and humiliating harassment.

"And since I'm into it that far," he told himself, "I might as well go all the way. I think I'll have a quiet talk with this Minister of Public Welfare."

But he could visualize that august individual shaking his head mockingly and saying, "Sorry. We have no records. No records at all. Be very happy to help you if I could. I knew your foster father. But without records—"

There were drugs, talk pills and anti-hib sprays and truth serums in a multitude of types, each with complicated medical and investigative uses. None of them were available to casual purchasers, no questions asked.

Sandler prowled the streets until he found a doctor's office. He intentionally avoided looking at the name, concentrating on the faded word "Psychiatrist," as he climbed the worn stairway. He emerged in a hallway that reeked of a strange mixture of odors, most indefinable and probably unmentionable. On the street level there had been a pawnbroker's establishment. On the floors above were dwelling units. He could hear squalling children and snarling mothers. This was the reverse side of the polished, gem-like capital of the galaxy. The night side. The foul, indescribable slum side.

The consultation room was jammed with the slovenly dregs of humanity: The aged, the infirm, the addicts, the alcoholics, all shabbily dressed, all waiting with dumbly inexpressive faces for the forces of healing to probe their crumbling minds.

Sandler turned aside and edged his way along the filthy hallway. Again avoiding the doctor's name, he pressed his ear to a door.

". . . Mrs. Schultz," a shrill male voice said. "Then I'll see you Tuesday at eleven."

Shuffling footsteps. A door opening. The shrill voice asking, "Who's next?" And then, as the visiphone gong chimed musically, "Just a moment, please."

The door closed. The visiphone mumbled inaudibly. The shrill voice piped, "What's that you say? Oh, pills! Yes, as soon as I can get there."

Footsteps moved urgently about the room and suddenly approached the door. Sandler stepped back as the lock clicked and raised his flame pistol. The doctor halted with the door half-opened, his wrinkled face transfixed with amazement. Sandler pushed through and closed the door after him as the doctor backed away.

The doctor cackled mockingly. "I don't suppose, young man, that you've called for professional assistance."

"I want to buy something," Sandler said.

"You've come to the wrong place. I'm a psychiatrist. I don't kept addictive drugs in my office. If I did, in this neighborhood, it'd be broken into ten times a night."

"I don't want addictive drugs," Sandler said.

"I have an emergency. A man has been injured in a street brawl. They call a psychiatrist to treat a bump on the head—but then, there aren't any other doctors in this neighborhood. Please state your business quickly."

He was a mere wisp of a man, gaunt, the pink of his head radiant beneath his sparse white hair. Sandler remembered the riffraff in the waiting room and regarded him with admiration. He was a real doctor, a doctor who lived only to serve.

He said firmly, "I want a hypodermic syringe and a maximum dose of truth serum."

The doctor scrutinized him with professional interest. "You don't look like a bad man."

"I'm a wronged man," Sandler said wearily. "I've harmed no one, I've violated no law, but the police are looking for me and an agency of the government has tried to murder me. I ask you in the name of justice to sell me what I want and forget about it."

"The police have truth serum," the doctor said. "I might forget, but could you?"

"I've done everything I could to protect you. I don't know your name. I'm a stranger in Galaxia, and once I leave your office I'll never be able to find my way back here."

"Even so, it would be safer for me to report it. Tomorrow—supposing I report it tomorrow?"

Sandler nodded.

"Well, then—I can't sell the things to you. Look." He got out a hypodermic syringe and filled it. "I'm ready for my next patient. And I get an emergency call, and in my hurry I forget to lock the door. I'm an old man, and I won't miss the thing until tomorrow. So?"

Sandler stepped aside, and the doctor hurried away. He grabbed the syringe and slipped a hundred-credit note into the doctor's desk. From the general character of his practice, Sandler thought he might need the money.

Sandler hurried down the stairs, saw the doctor tottering along the street, and turned in the opposite direction.

IV

The official residence of Jan Vildson, the Minister of Public Welfare, occupied a choice location at the intersection of Centaurian and Solar Avenues. Its grounds were enclosed on three sides by a towering, vine-covered wall. On the fourth was a tall commercial building, its wall windowless to the eighth story.

Sandler had circled the place a dozen times during the afternoon, gaping like an awed tourist while he made his plans. He'd expended a small fortune in air cab fares, riding back and forth to catch a passing glimpse of the mansion. He had prowled the neighborhood to set up alternate escape routes.

But he felt more determined than confident as he stood on Centaurian Avenue and watched the ground cab speed away. It was shortly before midnight, but the artificial "moons" that dotted the sky over Galaxia bathed the spacious avenue in light. He shouldered his heavy bag and hurried toward the minister's residence.

He reached the wall and crouched there under a steady whir of air traffic, seeking a shadow where there was none. From his bag he took a heavy, triangular-shaped building stone and tossed it so that its looping trajectory just cleared the wall. Then he raced along the street, tossing stones as he ran and hoping that at least one of them would trigger the mansion's alarm system. As he turned onto Solar Avenue he could hear a gong booming faintly, far away. He ran frantically, reached the far corner of the wall, and hauled himself up on the clinging vines.

On the other side he slid to the ground and sprinted for the cover of weird-looking, spiral-leaved shrubs. Men were dashing about at the other end of the grounds, and their shouts reached him faintly. He heard the excited yelp of a dog. Crouching, he ran from shrub to shrub and finally hurled himself into the tall, sprawling density of a flower bed. The flowers were of some exotic species, and they were in full bloom. The heavy sweet scent overpowered and stifled him, and he lay gasping for breath.

The alarm continued to sound. More men arrived, and a squadron of patrol cars swooped down and landed in an open space near the mansion. Sandler kept his head down, sank his fingers into the rich, moist soil, and waited.

His racing pulse counted off the minutes. Then the alarm stopped suddenly. Two of the searchers came trudging back and met a third man near the gate.

"Some idiot threw stones over the wall," one of them said.

The patrol cars lifted gracefully, one at a time, circled, and moved off in formation. Other men came straggling back in twos and threes. There was more grumbling conversation as they disappeared around the corner of the mansion.

A sentry resumed his plodding circuit of the grounds. With his head raised cautiously above the flowers, Sandler timed his movements and began planning a route of approach.

His first sprint carried him across twenty feet of open lawn to the cover of a large tree. He moved in spurts separated by maddening intervals of crouched waiting. After forty minutes of cautious maneuvering he was huddled in the scant shadow of a flowering bush studying a balcony that extended out over an artistically landscaped terrace. At one side, flowering vines wove their way up a metal framework. Sandler watched the sentry and waited.

The sentry moved out of sight behind the building. Sandler ran, leaped, and hauled himself up the vines. Thorns stabbed at him, ripping his hands and clothing. He stumbled across the balcony and tried the door. It opened easily. He stepped through, closed it silently, and squinted into the darkness.

Suddenly a beam of light struck him full in the face, blinding him. "All right, Fritz. See if he's armed," a crisp voice said.

Sandler closed his eyes and stood with fists clenched. Hands moved expertly over his body, spun him around roughly, and removed his pistol. The room lights came on, and Sandler saw three men watching him alertly. Two of them had flame pistols leveled unwaveringly at his stomach.

The crisp voice spoke again. "You're a patient man, friend. But then—so am I. I've been watching you for the last half-hour." He turned to the others. "I can handle him. I'll call you if I need you."

The door closed behind them, and he gestured with his pistol. "Now, then. You will sit down there and place your hands on the table. Right. Jan Vildson is my name. Minister of Public Welfare. And you are Thomas Jefferson Sandler. What can I do for you?"

The minister was an elderly man, but swarthy, robust-looking, and without a touch of gray in his black hair. He looked a youthful sixty-five and could have been fifteen years older.

"You surprise me," Sandler said boldly. "You hardly look like a scoundrel."

"I was thinking the same about you, young man. I've known you for longer than you think. I knew your adopted father well. He had high hopes for you. On your performance of the past two days I'd say you were quite capable of fulfilling his hopes. You show a commendable determination. It's a pity you squander it on trivialities."

"If my objective is so trivial," Sandler said, "why is the government going to such extremes to make me fail?"

The minister seated himself on the opposite side of the wide table and laid his pistol in front of him. "Trivial or not, your objective is certainly futile. The information you want was destroyed years ago—long before I became Minister of Public Welfare."

"The planet of my origin is clearly indicated on my record card."

"The planet's *number* is indicated. The number refers to a list of several hundred planets from which orphan children were taken for adoption. The number has no meaning without that list, and all copies of the list have been destroyed."

"Why was the list destroyed?"

The minister shook his head slowly. "Perhaps for the most noble of reasons, perhaps for stupid bureaucratic expediency, perhaps for criminal reasons—though I don't know what they could have been. It doesn't matter. We can't undo it now, we can't undestroy something that's been destroyed. I'm sincere, and everyone else has been sincere, in telling you to forget the whole business."

He paused, and Sandler waited silently.

"Now here is what I suggest," the minister went on. "You're in trouble, but it isn't serious trouble. I believe I can arrange to keep the whole affair quiet. I'll see that you get to the port and onto an outgoing ship. There will be no police report on your performance of this evening. After all, you are the son of an old friend. What do you say?"

"Will you answer a few questions?"

"Gladly, if I have the answers."

"The Department of Public Censorship is under your control, isn't it?"

"It is."

"Why have you banned performances of the 'Homing Song'?"
The minister looked puzzled. "The 'Homing Song'? Banned?"

"Bad for public morale. Or so your censors say."

"I've heard the song. Who hasn't? But I don't recall anything— *banned*, you say? I'll have to look into that."

"Banned without public notice. I was arrested for asking a professional performer to sing it."

The minister shook his head perplexedly.

"What government official gave the order to have me murdered?" Sandler asked. "Was it you?"

The minister slowly rose to his feet. "Murdered? Someone ordered you murdered?"

"I was fired on from an air car. Fortunately I ducked in time, but it made a mess of my hotel room."

The minister dropped back into his chair. "That's not true," he protested. "It can't be true."

Sandler dove across the table and seized the pistol. He regained his seat, breathing heavily, and held the weapon under the table. "If your men check up, you'll tell them everything is under control."

The minister had a hurt expression on his face. "You tricked me. I've tried to be nice to you, Sandler. I've given you every consideration—"

"Shut up!" Sandler snapped. "I'm a nobody, and I don't expect special consideration. However important my foster father may have been, I'm a nobody. All I want to do is go home. Why is the Federation Government determined to do anything in its power, legal and illegal, up to and including murder, to keep me from doing that? Why would it prefer me dead rather than answer questions about my home planet?"

"You shouldn't make such reckless accusations. Why would the government want to kill you?"

"No one outside the government cares what I do. I haven't any other enemies, and it isn't coincidence that my arrest and the attempted murder came immediately after I started these inquiries. Now—the planet's number is One eighty-seven. What is it, and where is it?"

"I told you the truth. To the best of my knowledge, there isn't a copy of that list in existence."

Sandler loosened his shirt and gripped the hypodermic syringe he had taped to his arm. "I've had enough of your kind of truth. Now I want my kind. Bare your arm, please."

The minister straightened up in alarm. "What's that you have?"

"Truth serum. I mean you no harm, but I'm going to have the truth if I have to kill you to get it."

"You don't believe me?" the minister croaked, his frightened eyes focused on the needle. "Think of it. Old T. J.'s son calling me a liar. Do you know, Sandler, I held you on my lap when you weren't more than six years old?"

The screen on the far wall flickered to life. One of the minister's guards glanced at them suspiciously. "Everything all right, sir?"

Sandler's hand tensed on the pistol.

"Everything's all right," the minister said weakly. The screen darkened.

Sandler rounded the table and stood waiting. "Bare your arm," he ordered.

"That's dangerous," the minister protested. He looked at Sandler's face, shrugged, and slipped out of his coat. "If that's all that will satisfy you—"

He rolled up his sleeve, and Sandler inexpertly jabbed the needle into his arm. He walked back to his chair and tossed the syringe under the table.

He watched the minister anxiously, wishing he'd got more information from the doctor. He hadn't any idea how much time the serum might require to take effect. The minister leaned back in his chair, eyes closed, breathing deeply.

Finally Sandler asked, "What is planet One eighty-seven?"

"Don't—know. List—destroyed."

"Who would have a copy of the list?"

"Destroyed—long ago."

"Why was the list destroyed?"

The minister doubled up suddenly, clutching both hands to his heart. His breath came in whistling gasps, his face was white and taut, and his teeth were clenched in searing agony. Sandler dashed around the table and bent over him in alarm.

He remembered belatedly that he had casually asked the doctor for a maximum dose of truth serum—and that a maximum dose might be too much for a man of eighty. It was too much. The minister was dying.

Sandler hurried to the balcony and looked out across the grounds. The sentry was not in sight. He slid quickly to the ground and ran. There was no time to worry about taking cover. He reached the wall and was going over the top when a light flashed in the balcony's open door. At the same time the alarm gong boomed urgently.

Sandler drove himself in merciless, headlong flight for two long blocks to an air train station. He hurtled down the moving escalator stairs, thrust a token into the turnstile, and pushed through, glancing anxiously at the clock, He had spent an hour, that afternoon, memorizing train schedules. He was waiting on the right platform twenty-five seconds later when a train glided smoothly to a stop. He boarded it, transferred at the next station, and rode the trains until dawn, leaving a meandering, crisscrossing trail through subterranean Galaxia.

He spent the day in a squalid hotel, and that evening he wove another meandering trail out to the port. He collected his belongings, and with the wile of a veteran spacer stowed away on a lumbering ore freighter that lifted at midnight for Mars. The freighter's crew smuggled him past Mars Customs, and he bought forged identity papers and shipped as a common spacer on a ship outward bound from the Solar System.

He stood in an observation port for a last, contemptuous look at Earth—a brittle spark thrown off by a shrinking sun.

V

Thomas Jefferson Sandler III drifted slowly across the galaxy, a derelict caught in weirdly eccentric currents. He shipped as a spacer when he found a post. He stowed away. Once he joined a hopeful group of immigrants in their cramped quarters. He piloted a cargo of smuggled gold from Lamruth to Emmoy. On Kilfton he was recognized, and he killed two guards in escaping.

Or perhaps they recovered. He never heard what happened to them, or cared.

Twice he encountered Marty Worrel, but he cautiously kept his distance. The little musician had a pronounced talent for fomenting disturbances—as on Hillan, where he got up on a table in a crowded tavern and sang his "Homing Song." Sandler made a hurried exit before the police appeared. He could not risk being associated with any kind of disturbance.

He drifted on, moving always outward from Earth, following the long axis of the galaxy. In Sector 187 he invaded the private residence of the Sector Commissioner, thinking that the number on his identification card might refer to sector rather than to planet. The commissioner persisted in his declarations of ignorance with Sandler's fingers about his throat. Sandler left him unconscious, stowed away once more, and drifted onward. He waylaid a dozen sector Chiefs of Public Welfare. He attempted to bribe government officials, and he threatened them with violence and sudden death, and he learned nothing.

The months drifted by and became years. Sandler moved from planet to planet, searching for a color of sky, for anything that would match his few blurred recollections of home. Hot worlds and cold, wet worlds and dry, he studied them hopefully from an observation port, wandered their surfaces until disillusion seized him, and then left without a backward glance.

Three years after leaving Earth, he stood staring at the dingy, gray face of one more planet as his ship flashed downward, and he felt depressed. Usually a new planet offered some hope, but not this one. Twisting clouds of dust erupted and slowly spread their heavy film across its surface. It was Stanruth; barren, lifeless, waterless world, but a world rich in minerals, so there was a colony, and there were humans who sought wealth, and found it or failed to find it, and fled homeward. No one would call Stanruth "home."

"But then—who can say?" Sandler muttered. Some day, perhaps children born on that blighted planet might see it as a place of beauty.

> The barren loam
> Of any home
> Is flower-crowned.

To Sandler, it was no more than a steppingstone that he must touch in passing. It was one strange world of many in the weary fabric of his existence, of his coming and going, of his hiding, of his seeking and not finding.

The ship landed, and he tensed himself for the inevitable customs inspection. His handsome, young-looking face had undergone transformation. He had scarred it hideously. His head was shaven bald. He wore a bushy, uncouth beard. His body was a weird gallery of spacer tattoos. But he knew that sooner or later a sharp-eyed official would recognize him and his search would be over.

He passed through customs almost unnoticed and moved on into the stark, treeless town. The building stones were fused sand. Sand drifted everywhere, and even the feet of a slow-moving pedestrian stirred up clouds of dust.

Sandler entered a squalid tavern, where a tumbler of water cost a credit and a bottle of good whisky was only a rumor at any price. He glanced about the smoke-filled interior and saw, huddled in a dark corner, a familiar figure: that little man of enormous talent and small worth, Marty Worrel.

Worrel's apparent sobriety intrigued Sandler, and he slid onto a fused-sand bench across the table from him and said, "Hello."

Worrel stared without a spark of recognition. "Do I know you?"

Sandler leaned forward and whispered, "From far I come, a drifting scum upon the void."

Worrel winced and glanced about cautiously. "Whoever you are," he said, "you've changed."

"You haven't changed. I thought that song would make you a billionaire with a big estate and a dozen air cars. I suppose someone stole it from you. You've been wearing the same suit for the last four years. It doesn't even look as though you've had it off."

"Clothes," Worrel said disgustedly. "Rags to hide the body's immodesty. The soul fashions its own raiment." He signaled for drinks and waved Sandler's money away. "I *am* a billionaire. A millionaire, anyway. Someone copyrighted that song for me. I didn't even know about it. I have money in the banks of half the planets of the galaxy. And what's money? The dowry of evil. The prop of tyranny. The strangling nourishment of greed. It corrodes the soul. It buys a woman's honor and a man's integrity. It lays waste to the body and stifles happiness. We are wanderers all, we puny humans, seeking wealth to buy the unattainable. You want money. I'll give you money. Hell, I'll give it all to you."

He slumped forward, spilling his expensive whisky, and sobbed brokenly with his face buried in his hands.

Sandler straightened up in alarm. "You're drunk," he said disgustedly.

"I'm always drunk. What else is there? One must be either drunk or sober, and I'm drunk. Money can buy *that*. Money buys whisky and whisky benumbs the senses and benumbed senses crave whisky and whisky requires money and money buys whisky and whisky benumbs the senses—"

He sobbed again and began to sing, in a cracked, nasal voice. "Home is that place in deepest space where memories burn."

Sandler leaned over and slapped Worrel's face. Worrel's head snapped back, and he shook himself, stared oddly at Sandler for a moment, and signaled for another drink. "What are you doing here?" he asked.

"Seeking the unattainable. Without money."

"You are a wise man. A wise, noble, generous, virtuous, deserving, admirable, good, worthy, unculpable—" He paused and squinted doubtfully. "What did you say your name was?"

"I didn't," Sandler said.

"No-Name. It's best that way. A name is but a label applied at birth through the connivance of dishonorable parents. I like you, No-Name. What did you say you were seeking?"

Sandler glanced about them cautiously. More spacers had come in, and the place rocked with their boisterous laughter. Bartenders and serving girls were rushing about frantically. The dingy corner was ignored, but Sandler leaned forward and said in a whisper, "Home."

Worrel paused with his glass in mid-air, face pale, manner unaccountably sober. "We must talk," he said. He drained his glass and screamed, "Bottle of whisky!" A serving girl hurried over. Worrel paid her and gripped Sandler's arm. "Come. We must talk."

He led Sandler from the tavern and along the dusty street. They entered a shabby, sand-eroded rooming house and climbed three flights of stairs to Worrel's room. It was virtually unfurnished. The bed was a pile of filthy blankets in one corner. In another corner was a pile of empty bottles. A bench of fused sand stood against one wall. Powdery dust covered everything.

Worrel seated Sandler on the bench, dashed out again, and returned with a pair of tumblers. He poured the drinks with trembling fingers and squatted on the floor.

"Tell me," he said. "Tell me everything."

Sandler sketched out the story of his frustrated efforts to find his home planet, carefully omitting any hint of criminal activity.

"But you did find the number of your planet," Worrel said excitedly. "What is it?"

"One eighty-seven."

Worrel got slowly to his feet. He fumbled in an inside pocket, produced a card, and handed it to Sandler: A photograph of a Ministry of Public Welfare record card concerning a child identified as Marty Worrel. And this photograph was complete. In the upper right corner Sandler read, "Source: 187."

Worrel snatched the card and stood in front of Sandler, body tense, eyes gleaming, his small, wrinkled face alight with tremendous excitement. "Brother!" he whispered.

Sandler nodded slowly. "I suppose I could be your brother."

"And we have a sister. Come!"

He gripped Sandler's arm, hurried him down a flight of stairs, and rushed him into a room on the floor below. This room was neatly furnished, tidy, almost free from dust. Its sole occupant was a young woman, who started up and hastily draped a robe over her bare limbs as they entered.

"Another one!" Worrel called. "Another One eighty-seven."

"No!" she exclaimed. She stared wide-eyed at Sandler, disbelief showing in her lovely face. "You look—well, so old for a space-orphan."

"Space-orphan?" Sandler echoed.

"From far we come, a drifting scum upon the void," Worrel chanted. "Space-orphans are we, and space-orphans we shall ever be. Cast us adrift in time, wrap us gently in the empty shroud of space, and lull us to sleep with the clanging music of the spheres. No one cares, and nothing else matters. Home is a moonlet drear with atmosphere, and who gives a damn whether the homeless breathe or not?" He waved his bottle. "Let's drink to One eighty-seven, somewhere on the bottom side of nowhere."

"You're drunk again, Marty," the girl sighed.

"I'm drunk *yet*," he corrected. "Oh. Introductions. Miriam, this is No-Name. No-Name, this is Miriam." He thrust his head forward and looked inquiringly at Sandler. "You're sure you haven't got a name?"

"My adopted name is Thomas Jefferson Sandler."

"So that's who you are. I remember. You're a pilot. You've changed. Your own mother wouldn't recognize you." He laughed shrilly. "That's a joke. Your own mother—"

"How did you find out you were both from One eighty-seven?" Sandler asked.

"Bribery. Cost me fifty thousand. That's another use for money. It adapts itself to any dishonorable purpose."

Miriam was still watching Sandler with frank suspicion. "Marty, are you sure he's—I mean, he looks so *old*."

"He's a fugitive from injustice," Worrel said. "That ages one. On the other hand, how *do* I know you came from One eighty-seven?"

The girl turned her back to them and whirled around suddenly with a small pistol in her hand. "We can't afford to take chances," she said sharply. "Prove it!"

Sandler moved over to the wall and sat down on a bench. "My papers are forged," he said. "I'm wanted on every planet in the galaxy for murder, attempted murder, assault on highly placed oficials, smuggling, flouting of customs regulations, unlawful flight to avoid whatever charges may have been placed against me, and an odd assortment of other things. I had a photo of my record card, but I lost it long ago. What proof do you want?"

She hesitated. "Can you remember anything at all about home?"

"A color of sky," Sandler said slowly, "that I can't describe, but if I saw it I think I'd know. I've tried many times to remember, but it's all so vague. A mud hut, with narrow slits in the walls. A small boy hurrying proudly home carrying an ornt by the tail. A mother who is a shapeless figure without features, and who is also wonderful. A father who helps a small hand grip a spear that is much longer than the boy. An arnel cake. Not much, is it?"

The pistol disappeared. Miriam threw herself on him, gripped him tightly, and kissed him profusely.

"One of us," Worrel said and chanted loudly. "Three space-orphans are we. Three space-orphans we be. Two are you and one is me. I am a minority." He sat down on the floor and tipped up the bottle.

"Stop it, Marty," Miriam pleaded. "Maybe he has some ideas. Maybe we can plan."

Worrel got up abruptly. "Plan," he said. "You have a plan?"

"No," Sandler said. "I'm just drifting, I've killed one man and possibly more, and I've nearly choked several men to death, and all I can find out is that no one knows. One eighty-seven is just a number. We'd be as well off not to know it. Better off, maybe."

Worrel seemed oddly sober again. "I know a man," he said. "Commissioner of Sector Fifteen thirty-one. He's an old man, he's been around a long time, and he knows something about the space-orphans. He goes around looking for them and asking them questions. Me he won't talk to. Me he laughs at. You're a man of action. He won't laugh at you."

"I'll see him," Sandler said. "Who is he?"

"Name's Novin. Commissioner Novin. On Pronna."

"Then I'll go to Pronna."

"We'll all go to Pronna," Worrel said. "We'll leave today."

"There may not be a ship."

"There'll be a ship. I'll buy a ship with my filthy, filthy money. When we find One eighty-seven, I'll buy the planet and throw the Federation off. I'll buy a space fleet and demolish Earth. I'll buy paradise and populate it with space-orphans. What sector do you suppose paradise is in? Is that another number no one remembers?'' He sat down again and tilted the bottle.

VI

Worrel bought a ship, a rusted space-worn freighter, but Sandler had to qualify for a pilot's license under his assumed name, and it was a week before they could leave Stanruth. They made slow, plodding progress, stopping off at a dozen planets for Worrel to convert his bank accounts into cash.

On New Miloma they traded their freighter and half a million credits for a sleek space yacht that Worrel renamed, privately, the *187*. On Calmus they waited several days while Worrel completed complicated arrangements to withdraw some money from banks across half the galaxy. They landed on Filline for still more financial transactions and found the police waiting.

"Thomas Jefferson Sandler," the young captain said cheerfully. "The Galactic Bureau of Investigation has been wanting you badly for a long time."

"Sure," Sandler said. "How'd you locate me?"

"You made the mistake of qualifying—or should I say, requalifying—for a pilot's license. Your fingerprints went all the way to Earth, and eventually someone got around to making cross-checks. He was mostly pleasantly surprised. All of you are under arrest."

Worrel, caught in one of his rare moments of sobriety, turned on Sandler in panic. "Why'd you do it?" he hissed. "You didn't need a license. We could have sneaked off Stanruth and no one would have noticed."

"They always notice," Sandler said wearily. "Then all three of us would have been fugitives. This way it's only me." He turned to the captain. "Why bother these people? They didn't know who I was. They just hired a pilot."

"They'll have every opportunity to prove their innocence."

Sandler was flown out into the open country to a small, walled prison. He was treated with politeness and consideration. His cell was comfortable, his food excellent, and he was given fresh clothing. He shaved off his beard and began to feel better.

Through the months and years he had known that this day would arrive, and he faced it almost with a sensation of

homecoming. Ahead of him lay more futile quests, to Pronna, to
other planets; and more futile interviews with officials who could
not or would not talk; and more violence and more hiding. The
drifting scum, the space-orphan, was better off returned to the
void.

An elderly, dignified lawyer called on him that afternoon and
brought the welcome news that Worrel and Miriam had been
released. Worrel had hired him. He went over the file of charges
with Sandler, growing increasingly gloomy at each successive
item, and finally he recommended that Sandler plead insanity.

"They'll hold you for psych-treatment if you bring it off," he
said, "but that's better than death. The death penalty is still
revived for special cases—about one a century—and I think
they're going to make a special case out of you."

"Thanks," Sandler said dryly. "I'll think it over."

But he was determined that there would be no insanity plea for
Thomas Jefferson Sandler III. He wanted the entire sordid story
of his career in crime aired in open court. The government could
eliminate Sandler, but it couldn't eliminate the sensational publicity that attended a criminal trial.

Or couldn't it? Instead of a trial it could easily arrange a
convenient accident on the long trip back to Earth, and there
wouldn't be a thing that Sandler could do about that.

He went to bed, drifted off into a peaceful sleep, and was
awakened in the dim hours of early morning by an urgent
whisper.

"Sandler!"

He leaped to his feet. The cell door stood open, and Marty
Worrel was in the corridor prodding a guard with a flame pistol.

"Quick!" Worrel hissed.

Barefooted, half dressed, Sandler took Worrel's pistol and
hurried the guard on ahead of him. They found Miriam holding a
pair of guards at pistol point near the entrance. With quick,
deadly motions Sandler clubbed them into unconsciousness.

"Can we make the ship?" he demanded.

"We can try," Worrel said. "We've got an air car hidden
outside."

"Let's go!"

They sprinted across the brightly lighted yard to the prison
gate. The gate stood ajar, and a dead guard was crumpled in the
guardhouse, his face gruesome even in the shadows.

They moved through the gate and were running across the

glaring patch of light that surrounded the walls when a guard saw them. A shout rang out, and a heavy flame rifle burned the air above their heads.

"It's in a clearing in the woods," Miriam gasped.

The flame rifle fired again and missed. They were running in darkness, but Sandler knew they had only seconds before the rolling meadow would be lighted. The shadows of trees loomed far ahead of them. They stumbled across the slight depression of a water course, and Sandler guided them along it.

"It gives us some cover," he panted. "We'd better spread out. Running together we're too good a target. Miriam first."

They separated, running in single file along the water course. Trees loomed ahead of them.

The flame rifle snapped again, slicing between Sandler and Worrel. Sandler stopped, fired carefully, and heard a cry. He fired again, and shouts of alarm sounded behind him. "Slowed them down," he thought, and ran on.

Lights glowed suddenly, bathing the meadow in naked brilliance. Beams from a dozen rifles crackled about them. Miriam's piercing scream cut across the night, and Sandler flung himself to the ground and methodically cut down the silhouetted pursuers. He moved on a moment later and found Miriam bending over Worrel's prostrate figure.

"Go on," Worrel whispered urgently. "Don't worry about me. Go on!"

Without a word Sandler picked up the little musician and led Miriam into the safety of the trees. He carried Worrel gently, ignoring the gushing blood and the gaping emptiness that had been his right side.

They reached the air car. Sandler carefully placed Worrel on a seat, and Miriam bent over him with tears in her eyes as Sandler took the controls.

"No good at this sort of thing," Worrel whispered. "Gun in my hand scares me stiff. See what my filthy money brings me? Sordid end of a sordid beginning. One less glob of scum on the troubled face of time."

"Don't talk," Miriam pleaded.

"You should have left me there," Sandler said bitterly. "You two hadn't done anything wrong. You could have kept on looking. Now you'll be hunted along with me."

Worrel's words were pain-wracked sobs. "Needed you. Couldn't pull it off ourselves. I don't count, except for money. You two will make it."

Sandler brushed his hand across his wet eyes and lied bravely. "Nonsense. You'll make it."

"Sordid end of a sordid beginning." Worrel lurched forward. "If you make it—if you find One eighty-seven—take my ashes with you. Promise!"

"You'll make it right along with us," Sandler said.

"Promise!"

"Of course. But you'll make it."

Marty Worrel was dead when they reached the space port. They landed by their ship, and Sandler raced up the ramp with Worrel's dead body, wrenched open the sealed air lock, and hurried to the controls. Police cars were swarming down on the port, and they lifted just as officers and guards were fanning out to approach the ship.

Sandler busied himself for hours with a complex, zigzag course that would evade detection. Finally he relaxed and turned to Miriam.

"Maybe they don't know you were involved in that mess. I can drop you off somewhere, and you can find a new identity for yourself. The longer you're with me, the less chance you'll have."

She shook her head. "Pronna. Marty would have wanted it that way."

"Yes," he said. "I suppose so." He took her hand and stroked it gently. She attracted him as no woman had ever attracted him, and yet—

"You're a brave woman," he said, and added quickly, to be quite safe, "sister."

She smiled wanly. "No. You're a brave man. Maybe a little reckless, but brave."

They slipped in on the night side of Pronna and landed in a forest clearing. For an exorbitant fee a village mortician cremated Marty Worrel's body and asked no questions. Miriam found lodgings in the village, and Sandler turned most of Worrel's money over to her.

"If I don't come back," he said, "forget about the ship. Forget about One eighty-seven. Forget about me. Go off to the other side of the galaxy and make a new life for yourself."

"You'll come back," she said. "And I'll be waiting."

It took Sandler three days to make his way halfway around the planet to the capital city. It took him only twenty minutes, under the cover of darkness, to make his way into the sector commissioner's sprawling residence. His fiendish efficiency amused him. "Getting to be an expert at this sort of thing," he told himself grimly.

He cornered a frightened servant, got detailed information about the house, and left the servant in a closet, bound and gagged. He found the commissioner's bedroom, awoke the old man, and blinded him with a light.

"I mean no harm to you or anyone else," he said softly. "I want information."

"You pick an irregular way asking for it," the commissioner said testily. "Can we sit down and talk peacefully, or do you have to blind me?"

Sandler turned his light aside, locked the door, and flipped on the room lights. The commissioner stopped rubbing his eyes and studied Sandler curiously. He was a small man, with a grotesquely wrinkled face and a shining bald head, but there was lively alertness, almost humor, in his dark eyes.

"Thomas Jefferson Sandler," he chuckled. "I've been averaging one bulletin a month on you for years. I suppose I should have expected this." He got to his feet and ceremoniously indicated a chair. "Please be seated. And put the gun away. I know you mean well, but I can't help thinking those things are known to go off accidentally."

Sandler pocketed his pistol, seated himself, and watched alertly while the commissioner slipped into a robe. He took the chair opposite Sandler and smiled at him benevolently.

"You interest me, Thomas Jefferson Sandler. I'm pleased that you took the trouble to call on me."

"Planet One eighty-seven," Sandler said. "What is it and where is it?"

The commissioner shook his head. "I don't know. I believe I can safely say that no one knows. Such records as were kept were all in the files of the Ministry of Public Welfare on Earth, and my confidential information is that they were destroyed years ago."

"I've heard so many lies," Sandler said wearily. "How do I know you're telling the truth?"

Commissioner Novin held up his hand. "No truth serum, please. On my word as a sector commissioner, and a galactic citizen, and a fellow human being, that is the truth."

"I've learned that violence doesn't really solve anything, so I'll believe you. I'll offer you my thanks and apologies and leave."

"Oh, don't go," the commissioner exclaimed. "I don't know about planet One eighty-seven, but I may be able to help you. As I said, you interest me. By profession I'm a psychologist, and I've been following your career carefully. I've also studied the problem of what you probably call the space-orphans. I have my ways of finding out things, and I know somewhat more about the matter than the authorities on Earth. My position out here places me much closer to the problem. Sit down, please, and I'll tell you what I know."

Suspecting a trap, hand clutching the pistol in his pocket, Sandler sat down.

"I believe some background information is in order," Commissioner Novin said. "Among us humans, fads are peculiar things. Sometimes they are mildly eccentric, and sometimes they reach the point of absolute mania. At the present time, for example, large families are something of a fad among the wealthy. One measure of a man's success in life is the number of children he has. It is also a measure of a woman's adequacy as a wife. The fad is a mild one, treated somewhat humorously but nevertheless sincerely. Perhaps you've encountered it yourself."

"In recent years I've had very little social contact with wealthy families," Sandler said dryly.

"I consider this fad to be a direct reaction to a fad of roughly twenty to forty years ago in which women considered it a very real stigma to bear even one child. That fad did reach the point of mania and resulted in a craze for adopted children. Fortunately for the human race it was a passing thing, and it never touched the lower classes at all. It was not even pursued by a majority of the upper classes, but only by a small, closely knit, socially select group that centered in the Earth sector. The unfortunate consequences resulted from the fact that the group had financial and political influence all out of proportion to its numbers.

"The craze for adopted children quickly exhausted the supply, and political pressures resulted. The Ministry of Public Welfare set up a special department and began to search the galaxy for children available for adoption. And it encountered a stubborn obstacle. The well-organized, civilized planets had their own laws concerning such children, and they flatly refused to permit meddling by the Ministry of Public Welfare. The situation grew more critical, and the political pressure became enormous. And finally a solution was found. Do you mind if I smoke?''

Sandler shook his head. The commissioner produced a bulging cigar from the pocket of his gown, lit it, and waved it at Sandler, who was listening intently.

"The solution," the commissioner said, "was simple. The Federation is constantly expanding and constantly discovering new, inhabited planets. The people of many of those planets have at best a primitive civilization. A high percentage of them could be termed 'savages.' We don't need to go into the conflicting migration and evolution theories which try to account for the presence of humans on these newly discovered planets. The point is, humans are constantly being discovered and many of them are living under rather primitive conditions. Where there were no obvious difficulties, such as distinctive racial characteristics or an apparent low level of intelligence, children from these planets were—taken."

"Stolen?" Sandler gasped.

"If you like. 'Appropriated' is a more apt term, with the government proceeding as though it had a legal right to such action. The children were transported to Earth, educated to the normal level of a civilized child of their age, and distributed to the adoption-crazed wealthy."

"Inhuman!" Sandler muttered.

"Decidedly. I was, for a time, local administrator on one of those planets, and one day a converted battle cruiser dropped down on us with a skeleton detachment of pediatricians and nurses and orders from highest authority. They processed the native children carefully, picked out a shipload, and left." He pointed his cigar at Sandler. "They did it kindly, I suppose, but never as long as I live will I forget the plight of those unfortunate parents. Ships dropped in periodically as long as I remained on that planet."

"Inhuman," Sandler muttered again.

"Governments frequently tend to become inhuman. So do laws. The Federation Government is a huge, complicated, impersonal thing. Supposing a need for a certain metal develops. The government locates a planet rich in that metal that has a primitive population and literally strips it. Later, when the planet develops a technology and its own need for the metal, the supply is exhausted. This stripping of a helpless planet of its natural resources was called 'colonial exploitation' by the ancients. It was done frequently, and it's still being done."

He blew a cloud of smoke in the general direction of the ceiling and said slowly, looking intently at Sandler and weighing every word, "In the eyes of the government, those children were just another natural resource, there for the taking."

Sandler managed to control his anger and keep his voice steady. "Up until now I've regretted the murders I've had to commit. But no longer."

"Ah! But those you murdered were in no way responsible for the crime. The craze for adopted children waned long ago, and eventually government officials began to foresee unfortunate long-range consequences. The exploitation was halted, but that did not eradicate its terrible impact on native populations. Some native parents, after being deprived of one child after another, stopped having children. And today, some of those planets are almost depopulated."

A violent pounding shook the door, and Sandler leaped to his feet. The servant babbled hysterically, and the commissioner shouted, "All right. Go to bed. I'll tell the police myself in the morning."

Sandler took a deep breath and resumed his seat. "That still doesn't explain all the secrecy over this."

"Politics," the commissioner said. "Sordid politics. The Expansionist Party has been in power for more than a hundred and seventy-five years. It intends to remain in power indefinitely. Its margin has always been comfortable but never overwhelming, and now some of these exploited planets are approaching the point where they must be given full membership in the Federation. The Expansionist Party must admit them, because to refuse would be to abandon its own principles. It would certainly lead to defeat. On the other hand, if all the details of that miserable exploitation were made public, the opposition would certainly control those new planets, and a good many of the old planets would turn against the Expansionists. A party in power for a hundred and seventy-five years becomes firmly entrenched. It develops ways of silencing criticism. It permits opposition—it has to—but only up to a point. So the adoption scandal has been suppressed, and the Expansionists will go to any extreme to keep it that way."

"Even murder," Sandler said. "You may not believe it, but

my career in crime started back on Earth when the government tried to have me murdered.''

"Not the government. The Expansionist Party. What you were doing couldn't have harmed the government.''

"I'm grateful for your information. Now I'm able to understand why I'm a space-orphan, but that doesn't help me to find planet One eighty-seven.''

"This might," the commissioner said. "The Expansionist Party has already been defeated. It doesn't realize it, yet, but the next election, or the one after that, will bring us a new government. A number of those planets are in my sector, and during the past few years—in fact, ever since that odd 'Homing Song' went around the galaxy—space-orphans have been coming home by the thousands. They've dropped everything, wherever they were, and come home. Some even left wives or husbands and children.''

"How did they know where their homes were?" Sandler demanded.

"As a psychologist, I find that question intriguing. How *did* they know? I've talked with many of them, and they did not even go so far as to discover their planet numbers. They simply decided to come home. On the other hand, others, such as you, have searched widely about the galaxy without a glimmer of an idea as to where their home planet might be. Can you account for that?''

Sandler shook his head.

The commissioner discarded his shrunken cigar and lit another. "I have a theory," he said. "I give it to you for what it's worth and wish you luck. It is a well-known fact that many animals have a kind of homing instinct. So do many primitive peoples. Few civilized peoples retain any of it. The space-orphans are not far removed from primitiveness, and evidently they retain that homing instinct. With sufficient motivation, and the song gave them that motivation, they got themselves ships, and said, in effect, let's go that way, and went home.''

"Across *space?*" Sandler said incredulously. "That's impossible!''

"Of course it is. Any intelligent, civilized man realizes that, but the fact remains that they've been coming by the thousands and tens of thousands.''

"I can't believe it.''

"No. That's why you interest me. Lose a primitive human, and his instinct takes him home. Lose a civilized man, and he looks around for a map or a chart. You're a trained pilot and navigator, and you know far too much about space travel to attempt to rely on instinct for anything. You consult a star chart, and you make complicated mathematical computations, and you know they will take you where you want to go. But if you can't find your destination on a chart, if your objective is some vague entity like 'home,' you're completely frustrated. Your homing instinct has been civilized out of you."

Sandler said, "Yes . . . yes . . ." And he thought about Marty Worrel. Worrel the wanderer. Sandler the wanderer. If the theory were even remotely correct, the wanderers had carried their defeat within them. Worrel's foster father had been a space line executive, and Marty had been traveling almost since he was adopted. He'd even had rudimentary training in stellar navigation. Like Sandler, he'd been civilized.

But there was Miriam. Would she have found her way home if she hadn't burdened herself with Worrel and Sandler?

Sandler got up wearily, raising with him the crushing burden of wasted years and wasted lives. "I'm grateful," he said. "If anyone back there on Earth had been decent enough—"

The commissioner raised a hand. "I know you're no criminal. As I said, I saw it happen, and I'll never forget it."

"If I'm able, I'll test your theory."

"Please let me know how you make out."

"If it's at all possible, I will."

The commissioner ushered Sandler through the silent house and stopped once to open a safe and stuff a bundle of currency into his hand. "It might be best if the police think a common thief was here tonight," he said. "I'll give you a couple of hours' start before I call them."

Solemnly Sandler shook the commissioner's hand.

Three days and a night later, Sandler and Miriam shot spaceward under the cover of darkness. When they reached deep space, Sandler turned to Miriam. "It's up to you, now," he said.

She smiled sadly. "I've always known, but I was afraid to trust myself. It's that way."

VII

Sandler set the ship down into the dawn, into the blue sky that was not blue, into the radiant pink of the promising new day. The planet was called Analon on their charts. They walked down the ramp and stood looking about tremulously as a ground car bounced toward them from the terminal building. A man Sandler's age leaped out and approached them, studying their faces. Suddenly he smiled.

"Welcome home," he said.

Other cars left the terminal and started toward them. "Why did you land here?" the stranger said. "Most of us are putting down in out-of-the-way places. Doesn't do to have this oaf of an administrator know too much. I suppose it doesn't matter now, though."

"Then there are—others?" Sandler asked.

"Enough to scare this administrator if he learned the truth. More than a hundred thousand, and they're still coming. Do you two remember anything? Family names? Places?"

Sandler shook his head, but Miriam said quickly, "My mother's name was Lilga."

"A common name, but we'll do some checking."

The other cars drew up and stopped, and their occupants sat waiting. He chuckled softly. "I have a kind of semi-official position of which the administrator does not approve. I'm head of a settlers' committee, which gives me the right to an exclusive interview before they haul you off for the formalities. Krig is the name, incidentally. We're all adopting our original names if we can find out what they were. And you'll have to learn to speak Analonian, though the old language is already pepped up to the point where you wouldn't recognize it even if you remembered it."

He took their names, descriptions, educational training, and occupations. He inquired about identification marks that might have survived from childhood. He carefully spoke the names of prominent places on Analon to see if they recognized any.

"We'll go into this more thoroughly later on," he said. "We'll do our best to locate your parents if they're still alive, and to help you get together with any brothers or sisters who've returned. The Federation—" He spat the word angrily. "The Federation took all the children in a certain age range. All of them. We estimate that a minimum quarter of a million children were stolen from Analon. Then the Federation pulled out abruptly. Didn't even bother to leave medical or observation teams, but it did leave a lot of alien bacteria, and the population was nearly wiped out. We have a few scores to settle with the Federation.

Any day, now, we're going to throw out the administrator and run this planet ourselves.''

Krig stepped back and nodded at the waiting officials. ''These two have the committee's approval,'' he called.

A young officer walked toward them waving a folder. ''These people aren't settlers,'' he said.

Krig looked at him coldly. ''Of course they're settlers.''

''No. They're going back to Earth and settle down to a nice multiple prison sentence. Or worse. Glad you dropped in here, Thomas Jefferson Sandler. This means a promotion for me. Consider yourself under arrest. I've already notified Sector Headquarters to send a ship for you.''

''What'd he do?'' Krig asked.

''Both of them. The girl is an accomplice, at least. Here—read it yourself. There's six pages.''

Krig leafed through the folder, and then he stepped close to Sandler. ''Did you really do all of this?''

''I wanted to come home,'' Sandler said bitterly. ''They tried to stop me.''

Sympathy touched Krig's face. ''We need people like you,'' he said softly. ''It's time we started running this planet our own way. We'll have you out by midnight.''

The officer tucked the file under his arm and jerked a thumb toward the ground car. Soldiers closed in on them. Sandler fumbled in his pocket and brought out a small plastic container. He broke the seal and tossed the contents to the searching wind.

''Welcome home, Marty,'' he whispered.

On a distant planet, the commissioner of Sector 1389 was jerked from a pleasantly sound slumber by the urgently clanging gong of his visiphone. Sleepily he stumbled toward it, listened for a few seconds to the incoherent babbling of a subclerk, and screamed, ''Idiot!''

He cut the connection and returned to his bed muttering angrily to himself. ''Revolution, indeed!''

The fool should have known that the native population on Analon was practically extinct!

Down to the Worlds of Men

by *Alexei Panshin*

I

The horses and packs were loaded before we went aboard the
scout ship. The scout bay is no more than a great oversized
airlock with a dozen small ships squatting over their tubes, but it
was the last of the Ship that I might ever see, so I took a long
final look from the top of the ramp.

There were sixteen of us girls and thirteen boys. We took our
places in the seats in the center of the scout. Riggy Allen made a
joke that nobody bothered to laugh at, and then we were all
silent. I was feeling lost and just beginning to enjoy it when
Jimmy Dentremont came over to me. He's redheaded and has a
face that makes him look about ten. An intelligent runt like me.

He said what I expected. "Mia, do you want to go partners if
we can get together when we get down?"

I guess he thought that because we were always matched on
study I liked him. Well, I did when I wasn't mad at him, but
now I had that crack he'd made about being a snob in mind, so I
said, "Not likely. I want to come back alive." It wasn't fair, but
it was a good crack and he went back to his place without saying
anything.

My name is Mia Havero. I'm fourteen, of course, or I wouldn't
be telling this. I'm short, dark, and scrawny, though I don't
expect that scrawniness to last much longer. Mother is very
good-looking. In the meantime, I've got brains as a consolation.

After we were all settled, George Fuhonin, the pilot, raised
the ramps. We sat there for five minutes while they bled air out
of our tube and then we just . . . dropped. My stomach turned

flips. We didn't have to leave that way, but George thinks it's fun to be a hot pilot.

Thinking it over, I was almost sorry I'd been stinking to Jimmy D. He's the only competition I have my own age. The trouble is, you don't go partners with the competition, do you? Besides, there was still that crack about being a snob.

The planet chosen for our Trial was called Tintera. The last contact the Ship had had with it—and we were the ones who dropped them—was almost 150 years ago. No contact since. That had made the council debate a little before they dropped us there, but they decided it was all right in the end. It didn't make any practical difference to us kids because they never tell you anything about the place they're going to drop you. All I knew was the name. I wouldn't have known that much if Daddy weren't chairman of the council.

I felt like crawling in a corner of the ship and crying, but nobody else was breaking down, so I didn't. I did feel miserable. I cried when I said good-bye to Mother and Daddy—a real emotional scene—but that wasn't in public.

It wasn't the chance of not coming back that bothered me really, because I never believed that I wouldn't. The thought that made me unhappy was that I would have to be on a planet for a whole month. Planets make me feel wretched.

The gravity is always wrong, for one thing. Either your arches and calves ache or every time you step you think you're going to trip on a piece of fluff and break your neck. There are vegetables everywhere and little grubby things just looking for *you* to crawl on. If you can think of anything creepier than that, you've got a real nasty imagination. Worst of all, planets stink. Every single one smells—I've been on enough to know that. A planet is all right for a mud-eater, but not for me.

We have a place in the Ship like that—the Third Level—but it's only a thousand square miles and anytime it gets on your nerves you can go up a level or down a level and be back in civilization.

When we reached Tintera, they started dropping us. We swung over the sea from the morning side and then dropped low over gray-green forested hills. Finally George spotted a clear area and dropped into it. They don't care what order you go in, so Jimmy D. jumped up, grabbed his gear and then led his horse down the ramp. I think he was still smarting from the slap I'd given him.

In a minute we were airborne again. I wondered if I would ever see Jimmy—if he would get back alive.

It's no game we play. When we turn fourteen, they drop us on the nearest colonized planet and come back one month later. That may sound like fun to you, but a lot of us never come back alive.

Don't think I was helpless. I'm hell on wheels. They don't let us grow for fourteen years and then kick us out to die. They prepare us. They do figure, though, that if you can't keep yourself alive by the time you're fourteen, you're too stupid, foolish, or unlucky to be any use to the Ship. There's sense behind it. It means that everybody on the Ship is a person who can take care of himself if he has to. Daddy says that something has to be done in a closed society to keep the population from decaying mentally and physically, and this is it. And it helps to keep the population steady.

I began to check my gear out—sonic pistol, pickup signal so I could be found at the end of the month, saddle and cinches, food and clothes. Venie Morlock has got a crush on Jimmy D., and when she saw me start getting ready to go, she began to check her gear, too. At our next landing, I grabbed Ninc's reins and cut Venie out smoothly. It didn't have anything to do with Jimmy. I just couldn't stand to put off the bad moment any longer.

The ship lifted impersonally away from Ninc and me like a rising bird, and in just a moment it was gone. Its gray-blue color was almost the color of the half-overcast sky, so I was never sure when I saw it last.

II

The first night was hell, I guess because I'm not used to having the lights out. That's when you really start to feel lonely, being alone in the dark. When the sun disappears, somehow you wonder in your stomach if it's really going to come back. But I lived through it—one day in thirty gone.

I rode in a spiral search pattern during the next two days. I had three things in mind—stay alive, find people, and find some of the others. The first was automatic. The second was to find out if there was a slot I could fit into for a month. If not, I would have to find a place to camp out, as nasty as that would be. The third was to join forces, though not with that meatball Jimmy D.

No, he isn't really a meatball. The trouble is that I don't take nothing from nobody, especially him, and he doesn't take nothing from nobody, especially me. So we do a lot of fighting.

I had a good month for Trial. My birthday is in November—too close to Year End Holiday for my taste, but this year it was all right. It was spring on Tintera, but it was December in the Ship, and after we got back we had five days of Holiday to celebrate. It gave me something to look forward to.

In two days of riding, I ran onto nothing but a few odd-looking animals. I shot one small one and ate it. It turned out to taste pretty good, though not as good as a slice from Hambone No. 4, to my mind the best meat vat on the Ship. I've eaten things so gruey-looking that I wondered that anybody had the guts to try them in the first place and they've turned out to taste good. And I've seen things that looked good that I couldn't keep on my stomach. So I guess I was lucky.

On the third day, I found the road. I brought Ninc down off the hillside, losing sight of the road in the trees, and then reaching it in the level below. It was narrow and made of sand spread over a hard base. Out of the marks in the sand, I could pick out the tracks of horses and both narrow and wide wheels. Other tracks I couldn't identify.

One of the smartest moves in history was to include horses when they dropped the colonies. I say "they" because, while we did the actual dropping, the idea originated with the whole evac plan back on Earth. Considering how short a time it was in which the colonies were established, there was no time to set up industry, so they had to have draft animals.

The first of the Great Ships was finished in 2025. One of the eight, as well as the two that were being built then, went up with everything else in the solar system in 2041. In that sixteen years 112 colonies were planted. I don't know how many of those planets had animals that *could* have been substituted but, even if they had, they would have had to be domesticated from scratch. That would have been stupid. I'll bet that half the colonies would have failed if they hadn't had horses.

We'd come in from the west over the ocean, so I traveled east on the road. That much water makes me nervous, and roads have to go somewhere.

I came on my first travelers three hours later. I rounded a tree-lined bend, ducking an overhanging branch, and pulled Ninc to a stop. There were five men on horseback herding a bunch of the ugliest creatures alive.

They were green and grotesque. They had squat bodies, long limbs, and knobby bulges at their joints. They had square, flat animal masks for faces. But they walked on their hind legs and they had paws that were almost hands, and that was enough to make them seem almost human. They made a wordless, chilling, lowing sound as they milled and plodded along.

I started Ninc up again and moved slowly to catch up with them. All the men on horseback had guns in saddle boots. They looked as nervous as cats with kittens. One of them had a string of packhorses on a line, and he saw me and called to another who seemed to be the leader. That one wheeled his black horse and rode back toward me.

He was a middle-aged man, maybe as old as my daddy. He was large and he had a hard face. Normal enough, but hard. He pulled to a halt when we reached each other, but I kept going. He had to come around and follow me. I believe in judging a person by his face. A man can't help the face he owns, but he can help the expression he wears on it. If a man looks mean, I generally believe that he is. This one looked mean. That was why I kept riding.

He said, "What be you doing out here, boy? Be you out of your head? There be escaped Losels in these woods."

I told you I hadn't finished filling out yet, but I hadn't thought it was that bad. I wasn't ready to make a fight over the point, though. Generally, I can't keep my bloody mouth shut, but now I didn't say anything. It seemed smart.

"Where be you from?" he asked.

I pointed to the road behind us.

"And where be you going?"

I pointed ahead. No other way to go.

He seemed exasperated. I have that effect sometimes. Even on Mother and Daddy, who should know better.

We were coming up on the others now, and the man said, "Maybe you'd better ride on from here with us. For protection."

He had an odd way of twisting his sounds, almost as though he had a mouthful of mush. I wondered whether he was just an oddball or whether everybody here spoke the same way. I'd never heard International English spoken any way but one, even on the planet Daddy made me visit with him.

One of the other outriders came easing by then. I suppose they'd been watching us all the while. He called to the hard man.

"He be awfully small, Horst. I doubt me a Losel'd even notice him at all. We mought as well throw him back again."

The rider looked at me. When I didn't dissolve in terror as he expected, he shrugged and one of the other men laughed.

The hard man said to the others, "This boy will be riding along with us to Forton for protection."

I looked down at the plodding, unhappy creatures they were driving along and one looked back at me with dull, expressionless, golden eyes. I felt uncomfortable.

I said, "I don't think so."

What the man did then surprised me. He said, "I do think so," and reached for the rifle in his saddle boot.

I whipped my sonic pistol out so fast that he was caught leaning over with the rifle half out. His jaw dropped. He knew what I held and he didn't want to be fried.

I said, "Ease your rifles out and drop them gently to the ground."

They did, watching me all the while with wary expressions.

When all the rifles were on the ground, I said, "All right, let's go."

They didn't want to move. They didn't want to leave the rifles. I could see that. Horst didn't say anything. He just watched me with narrowed eyes. But one of the others held up a hand and in wheedling tones said, "Look here, kid . . . ."

"Shut up," I said, in as mean a voice as I could muster, and he did. It surprised me. I didn't think I sounded *that* mean. I decided he just didn't trust the crazy kid not to shoot.

After twenty minutes of easy riding for us and hard walking for the creatures, I said, "If you want your rifles, you can go back and get them now." I dug my heels into Ninc's sides and rode on. At the next bend I looked back and saw four of them holding their packhorses and the creatures still while one beat a dust-raising retreat down the road.

I put this episode in the "file and hold for analysis" section in my mind and rode on, feeling good. I think I even giggled once. Sometimes I even convince myself that I'm hell on wheels.

III

When I was nine, my Daddy gave me a painted wooden doll that my great-grandmother brought from Earth. The thing is that inside it, nestled one in another, are eleven more dolls, each one smaller than the last. I like to watch people when they open it for the first time.

My face must have been like that as I rode along the road.

The country leveled into a great rolling valley and the trees gave way to great farms and fields. In the fields, working, were some of the green creatures, which surprised me since the ones I'd seen before hadn't seemed smart enough to count to one, let alone do any work.

But it relieved me. I thought they might have been eating them or something.

I passed two crossroads and started to meet more people, but nobody questioned me. I met people on horseback, and twice I met trucks moving silently past. And I overtook a wagon driven by the oldest man I've seen in my life. He waved to me, and I waved back.

Near the end of the afternoon I came to the town, and there I received a jolt that sickened me.

By the time I came out on the other side, I was sick. My hands were cold and sweaty and my head was spinning, and I wanted to kick Ninc to a gallop.

I rode slowly in, looking all around, missing nothing. The town was all stone, wood, and brick. Out of date. Out of time, really. There were no machines more complicated than the trucks I'd seen earlier. At the edge of town, I passed a newspaper office with a headline pasted in the window—INVASION! I remember that. I wondered about it.

But I looked most closely at the people. In all that town, I didn't see one girl over ten years old and no grown-up women at all. There were little kids, there were boys and there were men, but no girls. All the boys and men wore pants, and so did I, which must have been why Horst and his buddies assumed I was a boy. It wasn't flattering, but I decided I'd not tell anybody different until I found what made the clocks tick on this planet.

But that wasn't what bothered me. It was the kids. My God! They swarmed. I saw a family come out of a house—a father and *four* children. It was the most foul thing I've ever seen. It struck me then—these people were Free Birthers! I felt a wave of nausea and I closed my eyes until it passed.

The first thing you learn in school is that if it weren't for idiot and criminal people like these, Earth would never have been destroyed. The evacuation would never have had to take place, and eight billion people wouldn't have died. There wouldn't have *been* eight billion people. But, no. They bred and they spread and they devoured everything in their path like a cancer. They gobbled up all the resources that Earth had and crowded and shoved one another until the final war came.

I am lucky. My great-great-grandparents were among those who had enough foresight to see what was coming. If it hadn't been for them and some others like them, there wouldn't be any humans left anywhere. And I wouldn't be here. That may not scare you, but it scares me.

What happened before, when people didn't use their heads and wound up blowing the solar system apart, is something nobody should forget. The older people don't let *us* forget. But these people had, and that the council should know.

For the first time since I landed on Tintera, I felt *really* frightened. There was too much going on that I didn't understand. I felt a blind urge to get away, and when I reached the edge of town, I whomped Ninc a good one and gave him his head.

I let him run for almost a mile before I pulled him down to a walk again. I couldn't help wishing for Jimmy D. Whatever else he is, he's smart and brains I needed.

How do you find out what's going on? Eavesdrop? That's a lousy method. For one thing, people can't be depended on to talk about the things you want to hear. For another, you're likely to get caught. Ask somebody? Who? Make the mistake of bracing a fellow like Horst and you might wind up with a sore head and an empty pocket. The best thing I could think of was to find a library, but that might be a job.

I'd had two bad shocks on this day, but they weren't the last. In the late afternoon, when the sun was starting to sink and a cool wind was starting to ripple the tree leaves, I saw the scout ship high in the sky. The dying sun colored it a deep red. Back again? I wondered what had gone wrong.

I reached down into my saddlebag and brought out my contact signal. The scout ship swung up in the sky in a familiar movement calculated to drop the stomach out of everybody aboard.

George Fuhonin's style. I triggered the signal, my heart turning flips all the while. I didn't know why he was back, but I wasn't really sorry.

The ship swung around until it was coming back on a path almost over my head, going in the same direction. Then it went into a slip and started bucking so hard that I knew this wasn't hot piloting at all, just plain idiot stutter-fingered stupidity at the controls. As it skidded by me overhead, I got a good look at it and knew that it wasn't one of ours. Not too different, but not ours.

One more enigma. Where was it from? Not here. Even if you know how, and we wouldn't tell these mud-eaters how, a scout ship is something that takes an advanced technology to build.

I felt defeated and tired. Not much farther along the road I came to a campsite with two wagons pulled in for the night, and I couldn't help but pull in myself. The campsite was large and had two permanent buildings on it. One was a well enclosure and the other was little more than a high-walled pen. It didn't even have a roof.

I set up camp and ate my dinner. In the wagon closest to me were a man, his wife, and their three children. The kids were running around and playing, and one of them ran close to the high-walled pen. His father came and pulled him away.

The kids weren't to blame for their parents, but when one of them said hello to me, I didn't even answer. I know how lousy I would feel if I had two or three brothers and sisters, but it didn't strike me until that moment that it wouldn't even seem out of the ordinary to these kids. Isn't that horrible?

About the time I finished eating, and before it grew dark, the old man I had seen earlier in the day drove his wagon in. He fascinated me. He had white hair, something I had read about in stories but had never seen before.

When nightfall came, they started a large fire. Everybody gathered around. There was singing for a while, and then the father of the children tried to pack them off to bed. But they weren't ready to go, so the old man started telling them a story. In the old man's odd accent, and sitting there in the campfire light surrounded by darkness, it seemed just right.

It was about an old witch named Baba Yaga who lived in the forest in a house that stood on chicken legs. She was the nasty stepmother of a nice little girl, and to get rid of the kid she sent her on a phony errand into the deep dark woods at nightfall. I could appreciate the poor girl's position. All the little girl had to help her were the handkerchief, the comb, and the pearl that she had inherited from her dear dead mother. But, as it turned out, they were just enough to defeat nasty old Baba Yaga and bring the girl safely home.

I wished for the same for myself.

The old man had just finished and they were starting to drag the kids off to bed when there was a commotion on the road at the edge of the camp. I looked but my eyes were adjusted to the light of the fire and I couldn't see far into the dark.

A voice there said, "I'll be damned if I'll take another day like this one, Horst. We should have been here hours ago. It be your fault we're not."

Horst growled a retort. I decided that it was time for me to leave the campfire. I got up and eased away as Horst and his men came up to the fire, and cut back to where Ninc was parked. I grabbed up my blankets and mattress and started to roll them up. I had a pretty good idea now what they used the high-walled pen for.

I should have known that they would have to pen the animals up for the night. I should have used my head. I hadn't, and now it was time to take leave.

I never got the chance.

I was just heaving the saddle up on Ninc when I felt a hand on my shoulder and I was swung around.

"Well, well. Horst, look who we have here," he called. It was the one who'd made the joke about me being beneath the notice of a Losel. He was alone with me now, but with that call the others would be up fast.

I brought the saddle around as hard as I could and then up, and he went down. He started to get up again, so I dropped the saddle on him and reached inside my jacket for my gun. Somebody grabbed me then from behind and pinned my arms to my side.

I opened my mouth to scream—I have a good scream—but a rough smelly hand clamped down over it before I had a chance to get more than a lungful of air. I bit down hard—5000 pounds psi, I'm told—but he didn't let me go. I started to kick, but Horst jerked me off my feet and dragged me off.

When we were behind the pen and out of earshot of the fire,

he stopped dragging me and dropped me in a heap. "Make any noise," he said, "and I'll hurt you."

That was a silly way to put it, but somehow it said more than if he'd threatened to break my arm or my head. It left him a latitude of things to do if he pleased. He examined his hand. There was enough moonlight for that. "I ought to club you anyway," he said.

The one I'd dropped the saddle on came up then. The others were putting the animals in the pen. He started to kick me, but Horst stopped him.

"No," he said. "Look through the kid's gear, bring the horse and what we can use."

The other one didn't move. "Get going, Jack," Horst said in a menacing tone and they stood toe to toe for a long moment before Jack finally backed down. It seemed to me that Horst wasn't so much objecting to me being kicked, but rather was establishing who did the kicking in his bunch.

But I wasn't done yet, I was scared, but I still had the pistol under my jacket.

Horst turned back to me and I said, "You can't do this and get away with it."

He said, "Look, boy. You may not know it, but you be in a lot of trouble. So don't give me a hard time."

He still thought I was a boy. It was not time to correct him, but I didn't like to see the point go unchallenged. It was unflattering.

"The courts won't let you get away with this," I said. I'd passed a courthouse in the town with a carved motto over the doors: EQUAL JUSTICE UNDER THE LAW or TRUTH OUR SHIELD AND JUSTICE OUR SWORD or something stuffy like that.

He laughed, not a phony, villain-type laugh, but a real laugh, so I knew I'd goofed.

"Boy, boy. Don't talk about the courts. I be doing you a favor. I be taking what I can use of your gear, but I be letting you go. You go to court and they'll take everything and lock you up besides. I be leaving you your freedom."

"Why would they be doing that?" I asked. I slipped my hand under my jacket.

"Every time you open your mouth you shout that you be off one of the Ships," Horst said. "That be enough. They already have one of you brats in jail in Forton."

I was about to bring my gun out when up came Jack leading Ninc, with all my stuff loaded on. I mentally thanked him.

He said, "The kid's got some good equipment. But I can't make out what this be for." He held out my pickup signal.

Horst looked at it, then handed it back. "Throw it away," he said.

I leveled my gun at them—Hell on Wheels strikes again! I said, "Hand that over to me."

Horst made a disgusted sound.

"Don't make any noise," I said, "or you'll fry. Now hand it over."

I stowed it away, then paused with one hand on the leather horn of the saddle. "What's the name of the kid in jail in Forton?"

"I can't remember," he said. "But it be coming to me. Hold on."

I waited. Then suddenly my arm was hit a numbing blow from behind and the gun went flying. Jack pounced after it and Horst said, "Good enough," to the others who'd come up behind me.

I felt like a fool.

Horst stalked over and got the signal. He dropped it on the ground and said in a voice far colder than mine could ever be, because it was natural and mine wasn't, "The piece be yours." Then he tromped on it until it cracked and fell apart.

Then he said, "Pull a gun on me twice. Twice." He slapped me so hard that my ears rang. "You dirty little punk."

I said calmly, "You big louse."

It was a time I would have done better to keep my mouth shut. All I can remember is a flash of pain as his fist crunched against the side of my face and then nothing.

Brains are no good if you don't use them.

IV

I remember pain and sickness, and motion, but my next clear memory is waking in a bed in a house. I had a feeling that time had passed, but how much I didn't know. I looked around and found the old man who had told the story was sitting by my bed.

"How be you feeling this morning, young lady?" he asked. He had white hair and a seamed face and his hands were gnarled and old. His face was red, and the red and the white of his hair made a sharp contrast with the bright blue of his deep-set eyes. It was a good face.

"Not very healthy," I said. "How long has it been?"

"Two days," he said. "You'll get over it soon enough. I be Daniel Kutsov. And you?"

"I'm Mia Havero."

"I found you dumped in a ditch after Horst Fanger and his boys had left you," he said. "A very unpleasant man . . . as I suppose he be bound to be, herding Losels."

"Those green things were Losels? Why are they afraid of them?"

"The ones you saw beed drugged. They wouldn't obey otherwise. Once in a while a few be stronger than the drug and they escape to the woods. The drug cannot be so strong that they cannot work. So the strongest escape. They be some danger to most people, and a great danger to men like Horst Fanger who buy them from the ships. Every so often, hunters go out to thin them down."

"That seems like slavery," I said, yawning.

It was a stupid thing to say, like some comment about the idiocy of a Free Birth policy. Not the sentiment, but the timing.

Mr. Kutsov treated the comment with more respect than it deserved. "Only God can decide a question like that," he said gently. "Be it slavery to use my horses to work for me? I don't know anyone who would say so. A man be a different matter, though. The question be whether a Losel be like a horse or like a man, and that I can't answer. Now go to sleep again and in a while I will bring you some food."

He left then, but I didn't go to sleep. I was in trouble. I had no way to contact the scout ship. There was only one way out, and that was to find somebody else who did have his signal. That wasn't going to be easy.

Mr. Kutsov brought me some food later in the day, and I asked him then, "Why are you doing all this for me?"

He said, "I don't like to see children hurt, by people like Horst Fanger or by anyone."

"But I'm from one of the Ships," I said. "You know that, don't you?"

Mr. Kutsov nodded. "Yes, I know that."

"I understand that is pretty bad around here."

"With some people, true. But all the people who hate the Ships don't realize that if it beedn't for the Ships they wouldn't be here at all. They hold their grudge too close to their hearts. There be some of us who disagree with the government though it has lost us our families or years from our lives, and we would not destroy what we cannot agree with. When such an one as Horst Fanger uses this as an excuse to rob and injure a child, I will not agree. He has taken all that you have and there be no way to reclaim it, but what I can give of my house be yours.''

I thanked him as best I could and then I asked him what the grudge was that they held against the Ships.

"It ben't a simple thing," he said. "You have seen how poor and backward we be. We realize it. Now and again, when you decide to stop, we see you people from the Ships. And you ben't poor or backward. You could call what we feel jealousy, if you wanted, but it be more than that and different. When we beed dropped here, there been no scientists or technicians among us. I can understand. Why should they leave the last places where they had a chance to use and develop their knowledge for a backward planet where there is no equipment, no opportunity? What be felt here be that all the men who survived the end of Earth and the solar system be the equal heirs of man's knowledge and accomplishment. But by bad luck, things didn't work out that way. So ideas urged by the Ships be ignored, and the Ships be despised, and people from the Ships be treated as shamefully as you have beed or worse.''

I could think of a good example of an idea that the Ships had emphasized that had been ignored elsewhere. Only it was more than an idea or an opinion. It was a cold and deadly lesson taught by history. It was: Man is an organism that ultimately destroys itself unless he regulates his own size and growth. That was what I was taught.

I said, "I can understand how they might feel that way, but it's not fair. We pretty much support ourselves. As much as we can, we reuse things and salvage things, but we still need raw materials. The only thing we have to trade is knowledge. If we didn't have anything to trade for raw materials, that would be the end of us. Do we have a choice?''

"I don't hold you to blame," Mr. Kutsov said slowly, "but I can't help but to feel that you have made a mistake and that it will hurt you in the end.''

I didn't say it, but I thought—when you lay blame, whom do

you put it on? People who are obviously sick like these mud-eaters, or people who are normal like us?

After I got better, I had the run of Mr. Kutsov's house. It was a small place near the edge of Forton, surrounded by trees and with a small garden, Mr. Kutsov made a regular shipping run through the towns to the coast and back every second week. It was not a profitable business, but he said that at his age, profit was no longer very important. He was very good to me, but I didn't understand him.

He gave me lessons before he let me go outside into the town. Women were second-class citizens around here, but prejudice of that sort wasn't in Mr. Kutsov. Dressed as I was, as scrawny as I am, when people saw me here, they saw a boy. People see what they expect to see. I could get away with my sex, but not my accent. I might sound right on seven Ships and on III other planets, but here I was wrong. And I had two choices—sound right or shut up. One of these choices was impossible for me, so I set out to learn to sound like a Tinteran born and bred, with Mr. Kutsov's aid.

It was a long time before he was willing to give me a barely passing grade. He said, "All right. You should keep listening to people and correcting yourself, but I be satisfied. You talk as though you have a rag in your mouth, but I think you can get by."

Before I went out into town, I found out one more important thing. It was the answer to a question that I didn't ask Mr. Kutsov. I'd been searching for it in old newspapers, and at last I found the story I was looking for. The last sentence read: "After sentencing, Dentermount was sent to the territorial jail in Forton to serve his three-month term."

I thought, they misspelled his name. And then I thought, trust it to be Jimmy D. He gets in almost as much trouble as I do.

Though you may think it strange, my first stop was the library.

I've found that it helps to be well researched. I got what I could from Mr. Kutsov's books during the first days while he was outdoors working in his garden. In his library, I found a novel that he had written himself called *The White Way*.

He said, "It took me forty years to write it, and I have spent forty-two years since living with the political repercussions. It has beed an interesting forty-two years, but I am not sure that I would do it again. Read the book if you be interested."

I did read it, though I couldn't understand what the fuss was about. It seemed reasonable to me. But these mud-eaters were crazy anyway. I couldn't help but think that he and Daddy would have found a lot in common. They were both fine, tough-minded people, and though you would never know it to look at them, they were the same age. Except that at the age of eighty Mr. Kutsov was old, and at the age of eighty Daddy was not.

It cost me an effort to walk through the streets of Forton, but after my third trip, the pain was less, though the number of children still made me sick.

In the library, I spent four days getting a line on Tintera. I read their history. I studied their geography and, as sneakily as I could, I tore out the best local maps I could find.

On my trips through town, I took the time to look up Horst Fanger's place of business. It was a house, a shed and pen for the Losels, a stable, a truck garage (one truck—broken down) and a sale block, all housed in one rambling, shanty building. Mr. Horst Fanger was apparently a big man. Big deal.

When I was ready, I scouted out the jail. It was a raw unpleasant day, the sort that makes me hate planets, and rain was threatening when I reached the jailpen. It was a solid three-story building of great stone blocks, shaped like a fortress and protected by bars, an iron-spike fence, and two nasty-looking dogs. On my second trip around, the rain began. I beat it to the front and dodged in the entrance.

I was standing there shaking the rain off when a man in a green uniform came stalking out of one of the offices that lined the first-floor hallway. My heart stopped for a moment, but he went right by without giving me a second look and went upstairs. That gave me some confidence and so I started poking around.

I had covered the bulletin boards and the offices on one side of the hall when another man in green came into the hall and made straight for me. I didn't wait, I walked toward him, too. I said, as wide-eyed and innocent as I could, "Can you help me, sir?"

"Well, that depends. What sort of help do you need?" He was a big, rather slow man with one angled cloth bar on his shirt front over one pocket and a plate that said ROBARDS pinned over the pocket on the other side. He seemed good-natured.

I said, "Jerry had to write about the capital, and Jimmy got the governor, and I got *you*."

"Hold on there. First, what be your name?"

"Billy Davidow," I said. "I don't know what to write, sir, and I thought you could show me around and tell me things."

"I be sorry, son," he said. "We be pretty caught up today. Could you make it some other afternoon or maybe some evening?"

I said slowly, "I have to hand the paper in this week."

After a minute, he said, "All right. I'll take you around. But I can't spare much time. It'll have to be a quick tour."

The offices were on the first floor. Storage rooms, an arms room, and a target range were in the basement. Most of the cells were on the second floor, with the very rough cases celled on the third.

"If the judge says maximum security, they go on the third, everybody else on the second unless we have an overflow. Have a boy upstairs now."

My heart sank.

"A real bad actor. Killed a man."

Well, that wasn't Jimmy. Not with a three-month sentence.

Maximum security had three sets of barred doors plus an armed guard. Sgt. Robards pointed it all out to me. "By this time next week, it will all be full in here," he said sadly. "The governor has ordered a roundup of all political agitators. The Anti-Redemptionists be getting out of hand and he be going to cool them off. Uh, don't put that in your paper."

"Oh, I won't," I said, crossing off on my notes.

The ordinary cells on the second floor weren't behind barred doors and I got a guided tour. I stared Jimmy D. right in the face, but he had the brains to keep his mouth shut.

When we had finished, I thanked Sgt. Robards enthusiastically. "It sure has been swell, sir."

"Not at all, son," he said. "I enjoyed it myself. If you have time some evening, drop by when I have the duty. My schedule bees on the bulletin board."

"Thank you, sir," I said. "Maybe I will."

V

Before I scouted the jail I had only vague notions of what I was going to do to spring Jimmy D. I had spent an hour or so, for instance, toying with the idea of forcing the territorial governor to release Jimmy at the point of a gun. I spent that much time with it because the idea was fun to think about, but I dropped it because it was stupid.

I finally decided on a very simple course of action, one that could easily go wrong. It was my choice because it was the only thing I could pull off by myself that had a chance of working.

Before I left the jail building, I copied down Sgt. Robards's duty schedule from the bulletin board. Then I went home.

I spent the next few days shoplifting. Mr. Kutsov was laying in supplies, too, loading his wagon for his regular trip. I helped him load up, saving my shopping for my spare time. Mr. Kutsov wanted me to go along with him, but I couldn't, of course, and I couldn't tell him why. He didn't want to argue and he couldn't *make* me do anything I didn't want to do, so I had an unfair advantage. I just dug in my heels.

Finally he agreed it was all right for me to stay alone in the house while he was gone. It was what I wanted, but I didn't enjoy the process of getting my own way as much as I did at home. There it is a more even battle.

The day he picked to leave was perfect for my purposes. Mr. Kutsov said, "I'll be back in six days. Be you sure that you will be all right?"

I said, "Yes, I'll be careful. You be careful, too."

"I don't think it matters much any more at my age," he smiled. "Stay out of trouble."

"I'll try," I said, and waved good-bye. That was what I meant to do, stay out of trouble.

Back in the house I wrote a note of explanation for Mr. Kutsov and thanked him for all he had done. Then I dug my two small packs out of hiding and I was ready.

I set out just after dark. It was sprinkling lightly, but I didn't mind it. It surprised me, but I enjoyed the feel of the spray on my face. In one pocket I had pencil and paper for protective coverage. In another pocket I had a single sock and a roll of tape.

Just before I got to the jail, I filled the sock with wet sand.

Inside there were lights on in only two first-floor offices. Sgt. Robards was in one of them.

"Hello, Sgt. Robards," I said, going in. "How be you tonight?"

"Well enough," he said. "It be pretty slow down here tonight. They be busy up on the third floor tonight, though."

"Oh?"

"They be picking up those Anti-Redemptionists tonight. How did your paper go?"

"I handed it in," I said. "I should get a good grade with your help."

"Oh, you found out everything you needed to know."

"Oh, yes. I just came by to visit tonight. I wondered if you'd show me the target range again. That was keen."

"Sure," he said. "Would you like to see me pop some targets? I be the local champion, you know."

"Gee, would you?"

We went downstairs, Sgt. Robards leading the way. This was the place I'd picked to drop him. He was about to slip the key in the door to the range when I slugged him across the back of the neck with my sock full of sand. I grabbed him and eased him down.

I tried the keys on either side of the target door key and opened the arsenal on the second try. I dragged him in there and got out my roll of tape. I took three quick turns about his ankles, then did the same with his wrists. I finished by putting a bar and two crosspieces over the mouth.

I picked out two weapons then. They had no sonics, of course, so I picked out two of the smallest and lightest pistols in the room. I figured out what cartridges fit them, and then dropped guns and cartridge clips into my pocket.

I swung the door shut and locked it again, leaving Sgt. Robards inside. I stood for a moment in the corridor with the keys in my hand. There were only ten keys, not enough to cover each individual cell. Yet Sgt. Robards had clinked these keys and said that he could unlock the cells.

Maybe I would have done better to stick up the territorial governor.

Well, here goes.

I eased up to the first floor. Nobody came out of the second office to check on the noise made by my pounding heart, which surprised me. Then up to the second floor. It was dark here, but light from the first and third floors leaking up and down the stairs made things bright enough for me to see what I was doing. There were voices on the third floor and somebody laughed up there. I held my breath and moved quietly to Jimmy's cell.

I whispered, "Jimmy!" and he came alert and moved to the door.

"Am I glad to see you," he whispered back.

I held up the keys. "Do any of these fit?"

"Yes, the D key. The D key. It fits the four cells in this corner."

I fumbled through until I had the key tagged D. I opened the cell with as few clinking noises as possible. "Come on," I said. "We've got to get out of here in a hurry."

He slipped out and pushed the door shut behind him. We headed for the stairs and were almost there when I heard somebody coming up. Jimmy must have heard it, too, because he grabbed my arm and pulled me back. We flattened out as best we could.

Talk about walking right into it! The policeman looked over at us and said, "What are you doing up here, Robards? Hey, you're not . . ."

I stepped out and brought out one of the pistols. I said, "Easy now. If things go wrong for us, I have nothing to lose by shooting you, If you want to live, play it straight."

He apparently believed me, because he put his hands where I could see them and shut up.

I herded him into Jimmy's cell and let Jimmy do the honors with the loaded sock. We taped him up and while Jimmy was locking him in, I heard somebody in one of the cells behind me say, "Shut up, there," to somebody else. I turned and said, "Do you want to get shot?"

The voice was collected. "No. No trouble here."

"Do you want to be let out?"

The voice was amused. "I don't think so. Thank you just the same."

Jimmy finished and I asked, "Where is your signal? We have to have that."

"In the basement with the rest of my gear."

The signal was all we took. When we were three blocks away and on a dark side street, I handed Jimmy his gun and ammunition. As he took them, he said, "Tell me something, Mia. Would you really have shot him?"

I said, "I couldn't have. I hadn't loaded my gun yet."

I led him through town following the back ways I'd worked out before. Somebody once said that good luck is no more nor less than careful preparation, and this time I meant to have good luck. I led Jimmy toward the Losel-selling district.

Jimmy is short and redheaded with a face that makes him look about four years younger than he is. That's a handicap anytime.

When you stand out anyway, it's likely to make you a little bit tart. But Jimmy's all right most of the time.

He said, "We're in trouble."

"That's brilliant."

"No," Jimmy said. "They have a scout ship from one of the other Ships. This is going to sound wild, but they intend to use the scout to take over a Ship and then use that to destroy the rest of the Ships. They're going to try. The police are rounding up everybody who is opposed who has any influence and are putting them in jail."

"So what?"

"Mia, are you mad at me for something?"

"What makes you think so?"

"You're being bitter about something."

"If you must know, it's that crack you made about me being a snob."

"That was a month ago."

"I still resent it."

"Why?" Jimmy asked. "It's true. You think that because you're from a Ship you're automatically better than any mud-eater. That makes you a snob."

"Well, you're no better," I said.

"Maybe not, but I don't pretend. Hey, look, we can't get anywhere if we fight and we've got to stick together. I'll tell you what. I'll apologize. I'm sorry I said it, even if it is true. Make up?"

"Okay," I said. But that was a typical trick of his. Get the last blow in and then call the whole thing off.

When we got to Horst Fanger's place, I said, "I've got our packs all set up. This is where we get our horses." I'd left this until last, not wanting people running around looking for stolen horses while I was trying to break somebody out of the police jailpen. Besides, for this I wanted somebody along as lookout.

There was a fetid, unwashed odor that hung about the pens that the misting rain did nothing to dispel. We slipped by the pens, the Losels watching us but making no noise, and came to the stables, which smelled better. Jimmy stood guard while I broke the lock and slipped inside.

Ninc was there, good old Nincompoop, and a quick search turned up his saddle as well. I saddled him up and then stood watch while Jimmy picked himself out a horse and gear. I did one last thing before I left. I took out the pencil and paper in my pocket and wrote in *correct* Inter E, in great big letters: I'M A GIRL, YOU STINKER. I hung it on a nail. It may have been childish, but it felt good.

We rode from there to Mr. Kutsov's house, still following back alleys. As we rode, I told Jimmy about Mr. Kutsov and what he'd done for me.

When we got there we rode around to the back.

"Hold the horses," I said. "I'll slip in and get the packs. They're just inside."

We both dismounted and Jimmy took Ninc's reins. I bounded up the steps.

Mr. Kutsov was waiting in the dark inside. He said, "I read your note."

"Why did you come back?" I asked.

He smiled. "It didn't seem right to leave you here by yourself. I be sorry. I think I underestimated you. Be that Jimmy Dentremont outside?"

"You're not mad?"

"No. I ben't angry. I understand why you couldn't tell me."

For some reason, I started crying and couldn't stop. The tears ran down my face. "I'm sorry," I said. "I'm sorry."

The front door signal sounded then and Mr. Kutsov answered the door. A green-uniformed policeman stood in the doorway. "Daniel Kutsov?" he asked.

Instinctively, I shrank back out of sight of the doorway. I swiped at my face with my sleeve.

Mr. Kutsov said, "Yes. What can I do for you?"

The policeman moved one step inside the house where I could see him again. He said in a flat voice, "I have a warrant for your arrest."

There was only one light on in the house, in the front room. From the shadows at the rear I watched them both. The policeman had a hard mask for a face, no more human than a Losel. Mr. Kutsov was determined and I had the feeling that he had forgotten my presence.

"To jail again? For my book?" He shook his head. "No."

"It be nothing to do with any book I know of, Kutsov. It be known that you be an Anti-Redemptionist. So come along." He grasped Mr. Kutsov's arm.

Mr. Kutsov shook loose. "No. I won't go to jail again. It be no crime to be against stupidity. I won't go."

The policeman said, "You be coming whether you want to or not. You be under arrest."

Mr. Kutsov's voice had never shown his age before, but it shook now. "Get out of my house!"

A sense of coming destruction grew on me as I saw the policeman lift his gun from its holster and say, "You be coming if I have to shoot."

Mr. Kutsov swung his fist at the policeman and missed and, as though the man could afford to let nothing pass without retaliation, he swung the barrel of his pistol dully against the side of Mr. Kutsov's head. It rocked Mr. Kutsov, but he didn't fall. He raised his fist again. The policeman struck once more and waited but Mr. Kutsov still didn't fall. Instead, he swung again, and for the first time he landed, a blow that bounced weakly off the man's shoulder. Almost inevitably, it seemed, the policeman raised his pistol and fired directly at Mr. Kutsov, and then again, and as the second report rang Mr. Kutsov slid to the floor.

The silence was loud and gaunt. The policeman stood looking down at him and said, "Old fool!" under his breath. Then he came to himself and looked around. Then he picked a candlestick off the table and dropped it with a thud by Mr. Kutsov's empty outstretched hand.

The noise was a release for me and I moved for the first time. The policeman grunted and looked up and we stared at each other. Then again, slowly, he raised his gun and pointed it at me.

I heard a snickering sound and the three reports rang out, one following another. The policeman stood for a moment, balanced himself and then, like a crumpled sheet of paper, he fell to the floor. I didn't even look at Jimmy behind me. I started to cry and I went to Mr. Kutsov, passing by the policeman without even looking at him. As I bent down beside him, his eyes opened and he looked at me.

I couldn't stop crying. I held his head and cried. "I'm sorry," I said. "I'm sorry."

He smiled and said faintly, but clearly, "It be all right." After a minute he closed his eyes, and then he died.

After another minute, Jimmy touched my arm and said, "There's nothing we can do. Let's leave now, Mia, while we still can."

Outside, it was still raining. Standing in the rain I felt deserted.

VI

The final morning on Tintera was a fine day. We and the horses were in a rock-enclosed aerie where we had dodged the day before for shelter. In the aerie were grass and a small rock spring, and this day, the final day, was bright with blue and piled clouds riding high.

From where we sat, looking from the top of the rock wall, we could see over miles of expanse. Lower hills and curving valleys all covered with a rolling carpet of trees, a carpet of varying shades of gray and green. There were some natural upland meadows, and clearings in the valleys, and far away a line drawn in the trees that might be the path of a river. Down there, under that carpet, were all sorts of things—wild Losels, men hunting us, and—perhaps—some of the others from the Ship. We had seen the Losels and they had seen us; they had gone their way and we had gone ours. The men hunting us for blowing up their scout ship we hadn't seen for four days, and even then they hadn't seen us. As for the others, we hadn't seen them at all. But they might be there, under the anonymous carpet.

Jimmy got up from the ground and brushed himself off. He brought the signal over to me and said, "Should I, or do you want to?"

"Go ahead," I said.

He triggered it.

George Fuhonin was piloting and we were the sixth and seventh aboard. The other five crowded around and helped us put our gear away. Jimmy went on inside and I went upstairs to talk to George.

I was up there by the time we were airborne. "Hello, Halfpint," George said.

"Hi, Georgie-Worgie," I said, dealing blow for blow. "Have you had any trouble picking us up?"

"No trouble yet. You trying to wish me problems?"

"No," I said. "This is a real nasty planet. They had Jimmy D. locked up in jail. They hate everybody from the Ships."

"Oh." George raised his eyebrows. "Well, that might explain the board." He pointed to the board of lights above and to his left. Twenty-nine were marked for the twenty-nine of us. Of the twenty-nine, only twelve were lit. "The last light came on two hours ago. If there aren't any more, this will be the most fatal Trial Group I've ever picked up."

I stayed upstairs through two more pickups. Joe Fernandez-Fragoso, and then another double of which Venie Morlock was one-half. I went downstairs to say hello to her.

We were just settling down when George set off the alarm. He was speaking in the elder brother tone that I can't stand.

"All right, kids—shut up and listen. One of our people is down there. I didn't get close enough to see who. Whoever it is is surrounded by some of the local peasantry and we've got to bust him out. I'm going to buzz down and try to land on some of them. Then I want all of you outside and laying down a covering fire. Got that? I'm starting on down now."

Some of the kids had their weapons with them, but Jimmy and I didn't. We hopped for the gear racks and got out our pistols. There were ten of us and four ramps to the outside. Jimmy and I had No. 3 to ourselves. George is a hotrodder, as I've said, and after he gave us a long moment to get in place, he started down, a stomach-heaving swoop. Then he touched down light as a feather and dropped the ramps.

Jimmy and I dived down the ramp and I went left and he went right. We were on a slight slope facing down and my momentum and the slant put me right where I wanted to be—flat on my face. I rolled behind a tree and looked over to see Jimmy almost hidden in a bush.

Here, hundreds of miles from where we had been picked up, it was misting under a familiar rolled gray sky. In my ears was the sound of gunfire from the other side of the ship and from below us. Our boy was pinned fifty yards down the slope behind some rocks that barely protected him. He was fighting back. I could see the sighting beam of his sonic pistol slapping out. About thirty feet away from him toward us was the body of his horse. I recognized him then—a meatball named Riggy Allen.

I took all this in in seconds, and then I raised my pistol and fired, aiming at his attackers. They were dug in behind trees and rocks, at least partly hidden from Riggy as he was hidden from them. From where we were, though, above and looking down, they could be picked out. The distance was too great for my shot and it plowed up earth ten feet short, but the man I aimed at ducked back behind cover.

There was a certain satisfaction in one of these guns. Where a sonic pistol is silent, these made enough noise that you knew you were doing something. And when you missed with a sonic pistol, all you could expect at most was a shriveled branch or a sere and yellow leaf, but a miss with this gun could send up a gout of earth or drive a hole in a tree big enough to scare the steadiest man you can find.

I aimed higher and started to loft my shots in. Jimmy was doing the same thing, and the net effect was to keep their heads down. Riggy finally got the idea after a long moment. He stood up and started racing up the hill. Then my gun clicked empty, and a second later the firing to my right stopped. I started to fumble for another clip.

As our fire stopped, those heads popped back up again and took in the situation. They began to fire again and our boy Riggy took a long step and then dived over the body of his horse and went flat.

In a moment I was firing again, and then Jimmy was, too, and Riggy was up and running again. Then I started thinking clearly and held my fire while Jimmy emptied his clip. The instant he stopped, I started again, a regular squeeze, squeeze, squeeze. As I finished, Jimmy opened with his new clip and then Riggy was past us and up the ramp. He went flat in the doorway there and started firing his sonic pistol; its range was greater than our peashooters and he hosed the whole area down while Jimmy and I sprinted for the ramp.

As we hit the inside of the ship, I yelled, "Raise No. 3!" George had either been watching or listening, because it lifted smoothly up and locked in place.

Shots were still coming from the other sides of the ship, so I yelled at Jimmy to go left. Riggy just stood there for a moment fuzzy-headed, but Jimmy gave him a shove to the right and he finally got the idea. I cut through the middle. In the doorway of No. 1, I skidded flat on my face again and looked for targets. I dropped all my clips in front of me and began to fire. When the clip was empty, in two quick motions I pulled out the old one and slapped in the new and fired again. The three I was covering for used their heads and slipped in one at a time.

As the second one came aboard, I heard Jimmy's voice call from my left to raise No. 2. My third was Venie Morlock and as she ran aboard, I couldn't resist tripping her flat. I yelled to George to raise No. 1.

Venie glared at me and demanded, "What was that for?" as the ramp swung up.

"Just making sure you didn't get shot," I said, lying.

A second later, Riggy yelled that his side was okay and the last ramp was raised. My last view of Tintera was of a rain-soaked hillside and men doing their best to kill us, which all seems appropriate somehow. As the last ramp locked in place, George lifted the ship again and headed for the next pickup.

I went over to say hello to Riggy. He'd been completely unhurt by the barrage, but he had a great gash on his arm that was just starting to heal. He *said* that he was minding his own business in the woods one day when a Losel jumped out from behind a bush and slashed him. That may sound reasonable to you, but you don't know Riggy. I do. My opinion is that it was probably the other way around—the Losel was walking along in the woods one day, minding his own business, when *Riggy* jumped out from a bush and scared him. That is the sort of thing Riggy is inclined to do.

Riggy had been sneaking a look at my gun, and now he said, "Where did you get that neat pistol? Let me see it."

I handed it over.

After a minute of inspection, Riggy asked, "You wouldn't want to trade, would you?"

"For your sonic pistol?"

"Yes. You want to?"

I considered it for a minute, and then I said, "All right," and we traded. There is a certain amount of satisfaction in shooting an antique like that, but I know which is the more effective weapon. Besides, I only had one full clip of ammunition left.

There is a certain amount of prestige in coming back alive from Survival. It's your key to adulthood. There were no brass bands waiting for us when we got back, but our families were there, and that was enough.

The fifteen of us went down the lowered ramp, and when I stood again on solid rock, I looked around that ugly, bare scout bay and just drank it in. Home.

I turned to Jimmy then and I said, "Jimmy, it's a relief to be back, isn't it? And that isn't snobbery. It might have been before, but I don't think I am now."

And Jimmy nodded.

The waiting room wasn't bare. They had the decorations up for Year End, colored mobiles with lights that ranged through the spectrum, and more decorations on the walls. In the crowd of people waiting for us, I saw Jimmy's mother and her present husband, and Jimmy's father and *his* wife. When they saw Jimmy, they started waving and shouting.

Just as I said, "I'll see you tonight," I saw Mother and Daddy standing off to one side, and I waved. It was as though I had left the real world entirely for a month, and now at last I was back where things were going on and I wasn't missing a thing. I ran to them and I kissed Mother and hugged Daddy. Mother was crying.

I leaned back in Daddy's arms and looked up at him. He put a measuring hand over my head and said, "Mia, I believe you've grown some."

It might be so. I felt taller.

GOVERNANCE

As pointed out in the introduction, empires are not always ruled by emperors. The key features are, according to *Funk and Wagnalls Standard Dictionary*, "a union of dispersed territories, dominions, colonies, states, and unrelated peoples under one sovereign rule." But this supreme authority of the state can even be held by a body of persons, as in the Foundation series. All that is necessary is that, as opposed to a confederation or league, the supreme authority be supreme. That is, it should have the means of enforcing its will upon its subunits and their members.

As discussed in John F. Carr's fascinating introduction to *Empire* (1982), "Ministry of Disturbance" is part of H. Beam Piper's Empire portion of his future history. It examines a ruler's pressures and decisions, suggesting his or her job is not as easy as we might initially think it is. Yet despite that, and Piper's assertions to the contrary, imperial candidates have always been easy to find.

One person, or even a small group of persons, cannot possibly administer all rules and regulations necessary for the proper functioning of any society, let alone an empire. To ensure survival, a bureaucracy must develop, one that can give stability by carrying out policies and making delegated decisions even though the rulers change. "Blind Alley" by Isaac Asimov tells the story of one such galactic administrator and of how he discovers a wrong and attempts to correct it through skillful manipulation of the system. Like *Pebble in the Sky* (1950), *The Stars Like Dust* (1951), and *The Currents of Space* (1952), it is set in the Foundation universe, but is not part of the mainstream series:

Foundation (1951), *Foundation and Empire* (1952), *Second Foundation* (1953), and *Foundation's Edge* (1982).

Appropriate punishment for those who break the rules is an important part of any social system. Failure to punish leads to chaos, but unfair punishment may provoke revolution. In "A Planet Named Shayol," one of the most memorable science fiction stories ever written, Cordwainer Smith describes how the Lords of the Instrumentality (who appear to constitute a confederation) terminate the last and greatest of the old empire's prisons. *You Will Never Be the Same* (1963), *The Best of Cordwainer Smith* (1975), and *Norstrilia* (1975) include other works of this series.

Ministry of Disturbance

by *H. Beam Piper*

The symphony was ending, the final triumphant paean soaring up and up, beyond the limit of audibility. For a moment, after the last notes had gone away, Paul sat motionless, as though some part of him had followed. Then he roused himself and finished his coffee and cigarette, looking out the wide window across the city below—treetops and towers, roofs and domes and arching skyways, busy swarms of aircars glinting in the early sunlight. Not many people cared for João Coelho's music, now, and least of all for the Eighth Symphony. It was the music of another time, a thousand years ago, when the Empire was blazing into being out of the long night and hammering back the Neo-barbarians from world after world. Today people found it perturbing.

He smiled faintly at the vacant chair opposite him, and lit another cigarette before putting the breakfast dishes on the serving-robot's tray, and, after a while, realized that the robot was still beside his chair, waiting for dismissal. He gave it an instruction to summon the cleaning robots and sent it away. He could as easily have summoned them himself, or let the guards who would be in checking the room do it for him, but maybe it made a robot feel trusted and important to relay orders to other robots.

Then he smiled again, this time in self-derision. A robot couldn't feel important, or anything else. A robot was nothing but steel and plastic and magnetized tape and photomicropositronic circuits, whereas a man—His Imperial Majesty Paul XXII, for instance—was nothing but tissues and cells and colloids and electro-neuronic circuits. There was a difference; anybody knew that. The trouble was that he had never met anybody—which included physicists, biologists, psychologists, psionicists, philosophers and theologians—who could define the difference in satisfactorily exact terms. He watched the robot pivot on its treads and glide away, trailing steam from its coffee pot. It might be silly to treat robots like people, but that wasn't as bad as treating people like robots, an attitude which was becoming entirely too prevalent. If only so many people didn't act like robots!

He crossed to the elevator and stood in front of it until a tiny electroencephalograph inside recognized his distinctive brainwave pattern. Across the room, another door was popping open in response to the robot's distinctive wave pattern. He stepped inside and flipped a switch—there were still a few things around that had to be manually operated—and the door closed behind him and the elevator gave him an instant's weightlessness as it started to drop forty floors.

When it opened, Captain-General Dorflay of the Household Guard was waiting for him, with a captain and ten privates. General Dorflay was human. The captain and his ten soldiers weren't. They wore helmets, emblazoned with the golden sun and superimposed black cogwheel of the Empire, and red kilts and black ankle boots and weapons belts, and the captain had a narrow gold-laced cape over his shoulders, but for the rest, their bodies were covered with a stiff mat of black hair, and their faces were slightly like terriers'. (For all his humanity, Captain-General Dorflay's face was more like a bulldog's.) They were hillmen from the southern hemisphere of Thor, and as a people they made excellent mercenaries. They were crack shots, brave and crafty fighters, totally uninterested in politics off their own planet, and, because they had grown up in a patriarchal-clan society, they were fanatically loyal to anybody whom they accepted as their chieftain. Paul stepped out and gave them an inclusive nod.

"Good morning, gentlemen."

"Good morning, Your Imperial Majesty," General Dorflay said, bowing the couple of inches consistent with military dignity. The Thoran captain saluted by touching his forehead, his heart, which was on the right side, and the butt of his pistol. Paul complimented him on the smart appearance of his detail, and the captain asked how it could be otherwise, with the example and inspiration of his imperial majesty. Compliment and response could have been a playback from every morning of the ten years of his reign. So could Dorflay's question: "Your Majesty will proceed to his study?"

He wanted to say, "No, to Nifflheim with it; let's get an aircar and fly a million miles somewhere," and watch the look of shocked incomprehension on the captain-general's face. He couldn't do that, though; poor old Harv Dorflay might have a heart attack. He nodded slowly.

"If you please, General."

Dorflay nodded to the Thoran captain, who nodded to his men. Four of them took two paces forward; the rest, unslinging weapons, went scurrying up the corridor, some posting themselves along the way and the rest continuing to the main hallway. The captain and two of his men started forward slowly; after they had gone twenty feet, Paul and General Dorflay fell in behind them, and the other two brought up the rear.

"Your Majesty," Dorflay said, in a low voice, "let me beg you to be most cautious. I have just discovered that there exists a treasonous plot against your life."

Paul nodded. Dorflay was more than due to discover another treasonous plot; it had been ten days since the last one.

"I believe you mentioned it, General. Something about planting loose strontium-90 in the upholstery of the Audience Throne, wasn't it?"

And before that, somebody had been trying to smuggle a fission bomb into the Palace in a wine cask, and before that, it was a booby trap in the elevator, and before that, somebody was planning to build a submachine gun into the viewscreen in the study, and—

"Oh, no, Your Majesty; that was— Well, the persons involved in that plot became alarmed and fled the planet before I could arrest them. This is something different, Your Majesty. I have learned that unauthorized alterations have been made on one of the cooking-robots in your private kitchen, and I am positive that the object is to poison Your Majesty."

They were turning in the main hallway, between the rows of portraits of past emperors, Paul and Rodrik, Paul and Rodrik, alternating over and over on both walls. He felt a smile growing on his face, and banished it.

"The robot for the meat sauces, wasn't it?" he asked.

"Why—! Yes, Your Majesty."

"I'm sorry, General. I should have warned you. Those alterations were made by roboticists from the Ministry of Security;

they were installing an adaptation of a device used in the criminalistics-labs, to insure more uniform measurements. They'd done that already for Prince Travann, the Minister, and he'd recommended it to me.''

That was a shame, spoiling poor Harv Dorflay's murder plot. It had been such a nice little plot, too; he must have had a lot of fun inventing it. But a line had to be drawn somewhere. Let him turn the Palace upside down hunting for bombs; harass ladies-in-waiting whose lovers he suspected of being hired assassins; hound musicians into whose instruments he imagined firearms had been built; the emperor's private kitchen would have to be off limits.

Dorflay, who should have been looking crestfallen but relieved, stopped short—shocking breach of Court etiquette—and was staring in horror.

"Your Majesty! Prince Travann did that openly and with your consent? But, Your Majesty, I am convinced that it is Prince Travann himself who is the instigator of every one of these diabolical schemes. In the case of the elevator, I became suspicious of a man named Samml Ganner, one of Prince Travann's secret police agents. In the case of the gun in the viewscreen, it was a technician whose sister is a member of the household of Countess Yirzy, Prince Travann's mistress. In the case of the fission bomb—"

The two Thorans and their captain had kept on for some distance before they had discovered that they were no longer being followed, and were returning. He put his hand on General Dorflay's shoulder and urged him forward.

"Have you mentioned this to anybody?"

"Not a word, Your Majesty. This Court is so full of treachery that I can trust no one, and we must never warn the villain that he is suspected—"

"Good. Say nothing to anybody." They had reached the door of the study now. "I think I'll be here until noon. If I leave earlier, I'll flash you a signal."

He entered the big oval room, lighted from overhead by the great star-map in the ceiling, and crossed to his desk, with the viewscreens and reading screens and communications screens around it, and as he sat down, he cursed angrily, first at Harv Dorflay and then, after a moment's reflection, at himself. He was the one to blame; he'd known Dorflay's paranoid condition for years. Have to do something about it. Any psycho-medic would certify him; be no problem at all to have him put away. But be blasted if he'd do that. That was no way to repay loyalty, even insane loyalty. Well, he'd find a way.

He lit a cigarette and leaned back, looking up at the glowing swirl of billions of billions of tiny lights in the ceiling. At least, there were supposed to be billions of billions of them; he'd never counted them, and neither had any of the seventeen Rodriks and sixteen Pauls before him who had sat under them. His hand moved to a control button on his chair arm, and a red patch, roughly the shape of a pork chop, appeared on the western side.

That was the Empire. Every one of the thousand three hundred and sixty-five inhabited worlds, a trillion and a half intelligent beings, fourteen races—fifteen if you counted the Zarathustran Fuzzies, who were almost able to qualify under the talk-and-build-a-fire rule. And that had been the Empire when Rodrik VI had seen the map completed, and when Paul II had built the Palace, and when Stevan IV, the grandfather of Paul I, had proclaimed Odin the Imperial planet and Asgard the capital city. There had been some excuse for staying inside that patch of stars then; a newly-won Empire must be consolidated within before it can safely be expanded. But that had been over eight centuries ago.

He looked at the Daily Schedule, beautifully embossed and neatly slipped under his desk glass. Luncheon on the South Upper Terrace, with the Prime Minister and the Bench of Imperial Counselors. Yes, it was time for that again; that happened as inevitably and regularly as Harv Dorflay's murder plots. And in the afternoon, a Plenary Session, Cabinet and Counselors. Was he going to have to endure the Bench of Counselors twice in the same day? Then the vexation was washed out of his face by a spreading grin. Bench of Counselors; that was the answer! Elevate Harv Dorflay to the Bench. That was what the Bench was for, a gold-plated dustbin for the disposal of superannuated dignitaries. He'd do no harm there, and a touch of outright lunacy might enliven and even improve the Bench.

And in the evening, a banquet, and a reception and ball, in honor of His Majesty Ranulf XIV, Planetary King of Durendal, and First Citizen Zhorzh Yaggo, People's Manager-in-Chief of and for the Planetary Commonwealth of Aditya. Bargain day; two planetary chiefs of state in one big combination deal. He wondered what sort of prizes he had drawn this time, and closed his eyes, trying to remember. Durendal, of course, was one of the Sword-Worlds, settled by refugees from the losing side of the System States War in the time of the old Terran Federation, who had reappeared in Galactic history a few centuries later as the Space Vikings. They all had monarchial and rather picturesque governments; Durendal, he seemed to recall, was a sort of quasi-feudalism. About Aditya he was less sure. Something unpleasant, he thought; the titles of the government and its head were suggestive.

He lit another cigarette and snapped on the reading screen to see what they had piled onto him this morning, and then swore when a graph chart, with jiggling red and blue and green lines, appeared. Chart day, too. Everything happens at once.

It was the interstellar trade situation chart from Economics. Red line for production, green line for exports, blue for imports, sectioned vertically for the ten Viceroyalties and subsectioned for the Prefectures, and with the magnification and focus controls he could even get data for individual planets. He didn't bother with that, and wondered why he bothered with the charts at all. The stuff was all at least twenty days behind date, and not uniformly so, which accounted for much of the jiggling. It had been transmitted from Planetary Proconsulate to Prefecture, and from Prefecture to Viceroyalty, and from there to Odin, all by ship. A ship on hyperdrive could log light-years an hour, but radio waves still had to travel 186,000 mps. The supplementary chart for the past five centuries told the real story—three perfectly level and perfectly parallel lines.

It was the same on all the other charts. Population fluctuating slightly at the moment, completely static for the past five centuries. A slight decrease in agriculture, matched by an increase in synthetic food production. A slight population movement toward the more urban planets and the more densely populated centers. A trend downward in employment—nonworking population increasing by about .0001 per cent annually. Not that they were building better robots; they were just building them faster than they wore out. They all told the same story—a stable economy, a static population, a peaceful and undisturbed Empire; eight centuries, five at least, of historyless tranquillity. Well, that was what everybody wanted, wasn't it?

He flipped through the rest of the charts, and began getting summarized Ministry reports. Economics had denied a request from the Mining Cartel to authorize operations on a couple of

uninhabited planets; danger of local market gluts and overstim-
ulation of manufacturing. Permission granted to Robotics Cartel
to—Request from planetary government of Durendal for increase
of cereal export quotas under consideration—they wouldn't want
to turn that down while King Ranulf was here. Impulsively, he
punched out a combination on the communication screen and got
Count Duklass, Minister of Economics.

Count Duklass had thinning red hair and a plump, agreeable,
extrovert's face. He smiled and waited to be addressed.

"Sorry to bother Your Lordship," Paul greeted him. "What's
the story on this export quota request from Durendal? We have
their king here, now. Think he's come to lobby for it?"

Count Duklass chuckled. "He's not doing anything about it,
himself. Have you met him yet, sir?"

"Not yet. He's to be presented this evening."

"Well, when you see him—I think the masculine pronoun is
permissible—you'll see what I mean, sir. It's this Lord Koreff,
the Marshal. He came here on business, and had to bring the
king along, for fear somebody else would grab him while he was
gone. The whole object of Durendalian politics, as I understand,
is to get possession of the person of the king. Koreff was on my
screen for half an hour; I just got rid of him. Planet's pretty
heavily agricultural, they had a couple of very good crop years in
a row, and now they have grain running out their ears, and they
want to export it and cash in."

"Well?"

"Can't let them do it, Your Majesty. They're not suffering
any hardship; they're just not making as much money as they
think they ought to. If they start dumping their surplus into
interstellar trade, they'll cause all kinds of dislocations on other
agricultural planets. At least, that's what our computers all
say."

And that, of course, was gospel. He nodded.

"Why don't they turn their surplus into whisky? Age it five or
six years and it'd be on the luxury goods schedule and they could
sell it anywhere."

Count Duklass' eyes widened. "I never thought of that, Your
Majesty. Just a microsec; I want to make a note of that. Pass it
down to somebody who could deal with it. That's a wonderful
idea, Your Majesty!"

*   *   *

He finally got the conversation to an end, and went back to the reports. Security, as usual, had a few items above the dead level of bureaucratic procedure. The planetary king of Excalibur had been assassinated by his brother and two nephews, all three of whom were now fighting among themselves. As nobody had anything to fight with except small arms and a few light cannon, there would be no intervention. There had been intervention on Behemoth, however, where a whole continent had tried to secede from the planetary republic and the Imperial Navy had been requested to send a task force. That was all right, in both cases. No interference with anything that passed for a planetary government, but only one sovereignty on any planet with nuclear weapons, and only one supreme sovereignty in a galaxy with hyperdrive ships.

And there was rioting on Amaterasu, because of public indignation over a fraudulent election. He looked at that in incredulous delight. Why, here on Odin there hadn't been an election in the past six centuries that hadn't been utterly fraudulent. Nobody voted except the nonworkers, whose votes were bought and sold wholesale, by gangster bosses to pressure groups, and no decent person would be caught within a hundred yards of a polling place on an election day. He called the Minister of Security.

Prince Travann was a man of his own age—they had been classmates at the University—but he looked older. His thin face was lined, and his hair was almost completely white. He was at his desk, with the Sun and Cogwheel of the Empire on the wall behind him, but on the breast of his black tunic he wore the badge of his family, a silver planet with three silver moons. Unlike Count Duklass, he didn't wait to be spoken to.

"Good morning, Your Majesty."

"Good morning, Your Highness; sorry to bother you. I just caught an interesting item in your report. This business on Amaterasu. What sort of a planet is it, politically? I don't seem to recall."

"Why, they have a republican government, sir; a very complicated setup. Really, it's a junk heap. When anything goes badly, they always build something new into the government, but they never abolish anything. They have a president, a premier, and an executive cabinet, and a tricameral legislature, and two complete and distinct judiciaries. The premier is always the presidential candidate getting the next highest number of votes. In the present instance, the president, who controls the planetary militia, is accusing the premier, who controls the police, of fraud in the election of the middle house of the legislature. Each is supported by the judiciary he controls. Practically every citizen belongs either to the militia or the police auxiliaries. I am looking forward to further reports from Amaterasu," he added dryly.

"I daresay they'll be interesting. Send them to me in full, and redstar them, if you please, Prince Travann."

He went back to the reports. The Ministry of Science and Technology had sent up a lengthy one. The only trouble with it was that everything reported was duplication of work that had been done centuries before. Well, no. A Dr. Dandrik, of the physics department of the Imperial University here in Asgard announced that a definite limit of accuracy in measuring the velocity of accelerated subnucleonic particles had been established—16.067543333—times light-speed. That seemed to be typical; the frontiers of science, now, were all decimal points. The Ministry of Education had a little to offer; historical scholarship was still active, at least. He was reading about a new trove of source-material that had come to light on Uller, from the Sixth Century Atomic Era, when the door screen buzzed and flashed.

He lit it, and his son Rodrik appeared in it, with Snooks, the little red hound, squirming excitedly in the Crown Prince's arms. The dog began barking at once, and the boy called through the phone:

"Good morning, father; are you busy?"

"Oh, not at all." He pressed the release button. "Come on in."

Immediately, the little hound leaped out of the princely arms and came dashing into the study and around the desk, jumping onto his lap. The boy followed more slowly, sitting down in the deskside chair and drawing his foot up under him. Paul greeted Snooks first—people can wait, but for little dogs everything has to be right now—and rummaged in a drawer until he found some wafers, holding one for Snooks to nibble. Then he became aware that his son was wearing leather shorts and tall buskins.

"Going out somewhere?" he asked, a trifle enviously.

"Up in the mountains, for a picnic. Olva's going along."

And his tutor, and his esquire, and Olva's companion-lady, and a dozen Thoran riflemen, of course, and they'd be in continuous screen-contact with the Palace.

"That ought to be a lot of fun. Did you get all your lessons done?"

"Physics and math and galactiography," Rodrik told him. "And Professor Guilsan's going to give me and Olva our history after lunch."

They talked about lessons, and about the picnic. Of course, Snooks was going on the picnic, too. It was evident, though, that Rodrik had something else on his mind. After a while, he came out with it.

"Father, you know I've been a little afraid, lately," he said.

"Well, tell me about it, son. It isn't anything about you and Olva, is it?"

Rod was fourteen; the little Princess Olva thirteen. They would be marriageable in six years. As far as anybody could tell, they were both quite happy about the marriage which had been arranged for them years ago.

"Oh, no; nothing like that. But Olva's sister and a couple others of mother's ladies-in-waiting were to a psi-medium, and the medium told them that there were going to be changes. Great and frightening changes was what she said."

"She didn't specify?"

"No. Just that: great and frightening changes. But the only change of that kind I can think of would be . . . well, something happening to you."

Snooks, having eaten three wafers, was trying to lick his ear. He pushed the little dog back into his lap and pummeled him gently with his left hand.

"You mustn't let mediums' gabble worry you, son. These psi-mediums have real powers, but they can't turn them off and on like a water tap. When they don't get anything, they don't like to admit it, so they invent things. Always generalities like that; never anything specific."

"I know all that." The boy seem offended, as though somebody were explaining that his mother hadn't really found him out in the rose garden. "But they talked about it to some of their friends, and it seems that other mediums are saying the same thing. Father, do you remember when the Haval Valley generator blew up? All over Odin, the mediums had been talking about a terrible accident, for a month before that happened."

"I remember that." Harv Dorflay believed that somebody had been falsely informed that the emperor would visit the plant that day. "These great and frightening changes will probably turn out to be a new fad in abstract sculpture. Any change frightens most people."

They talked more about mediums, and then about aircars and aircar racing, and about the Emperor's Cup race that was to be flown in a month. The communications screen began flashing and buzzing, and after he had silenced it with the busy-button for the third time, Rodrik said that it was time for him to go, came around to gather up Snooks, and went out, saying that he'd be home in time for the banquet. The screen began to flash again as he went out.

It was Prince Ganzay, the Prime Minister. He looked as though he had a persistent low-level toothache, but that was his ordinary expression.

"Sorry to bother Your Majesty. It's about these chiefs-of-state. Count Gadvan, the Chamberlain, appealed to me, and I feel I should ask your advice. It's the matter of precedence."

"Well, we have a fixed rule on that. Which one arrived first?"

"Why, the Adityan, but it seems King Ranulf insists that he's entitled to precedence, or, rather, his Lord Marshal does. This Lord Koreff insists that his king is not going to yield precedence to a commoner."

"Then he can go home to Durendal!" He felt himself growing angry—all the little angers of the morning were focusing on one spot. He forced the harshness out of his voice. "At a court function, somebody has to go first, and our rule is order of arrival at the Palace. That rule was established to avoid violating the principle of equality to all civilized peoples and all planetary governments. We're not going to set it aside for the King of Durendal, or anybody else."

Prince Ganzay nodded. Some of the toothache expression had gone out of his face, now that he had been relieved of the decision.

"Of course, Your Majesty." He brightened a little. "Do you think we might compromise? Alternate the precedence, I mean?"

"Only if this First Citizen Yaggo consents. If he does, it would be a good idea."

"I'll talk to him, sir." The toothache expression came back. "Another thing, Your Majesty. They've both been invited to attend the Plenary Session, this afternoon."

"Well, no trouble there; they can enter by different doors and sit in visitors' boxes at opposite ends of the hall."

"Well, sir, I wasn't thinking of precedence. But this is to be an Elective Session—new Ministers to replace Prince Havaly, of Defense, deceased, and Count Frask, of Science and Technology, elevated to the Bench. There seems to be some difference of opinion among some of the Ministers and Counselors. It's very possible that the Session may degenerate into an outright controversy."

"Horrible," Paul said seriously. "I think, though, that our distinguished guests will see that the Empire can survive difference of opinion, and even outright controversy. But if you think it might have a bad effect, why not postpone the election?"

"Well—It's been postponed three times, already, sir."

"Postpone it permanently. Advertise for bids on two robot Ministers, Defense, and Science and Technology. If they're a success, we can set up a project to design a robot emperor."

The Prime Minister's face actually twitched and blanched at the blasphemy. "Your Majesty is joking," he said, as though he wanted to be reassured on the point.

"Unfortunately, I am. If my job could be robotized, maybe I could take my wife and my son and our little dog and go fishing for a while."

But, of course, he couldn't. There were only two alternatives: the Empire or Galactic anarchy. The galaxy was too big to hold general elections, and there had to be a supreme ruler, and a positive and automatic—which meant hereditary—means of succession.

"Whose opinion seems to differ from whose, and about what?" he asked.

"Well, Count Duklass and Count Tammsan want to have the Ministry of Science and Technology abolished, and its functions and personnel distributed. Count Duklass means to take over the technological sections under Economics, and Count Tammsan will take over the science part under Education. The proposal is going to be introduced at this Session by Count Guilfred, the Minister of Health and Sanity. He hopes to get some of the bio- and psycho-science sections for his own Ministry."

"That's right. Duklass gets the hide, Tammsan gets the head and horns, and everybody who hunts with them gets a cut of the meat. That's good sound law of the chase. I'm not in favor of it, myself. Prince Ganzay at this session, I wish you'd get Captain-General Dorflay nominated for the Bench. I feel that it is about time to honor him with elevation."

"General Dorflay? But why, Your Majesty?"

"Great galaxy, do you have to ask? Why, because the man's a

raving lunatic. He oughtn't even to be trusted with a sidearm, let alone five companies of armed soldiers. Do you know what he told me this morning?"

"That somebody is training a Nidhog swamp-crawler to crawl up the Octagon Tower and bite you at breakfast, I suppose. But hasn't that been going on for quite a while, sir?"

"It was a gimmick in one of the cooking robots, but that's aside from the question. He's finally named the master mind behind all these nightmares of his, and who do you think it is? Yorn Travann!"

The Prime Minister's face grew graver than usual. Well, it was something to look grave about; some of these days—

"Your Majesty, I couldn't possibly agree more about the general's mental condition, but I really should say that, crazy or not, he is not alone in his suspicions of Prince Travann. If sharing them makes me a lunatic, too, so be it, but share them I do."

Paul felt his eyebrows lift in surprise. "That's quite too much and too little, Prince Ganzay," he said.

"With your permission, I'll elaborate. Don't think that I suspect Prince Travann of any childish pranks with elevators or viewscreens or cooking-robots," the Prime Minister hastened to disclaim, "but I definitely do suspect him of treasonous ambitions. I suppose Your Majesty knows that he is the first Minister of Security in centuries who has assumed personal control of both the planetary and municipal police, instead of delegating his *ex officio* powers.

"Your Majesty may not know, however, of some of the peculiar uses he has been making of those authorities. Does Your Majesty know that he has recruited the Security Guard up to at least ten times the strength needed to meet any conceivable peace-maintenance problem on this planet, and that he has been piling up huge quantities of heavy combat equipment—guns up to 200-millimeter, heavy contragravity, even gun-cutters and bomb-and-rocket boats? And does Your Majesty know that most of this armament is massed within fifteen minutes' flight-time of this Palace? Or that Prince Travann has at his disposal from two and a half to three times, in men and firepower, the combined strength of the Planetary Militia and the Imperial Army on this planet?"

"I know. It has my approval. He's trying to salvage some of the young nonworkers through exposing them to military discipline. A good many of them, I believe, have gone off planet on their discharge from the SG and hired as mercenaries, which is a far better profession than vote-selling."

"Quite a plausible explanation; Prince Travann is nothing if not plausible," the Prime Minister agreed. "And does Your Majesty know that, because of repeated demands for support from the Ministry of Security, the Imperial Navy has been scattered all over the Empire, and that there is not a naval craft bigger than a scout-boat within fifteen hundred light-years of Odin?"

That was absolutely true. Paul could only nod agreement. Prince Ganzay continued:

"He has been doing some peculiar things as Police Chief of Asgard, too. For instance, there are two powerful nonworkers' voting-bloc bosses, Big Moogie Blisko and Zikko the Nose—I assure Your Majesty that I am not inventing these names; that's what the persons are actually called—who have been enjoying the favor and support of Prince Travann. On a number of occasions, their smaller rivals, leaders of less important gangs, have been arrested, often on trumped-up charges, and held incommunicado until either Moogie or Zikko could move into their territories and annex their nonworker followers. These two bloc-bosses are subsidized, respectively, by the Steel and Shipbuilding Cartels and by the Reaction Products and Chemical Cartels, but actually, they are controlled by Prince Travann. They, in turn, control between them about seventy per cent of the nonworkers in Asgard."

"And you think this adds up to a plot against the Throne?"

"A plot to seize the Throne, Your Majesty."

"Oh, come, Prince Ganzay! You're talking like Dorflay!"

"Hear me out, Your Majesty. His Imperial Highness is fourteen years old; it will be eleven years before he will be legally able to assume the powers of emperor. In the dreadful event of your immediate death, it would mean a regency for that long. Of course, your Ministers and Counselors would be the ones to name the Regent, but I know how they would vote with Security Guard bayonets at their throats. And regency might not be the limit of Prince Travann's ambitions."

"In your own words, quite plausible, Prince Ganzay. It rests, however, on a very questionable foundation. The assumption that Prince Travann is stupid enough to want the Throne."

He had to terminate the conversation himself and blank the

screen. Viktor Ganzay was still staring at him in shocked incredulity when his image vanished. Viktor Ganzay could not imagine anybody not wanting the Throne, not even the man who had to sit on it.

He sat, for a while, looking at the darkened screen, a little worried. Viktor Ganzay had a much better intelligence service than he had believed. He wondered how much Ganzay had found out that he hadn't mentioned. Then he went back to the reports. He had gotten down to the Ministry of Fine Arts when the communications screen began calling attention to itself again.

When he flipped the switch, a woman smiled out of it at him. Her blond hair was rumpled, and she wore a dressing gown; her smile brightened as his face appeared in her screen.

"Hi!" she greeted him.

"Hi, yourself. You just get up?"

She raised a hand to cover a yawn. "I'll bet you've been up reigning for hours. Were Rod and Snooks in to see you yet?"

He nodded. "They just left. Rod's going on a picnic with Olva in the mountains." How long had it been since he and Marris had been on a picnic—a real picnic, with less than fifty guards and as many courtiers along? "Do you have much reigning to do, this afternoon?"

She grimaced. "Flower Festivals. I have to make personal tri-di appearances, live, with messages for the loving subjects. Three minutes on, and a two-minute break between. I have forty for this afternoon."

"Ugh! Well, have a good time, sweetheart. All I have is lunch with the Bench, and then this Plenary Session." He told her about Ganzay's fear of outright controversy.

"Oh, fun! Maybe somebody'll pull somebody's whiskers, or something. I'm in on that, too."

The call-indicator in front of him began glowing with the code-symbol of the Minister of Security.

"We can always hope, can't we? Well, Yorn Travann's trying to get me, now."

"Don't keep him waiting. Maybe I can see you before the Session. She made a kissing motion with her lips at him, and blanked the screen.

He flipped the switch again, and Prince Travann was on the screen. The Security Minister didn't waste time being sorry to bother him.

"Your Majesty, a report's just come in that there's a serious riot at the University; between five and ten thousand students are attacking the Administration Center, lobbing stench bombs into it, and threatening to hang Chancellor Khane. They have already overwhelmed and disarmed the campus police, and I've sent two companies of the Gendarme riot brigade, under an officer I can trust to handle things firmly but intelligently. We don't want any indiscriminate stunning or tear-gassing or shooting; all sorts of people can have sons and daughters mixed up in a student riot.''

"Yes. I seem to recall student riots in which the sons of his late Highness Prince Travann and his late Majesty Rodrik XXI were involved." He deliberated the point for a moment, and added: "This scarcely sounds like a frat-fight or a panty-raid, though. What seems to have triggered it?''

"The story I got—a rather hysterical call for help from Khane himself—is that they're protesting an action of his in dismissing a faculty member. I have a couple of undercovers at the University, and I'm trying to contact them. I sent more undercovers, who could pass for students, ahead of the Gendarmes to get the student side of it and the names of the ringleaders." He glanced down at the indicator in front of him, which had begun to glow. "If you'll pardon me, sir, Count Tammsan's trying to get me. He may have particulars. I'll call Your Majesty back when I learn anything more.''

There hadn't been anything like that at the University within the memory of the oldest old grad. Chancellor Khane, he knew, was a stupid and arrogant old windbag with a swollen sense of his own importance. He made a small bet with himself that the whole thing was Khane's fault, but he wondered what lay behind it, and what would come out of it. Great plagues from little microbes start. Great and frightening changes—

The screen got itself into an uproar, and he flipped the switch. It was Viktor Ganzay again. He looked as though his permanent toothache had deserted him for the moment.

"Sorry to bother Your Majesty, but it's all fixed up," he reported. "First Citizen Yaggo agreed to alternate in precedence with King Ranulf, and Lord Koreff has withdrawn all his objections. As far as I can see, at present, there should be no trouble.''

"Fine. I suppose you heard about the excitement at the University?''

"Oh, yes, Your Majesty. Disgraceful affair!''

"Simply shocking. What seems to have started it, have you heard?" he asked. "All I know is that the students were protesting the dismissal of a faculty member. He must have been exceptionally popular, or else he got a more than ordinary raw deal from Khane."

"Well, as to that, sir, I can't say. All I learned was that it was the result of some faculty squabble in one of the science departments; the grounds for the dismissal were insubordination and contempt for authority."

"I always thought that when authority began inspiring contempt, it had stopped being authority. Did you say science? This isn't going to help Duklass and Tammsan any."

"I'm afraid not, Your Majesty." Ganzay didn't look particularly regretful. "The News Cartel's gotten hold of it and are using it; it'll be all over the Empire."

He said that as though it meant something. Well, maybe it did; a lot of Ministers and almost all the Counselors spent most of their time worrying about what people on planets like Chermosh and Zarathustra and Deirdre and Quetzalcoatl might think, in ignorance of the fact that interest in Empire politics varied inversely as the square of the distance to Odin and the level of corruption and inefficiency of the local government.

"I notice you'll be at the Bench luncheon. Do you think you could invite our guests, too? We could have an informal presentation before it starts. Can do? Good. I'll be seeing you there."

When the screen was blanked, he returned to the reports, ran them off hastily to make sure that nothing had been red-starred, and called a robot to clear the projector. After a while, Prince Travann called again.

"Sorry to bother Your Majesty, but I have most of the facts on the riot, now. What happened was that Chancellor Khane sacked a professor, physics department, under circumstances which aroused resentment among the science students. Some of them walked out of class and went to the stadium to hold a protest meeting, and the thing snowballed until half the students were in it. Khane lost his head and ordered the campus police to clear the stadium; the students rushed them and swamped them. I hope, for their sakes, that none of my men ever let anything like that happen. The man I sent, a Colonel Handrosan, managed to talk the students into going back to the stadium and continuing the meeting under Gendarme protection."

"Sounds like a good man."

"Very good, Your Majesty. Especially in handling disturbances. I have complete confidence in him. He's also investigating the background of the affair. I'll give Your Majesty what he's learned, to date. It seems that the head of the physics department, a Professor Nelse Dandrik, had been conducting an experiment, assisted by a Professor Klenn Faress, to establish more accurately the velocity of subnucleonic particles, beta micropositos, I believe. Dandrik's story, as relayed to Handrosan by Khane, is that he reached a limit and the apparatus began giving erratic results."

Prince Travann stopped to light a cigarette. "At this point, Professor Dandrik ordered the experiment stopped, and Professor Faress insisted on continuing. When Dandrik ordered the apparatus dismantled, Faress became rather emotional about it—obscenely abusive and threatening, according to Dandrik. Dandrik complained to Khane, Khane ordered Faress to apologize, Faress refused, and Khane dismissed Faress. Immediately, the students went on strike. Faress confirmed the whole story, and he added one small detail that Dandrik hadn't seen fit to mention. According to him, when these micropositos were accelerated beyond sixteen and a fraction times light-speed, they began registering at the target before the source registered the emission."

"Yes, I—*What did you say?*"

Prince Travann repeated it slowly, distinctly and tonelessly.

"That was what I thought you said. Well, I'm going to insist on a complete investigation, including a repetition of the experiment. Under direction of Professor Faress."

"Yes, Your Majesty. And when that happens, I mean to be on hand personally. If somebody is just before discovering time-travel, I think Security has a very substantial interest in it."

The Prime Minister called back to confirm that First Citizen Yaggo and King Ranulf would be at the luncheon. The Chamberlain, Count Gadvan, called with a long and dreary problem about the protocol for the banquet. Finally, at noon, he flashed a signal for General Dorflay, waited five minutes, and then left his desk and went out, to find the mad general and his wirchaired soldiers drawn up in the hall.

There were more Thorans on the South Upper Terrace, and after a flurry of porting and presenting and ordering arms and hand-saluting, the Prime Minister advanced and escorted him to where the Bench of Counselors, all thirty of them, total age close to twenty-eight hundred years, were drawn up in a rough crescent behind the three distinguished guests. The King of Durendal wore a cloth-of-silver leotard and pink tights, and a belt of gold links on which he carried a jeweled dagger only slightly thicker than a knitting needle. He was slender and willowy, and he had large and soulful eyes, and the royal beautician must have worked on him for a couple of hours. Wait till Marris sees this; oh, brother!

Koreff, the Lord Marshal, wore what was probably the standard costume of Durendal, a fairly long jerkin with short sleeves, and knee-boots, and his dress dagger looked as though it had been designed for use. Lord Koreff looked as though he would be quite willing and able to use it; he was fleshy and full-faced, with hard muscles under the flesh.

First Citizen Yaggo, People's Manager-in-Chief of and for the Planetary Commonwealth of Aditya, wore a one-piece white garment like a mechanic's coveralls, with the emblem of his government and the numeral 1 on his breast. He carried no dagger; if he had worn a dress weapon, it would probably have been a slide rule. His head was completely shaven, and he had small, pale eyes and a rat-trap mouth. He was regarding the Durendalians with a distaste that was all too evidently reciprocated.

King Ranulf appeared to have won the toss for first presentation. He squeezed the Imperial hand in both of his and looked up adoringly as he professed his deep honor and pleasure. Yaggo merely clasped both his hands in front of the emblem on his chest and raised them quickly to the level of his chin, saying: "At the service of the Imperial State," and adding, as though it hurt him, "Your Imperial Majesty." Not being a chief of state, Lord Koreff came third; he merely shook hands and said, "A great honor, Your Imperial Majesty, and the thanks, both of myself and my royal master, for a most gracious reception." The attempt to grab first place having failed, he was more than willing to forget the whole subject. There was a chance that finding a way to dispose of the grain surplus might make the difference between his staying in power at home or not.

Fortunately, the three guests had already met the Bench of Counselors. Immediately after the presentation of Lord Koreff, they all started the two hundred yards' march to the luncheon pavilion, the King of Durendal clinging to his left arm and First Citizen Yaggo stumping dourly on his right, with Prince Ganzay beyond him and Lord Koreff on Ranulf's left.

"Do you plan to stay long on Odin?" he asked the king.

"Oh, I'd *love* to stay for simply *months!* Everything is so *wonderful,* here in Asgard; it makes our little capital of Roncevaux seem so *utterly* provincial. I'm going to tell Your Imperial Majesty a secret. I'm going to see if I can lure some of your *wonderful* ballet dancers back to Durendal with me. Aren't I *naughty,* raiding Your Imperial Majesty's theaters?"

"In keeping with the traditions of your people," he replied gravely. "You Sword-Worlders used to raid everywhere you went."

"I'm afraid those bad old days are long past, Your Imperial Majesty," Lord Koreff said. "But we Sword-Worlders got around the galaxy, for a while. In fact, I seem to remember reading that some brethren from Morglay or Flamberge even occupied Aditya for a couple of centuries. Not that you'd guess it to look at Aditya now."

It was First Citizen Yaggo's turn to take precedence—the seat on the right of the throne chair. Lord Koreff sat on Ranulf's left, and, to balance him, Prince Ganzay sat beyond Yaggo and dutifully began inquiring of the People's Manager-in-Chief about the structure of his government, launching him on a monologue that promised to last at least half the luncheon. That left the King of Durendal to Paul; for a start, he dropped a compliment on the cloth-of-silver leotard.

King Ranulf laughed dulcetly, brushed the garment with his fingertips, and said that it was just a simple thing patterned after the Durendalian peasant costume.

"You have peasants on Durendal?"

"Oh, *dear,* yes! Such quaint, *charming* people. Of course, they're all poor, and they wear such *funny* ragged clothes, and travel about in rackety old aircars, it's a wonder they don't fall apart in the air. But they're so *wonderfully* happy and carefree. I often wish I were one of them, instead of king."

"Nonworking class, Your Imperial Majesty," Lord Koreff explained.

"On Aditya," First Citizen Yaggo declared, "there are no classes, and on Aditya everybody works. 'From each according to his ability; to each according to his need.' "

"On Aditya," an elderly Counselor four places to the right of him said loudly to his neighbor, "they don't call them classes, they call them sociological categories, and they have nineteen of

them. And on Aditya, they don't call them nonworkers, they call
them occupational reservists, and they have more of them than
we do."

"But of course, I was born a king," Ranulf said sadly and
nobly. "I have a duty to my people."

"No, they don't vote at all," Lord Koreff was telling the
Counselor on his left. "On Durendal, you have to pay taxes
before you can vote."

"On Aditya the crime of taxation does not exist," the First
Citizen told the Prime Minister.

"On Aditya," the Counselor four places down said to his
neighbor, "there's nothing to tax. The state owns all the property,
and if the Imperial Constitution and the Space Navy let them, the
State would own all the people, too. Don't tell me about Aditya.
First big-ship command I had was the old *Invictus*, 374, and she
was based on Aditya for four years, and I'd sooner have spent
that time in orbit around Nifflheim."

Now Paul remembered who he was; old Admiral—now Prince-
Counselor—Geklar. He and Prince-Counselor Dorflay would get
along famously. The Lord Marshal of Durendal was replying to
some objection somebody had made:

"No, nothing of the sort. We hold the view that every civil or
political right implies a civil or political obligation. The citizen
has a right to protection from the Realm, for instance; he therefore has the obligation to defend the Realm. And his right to
participate in the government of the Realm includes his obligation to support the Realm financially. Well, we tax only property;
if a nonworker acquires taxable property, he has to go to work to
earn the taxes. I might add that our nonworkers are very careful
to avoid acquiring taxable property."

"But if they don't have votes to sell, what do they live on?"
a Counselor asked in bewilderment.

"The nobility supports them; the landowners, the trading barons,
the industrial lords. The more nonworking adherents they have,
the greater their prestige." And the more rifles they could muster
when they quarreled with their fellow nobles, of course. "Besides,
if we didn't do that, they'd turn brigand, and it costs less to
support them than to have to hunt them out of the brush and hang
them."

"On Aditya, brigandage does not exist."

"On Aditya, all the brigands belong to the Secret Police, only on Aditya they don't call them Secret Police, they call them Servants of the People, Ninth Category.''

A shadow passed quickly over the pavilion, and then another. He glanced up quickly, to see two long black troop carriers, emblazoned with the Sun and Cogwheel and armored fist of Security, pass back of the Octagon Tower and let down on the north landing stage. A third followed. He rose quickly.

"Please remain seated, gentlemen, and continue with the luncheon. If you will excuse me for a moment, I'll be back directly." I hope, he added mentally.

Captain-General Dorflay, surrounded by a dozen officers, Thoran and human, had arrived on the lower terrace at the base of the Octagon Tower. They had a full Thoran rifle company with them. As he went down to them, Dorflay hurried forward.

"It has come, Your Majesty!" he said, as soon as he could make himself heard without raising his voice. "We are all ready to die with Your Majesty!"

"Oh, I doubt it'll come quite to that, Harv," he said. "But just to be on the safe side, take that company and the gentlemen who are with you and get up to the mountains and join the Crown Prince and his party. Here." He took a notepad from his belt pouch and wrote rapidly, sealing the note and giving it to Dorflay. "Give this to His Highness, and place yourself under his orders. I know; he's just a boy, but he has a good head. Obey him exactly in everything, but under no circumstances return to the Palace or allow him to return until I call you."

"Your Majesty is ordering me away?" The old soldier was aghast.

"An emperor who has a son can be spared. An emperor's son who is too young to marry can't. You know that."

Harv Dorflay was only mad on one subject, and even within the frame of his madness he was intensely logical. He nodded. "Yes, Your Imperial Majesty. We both serve the Empire as best we can. And I will guard the little Princess Olva, too." He grasped Paul's hand, said, "Farewell, Your Majesty!" and dashed away, gathering his staff and the company of Thorans as he went. In an instant, they had vanished down the nearest rampway.

The emperor watched their departure, and, at the same time, saw a big black aircar, bearing the three-mooned planet, argent on sable, of Travann, let down onto the south landing stage, and another troop carrier let down after it. Four men left the aircar—

Yorn, Prince Travann, and three officers in the black of the Security Guard. Prince Ganzay had also left the table; he came from one direction as Prince Travann advanced from the other. They converged on the emperor.

"What's happening here, Prince Travann?" Prince Ganzay demanded. "Why are you bringing all these troops to the Palace?"

"Your Majesty," Prince Travann said smoothly, "I trust that you will pardon this disturbance. I'm sure nothing serious will happen, but I didn't dare take chances. The students from the University are marching on the Palace—perfectly peaceful and loyal procession; they're bringing a petition for Your Majesty— but on the way, while passing through a nonworkers' district, they were attacked by a gang of hooligans connected with a voting-bloc boss called Nutchy the Knife. None of the students were hurt, and Colonel Handrosan got the procession out of the district promptly, and then dropped some of his men, who have since been reinforced, to deal with hooligans. That's still going on, and these riots are like forest fires; you never know when they'll shift and get out of control. I hope the men I brought won't be needed here. Really, they're a reserve for the riot work; I won't commit them, though, until I'm sure the Palace is safe."

He nodded. "Prince Travann, how soon do you estimate that the student procession will arrive here?" he asked.

"They're coming on foot, Your Majesty. I'd give them an hour, at least."

"Well, Prince Travann, will you have one of your officers see that the public-address screen in front is ready; I'll want to talk to them when they arrive. And meanwhile, I'll want to talk to Chancellor Khane, Professor Dandrik, Professor Faress and Colonel Handrosan, together. And Count Tammsan, too; Prince Ganzay, will you please screen him and invite him here immediately?"

"Now, Your Majesty?" At first, the Prime Minister was trying to suppress a look of incredulity; then he was trying to keep from showing comprehension. "Yes, Your Majesty; at once." He frowned slightly when he saw two of the Security Guard officers salute Prince Travann instead of the emperor before going away. Then he turned and hurried toward the Octagon Tower.

The officer who had gone to the aircar to use the radio returned and reported that Colonel Handrosan was bringing the Chancellor and both professors from the University in his command-car, having anticipated that they would be wanted. Paul nodded in pleasure.

"You have a good man there, Prince," he said. "Keep an eye on him."

"I know it, Your Majesty. To tell the truth, it was he who organized this march. Thought they'd be better employed coming here to petition you than milling around the University getting into further mischief."

The other officer also returned, bringing a portable viewscreen with him on a contragravity-lifter. By this time, the Bench of Counselors and the three off-planet guests had become anxious and left the luncheon pavilion in a body. The Counselors were looking about uneasily, noticing the black uniformed Security Guards who had left the troop carrier and were taking position by squads all around the emperor. First Citizen Yaggo, and King Ranulf and Lord Koreff, also seemed uneasy. They were avoiding the proximity of Paul as though he had the green death.

The viewscreen came on, and in it the city, as seen from an aircar at two thousand feet, spread out with the Palace visible in the distance, the golden pile of the Octagon Tower jutting up from it. The car carrying the pickup was behind the procession, which was moving toward the Palace along one of the broad skyways, with Gendarmes and Security Guards leading, following and flanking. There were a few Imperial and planetary and school flags, but none of the quantity-made banners and placards which always betray a planned demonstration.

Prince Ganzay had been gone for some time, now. When he returned, he drew Paul aside.

"Your Majesty," he whispered softly, "I tried to summon Army troops, but it'll be hours before any can get here. And the Militia can't be mobilized in anything less than a day. There are only five thousand Army Regulars on Odin, now, anyhow."

And half of them officers and noncoms of skeleton regiments. Like the Navy, the Army had been scattered all over the Empire—on Behemoth and Amida and Xipetotec and Astarte and Jotunnheim—in response to calls for support from Security.

"Let's have a look at this rioting, Prince Travann," one of the less decrepit Counselors, a retired general, said. "I want to see how your people are handling it."

The officers who had come with Prince Travann consulted briefly, and then got another pickup on the screen. This must have been a regular public pickup, on the front of a tall building.

It was a couple of miles farther away; the Palace was visible only as a tiny glint from the Octagon Tower, on the skyline. Half a dozen Security aircars were darting about, two of them chasing a battered civilian vehicle and firing at it. On rooftops and terraces and skyways, little clumps of Security Guards were skirmishing, dodging from cover to cover, and sometimes individuals or groups in civilian clothes fired back at them. There was a surprising absence of casualties.

"Your Majesty!" the old general hissed in a scandalized whisper. "That's nothing but a big fake! Look, they're all firing blanks! The rifles hardly kick at all, and there's too much smoke for propellant-powder."

"I noticed that." This riot must have been carefully prepared, long in advance. Yet the student riot seemed to have been entirely spontaneous. That puzzled him; he wished he knew just what Yorn Travann was up to. "Just keep quiet about it," he advised.

More aircars were arriving, big and luxurious, emblazoned with the arms of some of the most distinguished families in Asgard. One of the first to let down bore the device of Duklass, and from it the Minister of Economics, the Minister of Education, and a couple of other Ministers, alighted. Count Duklass went at once to Prince Travann, drawing him away from King Ranulf and Lord Koreff and talking to him rapidly and earnestly. Count Tammsan approached at a swift half-run.

"Save Your Majesty!" he greeted, breathlessly. "What's going on, sir? We heard something about some petty brawl at the University, that Prince Ganzay had become alarmed about, but now there seems to be fighting all over the city. I never saw anything like it; on the way here we had to go up to ten thousand feet to get over a battle, and there's a vast crowd on the Avenue of the Arts, and—" He took in the Security Guards. "Your Majesty, just what *is* going on?"

"Great and frightening changes." Count Tammsan started; he must have been to a psi-medium, too. "But I think the Empire is going to survive them. There may even be a few improvements, before things are done."

A blue-uniformed Gendarme officer approached Prince Travann, drawing him away from Count Duklass and speaking briefly to him. The Minister of Security nodded, then turned back to the Minister of Economics. They talked for a few moments longer, then clasped hands, and Travann left Duklass with his face wreathed in smiles. The Gendarme officer accompanied him as he approached.

"Your Majesty, this is Colonel Handrosan, the officer who handled the affair at the University."

"And a very good piece of work, colonel." He shook hands with him. "Don't be surprised if it's remembered next Honors Day. Did you bring Khane and the two professors?"

"They're down on the lower landing-stage, Your Majesty. We're delaying the students, to give Your Majesty time to talk to them."

"We'll see them now. My study will do." The officer saluted and went away. He turned to Count Tammsan. "That's why I asked Prince Ganzay to invite you here. This thing's become too public to be ignored; some sort of action will have to be taken. I'm going to talk to the students; I want to find out just what happened before I commit myself to anything. Well, gentlemen, let's go to my study."

Count Tammsan looked around, bewildered. "But I don't understand—" He fell into step with Paul and the Minister of Security; a squad of Security Guards fell in behind them. "I don't understand what's happening," he complained.

An emperor about to have his throne yanked out from under him, and a minister about to stage a *coup d' etat*, taking time out to settle a trifling academic squabble. One thing he did understand, though, was that the Ministry of Education was getting some very bad publicity at a time when it could be least afforded. Prince Travann was telling him about the hooligans' attack on the marching students, and that worried him even more. Non-working hooligans acted as voting-bloc bosses ordered; voting-bloc bosses acted on orders from the political manipulators of Cartels and pressure-groups, and action downward through the nonworkers was usually accompanied by action upward through influences to which ministers were sensitive.

There were a dozen Security Guards in black tunics, and as many Household Thorans in red kilts, in the hall outside the study, fraternizing amicably. They hurried apart and formed two ranks, and the Thoran officer with them saluted.

Going into the study, he went to his desk; Count Tammsan lit a cigarette and puffed nervously, and sat down as though he were afraid the chair would collapse under him. Prince Travann sank into another chair and relaxed, closing his eyes. There was a bit of wafer on the floor by Paul's chair, dropped by the little dog that morning. He stooped and picked it up, laying it on his desk, and sat looking at it until the door screen flashed and buzzed. Then he pressed the release button.

Colonel Handrosan ushered the three University men in ahead of him—Khane, with a florid, arrogant face that showed worry under the arrogance; Dandrik, gray-haired and stoop-shouldered, looking irritated; Faress, young, with a scrubby red mustache, looking bellicose. He greeted them collectively and invited them to sit, and there was a brief uncomfortable silence which everybody expected him to break.

"Well, gentlemen," he said, "we want to get the facts about this affair in some kind of order. I wish you'd tell me, as briefly and as completely as possible, what you know about it."

"There's the man who started it!" Khane declared, pointing at Faress.

"Professor Faress had nothing to do with it," Colonel Handrosan stated flatly. "He and his wife were in their apartment, packing to move out, when it started. Somebody called him and told him about the fighting at the stadium, and he went there at once to talk his students into dispersing. By that time, the situation was completely out of hand; he could do nothing with the students."

"Well, I think we ought to find out, first of all, why Professor Faress was dismissed," Prince Travann said. "It will take a good deal to convince me that any teacher able to inspire such loyalty in his students is a bad teacher, or deserves dismissal."

"As I understand," Paul said, "the dismissal was the result of a disagreement between Professor Faress and Professor Dandrik about an experiment on which they were working. I believe, an experiment to fix more exactly the velocity of accelerated subnucleonic particles. Beta micropositos, wasn't it, Chancellor Khane?"

Khane looked at him in surprise. "Your Majesty, I know nothing about that. Professor Dandrik is head of the physics department; he came to me, about six months ago, and told me that in his opinion this experiment was desirable. I simply deferred to his judgment and authorized it."

"Your Majesty has just stated the purpose of the experiment," Dandrik said. "For centuries, there have been inaccuracies in mathematical descriptions of subnucleonic events, and this experiment was undertaken in the hope of eliminating these inaccuracies." Before he could get into a lengthy mathematical explanation, Paul interrupted. "Yes, I understand that, professor.

But just what was the actual experiment, in terms of physical operations?"

Dandrik looked helpless for a moment. Faress, who had been choking back a laugh, interrupted:

"Your Majesty, we were using the big turbo-linear accelerator to project fast micropositos down an evacuated tube one kilometer in length, and clocking them with light, the velocity of which has been established almost absolutely. I will say that with respect to the light, there were no observable inaccuracies at any time, and until the micropositos were accelerated to $16.0675433331/3$ times light-speed, they registered much as expected. Beyond that velocity, however, the target for the micropositos began registering impacts before the source registered emission, although the light target was still registering normally. I notified Professor Dandrik about this, and—"

"You notified him. Wasn't he present at the time?"

"No, Your Majesty."

"Your Majesty, I am head of the physics department of the University. I have too much administrative work to waste time on the technical aspects of experiments like this," Dandrik interjected.

"I understand. Professor Faress was actually performing the experiment. You told Professor Dandrik what had happened. What then?"

"Why, Your Majesty, he simply declared that the limit of accuracy had been reached, and ordered the experiment dropped. He then reported the highest reading before this anticipation effect was observed as the newly established limit of accuracy in measuring the velocity of accelerated micropositos, and said nothing whatever in his report about the anticipation effect."

"I read a summary of the report. Why, Professor Dandrik, did you omit mentioning this slightly unusual effect?"

"Why, because the whole thing was utterly preposterous, that's why!" Dandrik barked, and then hastily added, "Your Imperial Majesty." He turned and glared at Faress; professors do not glare at galactic emperors. "Your Majesty, the limit of accuracy had been reached. After that, it was only to be expected that the apparatus would give erratic reports."

"It might have been expected that the apparatus would stop registering increased velocity relative to the light-speed standard, or that it would begin registering disproportionately," Faress said. "But, Your Majesty, I'll submit that it was not to be expected that it would register impacts before emissions. And I'll add this. After registering this slight apparent jump into the future, there was no proportionate increase in anticipation with further increase of acceleration. I wanted to find out why. But when Professor Dandrik saw what was happening, he became almost hysterical, and ordered the accelerator shut down as though he were afraid it would blow up in his face.''

"I think it has blown up in his face," Prince Travann said quietly. "Professor, have you any theory, or supposition, or even any wild guess, as to how this anticipation effect occurs?"

"Yes, Your Highness. I suspect that the apparent anticipation is simply an observational illusion, similar to the illusion of time-reversal experienced when it was first observed, though not realized, that positrons sometimes exceeded light-speed.''

"Why, that's what I've been saying, all along!" Dandrik broke in. "The whole thing is an illusion, due—''

"To having reached the limit of observational accuracy; I understand, Professor Dandrik. Go on, Professor Faress.''

"I think that beyond $16.0675433331/3$ times light-speed, the micropositos ceased to have any velocity at all, velocity being defined as rate of motion in four-dimensional spacetime. I believe they moved through the three spatial dimensions without moving at all in the fourth, temporal, dimension. They made that kilometer from source to target, literally, in nothing flat. Instantaneity.''

That must have been the first time he had actually come out and said it. Dandrik jumped to his feet with a cry that was just short of being a shriek.

"He's crazy! Your Majesty, you mustn't . . . that is, well, I mean— Please, Your Majesty, don't listen to him. He doesn't know what he's saying. He's raving!''

"He knows perfectly well what he's saying, and it probably scares him more than it does you. The difference is that he's willing to face it and you aren't.''

The difference was that Faress was a scientist and Dandrik was a science teacher. To Faress, a new door had opened, the first new door in eight hundred years. To Dandrik, it threatened invalidation of everything he had taught since the morning he had opened his first class. He could no longer say to his pupils, "You are here to learn from me." He would have to say, more humbly, *"We* are here to learn from the Universe.''

It had happened so many times before, too. The comfortable and established Universe had fitted all the known facts—and then new facts had been learned that wouldn't fit it. The third planet of the Sol system had once been the center of the Universe, and then Terra, and Sol, and even the galaxy, had been forced to abdicate centricity. The atom had been indivisible—until somebody divided it. There had been intangible substance that had permeated the Universe, because it had been necessary for the transmission of light—until it was demonstrated to be unnecessary and nonexistent. And the speed of light had been the ultimate velocity, once, and could be exceeded no more than the atom could be divided. And light-speed had been constant, regardless of distance from source, and the Universe, to explain certain observed phenomena, had been believed to be expanding simultaneously in all directions. And the things that had happened in psychology, when psi-phenomena had become too obvious to be shrugged away.

"And then, when Dr. Dandrik ordered you to drop this experiment, just when it was becoming interesting, you refused?"

"Your Majesty, I couldn't stop, not then. But Dr. Dandrik ordered the apparatus dismantled and scrapped, and I'm afraid I lost my head. Told him I'd punch his silly old face in, for one thing."

"You admit that?" Chancellor Khane cried.

"I think you showed admirable self-restraint in not doing it. Did you explain to Chancellor Khane the importance of this experiment?"

"I tried to, Your Majesty, but he simply wouldn't listen."

"But, Your Majesty!" Khane expostulated. "Professor Dandrik is head of the department, and one of the foremost physicists of the Empire, and this young man is only one of the junior assistant-professors. Isn't even a full professor, and he got his degree from some school away off-planet. University of Brannerton, on Gimli."

"Professor Faress, were you a pupil of Professor Vann Evaratt?" Prince Travann asked sharply.

"Why, yes, sir. I—"

"Ha, no wonder!" Dandrik crowed. "Your Majesty, that man's an out-and-out charlatan! He was kicked out of the University here ten years ago, and I'm surprised he could even get on the faculty of a school like Brannerton, on a planet like Gimli."

"Why, you stupid old fool!" Faress yelled at him. "You aren't enough of a physicist to oil robots in Vann Evaratt's lab!"

"There, Your Majesty," Khane said. "You see how much respect for authority this hooligan has!"

On Aditya, such would be unthinkable; on Aditya, everybody respects authority. Whether it's respectable or not.

Count Tammsan laughed, and he realized that he must have spoken aloud. Nobody else seemed to have gotten the joke.

"Well, how about the riot, now?" he asked. "Who started that?"

"Colonel Handrosan made an investigation on the spot," Prince Travann said. "May I suggest that we hear his report?"

"Yes indeed. Colonel?"

Handrosan rose and stood with his hands behind his back, looking fixedly at the wall behind the desk.

"Your Majesty, the students of Professor Faress' advanced subnucleonic physics class, postgraduate students, all of them, were told of Professor Faress' dismissal by a faculty member who had taken over the class this morning. They all got up and walked out in a body, and gathered outdoors on the campus to discuss the matter. At the next class break, they were joined by other science students, and they went into the stadium, where they were joined, half an hour later, by more students who had learned of the dismissal in the meantime. At no time was the gathering disorderly. The stadium is covered by a viewscreen pickup which is fitted with a recording device; there is a complete audiovisual of the whole thing, including the attack on them by the campus police.

"This attack was ordered by Chancellor Khane, at about 1100, the chief of the campus police was told to clear the stadium, and when he asked if he was to use force, Chancellor Khane told him to use anything he wanted to."

"I did not! I told him to get the students out of the stadium, but—"

"The chief of campus police carries a personal wire recorder," Handrosan said, in his flat monotone. "He has a recording of the order, in Chancellor Khane's own voice. I heard it myself. The police," he continued, "first tried to use gas, but the wind was against them. They then tried to use sono-stunners, but the students rushed them and overwhelmed them. If Your Majesty will permit a personal opinion, while I do not sympathize with their subsequent attack on the Administration Center, they were entirely within their rights in defending themselves in the stadium, and it's hard enough to stop trained and disciplined troops when they are winning. After defeating the police, they simply went on by what might be called the momentum of victory.''

"Then you'd say that it's positively established that the students were behaving in a peaceable and orderly manner in the stadium when they were attacked, and that Chancellor Khane ordered the attack personally?''

"I would, emphatically, Your Majesty.''

"I think we've done enough here, gentlemen.'' He turned to Count Tammsan. "This is, jointly, the affair of Education and Security. I would suggest that you and Prince Travann join in a formal and public inquiry, and until all the facts have been established and recorded and action decided upon, the dismissal of Professor Faress be reversed and he be restored to his position on the faculty.''

"Yes, Your Majesty,'' Tammsan agreed. "And I think it would be a good idea for Chancellor Khane to take a vacation till then, too.''

"I would further suggest that, as this microposito experiment is crucial to the whole question, it should be repeated. Under the personal direction of Professor Faress.''

"I agree with that, Your Majesty,'' Prince Travann said. "If it's as important as I think it is, Professor Dandrik is greatly to be censured for ordering it stopped and for failing to report this anticipation effect.''

"We'll consult about the inquiry, including the experiment, tomorrow, Your Highness,'' Tammsan told Travann.

Paul rose, and everybody rose with him. "That being the case, you gentlemen are all excused. The student's procession ought to be arriving, now, and I want to tell them what's going to be done. Prince Travann, Count Tammsan; do you care to accompany me?''

Going up to the central terrace in front of the Octagon Tower, he turned to Count Tammsan.

"I notice you laughed at that remark of mine about Aditya,'' he said. "Have you met the First Citizen?''

"Only on screen, sir. He was at me for about an hour, this morning. It seems that they are reforming the educational system on Aditya. On Aditya, everything gets reformed every ten years, whether it needs it or not. He came here to find somebody to take charge of the reformation.''

He stopped short, bringing the others to a halt beside him, and laughed heartily.

"Well, we'll send First Citizen Yaggo away happy; we'll make him a present of the most distinguished educator on Odin.''

"Khane?'' Tammsan asked.

"Khane. Isn't it wonderful; if you have a few problems, you have trouble, but if you have a whole lot of problems, they start solving each other. We get a chance to get rid of Khane, and create a vacancy that can be filled by somebody big enough to fill it; the Ministry of Education gets out from under a nasty situation; First Citizen Yaggo gets what he thinks he wants—''

"And if I know Khane, and if I know the People's Commonwealth of Aditya, it won't be a year before Yaggo has Khane shot or stuffs him into jail, and then the Space Navy will have an excuse to visit Aditya, and Aditya'll never be the same afterward,'' Prince Travann added.

The students massed on the front lawns were still cheering as they went down after addressing them. The Security Guards were conspicuously absent and it was a detail of red-kilted Thoran riflemen who met them as they entered the hall to the Session Chamber. Prince Ganzay approached, attended by two Household Guard officers, a human and a Thoran. Count Tammsan looked from one to the other of his companions, bewildered. The bewildering thing was that everything was as it should be.

"Well, gentlemen,'' Paul said, ''I'm sure that both of you will want to confer for a moment with your colleagues in the Rotunda before the Session. Please don't feel obliged to attend me further.''

Prince Ganzay approached as they went down the hall. "Your Majesty, what *is* going on here?'' he demanded querulously. "Just who is in control of the Palace—you or Prince Travann? And where is His Imperial Highness, and where is General Dorflay?''

"I sent Dorflay to join Prince Rodrik's picnic party. If you're upset about this, you can imagine what he might have done here.''

Prince Ganzay looked at him curiously for a moment. "I thought I understood what was happening,'' he said. "Now I— This business about the students, sir; how did it come out?''

Paul told him. They talked for a while, and then the Prime

Minister looked at his watch, and suggested that the Session ought to be getting started. Paul nodded, and they went down the hall and into the Rotunda.

The big semicircular lobby was empty, now, except for a platoon of Household Guards, and the Empress Marris and her ladies-in-waiting. She advanced as quickly as her sheath gown would permit, and took his arm; the ladies-in-waiting fell in behind her, and Prince Ganzay went ahead, crying: "My Lords, Your Venerable Highnesses, gentlemen; His Imperial Majesty!"

Marris tightened her grip on his arm as they started forward. "Paul!" she hissed into his ear. "What is this silly story about Yorn Travann trying to seize the Throne?"

"Isn't it? Yorn's been too close to the Throne for too long not to know what sort of a seat it is. He'd commit any crime up to and including genocide to keep off it."

She gave a quick skip to get into step with him. "Then why's he filled the Palace with these blackcoats? Is Rod all right?"

"Perfectly all right; he's somewhere out in the mountains, keeping Harv Dorflay out of mischief."

They crossed the Session Hall and took their seats on the double throne; everybody sat down, and the Prime Minister, after some formalities, declared the Plenary Session in being. Almost at once, one of the Prince-Counselors was on his feet begging His Majesty's leave to interrogate the Government.

"I wish to ask His Highness the Minister of Security the meaning of all this unprecedented disturbance, both here in the Palace and in the city," he said.

Prince Travann rose at once. "Your Majesty, in reply to the question of His Venerable Highness," he began, and then launched himself into an account of the student riot, the march to petition the emperor, and the clash with the nonworking class hooligans. "As to the affair at the University, I hesitate to speak on what is really the concern of His Lordship the Minister of Education, but as to the fighting in the city, if it is still going on, I can assure His Venerable Highness that the Gendarmes and Security Guards have it well in hand; the persons responsible are being rounded up, and, if the Minister of Justice concurs, an inquiry will be started tomorrow."

The Minister of Justice assured the Minister of Security that his Ministry would be quite ready to co-operate in the inquiry.

Count Tammsan then got up and began talking about the riot at
the University.

"What did happen, Paul?" Marris whispered.

"Chancellor Khane sacked a science professor for being too
interested in science. The students didn't like it. I think Khane's
successor will rectify that. Have a good time at the Flower
Festivals?"

She raised her fan to hide a grimace. "I made my schedule,"
she said. "Tomorrow, I have fifty more booked."

"Your Imperial Majesty!" The Counselor who had risen paused,
to make sure that he had the Imperial attention, before continuing:
"Inasmuch as this question also seems to involve a scientific
experiment, I would suggest that the Ministry of Science and
Technology is also interested, and since there is at present no
Minister holding that portfolio, I would suggest that the discussion be continued after a Minister has been elected."

The Minister of Health and Sanity jumped to his feet.

"Your Imperial Majesty; permit me to concur with the proposal of His Venerable Highness, and to extend it with the
subproposal that the Ministry of Science and Technology be
abolished, and its functions and personnel divided among the
other Ministries, specifically those of Education and of Economics."

The Minister of Fine Arts was up before he was fully seated.

"Your Imperial Majesty; permit me to concur with the proposal of Count Guilfred, and to extend it further with the proposal that the Ministry of Defense, now also vacant, be likewise
abolished, and its functions and personnel added to the Ministry
of Security under His Highness Prince Travann."

So that was it! Marris, beside him, said, "Well!" He had long
ago discovered that she could pack more meaning into that
monosyllable than the average counselor could into a half-hour's
speech. Prince Ganzay was thunderstruck, and from the Bench
of Counselors six or eight voices were babbling loudly at once.
Four Ministers were on their feet clamoring for recognition;
Count Duklass of Economics was yelling the loudest, so he got
it.

"Your Imperial Majesty; it would have been most unseemly
in me to have spoken in favor of the proposal of Count Guilfred,
being an interested party, but I feel no such hesitation in concur-
ring with the proposal of Baron Garatt, the Minister of Fine Arts.
Indeed, I consider it a most excellent proposal—"

"And I consider it the most diabolically dangerous proposal to be made in this Hall in the last six centuries!" old Admiral Geklar shouted. "This is a proposal to concentrate all the armed force of the Empire in the hands of one man. Who can say what unscrupulous use might be made of such power?"

"Are you intimating, Prince-Counselor, that Prince Travann is contemplating some tyrannical or subversive use of such power?" Count Tammsan, of all people, demanded.

There was a concerted gasp at that; about half the Plenary Session were absolutely sure that he was. Admiral Geklar backed quickly away from the question.

"Prince Travann will not be the last Minister of Security," he said.

"What I was about to say, Your Majesty, is that as matters stand, Security has a virtual monopoly on armed power on this planet. When these disorders in the city—which Prince Travann's men are now bringing under control—broke out, there was, I am informed, an order sent out to bring Regular Army and Planetary Militia into Asgard. It will be hours before any of the former can arrive, and at least a day before the latter can even be mobilized. By the time any of them get here, there will be nothing for them to do. Is that not correct, Prince Ganzay?"

The Prime Minister looked at him angrily, stung by the realization that somebody else had a personal intelligence service as good as his own, then swallowed his anger and assented.

"Furthermore," Count Duklass continued, "the Ministry of Defense, itself, is an anachronism, which no doubt accounts for the condition in which we now find it. The Empire has no external enemies whatever; all our defense problems are problems of internal security. Let us therefore turn the facilities over to the Ministry responsible for the tasks."

The debate went on and on; he paid less and less attention to it, and it became increasingly obvious that opposition to the proposition was dwindling. Cries of, "Vote! Vote!" began to be heard from its supporters. Prince Ganzay rose from his desk and came to the throne.

"Your Imperial Majesty," he said softly. "I am opposed to this proposition, but I am convinced that enough favor it to pass it, even over Your Majesty's veto. Before the vote is called, does Your Majesty wish my resignation?"

He rose and stepped down beside the Prime Minister, putting an arm over Prince Ganzay's shoulder.

"Far from it, old friend," he said, in a distinctly audible voice. "I will have too much need for you. But, as for the proposal, I don't oppose it. I think it an excellent one; it has my approval." He lowered his voice. "As soon as it's passed, place General Dorflay's name in nomination."

The Prime Minister looked at him sadly for a moment, then nodded, returning to his desk, where he rapped for order and called for the vote.

"Well, if you can't lick them, join them," Marris said as he sat down beside her. "And if they start chasing you, just yell, 'There he goes; follow me!' "

The proposal carried, almost unanimously. Prince Ganzay then presented the name of Captain-General Dorflay for elevation to the Bench of Counselors, and the emperor decreed it. As soon as the Session was adjourned and he could do so, he slipped out the little door behind the throne, into an elevator.

In the room at the top of the Octagon Tower, he laid aside his belt and dress dagger and unfastened his tunic, then sat down in his deep chair and called a serving robot. It was the one which had brought him his breakfast, and he greeted it as a friend; it lit a cigarette for him, and poured a drink of brandy. For a long time he sat, smoking and sipping and looking out the wide window to the west, where the orange sun was firing the clouds behind the mountains, and he realized that he was abominably tired. Well, no wonder; more Empire history had been made today than in the years since he had come to the Throne.

Then something behind him clicked. He turned his head, to see Yorn Travann emerge from the concealed elevator. He grinned and lifted his drink in greeting.

"I thought you'd be a little late," he said. "Everybody trying to climb onto the bandwagon?"

Yorn Travann came forward, unbuckling his belt and laying it with Paul's; he sank into the chair opposite, and the robot poured him a drink.

"Well, do you blame them? What would it have looked like to you, in their place?"

"A *coup d' etat.* For that matter, wasn't that what it was? Why didn't you tell me you were springing it?"

"I didn't spring it; it was sprung on me. I didn't know a thing about it till Max Duklass buttonholed me down by the landing stage. I'd intended fighting this proposal to partition Science and

Technology, but this riot blew up and scared Duklass and Tammsan and Guilfred and the rest of them. They weren't too sure of their majority—that's why they had the election postponed a couple of times—but they were sure that the riot would turn some of the undecided Counselors against them. So they offered to back me to take over Defense in exchange for my supporting their proposal. It looked too good to pass up.''

"Even at the price of wrecking Science and Technology?''

"It was wrecked, or left to rust into uselessness, long ago. The main function of Technology has been to suppress anything that might threaten this state of economic *rigor mortis* that Duklas calls stability, and the function of Science has been to let muttonheads like Khane and Dandrik dominate the teaching of science. Well, Defense has its own scientific and technical sections, and when we come to carving the bird, Duklass and Tammsan are going to see a lot of slices going onto my plate.''

"And when it's all cut up, it will be discovered that there is no provision for original research. So, it will please My Majesty to institute an Imperial Office of Scientific Research, independent of any Ministry, and guess who'll be named to head it.''

"Faress. And, by the way, we're all set on Khane, too. First Citizen Yaggo is as delighted to have him as we are to get rid of him. Why don't we get Vann Evaratt back, and give him the job?''

"Good. If he takes charge there at the opening of the next academic year, in ten years we'll have a thousand young men, maybe ten times that many, who won't be afraid of new things and new ideas. But the main thing is that now you have Defense, and now the plan can really start firing all jets.''

"Yes.'' Yorn Travann got out his cigarettes and lit one. Paul glanced at the robot, hoping that its feelings hadn't been hurt. "All these native uprisings I've been blowing up out of inter-tribal knife fights, and all these civil wars my people have been manufacturing; there'll be more of them, and I'll start yelling my head off for an adequate Space Navy, and after we get it, these local troubles will all stop, and then what'll we be expected to do? Scrap the ships?''

They both knew what would be done with some of them. It would have to be done stealthily, while nobody was looking, but some of those ships would go far beyond the boundaries of the Empire, and new things would happen. New worlds, new problems. Great and frightening changes.

"Paul, we agreed upon this long ago, when we were still boys at the University. The Empire stopped growing, and when things stop growing, they start dying, the death of petrifaction. And when petrifaction is complete, the cracking and the crumbling starts, and there's no way of stopping it. But if we can get people out onto new planets, the Empire won't die; it'll start growing again."

"You didn't start that thing at the University, this morning, yourself, did you?"

"Not the student riot, no. But the hooligan attack, yes. That was some of my own men. The real hooligans began looting after Handrosan had gotten the students out of the district. We collared all of them, including their boss, Nutchy the Knife, right away, and as soon as we did that, Big Moogie and Zikko the Nose tried to move in. We're cleaning them up now. By tomorrow morning there won't be one of these nonworkers' voting blocs left in Asgard, and by the end of the week they'll be cleaned up all over Odin. I have discovered a plot, and they're all involved in it."

"Wait a moment." Paul got to his feet. "That reminds me; Harv Dorflay's hiding Rod and Olva out in the mountains. I wanted him out of here while things were happening. I'll have to call him and tell him it's safe to come in, now."

"Well, zip up your tunic and put your dagger on; you look as though you'd been arrested, disarmed and searched."

"That's right." He hastily repaired his appearance and went to the screen across the room, punching out the combination of the screen with Rodrik's picnic party.

A young lieutenant of the Household Troops appeared in it, and had to be reassured. He got General Dorflay.

"Your Majesty! You are all right?"

"Perfectly all right, general, and it's quite safe to bring His Imperial Highness in. The conspiracy against the Throne has been crushed."

"Oh, thank the gods! Is Prince Travann a prisoner?"

"Quite the contrary, general. It was our loyal and devoted subject, Prince Travann, who crushed the conspiracy."

"But—but, Your Majesty—!"

"You aren't to be blamed for suspecting him, general. His agents were working in the very innermost councils of the conspirators. Every one of the people whom you suspected—

with excellent reason—was actually working to defeat the plot. Think back, general; the scheme to put the gun in the viewscreen, the scheme to sabotage the elevator, the scheme to introduce assassins into the orchestra with guns built into their trumpets— every one came to your notice because of what seemed to be some indiscretion of the plotters, didn't it?''

"Why . . . why, yes, Your Majesty!" By this time tomorrow, he would have a complete set of memories for each one of them. "You mean, the indiscretions were deliberate?"

"Your vigilance and loyalty made it necessary for them to resort to these fantastic expedients, and your vigilance defeated them as fast as they came to your notice. Well, today, Prince Travann and I struck back. I may tell you, in confidence, that every one of the conspirators is dead. Killed in this afternoon's rioting—which was incited for that purpose by Prince Travann."

"Then— Then there will be no more plots against your life?" There was a note of regret in the old man's voice.

"No more, Your Venerable Highness."

"But— What did Your Majesty call me?" he asked incredulously.

"I took the honor of being the first to address you by your new title, Prince-Counselor Dorflay."

He left the old man overcome, and blubbering happily on the shoulder of the Crown Prince, who winked at his father out of the screen. Prince Travann had gotten a couple of fresh drinks from the robot and handed one to him when he returned to his chair.

"He'll be finding the Bench of Counselors riddled with treason inside a week," Travann said. "You handled that just right, though. Another case of making problems solve each other."

"You were telling me about a plot you'd discovered."

"Oh, yes; this is one to top Dorflay's best efforts. All the voting-bloc bosses on Odin are in a conspiracy to start a civil war to give them a chance to loot the planet. There isn't a word of truth in it, of course, but it'll do to arrest and hold them for a few days, and by that time some of my undercovers will be in control of every nonworker vote on the planet. After all, the Cartels put an end to competition in every other business; why not a Voting Cartel, too? Then, whenever there's an election, we just advertise for bids."

"Why, that would mean absolute control—"

"Of the nonworking vote, yes. And I'll guarantee, personally, that in five years the politics of Odin will have become so unbearably corrupt and abusive that the intellectuals, the technicians, the business people, even the nobility, will be flocking to the polls to vote, and if only half of them turn out, they'll snow the nonworkers under. And that'll mean, eventually, an end to vote-selling, and the nonworkers'll have to find work. We'll find it for them."

"Great and frightening changes." Yorn Travann laughed; he recognized the phrase. Probably started it himself. Paul lifted his glass. "To the Minister of Disturbance!"

"Your Majesty!" They drank to each other, and then Yorn Travann said, "We had a lot of wild dreams, when we were boys; it looks as though we're starting to make some of them come true. You know, when we were in the University, the students would never have done what they did today. They didn't even do it ten years ago, when Vann Evaratt was dismissed."

"And Van Evaratt's pupil came back to Odin and touched this whole thing off." He thought for a moment. "I wonder what Faress has, in that anticipation effect."

"I think I can see what can come out of it. If he can propagate a wave that behaves like those micropositos, we may not have to depend on ships for communication. We may be able, someday, to screen Baldur or Vishnu or Aton or Thor as easily as you screened Dorflay, up in the mountains." He thought silently for a moment. "I don't know whether that would be good or bad. But it would be new, and that's what matters. That's the only thing that matters."

"Flower Festivals," Paul said, and, when Yorn Travann wanted to know what he meant, he told him. "When Princess Olva's Empress, she's going to curse the name of Klenn Faress. Flower Festivals, all around the galaxy, without end."

Blind Alley

by *Isaac Asimov*

Only once in Galactic History was an intelligent race of non-Humans discovered—
"Essays on History,"
by Ligurn Vier

I.

From: Bureau for the Outer Provinces
To: Loodun Antyok, Chief Public Administrator, A-8
   Subject: Civilian Supervisor of Cepheus 18, Administrative Position as,
   References:
   (a) Act of Council 2515, of the year 971 of the Galactic Empire, entitled, "Appointment of Officials of the Administrative Service, Methods for, Revision of."
   (b) Imperial Directive, Ja 2374, dated 243/975 G.E.
   1. By authorization of reference (a), you are hereby appointed to the subject position. The authority of said position as Civilian Supervisor of Cepheus 18 will extend over non-Human subjects of the Emperor living upon the planet under the terms of autonomy set forth in reference (b).
   2. The duties of the subject position shall comprise the general supervision of all non-Human internal affairs, co-ordination of authorized government investigating and reporting committees, and the preparation of semiannual reports on all phases of non-Human affairs.

                                   C. Morily, Chief, BuOuProv,
                                             12/977 G.E.

163

Loodun Antyok had listened carefully, and now he shook his round head mildly, "Friend, I'd like to help you, but you've grabbed the wrong dog by the ears. You'd better take this up with the Bureau."

Tomor Zammo flung himself back into his chair, rubbed his beak of a nose fiercely, thought better of whatever he was going to say, and answered quietly, "Logical, but not practical. I can't make a trip to Trantor now. You're the Bureau's representative on Cepheus 18. Are you entirely helpless?"

"Well, even as Civilian Supervisor, I've got to work within the limits of Bureau policy."

"Good," Zammo cried, "then, tell me what Bureau policy is. I head a scientific investigating committee, under direct Imperial authorization with, supposedly, the widest powers; yet at every angle in the road I am pulled up short by the civilian authorities with only the parrot shriek of 'Bureau policy' to justify themselves. What *is* Bureau policy? I haven't received a decent definition yet."

Antyok's gaze was level and unruffled. He said, "As I see it—and this is not official, so you can't hold me to it—Bureau policy consists in treating the non-Humans as decently as possible."

"Then, what authority have they—"

"*Ssh!* No use raising your voice. As a matter of fact, His Imperial Majesty is a humanitarian and a disciple of the philosophy of Aurelion. I can tell you quietly that it is pretty well-known that it is the Emperor himself who first suggested that this would be established. You can bet that Bureau policy will stick pretty close to Imperial notions. And you can bet that I can't paddle my way against *that* sort of current."

"Well, m'boy," the physiologist's fleshy eyelids quivered, "if you take that sort of attitude, you're going to lose your job. No, I won't have you kicked out. That's not what I mean at all. Your job will just fade out from under you, because nothing is going to be accomplished here!"

"Really? Why?" Antyok was short, pink, and pudgy, and his plump-cheeked face usually found it difficult to put on display any expression other than one of bland and cheerful politeness—but it looked grave now.

"You haven't been here long. I have." Zammo scowled. "Mind if I smoke?" The cigar in his hand was gnarled and strong and was puffed to life carelessly.

He continued roughly, "There's no place here for humani-

tarianism, administrator. You're treating non-Humans as if they
were Humans, and it won't work. In fact, I don't like the word
'non-Human.' They're animals.''

"They're intelligent," interjected Antyok, softly.

"Well, intelligent animals, then. I presume the two terms are
not mutually exclusive. Alien intelligences mingling in the same
space won't work, anyway."

"Do you propose killing them off?"

"Galaxy, no!" He gestured with his cigar. "I propose we
look upon them as objects for study, and only that. We could
learn a good deal from these animals if we were allowed to.
Knowledge, I might point out, that would be used for the
immediate benefit of the human race. *There's* humanity for
you. *There's* the good of the masses, if it's this spineless cult of
Aurelion that interests you."

"What, for instance, do you refer to?"

"To take the most obvious—You have heard of their chemistry,
I take it?"

"Yes," Antyok admitted. "I have leafed through most of the
reports on the non-Humans published in the last ten years. I
expect to go through more."

"Hmp. Well— Then, all I need say is that their chemical
therapy is extremely thorough. For instance, I have witnessed
personally the healing of a broken bone—what passes for a
broken bone with them, I mean—by the use of a pill. The bone
was whole in fifteen minutes. Naturally, none of their drugs are
any earthly use on Humans. Most would kill quickly. But if we
found out how they worked on the non-Humans—on the
animals—"

"Yes, yes. I see the significance."

"Oh, you do. Come, that's gratifying. A second point is that
these animals communicate in an unknown manner."

"Telepathy!"

The scientist's mouth twisted, as he ground out, "Telepathy!
Telepathy! Telepathy! Might as well say by witch brew. Nobody
knows anything about telepathy except its name. What is the
mechanism of telepathy? What is the physiology and the physics
of it? I would like to find out, but I can't. Bureau policy, if I
listen to you, forbids."

Antyok's little mouth pursed itself. "But— Pardon me, doctor,
but I don't follow you. How are you prevented? Surely the Civil
Administration has made no attempt to hamper scientific investi-

gation of these non-Humans. I cannot speak for my predecessor entirely, of course, but I myself—''

"No direct interference has occurred. I don't speak of that. But by the Galaxy, administrator, we're hampered by the spirit of the entire set-up. You're making us deal with humans. You allow them their own leader and internal autonomy. You pamper them and give them what Aurelion's philosophy would call 'rights.' I can't deal with their leader.''

"Why not?''

"Because he refuses to allow me a free hand. He refuses to allow experiments on any subject without the subject's own consent. The two or three volunteers we get are not too bright. It's an impossible arrangement.''

Antyok shrugged helplessly.

Zammo continued, "In addition, it is obviously impossible to learn anything of value concerning the brains, physiology, and chemistry of these animals without dissection, dietary experiments, and drugs. You know, administrator, scientific investigation is a hard game. Humanity hasn't much place in it.''

Loodun Antyok tapped his chin with a doubtful finger, "Must it be quite so hard? These are harmless creatures, these non-Humans. Surely, dissection— Perhaps, if you were to approach them a bit differently—I have the idea that you antagonize them. Your attitude might be somewhat overbearing.''

"Overbearing! I am not one of these whining social psychologists who are all the fad these days. I don't believe you can solve a problem that requires dissection by approaching it with what is called the 'correct personal attitude' in the cant of the times.''

"I'm sorry you think so. Sociopsychological training is required of all administrators above the grade of A-4.''

Zammo withdrew his cud of a cigar from his mouth and replaced it after a suitably contemptuous interval, "Then you'd better use a bit of your technique on the Bureau. You know, I *do* have friends at the Imperial court.''

"Well, now, I *can't* take the matter up with them, not baldly. Basic policy does not fall within my cognizance, and such things can only be initiated by the Bureau. But, you know, we might try an indirect approach on this.'' He smiled faintly, "Strategy.''

"What sort?''

Antyok pointed a sudden finger, while his other hand fell lightly on the rows of gray-bound reports upon the floor just next his chair, "Now, look, I've gone through most of these. They're dull, but contain *some* facts. For instance, when was the last non-Human infant born on Cepheus 18?

Zammo spent little time in consideration. "Don't know. Don't care either."

"But the Bureau would. There's *never* been a non-Human infant born on Cepheus 18—not in the two years the world has been established. Do you know the reason?"

The physiologist shrugged, "Too many possible factors. It would take study."

"All right, then. Suppose you write a report—"

"Reports! I've written twenty."

"Write another. Stress the unsolved problems. Tell them you must change your methods. Harp on the birth-rate problem. The Bureau doesn't dare ignore that. If the non-Humans die out, someone will have to answer to the Emperor. You see—"

Zammo stared, his eyes dark, "That will swing it?"

"I've been working for the Bureau for twenty-seven years. I know its ways."

"I'll think about it." Zammo rose and stalked out of the office. The door slammed behind him.

It was later that Zammo said to a co-worker, "He's a bureaucrat, in the first place. He won't abandon the orthodoxies of paper work and he won't risk sticking his neck out. He'll accomplish little by himself, yet maybe more than a little if we work through him."

From: Administrative Headquarters, Cepheus 18

To: BuOuProv

Subject: Outer Province Project 2563, Part II—Scientific Investigations of non-Humans of Cepheus 18, Co-ordination of,

References:

(a) BuOuProv letr. Cep-N-CM/jg, 100132, dated 302/975 G.E.

(b) AdHQ-Ceph18 letr. AA-LA/mn, dated 140/977 G.E.

Enclosure:

1. SciGroup 10, Physical & Biochemical Division, Report, entitled "Physiologic Characteristics of non-Humans of Cepheus 18, Part XI," dated 172/977 G.E.

1. Enclosure 1, included herewith, is forwarded for the information of the BuOuProv. It is to be noted that Section XII, paragraphs 1–16 of Encl. 1, concern possible changes in present BuOuProv policy with regard to Non-Humans with a view to facilitating physical and chemical investigations at present proceeding under authorization of reference (a)

2. It is brought to the attention of the BuOuProv that reference (b) has already discussed possible changes in investigating methods and that it remains the opinion of AdHQ-Ceph18 that such changes are as yet premature. It is nevertheless suggested that the question of non-Human birth rate be made the subject of a BuOuProv project assigned to AdHQ-Ceph18 in view of the importance attached by SciGroup 10 to the problem, as evidenced in Section V of Enclosure 1.

L. Antyok, Superv, AdHQ-Ceph18,
174/977

From: BuOuProv
To: AdHQ-Ceph18
Subject: Outer Province Project 2563—Scientific Investigations of non-Humans of Cepheus 18, Co-ordination of,
Reference:
(a) AdHQ-Ceph18 letr. AA-LA/mn, dated 174/977 G.E.

1. In response to the suggestion contained in paragraph 2 of reference (a), it is considered that the question of the non-Human birth rate does not fall within the cognizance of AdHQ-Ceph18. In view of the fact that SciGroup 10 has reported said sterility to be probably due to a chemical deficiency in the food supply, all investigations in the field are relegated to SciGroup 10 as the proper authority.

2. Investigating procedures by the various SciGroups shall continue according to current directives on the subject. No changes in policy are envisaged.

C. Morily, Chief, BuOuProv,
186/977 G.E.

II.

There was a loose-jointed gauntness about the news reporter which made him appear somberly tall. He was Gustiv Bannerd, with whose reputation was combined ability—two things which do not invariably go together despite the maxims of elementary morality.

Loodun Antyok took his measure doubtfully and said, "There's no use denying that you're right. But the SciGroup report was confidential. I don't understand how—"

"It leaked," said Bannerd, callously. "Everything leaks."

Antyok was obviously baffled, and his pink face furrowed slightly, "Then I'll just have to plug the leak here. I can't pass your story. All references to SciGroup complaints have to come out. You see that, don't you?"

"No." Bannerd was calm enough. "It's important; and I have my rights under the Imperial directive. I think the Empire should know what's going on."

"But it isn't going on," said Antyok, despairingly. "Your claims are all wrong. The Bureau isn't going to change its policy. I showed you the letters."

"You think you can stand up against Zammo when he puts the pressure on?" the newsman asked derisively.

"I will—if I think he's wrong."

"If!" stated Bannerd flatly. Then, in a sudden fervor, "Antyok, the Empire has something great here; something greater by a good deal than the government apparently realizes. They're destroying it. They're treating these creatures like animals."

"Really—" began Antyok, weakly.

"Don't talk about Cepheus 18. It's a zoo. It's a high-class zoo, with your petrified scientists teasing those poor creatures with their sticks poking through the bars. You throw them chunks of meat, but you cage them up. I know! I've been writing about them for two years now. I've almost been living with them."

"Zammo says—"

"Zammo!" This with hard contempt.

"Zammo says," insisted Antyok with worried firmness, "that we treat them too like humans as it is."

The newsman's straight, long cheeks were rigid, "Zammo is rather animal-like in his own right. He is a science-worshiper. We can do with less of them. Have you read Aurelion's works?" The last was suddenly posed.

"Umm. Yes. I understand the Emperor—"

"The Emperor tends towards us. That is good—better than the hounding of the last reign."

"I don't see where you're heading."

"These aliens have much to teach us. You understand? It is nothing that Zammo and his SciGroup can use; no chemistry, no telepathy. It's a way of life; a way of thinking. The aliens have no crime, no misfits. What effort is being made to study their philosophy? Or to set them up as a problem in social engineering?"

Antyok grew thoughtful, and his plump face smoothed out, "It is an interesting consideration. It would be a matter for psychologists—"

"No good. Most of them are quacks. Psychologists point out problems, but their solutions are fallacious. We need men of Aurelion. Men of The Philosophy—"

"But look here, we can't turn Cepheus 18 into . . . into a metaphysical study."

"Why not? It can be done easily."

"How?"

"Forget your puny test-tube peerings. Allow the aliens to set up a society free of Humans. Give them an untrammeled independence and allow an intermingling of philosophies—"

Antyok's nervous response came, "That can't be done in a day."

"We can start in a day."

The administrator said slowly, "Well, I can't prevent you from trying to start." He grew confidential, his mild eyes thoughtful, "You'll ruin your own game, though, if you publish SciGroup 10's report and denounce it on humanitarian grounds. The Scientists are powerful."

"And we of The Philosophy as well."

"Yes, but there's an easy way. You needn't rave. Simply point out that the SciGroup is not solving its problems. Do so unemotionally and let the readers think out your point of view for themselves. Take the birth-rate problem, for instance. *There's* something for you. In a generation, the non-Humans might die out, for all science can do. Point out that a more philosophical approach is required. Or pick some other obvious point. Use your judgment, eh?"

Antyok smiled ingratiatingly as he arose, "But, for the Galaxy's sake, don't stir up a bad smell."

Bannerd was stiff and unresponsive, "You may be right."

It was later that Bannerd wrote in a capsule message to a friend, "He is not clever, by any means. He is confused and has no guiding-line through life. Certainly utterly incompetent in his job. But he's a cutter and a trimmer, compromises his way around difficulties, and will yield concessions rather than risk a hard stand. He may prove valuable in that. Yours in Aurelion."

    From: AdHQ-Ceph18
    To: BuOuProv
    Subject: Birth rate of non-Humans on Cepheus 18, News Report
  on.
    References:
      (a) AdHQ-Ceph18 letr. AA-LA/mn, dated 174/977 G.E.

(b) Imperial Directive, Ja2374, dated 243/975 G.E.

Enclosures:

1-G. Bannerd news report, datelined Cepheus 18, 201/977 G.E.

2-G. Bannerd news report, datelined Cepheus 18, 203/977 G.E.

1. The sterility of non-Humans on Cepheus 18, reported to the BuOuProv in reference (a), has become the subject of news reports to the galactic press. The news reports in question are submitted herewith for the information of the BuOuProv as Enclosures 1 and 2. Although said reports are based on material considered confidential and closed to the public, the news reporter in question maintained his rights to free expression under the terms of reference (b).

2. In view of the unavoidable publicity and misunderstanding on the part of the general public now inevitable, it is requested that the BuOuProv direct future policy on the problem of non-Human sterility.

L. Antyok, Superv. AdHQ-Ceph18,
209/977 G.E.

From: BuOuProv
To: AdHQ-Ceph18
Subject: Birth rate of non-Humans on Cepheus 18, Investigation of.

References:

(a) *AdHQ-Ceph18 letr. AA-LA/mn, dated 209/977 G.E.*
(b) *AdHQ-Ceph18 letr. AA-LA/mn, dated 174/977 G.E.*

1. It is proposed to investigate the causes and the means of precluding the unfavorable birth-rate phenomena mentioned in references (a) and (b). A project is therefore set up, entitled, "Birth rate of non-Humans on Cepheus 18, Investigation of" to which, in view of the crucial importance of the subject, a priority of AA is given.

2. The number assigned to the subject project is 2910, and all expenses incidental to it shall be assigned to Appropriation number 18/78.

C. Morily, Chief, BuOuProv,
223/977 G.E.

III.

If Tomor Zammo's ill-humor lessened within the grounds of SciGroup 10 Experimental Station, his friendliness had not thereby increased. Antyok found himself standing alone at the viewing window into the main field laboratory.

The main field laboratory was a broad court set at the environmental conditions of Cepheus 18 itself for the discomfort of the experimenters and the convenience of the experimentees. Through the burning sand, and the dry, oxygen-rich air, there sparkled the hard brilliance of hot, white sunlight. And under the blaze, the brick-red non-Humans, wrinkled of skin and wiry of build, huddled in their squatting positions of ease, by ones and twos.

Zammo emerged from the laboratory. He paused to drink water thirstily. He looked up, moisture gleaming on his upper lip, "Like to step in there?"

Antyok shook his head definitely, "No, thank you. What's the temperature right now?"

"A hundred twenty, if there were shade. And they complain of the cold. It's drinking time now. Want to watch them drink?"

A spray of water shot upward from the fountain in the center of the court, and the little alien figures swayed to their feet and hopped eagerly forward in a queer, springy half-run. They milled about the water, jostling one another. The centers of their faces were suddenly disfigured by the projection of a long and flexible fleshy tube, which thrust forward into the spray and was withdrawn dripping.

It continued for long minutes. The bodies swelled and the wrinkles disappeared. They retreated slowly, backing away, with the drinking tube flicking in and out, before receding finally into a pink, wrinkled mass above a wide, lipless mouth. They went to sleep in groups in the shaded angles, plump and sated.

"Animals!" said Zammo, with contempt.

"How often do they drink?" asked Antyok.

"As often as they want. They can go a week if they have to. We water them every day. They store it under their skin. They eat in the evenings. Vegetarians, you know."

Antyok smiled chubbily, "It's nice to get a bit of firsthand information occasionally. Can't read reports all the time."

"Yes?"—noncommittally. Then, "What's new? What about the lacy-pants boys on Trantor?"

Antyok shrugged dubiously, "You can't get the Bureau to commit itself, unfortunately. With the Emperor sympathetic to the Aurelionists, humanitarianism is the order of the day. You know that."

There was a pause in which the administrator chewed his lip uncertainly. "But there's this birth-rate problem now. It's finally been assigned to AdHQ, you know—and double A priority, too."

Zammo muttered wordlessly.

Antyok said, "You may not realize it, but that project will now take precedence over all other work proceeding in Cepheus 18. It's important."

He turned back to the viewing window and said thoughtfully with a bald lack of preamble, "Do you think those creatures might be unhappy?"

"Unhappy!" The word was an explosion.

"Well, then," Antyok corrected hastily, "maladjusted. You understand? It's difficult to adjust an environment to a race we know so little of."

"Say—did you ever see the world we took them from?"

"I've read the reports—"

"Reports!"—infinite contempt. "I've *seen* it. This may look like desert out there to you, but it's a watery paradise to those devils. They have all the food and water they can get. They have a world to themselves with vegetation and natural water flow, instead of a lump of silica and granite where fungi were force-grown in caves and water had to be steamed out of gypsum rock. In ten years, they would have been dead to the last beast, and we saved them. Unhappy? Ga-a-ah, if they are, they haven't the decency of most animals."

"Well, perhaps. Yet I have a notion."

"A notion? What is your notion?" Zammo reached for one of his cigars.

"It's something that might help you. Why not study the creatures in a more integrated fashion? Let them use their initiative. After all, they did have a highly developed science. Your reports speak of it continually. Give them problems to solve."

"Such as?"

"Oh . . . oh," Antyok waved his hands helplessly. "Whatever you think might help most. For instance, spaceships. Get them into the control room and study their reactions."

"Why?" asked Zammo with dry bluntness.

"Because the reaction of their minds to tools and controls adjusted to the human temperament can teach you a lot. In addition, it will make a more effective bribe, it seems to me, than anything you've yet tried. You'll get more volunteers if they think they'll be doing something interesting."

"That's your psychology coming out. Hm-m-m. Sounds better

than it probably is. I'll sleep on it. And where would I get permission, in any case, to let them handle spaceships? I've none at *my* disposal, and it would take a good deal longer than it was worth to follow down the line of red tape to get one assigned to us.''

Antyok pondered, and his forehead creased lightly, "It doesn't *have* to be spaceships. But even so—If you would write up another report and make the suggestion yourself—strongly, you understand—I might figure out some way of tying it up with my birth-rate project. A double-A priority can get practically anything, you know, without questions.''

Zammo's interest lacked a bit even of mildness, "Well, maybe. Meanwhile, I've some basal metabolism tests in progress, and it's getting late. I'll think about it. It's got its points.''

From: AdHQ-Ceph18

To: BuOuProv

Subject: Outer Province Project 2910, Part I—Birth rate of non-Humans on Cepheus 18, Investigation of,

Reference:

(a) *BuOuProv letr. Ceph-N-CM/car, 115097, 223/977 G.E.*

Enclosure:

1. SciGroup 10, Physical & Biochemical Division report, Part XV, dated 220/977 G.E.

1. Enclosure 1 is forwarded herewith for the information of the BuOuProv.

2. Special attention is directed to Section V, Paragraph 3 of Enclosure 1 in which it is requested that a spaceship be assigned SciGroup 10 for use in expediting investigations authorized by the BuOuProv. It is considered by AdHQ-Ceph18 that such investigations may be of material use in aiding work now in progress on the subject project, authorized by reference (a). It is suggested, in view of the high priority placed by the BuOuProv upon the subject project, that immediate consideration be given the SciGroup's request.

L. Antyok, Superv. AdHQ-Ceph18,
240/977 G.E.

From: BuOuProv

To: AdHQ-Ceph18

Subject: Outer Province Project 2910—Birth rate of non-Humans on Cepheus 18, Investigation of.

Reference:

(a) AdHQ-Ceph18 letr. AA-LA/mn, dated 240/977 G.E.

1. Training Ship *AN-R*-2055 is being placed at the disposal of

AdHQ-Ceph18 for use in investigation of non-Humans on Cepheus 18 with respect to the subject project and other authorized OuProv projects, as requested in Enclosure 1 to reference (a).

2. It is urgently requested that work on the subject project be expedited by all available means.

C. Morily, Head, BuOuProv,
251/977 G.E.

IV.

The little, bricky creatures must have been more uncomfortable than his bearing would admit to. He was carefully wrapped in a temperature already adjusted to the point where his human companions steamed in their open shirts.

His speech was high-pitched and careful, "I find it damp, but not unbearably so at this low temperature."

Antyok smiled, "It was nice of you to come. I had planned to visit you, but a trial run in your atmosphere out there—" The smile had become rueful.

"It doesn't matter. You other worldlings have done more for us than ever we were able to do for ourselves. It is an obligation that is but imperfectly returned by the endurance on my part of a trifling discomfort." His speech seemed always indirect, as if he approached his thoughts sidelong, or as if it were against all etiquette to be blunt.

Gustiv Bannerd, seated in an angle of the room, with one long leg crossing the other, scrawled nimbly and said, "You don't mind if I record all this?"

The Cepheid non-Human glanced briefly at the journalist, "I have no objection."

Antyok's apologetics persisted, "This is not a purely social affair, sir. I would not have forced discomfort on you for that. There are important questions to be considered, and you are the leader of your people."

The Cepheid nodded, "I am satisfied your purposes are kindly. Please proceed."

The administrator almost wriggled in his difficulty in putting thoughts into words. "It is a subject," he said, "of delicacy, and one I would never bring up if it weren't for the overwhelming importance of the . . . uh . . . question. I am only the spokesman of my government—"

"My people consider the otherworld government a kindly one."

"Well, yes, they are kindly. For that reason, they are disturbed over the fact that your people no longer breed."

Antyok paused, and waited with worry for a reaction that did not come. The Cepheid's face was motionless except for the soft, trembling motion of the wrinkled area that was his deflated drinking tube.

Antyok continued, "It is a question we have hesitated to bring up because of its extremely personal angles. Noninterference is my government's prime aim, and we have done our best to investigate the problem quietly and without disturbing your people. But, frankly, we—"

"Have failed?" finished the Cepheid, at the other's pause.

"Yes. Or at least, we have not discovered a concrete failure to reproduce the exact environment of your original world; with, of course, the necessary modification to make it more livable. Naturally, it is thought there is some chemical shortcoming. And so I ask your voluntary help in the matter. Your people are advanced in the study of your own biochemistry. If you do not choose, or would rather not—"

"No, no, I can help." The Cepheid seemed cheerful about it. The smooth flat planes of his loose-skinned, hairless skull wrinkled in an alien response to an uncertain emotion. "It is not a matter that any of us would have thought would have disturbed you other-worldlings. That it does is but another indication of your well-meaning kindness. This world we find congenial, a paradise in comparison to our old. It lacks in nothing. Conditions such as now prevail belong in our legends of the Golden Age."

"Well—"

"But there is a something; a something you may not understand. We cannot expect different intelligences to think alike."

"I shall try to understand."

The Cepheid's voice had grown soft, its liquid undertones more pronounced, "We were dying on our native world; but we were fighting. Our science, developed through a history older than yours, was losing; but it had not yet lost. Perhaps it was because our science was fundamentally biological, rather than physical as yours is. Your people discovered new forms of energy and reached the stars. Our people discovered new truths of psychology and psychiatry and built up a working society free of disease and crime.

"There is no need to question which of the two angles of approach was the more laudable, but there is no uncertainty as to which proved more successful in the end. In our dying world, without the means of life or sources of power, our biological science could but make the dying easier.

"And yet we fought. For centuries past, we had been groping toward the elements of atomic power, and slowly the spark of hope had glimmered that we might break through the two-dimensional limits of our planetary surface and reach the stars. There were no other planets in our system to serve as stepping stones. Nothing but some twenty light-years to the nearest star, without the knowledge of the possibility of the existence of other planetary systems, but rather of the contrary.

"But there is something in all life that insists on striving; even on useless striving. There were only five thousand of us left in the last days. Only five thousand. And our first ship was ready. It was experimental. It would probably have been a failure. But already we had all the principles of propulsion and navigation correctly worked out."

There was a long pause, and the Cepheid's small black eyes seemed glazed in retrospect.

The newspaperman put in suddenly, from his corner, "And then we came?"

"And then you came," the Cepheid agreed simply. "It changed everything. Energy was ours for the asking. A new world, congenial and, indeed, ideal, was ours even without asking. If our problems of society had long been solved by ourselves, our more difficult problems of environment were suddenly solved for us, no less completely."

"Well?" urged Antyok.

"Well—it was somehow not well. For centuries, our ancestors had fought towards the stars, and now the stars suddenly proved to be the property of others. We had fought for life, and it had become a present handed to us by others. There is no longer any reason to fight. There is no longer anything to attain. All the universe is the property of your race."

"This world is yours," said Antyok, gently.

"By sufferance. It is a gift. It is not ours by right."

"You have earned it, in my opinion."

And now the Cepheid's eyes were sharply fixed on the other's countenance, "You mean well, but I doubt that you understand. We have nowhere to go, save this gift of a world. We are in a blind alley. The function of life is striving, and that is taken from us. Life can no longer interest us. We have no offspring—voluntarily. It is our way of removing ourselves from your way."

Absent-mindedly, Antyok had removed the fluoro-globe from the window seat, and spun it on its base. Its gaudy surface reflected light as it spun, and its three-foot-high bulk floated with incongruous grace and lightness in the air.

Antyok said, "Is that your only solution? Sterility?"

"We might escape still," whispered the Cepheid, "but where in the Galaxy is there place for us? It is all yours."

"Yes, there is no place for you nearer than the Magellanic Clouds if you wished independence. The Magellanic Clouds—"

"And you would not let us go of yourselves. You mean kindly, I know."

"Yes, we mean kindly—but we could not let you go."

"It is a mistaken kindness."

"Perhaps, but could you not reconcile yourselves? You have a world."

"It is something past complete explanations. Your mind is different. We could not reconcile ourselves. I believe, administrator, that you have thought of all this before. The concept of the blind alley we find ourselves trapped in is not new to you."

Antyok looked up, startled, and one hand steadied the fluoroglobe, "Can you read my mind?"

"It is just a guess. A good one, I think."

"Yes—but *can* you read my mind? The minds of humans in general, I mean. It is an interesting point. The scientists say you cannot, but sometimes I wonder if it is that you simply will not. Could you answer that? I am detaining you, unduly, perhaps."

"No . . . no—" But the little Cepheid drew his enveloping robe closer, and buried his face in the electrically-heated pad at the collar for a moment. "You other-worldlings speak of reading minds. It is not so at all, but it is assuredly hopeless to explain."

Antyok mumbled the old proverb, "One cannot explain sight to a man blind from birth."

"Yes, just so. This sense which you call 'mind reading,' quite erroneously, cannot be applied to us. It is not that we cannot receive the proper sensations, it is that your people do not transmit them, and we have no way of explaining to you how to go about it."

"Hm-m-m."

"There are times, of course, of great concentration or emotional tension on the part of an other-worldling when some of us who are more expert in this sense; more sharp-eyed, so to speak; detect vaguely *something*. It is uncertain; yet I myself have at times wondered—"

Carefully, Antyok began spinning the fluoro-globe once more. His pink face was set in thought, and his eyes were fixed upon the Cepheid. Gustiv Bannerd stretched his fingers and reread his notes, his lips moving silently.

The fluoro-globe spun, and slowly the Cepheid seemed to grow tense as well, as his eyes shifted to the colorful sheen of the globe's fragile surface.

The Cepheid said, "What is that?"

Antyok started, and his face smoothed into an almost chuckling placidity, "This? A Galactic fad of three years ago; which means that it is a hopelessly old-fashioned relic this year. It is a useless device but it looks pretty. Bannerd, could you adjust the windows to nontransmission?"

There was the soft click of a contact, and the windows became curved regions of darkness, while in the center of the room, the fluoro-globe was suddenly the focus of a rosy effulgence that seemed to leap outward in streamers. Antyok, a scarlet figure in a scarlet room, placed it upon the table and spun it with a hand that dripped red. As it spun, the colors changed with a slowly increasing rapidity, blended and fell apart into more extreme contrasts.

Antyok was speaking in an eerie atmosphere of molten, shifting rainbow, "The surface is of a material that exhibits variable fluorescence. It is almost weightless, extremely fragile, but gyroscopically balanced so that it rarely falls, with ordinary care. It is rather pretty, don't you think?"

From somewhere the Cepheid's voice came, "Extremely pretty."

"But it has outworn its welcome; outlived its fashionable existence."

The Cepheid's voice was abstracted, "It is very pretty."

Bannerd restored the light at a gesture, and the colors faded.

The Cepheid said, "That is something my people would enjoy." He stared at the globe with fascination.

And now Antyok rose. "You had better go. If you stay

longer, the atmosphere may have bad effects. I thank you humbly for your kindness."

"I thank you humbly for yours." The Cepheid had also risen.

Antyok said, "Most of your people, by the way, have accepted our offers to them to study the make-up of our modern spaceships. You understand, I suppose, that the purpose was to study the reactions of your people to our technology. I trust that conforms with your sense of propriety."

"You need not apologize. I, myself, have now the makings of a human pilot. It was most interesting. It recalls our own efforts—and reminds us of how nearly on the right track we were."

The Cepheid left, and Antyok sat, frowning.

"Well," he said to Bannerd, a little sharply. "You remember our agreement, I hope. This interview can't be published."

Bannerd shrugged, "Very well."

Antyok was at his seat, and his fingers fumbled with the small metal figurine upon his desk, "What do you think of all this, Bannerd?"

"I am sorry for them. I think I understand how they feel. We must educate them out of it. The Philosophy can do it."

"You think so?"

"Yes."

"We can't let them go, of course."

"Oh, no. Out of the question. We have too much to learn from them. This feeling of theirs is only a passing stage. They'll think differently, especially when we allow them the completest independence."

"Maybe. What do you think of the fluoro-globes, Bannerd? He liked them. It might be a gesture of the right sort to order several thousand of them. The Galaxy knows, they're a drug on the market right now, and cheap enough."

"Sounds like a good idea," said Bannerd.

"The Bureau would never agree, though. I know them."

The newsman's eyes narrowed, "But it might be just the thing. They need new interests."

"Yes? Well, we *could* do something. I could include your transcript of the interview as part of a report and just emphasize the matter of the globes a bit. After all, you're a member of The Philosophy and might have influence with important people, whose word with the Bureau might carry much more weight than mine. You understand—?"

"Yes," mused Bannerd. "Yes."

From: AdHQ-Ceph18
To: BuOuProv
Subject: OuProv Project 2910, Part II; Birth rate of non-Humans on Cepheus 18, Investigation of.
Reference:
　　(a) BuOuProv letr. Cep-N-CM/car, 115097, dated 223/977 G.E.
Enclosure:
　　1. Transcript of conversation between L. Antyok of AdHQ-Ceph18, and Ni-San, High Judge of the non-Humans on Cepheus 18.

1. Enclosure 1 is forwarded herewith for the information of the BuOuProv.

2. The investigation of the subject project undertaken in response to the authorization of reference (a) is being pursued along the new lines indicated in Enclosure 1. The BuOuProv is assured that every means will be used to combat the harmful psychological attitude at present prevalent among the non-Humans.

3. It is to be noted that the High Judge of the non-Humans on Cepheus 18 expressed interest in fluoro-globes. A preliminary investigation into this fact of non-Human psychology has been initiated.

　　　　　　　　　　　L. Antyok, Superv. AdHQ-Ceph18,
　　　　　　　　　　　272/977 G.E.

From: BuOuProv
To: AdHQ-Ceph18
Subject: OuProv Project 2910; Birth rate of non-Humans on Cepheus 18, Investigation of.
Reference:
　　(a) AdHQ-Ceph18 letr. AA-LA/mn, dated 272/977 G.E.

1. With reference to Enclosure 1 of reference (a), five thousand fluoro-globes have been allocated for shipment to Cepheus 18, by the Department of Trade.

2. It is instructed that AdHQ-Ceph18 make use of all methods of appeasing non-Humans' dissatisfaction, consistent with the necessities of obedience to Imperial proclamations.

　　　　　　　　　　　C. Morily, Chief, BuOuProv,
　　　　　　　　　　　283/977 G.E.

V.

The dinner was over, the wine had been brought in, and the cigars were out. The groups of talkers had formed, and the captain of the merchant fleet was the center of the largest. His brilliant white uniform quite outsparkled his listeners.

He was almost complacent in his speech: "The trip was nothing. I've had more than three hundred ships under me before this. Still, I've never had a cargo quite like this. What do you want with five thousand fluoro-globes on this desert, by the Galaxy!"

Loodun Antyok laughed gently. He shrugged. "For the non-Humans. It wasn't a difficult cargo, I hope."

"No, not difficult. But bulky. They're fragile, and I couldn't carry more than twenty to a ship, with all the government regulations concerning packing and precautions against breakage. But it's the government's money, I suppose."

Zammo smiled grimly. "Is this your first experience with government methods, captain?"

"Galaxy, no," exploded the spaceman. "I try to avoid it, of course, but you can't help getting entangled on occasion. And it's an abhorrent thing when you are, and that's the truth. The red tape! The paper work! It's enough to stunt your growth and curdle your circulation. It's a tumor, a cancerous growth on the Galaxy. I'd wipe out the whole mess."

Antyok said, "You're unfair, captain. You don't understand."

"Yes? Well, now, as one of these bureaucrats," and he smiled amiably at the word, "suppose you explain your side of the situation, administrator."

"Well, now," Antyok seemed confused, "government is a serious and complicated business. We've got thousands of planets to worry about in this Empire of ours and billions of people. It's almost past human ability to supervise the business of governing without the tightest sort of organization. I think there are something like four hundred million men today in the Imperial Administrative Service alone, and in order to co-ordinate their efforts and to pool their knowledge, you *must* have what you call red tape and paper work. Every bit of it, senseless though it may seem, annoying though it may be, has its uses. Every piece of paper is a thread binding the labors of four hundred million humans. Abolish the Administrative Service and you abolish the Empire; and with it, interstellar peace, order, and civilization."

"Come—" said the captain.

"No. I mean it." Antyok was earnestly breathless. "The rules and system of the Administrative set-up must be sufficiently all-embracing and rigid so that in case of incompetent officials, and sometimes one *is* appointed—you may laugh, but there are incompetent scientists, and newsmen, and captains, too—in case of incompetent officials, I say, little harm will be done. For, at the worst, the system can move by itself."

"Yes," grunted the captain, sourly, "and if a capable administrator should be appointed? He is then caught by the same rigid web and is forced into mediocrity."

"Not at all," replied Antyok, warmly. "A capable man can work within the limits of the rules and accomplish what he wishes."

"How?" asked Bannerd.

"Well . . . well—" Antyok was suddenly ill at ease. "One method is to get yourself an A-priority project, or double-A, if possible."

The captain leaned his head back for laughter, but never quite made it, for the door was flung open and frightened men were pouring in. The shouts made no sense at first. Then:

"Sir, the ships are gone. These non-Humans have taken them by force."

"What? All?"

"Every one. Ships and creatures—"

It was two hours later that the four were together again, alone in Antyok's office now.

Antyok said coldly, "They've made no mistakes. There's not a ship left behind, not even your training ship, Zammo. And there isn't a government ship available in this entire half of the Sector. By the time we organize a pursuit they'll be out of the Galaxy and halfway to the Magellanic Clouds. Captain, it was your responsibility to maintain an adequate guard."

The captain cried, "It was our first day out of space. Who could have known—"

Zammo interrupted fiercely, "Wait a while, captain. I'm beginning to understand. Antyok," his voice was hard, "you engineered this."

"I?" Antyok's expression was strangely cool, almost indifferent.

"You told us this evening that a clever administrator got a A-priority project assigned to accomplish what he wished. You got such a project in order to help the non-Humans escape."

"I did? I beg your pardon, but how could that be? It was you yourself in one of your reports that brought up the problem of the failing birth rate. It was Bannerd, here, whose sensational articles frightened the Bureau into making a double A-priority project out of it. I had nothing to do with it."

"*You* suggested that I mention the birth rate," said Zammo, violently.

"Did I?" said Antyok, composedly.

"And for that matter," roared Bannerd, suddenly, "you suggested that I mention the birth rate in my articles."

The three ringed him now and hemmed him in. Antyok leaned back in his chair and said easily, "I don't know what you mean by suggestions. If you are accusing me, please stick to evidence—legal evidence. The laws of the Empire go by written, filmed, or transcribed material, or by witnessed statements. All my letters as administrator are on file here, at the Bureau, and at other places. I never asked for a double-A-priority project. The Bureau assigned it to me, and Zammo and Bannerd are responsible for that. In print, at any rate."

Zammo's voice was an almost inarticulate growl, "You hoodwinked me into teaching the creatures how to handle a spaceship."

"It was *your* suggestion. I have your report proposing they be studied in their reaction to human tools on file. So has the Bureau. The evidence—the *legal* evidence, is plain. I had nothing to do with it."

"Nor with the globes?" demanded Bannerd.

The captain howled suddenly, "You had my ships brought here purposely. Five thousand globes! You knew it would require hundreds of craft."

"I never asked for globes," said Antyok, coldly. "That was the Bureau's idea, although I think Bannerd's friends of The Philosophy helped that along."

Bannerd fairly choked. He spat out, "You were asking that Cepheid leader if he could read minds. You were telling him to express interest in the globes."

"Come, now. You prepared the transcript of the conversation yourself, and that, too, is on file. You can't prove it." He stood up, "You'll have to excuse me. I must prepare a report for the Bureau."

At the door, Antyok turned, "In a way, the problem of the non-Humans is solved, even if only to their own satisfaction. They'll breed now, and have a world they've earned themselves. It's what they wanted.

"Another thing. Don't accuse me of silly things. I've been in the Service for twenty-seven years, and I assure you that my paper work is proof enough that I have been thoroughly correct in everything I have done. And captain, I'll be glad to continue our discussion of earlier this evening at your convenience and explain how a capable administrator can work through red tape and still get what he wants.''

It was remarkable that such a round, smooth baby-face could wear a smile quite so sardonic.

From: BuOuProv
To: Loodun Antyok, Chief Public Administrator, A-8
Subject: Administrative Service, Standing in.
Reference:
 (a) AdServ Court Decision 22874-Q, dated 1/978 G.E.
 1. In view of the favorable opinion handed down in reference (a) you are hereby absolved of all responsibility for the flight of non-Humans on Cepheus 18. It is requested that you hold yourself in readiness for your next appointment.

R. Horpritt, Chief, AdServ,
15/978 G.E.

A Planet Named Shayol

by *Cordwainer Smith*

I

There was a tremendous difference between the liner and the ferry in Mercer's treatment. On the liner, the attendants made gibes when they brought him his food.

"Scream good and loud," said one rat-faced steward, "and then we'll know it's you when they broadcast the sounds of punishment on the Emperor's birthday."

The other fat steward ran the tip of his wet red tongue over his thick purple-red lips one time and said, "Stands to reason, man. If you hurt all the time, the whole lot of you would die. Something pretty good must happen, along with the-whatchama-callit. Maybe you turn into a woman. Maybe you turn into two people. Listen, cousin, if it's real crazy fun, let me know. . . ." Mercer said nothing. Mercer had enough troubles of his own not to wonder about the daydreams of nasty men.

At the ferry it was different. The biopharmaceutical staff was deft, impersonal, quick in removing his shackles. They took off all his prison clothes and left them on the liner. When he boarded the ferry, naked, they looked him over as if he were a rare plant or a body on the operating table. They were almost kind in the clinical deftness of their touch. They did not treat him as a criminal, but as a specimen.

Men and women, clad in their medical smocks, they looked at him as though he were already dead.

He tried to speak. A man, older and more authoritative than the others, said firmly and clearly, "Do not worry about talking. I will talk to you myself in a very little time. What we are having

186

now are the preliminaries, to determine your physical condition. Turn around, please."

Mercer turned around. An orderly rubbed his back with a very strong antiseptic.

"This is going to sting," said one of the technicans, "but it is nothing serious or painful. We are determining the toughness of the different layers of your skin."

Mercer, annoyed by this impersonal approach, spoke up just as a sharp little sting burned him above the sixth lumbar vertebra. "Don't you know who I am?"

"Of course we know who you are," said a woman's voice. "We have it all in a file in the corner. The chief doctor will talk about your crime later, if you want to talk about it. Keep quiet now. We are making a skin test, and you will feel much better if you do not make us prolong it."

Honesty forced her to add another sentence: "And we will get better results as well."

They had lost no time at all in getting to work.

He peered at them sidewise to look at them. There was nothing about them to indicate that they were human devils in the antechambers of hell itself. Nothing was there to indicate that this was the satellite of Shayol, the final and uttermost place of chastisement and shame. They looked like medical people from his life before he committed the crime without a name.

They changed from one routine to another. A woman, wearing a surgical mask, waved her hand at a white table.

"Climb up on that, please."

No one had said "please" to Mercer since the guards had seized him at the edge of the palace. He started to obey her and then he saw that there were padded handcuffs at the head of the table. He stopped.

"Get along, please," she demanded. Two or three of the others turned around to look at both of them.

The second "please" shook him. He had to speak. These were people, and he was a person again. He felt his voice rising, almost cracking into shrillness as he asked her, "Please ma'am, is the punishment going to begin?"

"There's no punishment here," said the woman. "This is the satellite. Get on the table. We're going to give you your first skin-toughening before you talk to the head doctor. Then you can tell him all about your crime—"

"You know my crime?" he said, greeting it almost like a neighbor.

"Of course not," said she, "but all the people who come through here are believed to have committed crimes. Somebody thinks so or they wouldn't be here. Most of them want to talk about their personal crimes. But don't slow me down. I'm a skin technician, and down on the surface of Shayol you're going to need the very best work that any of us can do for you. Now get on that table. And when you are ready to talk to the chief you'll have something to talk about besides your crime."

He complied.

Another masked person, probably a girl, took his hands in cool, gentle fingers and fitted them to the padded cuffs in a way he had never sensed before. By now he thought he knew every interrogation machine in the whole empire, but this was nothing like any of them.

The orderly stepped back. "All clear, sir and doctor."

"Which do you prefer?" said the skin technician. "A great deal of pain or a couple of hours' unconsciousness?"

"Why should I want pain?" said Mercer.

"Some specimens do," said the technician, "by the time they arrive here. I suppose it depends on what people have done to them before they got here. I take it you did not get any of the dream-punishments."

"No," said Mercer. "I missed those." He thought to himself, I didn't know that I missed anything at all.

He remembered his last trial, himself wired and plugged in to the witness stand. The room had been high and dark. Bright blue light shone on the panel of judges, their judicial caps a fantastic parody of the episcopal mitres of long, long ago. The judges were talking, but he could not hear them. Momentarily the insulation slipped and he heard one of them say, "Look at that white, devilish face. A man like that is guilty of everything. I vote for Pain Terminal." "Not Planet Shayol?" said a second voice. "The dromozoa place," said a third voice. "That should suit him," said the first voice. One of the judicial engineers must then have noticed that the prisoner was listening illegally. He was cut off. Mercer then thought that he had gone through everything which the cruelty and intelligence of mankind could devise.

But this woman said he had missed the dream-punishments. Could there be people in the universe even worse off than himself? There must be a lot of people down on Shayol. They never came back.

He was going to be one of them; would they boast to him of what they had done, before they were made to come to this place?

"You asked for it," said the woman technician. "It is just an ordinary anesthetic. Don't panic when you awaken. Your skin is going to be thickened and strengthened chemically and biologically."

"Does it hurt?"

"Of course," said she. "But get this out of your head. We're not punishing you. The pain here is just ordinary medical pain. Anybody might get it if they needed a lot of surgery. The punishment, if that's what you want to call it, is down on Shayol. Our only job is to make sure that you are fit to survive after you are landed. In a way, we are saving your life ahead of time. You can be grateful for that if you want to be. Meanwhile, you will save yourself a lot of trouble if you realize that your nerve endings will all respond to the change in the skin. You had better expect to be very uncomfortable when you recover. But then, we can help that, too." She brought down an enormous lever and Mercer blacked out.

When he came to, he was in an ordinary hospital room, but he did not notice it. He seemed bedded in fire. He lifted his hand to see if there were flames on it. It looked the way it always had, except that it was a little red and a little swollen. He tried to turn in the bed. The fire became a scorching blast which stopped him in mid-turn. Uncontrollably, he moaned.

A voice spoke, "You are ready for some pain-killer."

It was a girl nurse. "Hold your head still," she said, "and I will give you half an amp of pleasure. Your skin won't bother you then."

She slipped a soft cap on his head. It looked like metal but it felt like silk.

He had to dig his fingernails into his palms to keep from threshing about on the bed.

"Scream if you want to," she said. "A lot of them do. It will just be a minute or two before the cap finds the right lobe in your brain."

She stepped to the corner and did something which he could not see.

There was the flick of a switch.

The fire did not vanish from his skin. He still felt it; but suddenly it did not matter. His mind was full of delicious pleasure which throbbed outward from his head and seemed to pulse down through his nerves. He had visited the pleasure palaces, but he had never felt anything like this before.

He wanted to thank the girl, and he twisted around in the bed to see her. He could feel his whole body flash with pain as he did so, but the pain was far away. And the pulsating pleasure which coursed out of his head, down his spinal cord and into his nerves was so intense that the pain got through only as a remote, unimportant signal.

She was standing very still in the corner.

"Thank you, nurse," said he.

She said nothing.

He looked more closely, though it was hard to look while enormous pleasure pulsed through his body like a symphony written in nerve-messages. He focused his eyes on her and saw that she too wore a soft metallic cap.

He pointed at it.

She blushed all the way down to her throat.

She spoke dreamily, "You looked like a nice man to me. I didn't think you'd tell on me. . . ."

He gave her what he thought was a friendly smile, but with the pain in his skin and the pleasure bursting out of his head, he really had no idea of what his actual expression might be. "It's against the law," he said. "It's terribly against the law. But it is nice."

"How do you think we stand it here?" said the nurse. "You specimens come in here talking like ordinary people and then you go down to Shayol. Terrible things happen to you on Shayol. Then the surface station sends up parts of you, over and over again. I may see your head ten times, quick-frozen and ready for cutting up, before my two years are up. You prisoners ought to know how we suffer," she crooned, the pleasure-charge still keeping her relaxed and happy, "you ought to die as soon as you get down there and not pester us with your torments. We can hear you screaming, you know. You keep on sounding like people even after Shayol begins to work on you. Why do you do it, Mr. Specimen?" She giggled sillily. "You hurt our feelings so. No wonder a girl like me has to have a little jolt now and then. It's real, real dreamy and I don't mind getting you ready to go down on Shayol." She staggered over to his bed. "Pull this cap off me, will you? I haven't got enough will power left to raise my hands." Mercer saw his hand tremble as he reached for the cap.

His fingers touched the girl's soft hair through the cap. As he tried to get his thumb under the edge of the cap, in order to pull it off, he realized that this was the loveliest girl he had ever touched. He felt that he had always loved her, that he always would. The cap came off. She stood erect, staggering a little before she found a chair to hold on to. She closed her eyes and breathed deeply.

"Just a minute," she said in her normal voice. "I'll be with you in just a minute. The only time I can get a jolt of this is when one of you visitors gets a dose to get over the skin trouble."

She turned to the room mirror to adjust her hair. Speaking with her back to him, she said, "I hope I didn't say anything about downstairs."

Mercer still had the cap on. He loved this beautiful girl who had put it on him. He was ready to weep at the thought that she had had the same kind of pleasure which he still enjoyed. Not for the world would he say anything which could hurt her feelings. He was sure she wanted to be told that she had not said anything about "downstairs"—probably shop talk for the surface of Shayol—so he assured her warmly, "You said nothing. Nothing at all."

She came over to the bed, leaned, kissed him on the lips. The kiss was as far away as the pain; he felt nothing; the Niagara of throbbing pleasure which poured through his head left no room for more sensation. But he liked the friendliness of it. A grim, sane corner of his mind whispered to him that this was probably the last time he would ever kiss a woman, but it did not seem to matter.

With skilled fingers she adjusted the cap on his head. "There, now. You're a sweet guy. I'm going to pretend-forget and leave the cap on you till the doctor comes."

With a bright smile she squeezed his shoulder.

She hastened out of the room.

The white of her skirt flashed prettily as she went out the door. He saw that she had very shapely legs indeed.

She was nice, but the cap . . . ah, it was the cap that mattered! He closed his eyes and let the cap go on stimulating the pleasure centers of his brain. The pain in his skin was still there, but it did not matter any more than did the chair standing in the corner. The pain was just something that happened to be in the room.

A firm touch on his arm made him open his eyes.

The older, authoritative-looking man was standing beside the bed, looking down at him with a quizzical smile.

"She did it again," said the old man.

Mercer shook his head, trying to indicate that the young nurse had done nothing wrong.

"I'm Doctor Vomact," said the older man, "and I am going to take this cap off you. You will then experience the pain again, but I think it will not be so bad. You can have the cap several more times before you leave here."

With a swift, firm gesture he snatched the cap off Mercer's head.

Mercer promptly doubled up with the inrush of fire from his skin. He started to scream and then saw that Doctor Vomact was watching him calmly.

Mercer gasped, "It is—easier now."

"I knew it would be," said the doctor. "I had to take the cap off to talk to you. You have a few choices to make."

"Yes, doctor," gasped Mercer.

"You have committed a serious crime and you are going down to the surface of Shayol."

"Yes," said Mercer.

"Do you want to tell me your crime?"

Mercer thought of the white palace walls in perpetual sunlight, and the soft mewing of the little things when he reached them. He tightened his arms, legs, back and jaw. "No," he said, "I don't want to talk about it. It's the crime without a name. Against the Imperial family . . ."

"Fine," said the doctor, "that's a healthy attitude. The crime is past. Your future is ahead. Now, I can destroy your mind before you go down—if you want me to."

"That's against the law," said Mercer.

Doctor Vomact smiled warmly and confidently. "Of course it is. A lot of things are against human law. But there are laws of science, too. Your body, down on Shayol, is going to serve science. It doesn't matter to me whether that body has Mercer's mind or the mind of a low-grade shellfish. I have to leave enough mind in you to keep the body going, but I can wipe out the historic you and give your body a better chance of being happy. It's your choice, Mercer. Do you want to be you or not?"

Mercer shook his head back and forth, "I don't know."

"I'm taking a chance," said Doctor Vomact, "in giving you this much leeway. I'd have it done if I were in your position. It's pretty bad down there."

Mercer looked at the full, broad face. He did not trust the comfortable smile. Perhaps this was a trick to increase his punishment. The cruelty of the Emperor was proverbial. Look at what he had done to the widow of his predecessor, the Dowager Lady Da. She was younger than the Emperor himself, and he had sent her to a place worse than death. If he had been sentenced to Shayol, why was this doctor trying to interfere with the rules? Maybe the doctor himself had been conditioned, and did not know what he was offering.

Doctor Vomact read Mercer's face. "All right. You refuse. You want to take your mind down with you. It's all right with me. I don't have you on my conscience. I suppose you'll refuse the next offer too. Do you want me to take your eyes out before you go down? You'll be much more comfortable without vision. I *know* that, from the voices that we record for the warning broadcasts. I can sear the optic nerves so that there will be no chance of your getting vision again."

Mercer rocked back and forth. The fiery pain had become a universal itch, but the soreness of his spirit was greater than the discomfort of his skin.

"You refuse that, too?" said the doctor.

"I suppose so," said Mercer.

"Then all I have to do is to get you ready. You can have the cap for a while, if you want."

Mercer said, "Before I put the cap on, can you tell me what happens down there?"

"Some of it," said the doctor. "There is an attendant. He is a man, but not a human being. He is a homunculus fashioned out of cattle material. He is intelligent and very conscientious. You specimens are turned loose on the surface of Shayol. The dromozoa are a special life-form there. When they settle in your body, B'dikkat—that's the attendant—carves them out with an anesthetic and sends them up here. We freeze the tissue cultures, and they are compatible with almost any kind of oxygen-based life. Half the surgical repair you see in the whole universe comes out of buds that we ship from here. Shayol is a very healthy place, as far as survival is concerned. You won't die."

"You mean," said Mercer, "that I am getting perpetual punishment."

"I didn't say that," said Doctor Vomact. "Or if I did, I was wrong. You won't die soon. I don't know how long you will live down there. Remember, no matter how uncomfortable you get, the samples which B'dikkat sends up will help thousands of people in all the inhabited worlds. Now take the cap."

"I'd rather talk," said Mercer. "It may be my last chance."

The doctor looked at him strangely. "If you can stand that pain, go ahead and talk."

"Can I commit suicide down there?"

"I don't know," said the doctor. "It's never happened. And to judge by the voices, you'd think they wanted to."

"Has anybody ever come back from Shayol?"

"Not since it was put off limits about four hundred years ago."

"Can I talk to other people down there?"

"Yes," said the doctor.

"Who punishes me down there?"

"Nobody does, you fool," cried Doctor Vomact. "It's not punishment. People don't like it down on Shayol, and it's better, I guess, to get convicts instead of volunteers. But there isn't anybody *against* you at all."

"No jailers?" asked Mercer, with a whine in his voice.

"No jailers, no rules, no prohibitions. Just Shayol, and B'dikkat to take care of you. Do you still want your mind and your eyes?"

"I'll keep them," said Mercer. "I've gone this far and I might as well go the rest of the way."

"Then let me put the cap on you for your second dose," said Doctor Vomact.

The doctor adjusted the cap just as lightly and delicately as had the nurse; he was quicker about it. There was no sign of his picking out another cap for himself.

The inrush of pleasure was like a wild intoxication. His burning skin receded into distance. The doctor was near in space, but even the doctor did not matter. Mercer was not afraid of Shayol. The pulsation of happiness out of his brain was too great to leave room for fear or pain.

Doctor Vomact was holding out his hand.

Mercer wondered why, and then realized that the wonderful, kindly, cap-giving man was offering to shake hands. He lifted his own. It was heavy, but his arm was happy, too.

They shook hands. It was curious, thought Mercer, to feel the handshake beyond the double level of cerebral pleasure and dermal pain.

"Good-by, Mr. Mercer," said the doctor, "Good-by and a good good night . . ."

II

The ferry satellite was a hospitable place. The hundreds of hours that followed were like a long, weird dream.

Twice again the young nurse sneaked into his bedroom with him when he was being given the cap and had a cap with him. There were baths which callused his whole body. Under strong local anesthetics, his teeth were taken out and stainless steel took their place. There were irradiations under blazing lights which took away the pain of his skin. There were special treatments for his fingernails and toenails. Gradually they changed into formidable claws; he found himself stropping them on the aluminum bed one night and saw that they left deep marks.

His mind never became completely clear.

Sometimes he thought that he was home with his mother, that he was little again, and in pain. Other times, under the cap, he laughed in his bed to think that people were sent to this place for punishment when it was all so terribly much fun. There were no trials, no questions, no judges. Food was good, but he did not think about it much; the cap was better. Even when he was awake, he was drowsy.

At last, with the cap on him, they put him into an adiabatic pod—a one-body missile which could be dropped from the ferry to the planet below. He was all closed in, except for his face.

Doctor Vomact seemed to swim into the room. "You are strong, Mercer," the doctor shouted, you are very strong! Can you hear me?"

Mercer nodded.

"We wish you well, Mercer. No matter what happens, remember you are helping other people up here."

"Can I take the cap with me?" said Mercer.

For an answer, Doctor Vomact removed the cap himself. Two men closed the lid of the pod, leaving Mercer in total darkness. His mind started to clear, and he panicked against his wrappings.

There was the roar of thunder and the taste of blood.

The next thing that Mercer knew, he was in a cool, cool room, much chillier than the bedrooms and operating rooms of the satellite. Someone was lifting him gently onto a table.

He opened his eyes.

An enormous face, four times the size of any human face Mercer had ever seen, was looking down at him. Huge brown eyes, cowlike in their gentle inoffensiveness, moved back and forth as the big face examined Mercer's wrappings. The face was that of a handsome man of middle years, clean-shaven, hair chestnut-brown, with sensual full lips and gigantic but healthy yellow teeth exposed in a half smile. The face saw Mercer's eyes open, and spoke with a deep friendly roar.

"I'm your best friend. My name is B'dikkat, but you don't have to use that here. Just call me Friend, and I will always help you."

"I hurt," said Mercer.

"Of course you do. You hurt all over. That's a big drop," said B'dikkat.

"Can I have a cap, please," begged Mercer. It was not a question; it was a demand; Mercer felt that his private inward eternity depended on it.

B'dikkat laughed. "I haven't any caps down here. I might use them myself. Or so they think. I have other things, much better. No fear, fellow, I'll fix you up."

Mercer looked doubtful. If the cap had brought him happiness on the ferry, it would take at least electrical stimulation of the brain to undo whatever torments the surface of Shayol had to offer.

B'dikkat's laughter filled the room like a bursting pillow.

"Have you ever heard of condamine?"

"No," said Mercer.

"It's a narcotic so powerful that the pharmacopeias are not allowed to mention it."

"You have that?" said Mercer hopefully.

"Something better. I have super-condamine. It's named after the New French town where they developed it. The chemists hooked in one more hydrogen molecule. That gave it a real jolt. If you took it in your present shape, you'd be dead in three minutes, but those three minutes would seem like ten thousand years of happiness to the inside of your mind." B'dikkat rolled his brown cow eyes expressively and smacked his rich red lips with a tongue of enormous extent.

"What's the use of it, then?"

"*You* can take it," said B'dikkat. "You can take it after you have been exposed to the dromozoa outside this cabin. You get all the good effects and none of the bad. You want to see something?"

What answer is there except *yes,* thought Mercer grimly; does he think I have an urgent invitation to a tea party?

"Look out the window," said B'dikkat, "and tell me what you see."

The atmosphere was clear. The surface was like a desert, ginger-yellow with streaks of green where lichen and low shrubs grew, obviously stunted and tormented by high, dry winds. The landscape was monotonous. Two or three hundred yards away there was a herd of bright pink objects which seemed alive, but Mercer could not see them well enough to describe them clearly. Further away, on the extreme right of his frame of vision, there was the statue of an enormous human foot, the height of a six-story building. Mercer could not see what the foot was connected to. "I see a big foot," said he, "but—"

"But what?" said B'dikkat, like an enormous child hiding the denouement of a hugely private joke. Large as he was, he would have been dwarfed by any one of the toes on that tremendous foot.

"But it can't be a real foot," said Mercer.

"It is," said B'dikkat. "That's Go-Captain Alvarez, the man who found this planet. After six hundred years he's still in fine shape. Of course, he's mostly dromozootic by now, but I think there is some human consciousness inside him. You know what I do?"

"What?" said Mercer.

"I give him six cubic centimeters of super-condamine and he snorts for me. Real happy little snorts. A stranger might think it was a volcano. That's what super-condamine can do. And you're going to get plenty of it. You're a lucky, lucky man, Mercer. You have me for a friend, and you have my needle for a treat. I do all the work and you get all the fun. Isn't that a nice surprise?"

Mercer thought, You're lying! Lying! Where do the screams come from that we have all heard broadcast as a warning on

Punishment Day? Why did the doctor offer to cancel my brain or
to take out my eyes?

The cow-man watched him sadly, a hurt expression on his
face. "You don't believe me," he said, very sadly.

"It's not quite that," said Mercer, with an attempt at heartiness,
"but I think you're leaving something out."

"Nothing much," said B'dikkat. "You jump when the
dromozoa hit you. You'll be upset when you start growing new
parts—heads, kidneys, hands. I had one fellow in here who grew
thirty-eight hands in a single session outside. I took them all off,
froze them and sent them upstairs. I take good care of everybody.
You'll probably yell for a while. But remember, just call me
Friend, and I have the nicest treat in the universe waiting for
you. Now, would you like some fried eggs? I don't eat eggs
myself, but most true men like them."

"Eggs?" said Mercer. "What have eggs got to do with it?"

"Nothing much. It's just a treat for you people. Get something in your stomach before you go outside. You'll get through
the first day better."

Mercer, unbelieving, watched as the big man took two pre-
cious eggs from a cold chest, expertly broke them into a little
pan and put the pan in the heat-field at the center of the table
Mercer had awakened on.

"Friend, eh?" B'dikkat grinned. "You'll see I'm a good
friend. When you go outside, remember that."

An hour later, Mercer did go outside.

Strangely at peace with himself, he stood at the door. B'dikkat
pushed him in a brotherly way, giving him a shove which was
gentle enough to be an encouragement.

"Don't make me put on my lead suit, fellow." Mercer had
seen a suit, fully the size of an ordinary space-ship cabin,
hanging on the wall of an adjacent room. "When I close this
door, the outer one will open. Just walk on out."

"But what will happen?" said Mercer, the fear turning around
in his stomach and making little grabs at his throat from the
inside.

"Don't start that again," said B'dikkat. For an hour he had
fended off Mercer's questions about the outside. A map? B'dikkat
had laughed at the thought. Food? He said not to worry. Other
people? They'd be there. Weapons? What for, B'dikkat had
replied. Over and over again, B'dikkat had insisted that he was

Mercer's friend. What would happen to Mercer? The same that happened to everybody else.

Mercer stepped out.

Nothing happened. The day was cool. The wind moved gently against his toughened skin.

Mercer looked around apprehensively.

The mountainous body of Captain Alvarez occupied a good part of the landscape to the right. Mercer had no wish to get mixed up with that. He glanced back at the cabin. B'dikkat was not looking out the window.

Mercer walked slowly, straight ahead.

There was a flash on the ground, no brighter than the glitter of sunlight on a fragment of glass. Mercer felt a sting in the thigh, as though a sharp instrument had touched him lightly. He brushed the place with his hand.

It was as though the sky fell in.

A pain—it was more than a pain: it was a living throb—ran from his hip to his foot on the right side. The throb reached up to his chest, robbing him of breath. He fell, and the ground hurt him. Nothing in the hospital-satellite had been like this. He lay in the open air, trying not to breathe, but he did breathe anyhow. Each time he breathed, the throb moved with his thorax. He lay on his back, looking at the sun. At last he noticed that the sun was violet-white.

It was no use even thinking of calling. He had no voice. Tendrils of discomfort twisted within him. Since he could not stop breathing, he concentrated on taking air in the way that hurt him least. Gasps were too much work. Little tiny sips of air hurt him least.

The desert around him was empty. He could not turn his head to look at the cabin. Is this it? he thought. Is an eternity of this the punishment of Shayol?

There were voices near him.

Two faces, grotesquely pink, looked down at him. They might have been human. The man looked normal enough, except for having two noses side by side. The woman was a caricature beyond belief. She had grown a breast on each cheek and a cluster of naked baby-like fingers hung limp from her forehead.

"It's a beauty," said the woman, "a new one."

"Come along," said the man.

They lifted him to his feet. He did not have strength enough to resist. When he tried to speak to them a harsh cawing sound, like the cry of an ugly bird, came from his mouth.

They moved with him efficiently. He saw that he was being dragged to the herd of pink things.

As they approached, he saw that they were people. Better, he saw that they had once been people. A man with the beak of a flamingo was picking at his own body. A woman lay on the ground; she had a single head, but beside what seemed to be her original body, she had a boy's naked body growing sidewise from her neck. The boy-body, clean, new, paralytically helpless, made no movement other than shallow breathing. Mercer looked around. The only one of the group who was wearing clothing was a man with his overcoat on sidewise. Mercer stared at him, finally realizing that the man had two—or was it three?—stomachs growing on the outside of his abdomen. The coat held them in place. The transparent peritoneal wall looked fragile.

"New one," said his female captor. She and the two-nosed man put him down.

The group lay scattered on the ground.

Mercer lay in a state of stupor among them.

An old man's voice said, "I'm afraid they're going to feed us pretty soon."

"Oh, no!" "It's too early!" "Not again!" "Protests echoed from the group.

The old man's voice went on, "Look, near the big toe of the mountain!"

The desolate murmur in the group attested their confirmation of what he had seen.

Mercer tried to ask what it was all about, but produced only a caw.

A woman—was it a woman?—crawled over to him on her hands and knees. Beside her ordinary hands, she was covered with hands all over her trunk and halfway down her thighs. Some of the hands looked old and withered. Others were as fresh and pink as the baby-fingers on his captress' face. The woman shouted at him, though it was not necessary to shout.

"The dromozoa are coming. This time it hurts. When you get used to the place, you can dig in—"

She waved at a group of mounds which surrounded the herd of people.

"They're dug in," she said.

Mercer cawed again.

"Don't you worry," said the hand-covered woman, and gasped as a flash of light touched her.

The lights reached Mercer too. The pain was like the first contact but more probing. Mercer felt his eyes widen as odd sensations within his body led to an inescapable conclusion: these lights, these things, these whatever-they-were, were feeding him and building him up.

Their intelligence, if they had it, was not human, but their motives were clear. In between the stabs of pain he felt them fill his stomach, put water in his blood, draw water from his kidneys and bladder, massage his heart, move his lungs for him.

Every single thing they did was well meant and beneficent in intent.

And every single action hurt.

Abruptly, like the lifting of a cloud of insects, they were gone. Mercer was aware of a noise somewhere outside—a brainless, bawling cascade of ugly noise. He started to look around. And the noise stopped.

It had been himself, screaming. Screaming the ugly screams of a psychotic, a terrified drunk, an animal driven out of understanding or reason.

When he stopped, he found he had his speaking voice again.

A man came to him, naked like the others. There was a spike sticking through his head. The skin had healed around it on both sides. "Hello, fellow," said the man with the spike.

"Hello," said Mercer. It was a foolishly commonplace thing to say in a place like this.

"You can't kill yourself," said the man with the spike through his head.

"Yes, you can," said the woman, covered with hands.

Mercer found that his first pain had disappeared. "What's happening to me?"

"You got a part," said the man with the spike. "They're always putting parts on us. After a while B'dikkat comes and cuts most of them off, except for the ones that ought to grow a little more. Like her," he added, nodding at the woman who lay with the boy-body growing from her neck.

"And that's all?" said Mercer. "The stabs for the new parts and the stinging for the feeding."

"No," said the man. "Sometimes they think we're too cold and they fill our insides with fire. Or they think we're too hot and they freeze us, nerve by nerve."

The woman with the boy-body called over, "And sometimes they think we're unhappy, so they try to force us to be happy. *I* think that's the worst of it all."

Mercer stammered, "Are you people—I mean—are you the only herd?"

The man with the spike coughed instead of laughing. "Herd! That's funny. The land is full of people. Most of them dig in. We're the ones who can still talk; we stay together for company. We get more turns with B'dikkat that way."

Mercer started to ask another question, but he felt the strength run out of him. The day had been too much.

The ground rocked like a ship on water. The sky turned black. He felt someone catch him as he fell. He felt himself being stretched out on the ground. And then, mercifully and magically, he slept.

III

Within a week, he came to know the group well. They were an absent-minded bunch of people. Not one of them ever knew when a dromozoon might flash by and add another part. Mercer was not stung again, but the incision he had obtained just outside the cabin was hardening. Spikehead looked at it when Mercer modestly undid his belt and lowered the edge of his trouser-top so they could see the wound.

"You've got a head," he said. "A whole baby head. They'll be glad to get that one upstairs when B'dikkat cuts it off you."

The group even tried to arrange his social life. They introduced him to the girl of the herd. She had grown one body after another, pelvis turning into shoulders and the pelvis below that turning into shoulders again until she was five people long. Her face was unmarred. She tried to be friendly to Mercer.

He was so shocked by her that he dug himself into the soft dry crumbly earth and stayed there for what seemed like a hundred years. He found later that it was less than a full day. When he came out, the long many-bodied girl was waiting for him.

"You didn't have to come out just for me," said she.

Mercer shook the dirt off himself.

He looked around. The violet sun was going down, and the sky was streaked with blues, deeper blues and trails of orange sunset.

He looked back at her. "I didn't get up for you. It's no use lying there, waiting for the next time."

"I want to show you something," she said. She pointed to a low hummock. "Dig that up."

Mercer looked at her. She seemed friendly. He shrugged and attacked the soil with his powerful claws. With tough skin and heavy digging-nails on the ends of his fingers, he found it was easy to dig like a dog. The earth cascaded beneath his busy hands. Something pink appeared down in the hole he had dug. He proceeded more carefully.

He knew what it would be.

It was. It was a man, sleeping. Extra arms grew down one side of his body in an orderly series. The other side looked normal.

Mercer turned back to the many-bodied girl, who had writhed closer.

"That's what I think it is, isn't it?"

"Yes," she said. "Doctor Vomact burned his brain out for him. And took his eyes out, too."

Mercer sat back on the ground and looked at the girl. "You told me to do it. Now tell me what for."

"To let you see. To let you know. To let you think."

"That's all?" said Mercer.

The girl twisted with startling suddenness. All the way down her series of bodies, her chests heaved. Mercer wondered how the air got into all of them. He did not feel sorry for her; he did not feel sorry for anyone except himself. When the spasm passed the girl smiled at him apologetically.

"They just gave me a new plant."

Mercer nodded grimly.

"What now, a hand? It seems you have enough."

"Oh, those," she said looking back at her many torsos. "I promised B'dikkat that I'd let them grow. He's *good*. But that man, stranger. Look at that man you dug up. Who's better off, he or we?"

Mercer stared at her. "Is that what you had me dig him up for?"

"Yes," said the girl.

"Do you expect me to answer?"

"No," said the girl, "not now."

"Who are you?" said Mercer.

"We never ask that here. It doesn't matter. But since you're new, I'll tell you. I used to be the Lady Da—the Emperor's stepmother."

"You!" he exclaimed.

She smiled, ruefully. "You're still so fresh you think it matters! But I have something more important to tell you." She stopped and bit her lip.

"What?" he urged. "Better tell me before I get another bite. I won't be able to think or talk then, not for a long time. Tell me now."

She brought her face close to his. It was still a lovely face, even in the dying orange of this violet-sunned sunset. "People never live forever."

"Yes," said Mercer. "I knew that."

"*Believe* it," ordered the Lady Da.

Lights flashed across the dark plain, still in the distance. Said she, "Dig in, dig in for the night. They may miss you."

Mercer started digging. He glanced over at the man he had dug up. The brainless body, with motions as soft as those of a starfish under water, was pushing its way back into the earth.

Five or seven days later, there was a shouting through the herd.

Mercer had come to know a half-man, the lower part of whose body was gone and whose viscera were kept in place with what resembled a translucent plastic bandage. The half-man had shown him how to lie still when the dromozoa came with their inescapable errands of doing good.

Said the half-man, "You can't fight them. They made Alvarez as big as a mountain, so that he never stirs. Now they're trying to make us happy. They feed us and clean us and sweeten us up. Lie still. Don't worry about screaming. We all do."

"When do we get the drug?" said Mercer.

"When B'dikkat comes."

B'dikkat came that day, pushing a sort of wheeled sled ahead of him. The runners carried it over the hillocks; the wheels worked on the surface.

Even before he arrived, the herd sprang into furious action. Everywhere, people were digging up the sleepers. By the time B'dikkat reached their waiting place, the herd must have uncovered twice their own number of sleeping pink bodies—men and women, young and old. The sleepers looked no better and no worse than the waking ones.

"Hurry!" said the Lady Da. "He never gives any of us a shot until we're all ready."

B'dikkat wore his heavy lead suit.

He lifted an arm in friendly greeting, like a father returning home with treats for his children. The herd clustered around him but did not crowd him.

He reached into the sled. There was a harnessed bottle which he threw over his shoulders. He snapped the locks on the straps. From the bottle there hung a tube. Midway down the tube there was a small pressure-pump. At the end of the tube there was a glistening hypodermic needle.

When ready, B'dikkat gestured for them to come closer. They approached him with radiant happiness. He stepped through their ranks and past them, to the girl who had the boy growing from her neck. His mechanical voice boomed through the loudspeaker set in the top of his suit.

"Good girl. Good, good girl. You get a big, big, present." He thrust the hypodermic into her so long that Mercer could see an air bubble travel from the pump up to the bottle.

Then he moved back to the others, booming a word now and then, moving with improbable grace and speed amid the people. His needle flashed as he gave them hypodermics under pressure. The people dropped to sitting position or lay down on the ground as though half-asleep.

He knew Mercer. "Hello, fellow. Now you can have the fun. It would have killed you in the cabin. Do you have anything for me?"

Mercer stammered, not knowing what B'dikkat meant, and the two-nosed man answered for him, "I think he has a nice baby head, but it isn't big enough for you to take yet."

Mercer never noticed the needle touch his arm.

B'dikkat had turned to the next knot of people when the super-condamine hit Mercer.

He tried to run after B'dikkat, to hug the lead spacesuit, to tell B'dikkat that he loved him. He stumbled and fell, but it did not hurt.

The many-bodied girl lay near him. Mercer spoke to her.

"Isn't it wonderful? You're beautiful, beautiful, beautiful. I'm so happy to be here."

The woman covered with growing hands came and sat beside them. She radiated warmth and good fellowship. Mercer thought that she looked very distinguished and charming. He struggled out of his clothes. It was foolish and snobbish to wear clothing when none of these nice people did.

The two women babbled and crooned at him.

With one corner of his mind he knew that they were saying nothing, just expressing the euphoria of a drug so powerful that the known universe had forbidden it. With most of his mind he was happy. He wondered how anyone could have the good luck to visit a planet as nice as this. He tried to tell the Lady Da, but the words weren't quite straight.

A painful stab hit him in the abdomen. The drug went after the pain and swallowed it. It was like the cap in the hospital, only a thousand times better. The pain was gone, though it had been crippling the first time.

He forced himself to be deliberate. He rammed his mind into focus and said to the two ladies who lay pinkly nude beside him in the desert, "That was a good bite. Maybe I will grow another head. That would make B'dikkat happy!"

The Lady Da forced the foremost of her bodies in an upright position. Said she, "I'm strong, too. I can talk. Remember, man, remember. People never live forever. We can die, too, we can die like real people. I do so believe in death!"

Mercer smiled at her through his happiness.

"Of course you can. But isn't this nice . . ."

With this he felt his lips thicken and his mind go slack. He was wide awake, but he did not feel like doing anything. In that beautiful place, among all those companionable and attractive people, he sat and smiled.

B'dikkat was sterilizing his knives.

Mercer wondered how long the super-condamine had lasted him. He endured the ministrations of the dromozoa without screams or movement. The agonies of nerves and itching of skin were phenomena which happened somewhere near him, but meant nothing. He watched his own body with remote, casual interest. The Lady Da and the hand-covered woman stayed near him. After a long time the half-man dragged himself over to the group with his powerful arms. Having arrived he blinked sleepily and friendlily at them, and lapsed back into the restful stupor from which he had emerged. Mercer saw the sun rise on occasion, closed his eyes briefly, and opened them to see stars shining. Time had no meaning. The dromozoa fed him in their mysterious way; the drug canceled out his needs for cycles of the body.

At last he noticed a return of the inwardness of pain.

The pains themselves had not changed; he had.

He knew all the events which could take place on Shayol. He remembered them well from his happy period. Formerly he had noticed them—now he felt them.

He tried to ask the Lady Da how long they had had the drug, and how much longer they would have to wait before they had it again. She smiled at him with benign, remote happiness; apparently her many torsos, stretched out along the ground, had a greater capacity for retaining the drug than did his body. She meant him well, but was in no condition for articulate speech.

The half-man lay on the ground, arteries pulsating prettily behind the half-transparent film which protected his abdominal cavity.

Mercer squeezed the man's shoulder.

The half-man woke, recognized Mercer and gave him a healthily sleepy grin.

" 'A good morrow to you, my boy.' That's out of a play. Did you ever see a play?"

"You mean a game with cards?"

"No," said the half-man, "a sort of eye-machine with real people doing the figures."

"I never saw that," said Mercer, "but I—"

"But you want to ask me when B'dikkat is going to come back with the needle."

"Yes," said Mercer, a little ashamed of his obviousness.

"Soon," said the half-man. That's why I think of plays. We all know what is going to happen. We all know when it is going to happen. We all know what the dummies will do"—he gestured at the hummocks in which the decorticated men were cradled—"and we all know what the new people will ask. But we never know how long a scene is going to take."

"What's a 'scene'?" asked Mercer. "Is that the name for the needle?"

The half-man laughed with something close to real humor. "No, no, no. You've got the lovelies on the brain. A scene is just a part of a play. I mean we know the order in which things happen, but we have no clocks and nobody cares enough to count days or to make calendars and there's not much climate here, so none of us know how long anything takes. The pain seems short and the pleasure seems long. I'm inclined to think that they are about two Earth-weeks each."

Mercer did not know what an "Earth-week" was, since he had not been a well-read man before his conviction, but he got nothing more from the half-man at that time. The half-man received a dromozootic implant, turned red in the face, shouted senselessly at Mercer, "Take it out, you fool! Take it out of me!"

When Mercer looked on helplessly, the half-man twisted over on his side, his pink dusty back turned to Mercer, and wept hoarsely and quietly to himself.

Mercer himself could not tell how long it was before B'dikkat came back. It might have been several days. It might have been several months.

Once again B'dikkat moved among them like a father; once again they clustered like children. This time B'dikkat smiled pleasantly at the little head which had grown out of Mercer's thigh—a sleeping child's head, covered with light hair on top and with dainty eyebrows over the resting eyes. Mercer got the blissful needle.

When B'dikkat cut the head from Mercer's thigh, he felt the knife grinding against the cartilage which held the head to his own body. He saw the child-face grimace as the head was cut; he felt the far, cool flash of unimportant pain, as B'dikkat dabbed the wound with a corrosive antiseptic which stopped all bleeding immediately.

The next time it was two legs growing from his chest.

Then there had been another head beside his own.

Or was that after the torso and legs, waist to toe-tips, of the little girl which had grown from his side?

He forgot the order.

He did not count time.

Lady Da smiled at him often, but there was no love in this place. She had lost the extra torsos. In between teratologies, she was a pretty and shapely woman; but the nicest thing about their relationship was her whisper to him, repeated some thousands of time, repeated with smiles and hope, "People never live forever."

She found this immensely comforting, even though Mercer did not make much sense out of it.

Thus events occurred, and victims changed in appearance, and new ones arrived. Sometimes B'dikkat took the new ones, resting in the everlasting sleep of their burned-out brains, in a ground-truck to be added to other herds. The bodies in the truck threshed and bawled without human speech when the dromozoa struck them.

Finally, Mercer did manage to follow B'dikkat to the door of the cabin. He had to fight the bliss of super-condamine to do it. Only the memory of previous hurt, bewilderment and perplexity made him sure that if he did not ask B'dikkat when he, Mercer, was happy, the answer would no longer be available when he needed it. Fighting pleasure itself, he begged B'dikkat to check the records and to tell him how long he had been there.

B'dikkat grudgingly agreed, but he did not come out of the doorway. He spoke through the public address box built into the cabin, and his gigantic voice roared out over the empty plain, so that the pink herd of talking people stirred gently in their happiness and wondered what their friend B'dikkat might be wanting to tell them. When he said it, they thought it exceedingly profound, though none of them understood it, since it was simply the amount of time that Mercer had been on Shayol:

"Standard years—eighty-four years, seven months, three days, two hours, eleven and one half minutes. Good luck, fellow."

Mercer turned away.

The secret little corner of his mind, which stayed sane through happiness and pain, made him wonder about B'dikkat. What persuaded the cow-man to remain on Shayol? What kept him happy without super-condamine? Was B'dikkat a crazy slave to his own duty or was he a man who had hopes of going back to his own planet some day, surrounded by a family of little cow-people resembling himself? Mercer, despite his happiness, wept a little at the strange fate of B'dikkat. His own fate he accepted.

He remembered the last time he had eaten—actual eggs from an actual pan. The dromozoa kept him alive, but he did not know how they did it.

He staggered back to the group. The Lady Da, naked in the dusty plain, waved a hospitable hand and showed that there was a place for him to sit beside her. There were unclaimed square miles of seating space around them, but he appreciated the kindliness of her gesture none the less.

IV

The years, if they were years, went by. The land of Shayol did not change.

Sometimes the bubbling sound of geysers came faintly across

the plain to the herd of men; those who could talk declared it to be the breathing of Captain Alvarez. There was night and day, but no setting of crops, no change of season, no generations of men. Time stood still for these people, and their load of pleasure was so commingled with the shocks and pains of the dromozoa that the words of the Lady Da took on very remote meaning.

"People never live forever."

Her statement was a hope, not a truth in which they could believe. They did not have the wit to follow the stars in their courses, to exchange names with each other, to harvest the experience of each for the wisdom of all. There was no dream of escape for these people. Though they saw the old-style chemical rockets lift up from the field beyond B'dikkat's cabin, they did not make plans to hide among the frozen crop of transmuted flesh.

Far long ago, some other prisoner than one of these had tried to write a letter. His handwriting was on a rock. Mercer read it, and so had a few of the others, but they could not tell which man had done it. Nor did they care.

The letter, scraped on stone, had been a message home. They could still read the opening: "Once, I was like you, stepping out of my window at the end of day, and letting the winds blow me gently toward the place I lived in. Once, like you, I had one head, two hands, ten fingers on my hands. The front part of my head was called a face, and I could talk with it. Now I can only write, and that only when I get out of pain. Once, like you, I ate foods, drank liquid, had a name. I cannot remember the name I had. You can stand up, you who get this letter. I cannot even stand up. I just wait for the lights to put my food in me molecule by molecule, and to take it out again. Don't think that I am punished any more. This place is not a punishment. It is something else."

Among the pink herd, none of them ever decided what was "something else."

Curiosity had died among them long ago.

Then came the day of the little people.

It was a time—not an hour, not a year: a duration somewhere between them—when the Lady Da and Mercer sat wordless with happiness and filled with the joy of super-condamine. They had nothing to say to one another; the drug said all things for them.

A disagreeable roar from B'dikkat's cabin made them stir mildly.

Those two, and one or two others, looked toward the speaker of the public address system.

The Lady Da brought herself to speak, though the matter was unimportant beyond words. "I do believe," said she, "that we used to call that the War Alarm."

They drowsed back into their happiness.

A man with two rudimentary heads growing beside his own crawled over to them. All three heads looked very happy, and Mercer thought it delightful of him to appear in such a whimsical shape. Under the pulsing glow of super-condamine, Mercer regretted that he had not used times when his mind was clear to ask him who he had once been. He answered it for them. Forcing his eyelids open by sheer will power, he gave the Lady Da and Mercer the lazy ghost of a military salute and said, "Suzdal, ma'am and sir, former cruiser commander. They are sounding the alert. Wish to report that I am . . . I am . . . I am not quite ready for battle."

He dropped off to sleep.

The gentle peremptories of the Lady Da brought his eyes open again.

"Commander, why are they sounding it here? Why did you come to us?"

"You, ma'am, and the gentleman with the ears seem to think best of our group. I thought you might have orders."

Mercer looked around for the gentleman with the ears. It was himself. In that time his face was almost wholly obscured with a crop of fresh little ears, but he paid no attention to them, other than expecting that B'dikkat would cut them all off in due course and that the dromozoa would give him something else.

The noise from the cabin rose to a higher, ear-splitting intensity.

Among the herd, many people stirred.

Some opened their eyes, looked around, murmured. "It's a noise," and went back to the happy drowsing with super-condamine.

The cabin door opened.

B'dikkat rushed out, *without* his suit. They had never seen him on the outside without his protective metal suit.

He rushed up to them, looked wildly around, recognized the Lady Da and Mercer, picked them up, one under each arm, and raced with them back to the cabin. He flung them into the double door. They landed with bone-splitting crashes, and found it amusing to hit the ground so hard. The floor tilted them into the room. Moments later, B'dikkat followed.

He roared at them, "You're people, or you were. You understand people; I only obey them. But this I will not obey. Look at that!"

Four beautiful human children lay on the floor. The two smallest seemed to be twins, about two years of age. There was a girl of five and a boy of seven or so. All of them had slack eyelids. All of them had thin red lines around their temples and their hair, shaved away, showed how their brains had been removed.

B'dikkat, heedless of danger from dromozoa, stood beside the Lady Da and Mercer, shouting.

"You're real people. I'm just a cow. I do my duty. My duty does not include this. These are *children*."

The wise, surviving recess of Mercer's mind registered shock and disbelief. It was hard to sustain the emotion, because the super-condamine washed at his consciousness like a great tide, making everything seem lovely. The forefront of his mind, rich with the drug, told him, "Won't it be nice to have some children with us!" But the undestroyed interior of his mind, keeping the honor he knew before he came to Shayol, whispered, "This is a crime worse than any crime we have committed! *And the Empire has done it.*"

"What have you done?" said the Lady Da. "What can we do?"

"I tried to call the satellite. When they knew what I was talking about, they cut me off. After all, I'm not people. The head doctor told me to do my work."

"Was it Doctor Vomact?" Mercer asked.

"Vomact?" said B'dikkat. "He died a hundred years ago, of old age. No, a new doctor cut me off. I don't have people-feeling, but I am Earth-born, of Earth blood. I have emotions myself. Pure cattle emotions! *This* I cannot permit."

"What have you done?"

B'dikkat lifted his eyes to the window. His face was illuminated by a determination which, even beyond the edges of the drug which made them love him, made him seem like the father of this world—responsible, honorable, unselfish.

He smiled. "They will kill me for it, I think. But I have put in the Galactic Alert—*all ships here.*"

The Lady Da, sitting back on the floor, declared, "But that's only for new invaders! It is a false alarm." She pulled herself together and rose to her feet. "Can you cut these things off me, right now, in case people come? And get me a dress. And do you have anything which will counteract the effects of the super-condamine?"

"That's what I wanted!" cried B'dikkat. "I will not take these children. You give me leadership."

There and then, on the floor of the cabin, he trimmed her down to the normal proportions of mankind.

The corrosive antiseptic rose like smoke in the air of the cabin. Mercer thought it all very dramatic and pleasant, and dropped off in catnaps part of the time. Then he felt B'dikkat trimming him too. B'dikkat opened a long, long drawer and put the specimens in; from the cold in the room it must have been a refrigerated locker.

He sat them both up against the wall.

"I've been thinking," he said. "There is no antidote for super-condamine. Who would want one? But I can give you the hypos from my rescue boat. They are supposed to bring a person back no matter what has happened to that person out in space."

There was a whining over the cabin roof. B'dikkat knocked a window out with his fist, stuck his head out of the window and looked up.

"Come on in," he shouted.

There was the thud of a landing craft touching ground quickly. Doors whirred. Mercer wondered, mildly, why people dared to land on Shayol. When they came in he saw that they were not people; they were Customs Robots, who could travel at velocities which people could never match. One wore the insigne of an inspector.

"Where are the invaders?"

"There are no—" began B'dikkat.

The Lady Da, imperial in her posture though she was completely nude, said in a voice of complete clarity, "I am a former Empress, the Lady Da. Do you know me?"

"No, ma'am," said the robot inspector. He looked as uncomfortable as a robot could look. The drug made Mercer think that it would be nice to have robots for company, out on the surface of Shayol.

"I declare this Top Emergency, in the ancient words. Do you understand? Connect me with the Instrumentality."

"We can't—" said the inspector.

"You can ask," said the Lady Da.

The inspector complied.

The Lady Da turned to B'dikkat. "Give Mercer and me those shots now. Then put us outside the door so the dromozoa can repair these scars. Bring us in as soon as a connection is made. Wrap us in cloth if you do not have clothes for us. Mercer can stand the pain."

"Yes," said B'dikkat, keeping his eyes away from the four soft children and their collapsed eyes.

The injection burned like no fire ever had. It must have been capable of fighting the super-condamine, because B'dikkat put them through the open window, so as to save time going through the door. The dromozoa, sensing that they needed repair, flashed upon them. This time the super-condamine had something else fighting it.

Mercer did not scream but he lay against the wall and wept for ten thousand years; in objective time, it must have been several hours.

The Customs robots were taking pictures. The dromozoa were flashing against them too, sometimes in whole swarms, but nothing happened.

Mercer heard the voice of the communicator inside the cabin calling loudly for B'dikkat. "Surgery Satellite calling Shayol. B'dikkat, get on the line!"

He obviously was not replying.

There were soft cries coming from the other communicator, the one which the customs officials had brought into the room. Mercer was sure that the eye-machine was on and that people in other worlds were looking at Shayol for the first time.

B'dikkat came through the door. He had torn navigation charts out of his lifeboat. With these he cloaked them.

Mercer noted that the Lady Da changed the arrangement of the cloak in a few minor ways and suddenly looked like a person of great importance.

They re-entered the cabin door.

B'dikkat whispered, as if filled with awe, "The Instrumentality has been reached, and a Lord of the Instrumentality is about to talk to you."

There was nothing for Mercer to do, so he sat back in a corner of the room and watched. The Lady Da, her skin healed, stood pale and nervous in the middle of the floor.

The room filled with an odorless intangible smoke. The smoke clouded. The full communicator was on.

A human figure appeared.

A woman, dressed in a uniform of radically conservative cut, faced the Lady Da.

"This is Shayol. You are the Lady Da. You called me."

The Lady Da pointed to the children on the floor. "This must not happen," she said. "This is a place of punishments, agreed upon between the Instrumentality and the Empire. No one said anything about children."

The woman on the screen looked down at the children.

"This is the work of insane people!" she cried.

She looked accusingly at the Lady Da. "Are you imperial?"

"I was an Empress, madam," said the Lady Da.

"And you permit this!"

"Permit it?" cried the Lady Da. "I had nothing to do with it." Her eyes widened. "I am a prisoner here myself. Don't you understand?"

The image-woman snapped, "No, I don't."

"I," said the Lady Da, "am a specimen. Look at the herd out there. I came from them a few hours ago."

"Adjust me," said the image-woman to B'dikkat. "Let me see that herd."

Her body, standing upright, soared through the wall in a flashing arc and was placed in the very center of the herd.

The Lady Da and Mercer watched her. They saw even the image lose its stiffness and dignity. The image-woman waved an arm to show that she should be brought back into the cabin. B'dikkat tuned her back into the room.

"I owe you an apology," said the image. "I am the Lady Johanna Gnade, one of the Lords of the Instrumentality."

Mercer bowed, lost his balance and had to scramble up from the floor. The Lady Da acknowledged the introduction with a royal nod.

The two women looked at each other.

"You will investigate," said the Lady Da, "and when you have investigated, please put us all to death. You know about the drug?"

"Don't mention it," said B'dikkat, "don't even say the name into a communicator. It is a secret of the Instrumentality!"

"I am the Instrumentality," said the Lady Johanna. "Are you in pain? I did not think that any of you were alive. I had heard of the surgery banks on your off-limits planet, but I thought that robots tended parts of people and sent up the new grafts by rocket. Are there any people with you? Who is in charge? Who did this to the children?''

B'dikkat stepped in front of the image. He did not bow. "I'm in charge."

"You're underpeople!" cried the Lady Johanna. "You're a cow!"

"A bull, ma'am. My family is frozen back on earth itself, and with a thousand years' service I am earning their freedom and my own. Your other questions, ma'am. I do all the work. The dromozoa do not affect me much, though I have to cut a part off myself now and then. I throw those away. They don't go into the bank. Do you know the secret rules of this place?"

The Lady Johanna talked to someone behind her on another world. Then she looked at B'dikkat and commanded, "Just don't name the drug or talk too much about it. Tell me the rest."

"We have," said B'dikkat very formally, "thirteen hundred and twenty-one people here who can still be counted on to supply parts when the dromozoa implant them. There are about seven hundred more, including Go-Captain Alvarez, who have been so thoroughly absorbed by the planet that it is no use trimming them. The Empire set up this place as a point of uttermost punishment. But the Instrumentality gave secret orders for *medicine*''—he accented the word strangely, meaning super-condamine—''to be issued so that the punishment would be counteracted. The Empire supplies our convicts. The Instrumentality distributes the surgical material.''

The Lady Johanna lifted her right hand in a gesture of silence and compassion. She looked around the room. Her eyes came back to the Lady Da. Perhaps she guessed what effort the Lady Da had made in order to remain standing erect while the two drugs, the super-condamine and the lifeboat drug, fought within her veins.

"You people can rest. I will tell you now that all things possible will be done for you. The Empire is finished. The Fundamental Agreement, by which the Instrumentality surrendered to the Empire a thousand years ago, has been set aside. We did not know that you people existed. We would have found out in time, but I am sorry we did not find out sooner. Is there anything we can do for you right away?"

"Time is what we all have," said the Lady Da. "Perhaps we

cannot ever leave Shayol, because of the dromozoa and the *medicine*. The one could be dangerous. The other must never be permitted to be known.''

The Lady Johanna Gnade looked around the room. When her glance reached him, B'dikkat fell to his knees and lifted his enormous hands in complete supplication.

''What do you want?'' said she.

''These,'' said B'dikkat, pointing to the mutilated children. ''Order a stop on children. Stop it now!'' He commanded her with the last cry, and she accepted his command. ''And lady—'' He stopped, as if shy.

''Yes? Go on.''

''Lady, I am unable to kill. It is not in my nature. To work, to help, but not to kill. What do I do with these?'' He gestured at the four motionless children on the floor.

''Keep them,'' she said. ''Just keep them.''

''I can't,'' he said. ''There's no way to get off this planet alive. I do not have food for them in the cabin. They will die in a few hours. And governments,'' he added wisely, ''take a long, long time to do things.''

''Can you give them the *medicine?*''

''No, it would kill them if I gave them that stuff first before the dromozoa have fortified their bodily processes.''

The Lady Johanna Gnade filled the room with tinkling laughter that was very close to weeping. ''Fools, poor fools, and the more fool I! If super-condamine works only *after* the dromozoa, what is the purpose of the secret?''

B'dikkat rose to his feet, offended. He frowned, but he could not get the words with which to defend himself.

The Lady Da, ex-empress of a fallen empire, addressed the other lady with ceremony and force: ''Put them outside, so they will be touched. They will hurt. Have B'dikkat give them the drug as soon as he thinks it safe. I beg your leave, my lady. . . .''

Mercer had to catch her before she fell.

''You've all had enough,'' said the Lady Johanna. ''A storm ship with heavily armed troops is on its way to your ferry satellite. They will seize the medical personnel and find out who committed this crime against children.''

Mercer dared to speak. ''Will you punish the guilty doctor?''

''*You* speak of punishment,'' she cried. ''You!''

''It's fair. I was punished for doing wrong. Why shouldn't he be?''

"Punish—punish!" she said to him. "We will cure that doctor. And we will cure you too, if we can."

Mercer began to weep. He thought of the oceans of happiness which super-condamine had brought him, forgetting the hideous pain and the deformities on Shayol. Would there be no next needle? He could not guess what life would be like off Shayol. Was there to be no more tender, fatherly B'dikkat coming with his knives?

He lifted his tear-stained face to the Lady Johanna Gnade and choked out the words, "Lady, we are all insane in this place. I do not think we want to leave."

She turned her face away, moved by enormous compassion. Her next words were to B'dikkat. "You are wise and good, even if you are not a human being. Give them all of the drug they can take. The Instrumentality will decide what to do with all of you. I will survey your planet with robot soldiers. Will the robots be safe, cow-man?"

B'dikkat did not like the thoughtless name she called him, but he held no offense. "The robots will be all right, ma'am, but the dromozoa will be excited if they cannot feed them and heal them. Send as few as you can. We do not know how the dromozoa live or die."

"As few as I can," she murmured. She lifted her hand in command to some technician unimaginable distances away. The odorless smoke rose about her and the image was gone.

A shrill cheerful voice spoke up. "I fixed your window," said the customs robot. B'dikkat thanked him absentmindedly. He helped Mercer and the Lady Da into the doorway. When they had gotten outside, they were promptly stung by the dromozoa. It did not matter.

B'dikkat himself emerged, carrying the four children in his two gigantic, tender hands. He lay the slack bodies on the ground near the cabin. He watched as the bodies went into spasm with the onset of the dromozoa. Mercer and the Lady Da saw that his brown cow eyes were rimmed with red and that his huge cheeks were dampened by tears.

Hours or centuries.

Who could tell them apart?

The herd went back to its usual life, except that the intervals between needles were much shorter. The once-commander, Suzdal, refused the needle when he heard the news. Whenever he could walk, he followed the customs robots around as they photographed, took soil samples, and made a count of the bodies. They were particularly interested in the mountain of the Go-Captain Alvarez and professed themselves uncertain as to whether there was organic life there or not. The mountain did appear to react to super-condamine, but they could find no blood, no heartbeat. Moisture, moved by the dromozoa, seemed to have replaced the once-human bodily processes.

V

And then, early one morning, the sky opened.

Ship after ship landed. People emerged, wearing clothes.

The dromozoa ignored the newcomers. Mercer, who was in a state of bliss, confusedly tried to think this through until he realized that the ships were loaded to their skins with communications machines; the "people" were either robots or images of persons in other places.

The robots swiftly gathered together the herd. Using wheel-barrows, they brought the hundreds of mindless people to the landing area.

Mercer heard a voice he knew. It was the Lady Johanna Gnade. "Set me high," she commanded.

Her form rose until she seemed one-fourth the size of Alvarez. Her voice took on more volume.

"Wake them all," she commanded.

Robots moved among them, spraying them with a gas which was both sickening and sweet. Mercer felt his mind go clear. The super-condamine still operated in his nerves and veins, but his cortical area was free of it. He thought clearly.

"I bring you," cried the compassionate feminine voice of the gigantic Lady Johanna, "the judgment of the Instrumentality on the planet Shayol.

"Item: the surgical supplies will be maintained and the dromozoa will not be molested. Portions of human bodies will be left here to grow, and the grafts will be collected by robots. Neither man nor homunculus will live here again.

"Item: the underman B'dikkat, of cattle extraction, will be rewarded by an immediate return to earth. He will be paid twice his expected thousand years of earnings."

The voice of B'dikkat, without amplification, was almost as loud as hers through the amplifier. He shouted his protest, "Lady, Lady!"

She looked down at him, his enormous body reaching to ankle height on her swirling gown, and said in a very informal tone, "What do you want?"

"Let me finish my work first," he cried, so that all could hear. "Let me finish taking care of these people."

The specimens who had minds all listened attentively. The brainless ones were trying to dig themselves back into the soft earth of Shayol, using their powerful claws for the purpose. Whenever one began to disappear, a robot seized him by a limb and pulled him out again.

"Item: cephalectomies will be performed on all persons with irrecoverable minds. Their bodies will be left here. Their heads will be taken away and killed as pleasantly as we can manage, probably by an overdosage of super-condamine."

"The last big jolt," murmured Commander Suzdal, who stood near Mercer. "That's fair enough."

"Item: the children have been found to be the last heirs of the Empire. An over-zealous official sent them here to prevent their committing treason when they grew up. The doctor obeyed orders without questioning them. Both the official and the doctor have been cured and their memories of this have been erased, so that they need have no shame or grief for what they have done."

"It's unfair," cried the half-man. "They should be punished as we were!"

The Lady Johanna Gnade looked down at him. "Punishment is ended. We will give you anything you wish, but not the pain of another. I shall continue.

"Item: since none of you wish to resume the lives which you led previously, we are moving you to another planet nearby. It is similar to Shayol, but much more beautiful. There are no dromozoa."

At this an uproar seized the herd. They shouted, wept, cursed, appealed. They all wanted the needle, and if they had to stay on Shayol to get it, they would stay.

"Item," said the gigantic image of the lady, overriding their babble with her great but feminine voice, "you will not have super-condamine on the new planet, since without dromozoa it would kill you. But there will be caps. *Remember the caps.* We will try to cure you and to make people of you again. But if you give up, we will not force you. Caps are very powerful; with medical help you can live under them many years."

A hush fell on the group. In their various ways, they were

trying to compare the electrical caps which had stimulated their pleasure-lobes with the drug which had drowned them a thousand times in pleasure. Their murmur sounded like assent.

"Do you have any questions?" said the Lady Johanna.

"When do we get the caps?" said several. They were human enough that they laughed at their own impatience.

"Soon," she said reassuringly, "very soon."

"Very soon," echoed B'dikkat, reassuring his charges even though he was no longer in control.

"Question," cried the Lady Da.

"My Lady . . . ?" said the Lady Johanna, giving the ex-empress her due courtesy.

"Will we be permitted marriage?"

The Lady Johanna looked astonished. "I don't know." She smiled. "I don't know any reason why not—"

"I claim this man Mercer," said the Lady Da. "When the drugs were deepest, and the pain was greatest, he was the one who always tried to think. May I have him?"

Mercer thought the procedure arbitrary but he was so happy that he said nothing. The Lady Johanna scrutinized him and then she nodded. She lifted her arms in a gesture of blessing and farewell.

The robots began to gather the pink herd into two groups. One group was to whisper in a ship over to a new world, new problems and new lives. The other group, no matter how much its members tried to scuttle into the dirt, was gathered for the last honor which humanity could pay their manhood.

B'dikkat, leaving everyone else, jogged with his bottle across the plain to give the mountainman Alvarez an especially large gift of delight.

CONCERNS

Empires have two major areas of concern: internal and external. Internal affairs include political stability, economics, and education, among others. Unfortunately, however, with the exception of the first category, this area has been virtually ignored by most science fiction writers. On the other hand, external affairs, including exploration, incorporation, and defense, have been written about extensively.

Exploration appears to be a major concern of young empires during relatively primitive times. Frederick Jackson Turner suggests in his classic book *The Frontier in American History* (1920) that a frontier provides us with psychological space and hope. Failure can be erased by a new start in a new land, a process which also removes dissidents and reduces disaffection in settled territories. The exploration story we have chosen for this volume is "Diabologic," by Eric Frank Russell. It takes place during the Empire of the Grand Council and is part of his currently uncollected Terran Space Scout series. (See *Six Worlds Yonder/The Space Willies*, 1958, for many of these stories.) And like most of Russell's work, it demonstrates how John W. Campbell, Jr.'s vision of the resourceful earthman can triumph over aliens by cleverness and guile.

After exploration, expanding empires face problems of incorporation. Independent colonies and alien races must be educated, persuaded, or conquered if there is to be both growth and secure boundaries. E. B. Cole believes that incorporation by Earth's Federation, as delineated in "Fighting Philosopher" and other stories (most of which were patched together as *The Philosophical Corps*, 1961), will be done benevolently and for the benefit of all parties—a position which probably is much less likely to be advanced today.

Older empires, staffed by those far removed from its origins, tend to become soft and cautious. Rulers are more concerned with protecting what they have from internal and external threats than they are with continued expansion. As Poul Anderson points out in "Honorable Enemies" and several other works (such as *Flandry of Terra*, 1961; *Agent of the Terran Empire*, 1965; and *Ensign Flandry*, 1966), it is the golden age before a fall. Men like Dominic Flandry can at best but delay the collapse that precedes the beginning of another, perhaps even greater cycle.

Diabologic

by *Eric Frank Russell*

He made one circumnavigation to put the matter beyond doubt. That was standard space-scout technique; look once on the approach, look again all the way around. It often happened that second and closer impressions contradicted first and more distant ones. Some perverse factor in the probability sequence frequently caused the laugh to appear on the other side of a planetary face.

Not this time, though. What he'd observed coming in remained visible right around the belly. This world was occupied by intelligent life of a high order. The unmistakable markings were there in the form of dockyards, railroad marshaling grids, power stations, spaceports, quarries, factories, mines, housing projects, bridges, canals, and a hundred and one other signs of a life that spawns fast and vigorously.

The spaceports in particular were highly significant. He counted three of them. None held a flightworthy ship at the moment he flamed high above them, but in one was a tubeless vessel undergoing repair. A long, black, snouty thing about the size and shape of an Earth-Mars tramp. Certainly not as big and racy-looking as a Sol-Sirius liner.

As he gazed down through his tiny control-cabin's armor-glass, he knew that this was to be contact with a vengeance. During long, long centuries of human expansion, more than seven hundred inhabitable worlds had been found, charted, explored and, in some cases, exploited. All contained life. A minority held intelligent life. But up to this moment nobody had found one other lifeform sufficiently advanced to cavort among the stars.

Of course, such a discovery had been theorized. Human adventuring created an exploratory sphere that swelled into the cosmos. Sooner or later, it was assumed, that sphere must touch another one at some point within the heavenly host. What would happen then was anybody's guess. Perhaps they'd fuse, making a bigger, shinier biform bubble. Or perhaps both bubbles would burst. Anyway, by the looks of it the touching-time was now.

If he'd been within reach of a frontier listening-post, he'd have beamed a signal detailing this find. Even now it wasn't too late to drive back for seventeen weeks and get within receptive range. But that would mean seeking a refueling dump while he was at it. The ship just hadn't enough for such a double run plus the return trip home. Down there they had fuel. Maybe they'd give him some and maybe it would suit his engines. And just as possibly it would prove useless.

Right now he had adequate power reserves to land here and eventually get back to base. A bird in the hand is worth two in the bush. So he tilted the vessel and plunged into the alien atmosphere, heading for the largest spaceport of the three.

What might be awaiting him at ground level did not bother him at all. The Terrans of today were not the nervy, apprehensive Terrans of the earthbound and lurid past. They had become space-sophisticated. They had learned to lounge around with a carefree smile and let the other lifeforms do the worrying. It lent an air of authority and always worked. Nothing is more intimidating than an idiotic grin worn by a manifest non-idiot.

Quite a useful weapon in the diabological armory was the knowing smirk.

His landing created a most satisfactory sensation. The planet's point-nine Earth-mass permitted a little extra dexterity in handling the ship. He swooped it down, curved it up, dropped tail-first, stood straddle-legged on the tail-fins, cut the braking blast and would not have missed centering on a spread handkerchief by more than ten inches.

They seemed to spring out of the ground the way people do when cars collide on a deserted road. Dozens of them, hundreds. They were on the short side, the tallest not exceeding five feet. Otherwise they differed from his own pink-faced, blue-eyed type no more than would a Chinese covered in fine gray fur.

Massing in a circle beyond range of his jet-rebound, they stared at the ship, gabbled, gesticulated, nudged each other, argued, and generally behaved in the manner of a curious mob that has discovered a deep, dark hole with strange noises issuing therefrom. The noteworthy feature about their behavior was that none were scared, none attempted to get out of reach, either openly or surreptitiously. The only thing about which they were wary was the chance of a sudden blast from the silent jets.

He did not emerge at once. That would have been an error—and blunderers are not chosen to pilot scout-vessels. Pre-exit rule number one is that air must be tested. What suited that crowd outside would not necessarily agree with him. Anyway, he'd have checked air even if his own mother had been smoking a cigar in the front row of the audience.

The Schrieber analyzer required four minutes in which to suck a sample through the Pitot tube, take it apart, sneer at the bits, make a bacteria count and say whether its lord and master could condescend to breathe the stuff.

He sat patiently while it made up its mind. Finally the needle on its half-red, half-white dial crawled reluctantly to mid-white. A fast shift would have pronounced the atmosphere socially acceptable. Slowness was the Schrieber's way of saying that his lungs were about to go slumming. The analyzer was and always had been a robotic snob that graded alien atmospheres on the caste system. The best and cleanest air was Brahman, pure Brahman. The worst was Untouchable.

Switching it off, he opened the inner and outer air-lock doors, sat in the rim with his feet dangling eighty yards above ground level. From this vantage-point he calmly surveyed the mob, his expression that of one who can spit but not be spat upon. The sixth diabological law states that the higher, the fewer. Proof: the sea gull's tactical advantage over man.

Being intelligent, those placed by unfortunate circumstances eighty yards deeper in the gravitational field soon appreciated their state of vertical disadvantage. Short of toppling the ship or climbing a polished surface, they were impotent to get at him. Not that any wanted to in any inimical way. But desire grows strongest when there is the least possibility of satisfaction. So they wanted him down there, face to face, merely because he was out of reach.

To make matters worse, he turned sidewise and lay within the rim, one leg hitched up and hands linked around the knee, then continued looking at them in obvious comfort. They had to stand. And they had to stare upward at the cost of a crick in the neck. Alternatively, they could adjust their heads and eyes to a crickless level and endure being looked at while not looking. Altogether, it was a hell of a situation.

The longer it lasted the less pleasing it became. Some of them shouted at him in squeaky voices. Upon those he bestowed a benign smile. Others gesticulated. He gestured back and the sharpest among them weren't happy about it. For some strange reason that no scientist had ever bothered to investigate, certain digital motions stimulate special glands in any part of the cosmos. Basic diabological training included a course in what was known as signal-deflation, whereby the yolk could be removed from an alien ego with one wave of the hand.

For a while the crowd surged restlessly around, nibbling the gray fur on the backs of their fingers, muttering to each other, and occasionally throwing sour looks upward. They still kept clear of the danger zone, apparently assuming that the specimen reclining in the lock-rim might have a companion at the controls. Next, they became moody, content to do no more than scowl futilely at the tail-fins.

That state of affairs lasted until a convoy of heavy vehicles arrived and unloaded troops. The newcomers bore riot sticks and handguns, and wore uniforms the color of the stuff hogs roll in. Forming themselves into three ranks, they turned right at a barked command, marched forward. The crowd opened to make way.

Expertly, they stationed themselves in an armed circle separating the ship from the horde of onlookers. A trio of officers paraded around and examined the tail-fins without going nearer than was necessary. Then they backed off, stared up at the air-lock rim. The subject of their attention gazed back with academic interest.

The senior of the three officers patted his chest where his heart was located, bent and patted the ground, forced pacific innocence into his face as again he stared at the arrival high above. The tilt of his head made his hat fall off, and in turning to pick it up he trod on it.

This petty incident seemed to gratify the one eighty yards higher because he chuckled, let go the leg he was nursing, leaned out for a better look at the victim. Red-faced under his furry complexion, the officer once more performed the belly and ground massage. The other understood this time. He gave a nod of gracious assent, disappeared into the lock. A few seconds later a nylon ladder snaked down the ship's side and the invader descended with monkey-like agility.

Three things struck the troops and the audience immediately he stood before them, namely, the nakedness of his face and hands, his greater size and weight, and the fact that he carried no visible weapons. Strangeness of shape and form was to be expected. After all, they had done some space-roaming themselves and knew of lifeforms more outlandish. But what sort of creature has the brains to build a ship and not the sense to carry means of defense?

They were essentially a logical people.

The poor saps.

The officers made no attempt to converse with this specimen from the great unknown. They were not telepathic, and space-experience had taught them that mere mouth-noises are useless until one side or the other has learned the meanings thereof. So by signs they conveyed to him their wish to take him to town where he would meet others of their kind more competent to establish contact. They were pretty good at explaining with their hands, as was natural for the only other lifeform that had found new worlds.

He agreed to this with the same air of a lord consorting with the lower orders that had been apparent from the start. Perhaps he had been unduly influenced by the Schrieber. Again the crowd made way while the guard conducted him to the trucks. He passed through under a thousand eyes, favored them with deflatory gesture number seventeen, this being a nod that acknowledged their existence and tolerated their vulgar interest in him.

The trucks trundled away leaving the ship with air-lock open, ladder dangling and the rest of the troops still standing guard around the fins. Nobody failed to notice that touch, either. He hadn't bothered to prevent access to the vessel. There was nothing to prevent experts looking through it and stealing ideas from another space-going race.

Nobody of that caliber could be so criminally careless. Therefore, it would not be carelessness. Pure logic said the ship's designs were not worth protecting from the stranger's viewpoint because they were long out of date. Or else they were unstealable because they were beyond the comprehension of a lesser people. Who the heck did he think they were? By the Black World of Khas, they'd show him!

A junior officer climbed the ladder, explored the ship's interior, came down, reported no more aliens within, not even a pet *lansim*, not a pretzel. The stranger had come alone. This item of information circulated through the crowd. They didn't care for it too much. A visit by a fleet of battleships bearing ten thousand they could understand. It would be a show of force worthy of their stature. But the casual arrival of one, and only one, smacked somewhat of the dumping of a missionary among the heathens of the twin worlds of Morantia.

Meanwhile, the trucks rolled clear of the spaceport, speeded up through twenty miles of country, entered a city. Here, the leading vehicle parted company from the rest, made for the western suburbs, arrived at a fortress surrounded by huge walls. The stranger dismounted and promptly got tossed into the clink.

The result of that was odd, too. He should have resented incarceration, seeing that nobody had yet explained the purpose of it. But he didn't. Treating the well-clothed bed in his cell as if it were a luxury provided as recognition of his rights, he sprawled on it full length, boots and all, gave a sigh of deep satisfaction and went to sleep. His watch hung close by his ear and compensated for the constant ticking of the auto-pilot, without which slumber in space was never complete.

During the next few hours guards came frequently to look at him and make sure that he wasn't finagling the locks or disintegrating the bars by means of some alien technique. They had not searched him and accordingly were cautious. But he snored on, dead to the world, oblivious to the ripples of alarm spread through a spatial empire.

He was still asleep when Parmith arrived bearing a load of picture books. Parmith, elderly and myopic, sat by the bedside and waited until his own eyes became heavy in sympathy and he found himself considering the comfort of the carpet. At that point he decided he must either get to work or lie flat. He prodded the other into wakefulness.

They started on the books. *Ah* is for *ahmud* that plays in the grass. *Ay* is for *aysid* that's kept under glass. *Oom* is for *oomtuck* that's found in the moon. *Uhm* is for *uhmlak*, a clown or buffoon. And so on.

Stopping only for meals, they were at it the full day and progress was fast. Parmith was a first-class tutor, the other an excellent pupil able to learn with remarkable speed. At the end of the first long session they were able to indulge in a brief and simple conversation.

"I am called Parmith. What are you called?"

"Wayne Hillder."

"Two callings?"

"Yes."

"What are many of you called?"

"Terrans."

"We are called Vards."

Talk ceased for lack of enough words and Parmith left. Within nine hours he was back accompanied by Gerka, a younger specimen who specialized in reciting words and phrases again and again until the listener could echo them to perfection. They carried on for another four days, working into late evening.

"You are not a prisoner."

"I know," said Wayne Hillder, blandly self-assured.

Parmith looked uncertain. "How do you know?"

"You would not dare to make me one."

"Why not?"

"You do not know enough. Therefore you seek common speech. You must learn from me—and quickly."

This being too obvious to contradict, Parmith let it go by and said, "I estimated it would take about ninety days to make you fluent. It looks as if twenty will be sufficient."

"I wouldn't be here if my kind weren't smart," Hillder pointed out.

Gerka registered uneasiness; Parmith was disconcerted.

"No Vard is being taught by us," he added for good measure. "Not having got to us yet."

Parmith said hurriedly, "We must get on with this task. An important commission is waiting to interview you as soon as you can converse with ease and clarity. We'll try again this *fth*-prefix that you haven't got quite right. Here's a tongue-twister to practice on. Listen to Gerka."

"*Fthon deas fthleman fathangafth*," recited Gerka, punishing his bottom lip.

"*Futhong deas—*"

"*Fthon*," corrected Gerka. "*Fthon deas fthleman fthangafth*."

"It's better in a civilized tongue. Wet evenings are gnatless *futhong—*"

"*Fthon!*" insisted Gerka, playing catapults with his mouth.

*   *   *

The commission sat in an ornate hall containing semicircular rows of seats rising in ten tiers. There were four hundred present. The way in which attendants and minor officials fawned around them showed that this was an assembly of great importance.

It was, too. The four hundred respresented the political and military power of a world that had created a space-empire extending through a score of solar systems and controlling twice as many planets. Up to a short time ago they had been, to the best of their knowledge and belief, the lords of creation. Now there was some doubt about it. They had a serious problem to settle, one that a later Terran historian irreverently described as "a moot point."

They ceased talking among themselves when a pair of guards arrived in charge of Hillder, led him to a seat facing the tiers. Four hundred pairs of eyes examined the stranger, some curiously, some doubtfully, some challengingly, many with unconcealed antagonism.

Sitting down, Hillder looked them over much as one looks into one of the more odorous cages at the zoo. That is to say, with faint distaste. Gently, he rubbed the side of his nose with a forefinger and sniffed. Deflatory gesture number twenty-two, suitable for use in the presence of massed authority. It brought its carefully calculated reward. Half a dozen of the most bellicose characters glared at him.

A frowning, furry-faced oldster stood up, spoke to Hillder as if reciting a well-rehearsed speech. "None but a highly intelligent and completely logical species can conquer space. It being self-evident that you are of such a kind, you will appreciate our position. Your very presence compels us to consider the ultimate alternatives of cooperation or competition, peace or war."

"There are no two alternatives to anything," Hillder asserted. "There is black and white and a thousand intermediate shades. There is yes and no and a thousand ifs, buts or maybes. For example: you could move farther out of reach."

Being tidy-minded, they didn't enjoy watching the thread of their logic being tangled. Neither did they like the resultant knot in the shape of the final suggestion. The oldster's frown grew deeper, his voice sharper.

"You should also appreciate your own position. You are one among countless millions. Regardless of whatever may be the strength of your kind, you, personally, are helpless. Therefore, it is for us to question and for you to answer. If our respective positions were reversed, the contrary would be true. That is logical. Are you ready to answer our questions?''

"I am ready."

Some showed surprise at that. Others looked resigned, taking it for granted that he would give all the information he saw fit and suppress the rest.

Resuming his seat, the oldster signaled to the Vard on his left, who stood up and asked, "Where is your base-world?"

"At the moment I don't know."

"You don't know?" His expression showed that he had expected awkwardness from the start. "How can you return to it if you don't know where it is?"

"When within its radio-sweep I pick up its beacon. I follow that."

"Aren't your space-charts sufficient to enable you to find it?"

"No."

"Why not?"

"Because," said Hillder, "it isn't tied to a primary. It wanders around."

Registering incredulity, the other said, "Do you mean that it is a planet broken loose from a solar system?"

"Not at all. It's a scout-base. Surely you know what that is?"

"I do not," snapped the interrogator. "What is it?"

"A tiny, compact world equipped with all the necessary contraptions. An artificial sphere that functions as a frontier outpost."

There was a deal of fidgeting and murmuring among the audience as individuals tried to weigh the implications of this news.

Hiding his thoughts, the questioner continued, "You define it as a frontier outpost. That does not tell us where your home-world is located."

"You did not ask about my home-world. You asked about my base-world. I heard you with my own two ears."

"Then where is your home-world?"

"I cannot show you without a chart. Do you have charts of unknown regions?"

"Yes." The other smiled like a satisfied cat. With a dramatic flourish he produced them, unrolled them. "We obtained them from your ship."

"That was thoughtful of you," said Hillder, disappointingly pleased. Leaving his seat he placed a fingertip on the topmost chart and said, "There! Good old Earth!" Then he returned and sat down.

The Vard stared at the designated point, glanced around at his fellows as if about to make some remark, changed his mind and said nothing. Producing a pen he marked the chart, rolled it up with the others.

"This world you call Earth is the origin and center of your empire?"

"Yes."

"The mother-planet of your species?"

"Yes."

"Now," he went on, firmly, "how many of your kind are there?"

"Nobody knows."

"Don't you check your own numbers?"

"We did once upon a time. These days we're too scattered around." Hillder pondered a moment, added helpfully, "I can tell you that there are four billions of us spread over three planets in our own solar system. Outside of those the number is a guess. We can be divided into the rooted and the rootless and the latter can't be counted. They won't let themselves be counted because somebody might want to tax them. Take the grand total as four billions plus."

"That tells us nothing," the other objected. "We don't know the size of the plus."

"Neither do we," said Hillder, visibly awed at the thought of it. "Sometimes it frightens us." He surveyed the audience. "If nobody's ever been scared by a plus, now's the time."

Scowling, the questioner tried to get at it another way. "You say you are scattered. Over how many worlds?"

"Seven hundred fourteen at last report. That's already out of date. Every report is eight to ten planets behind the times."

"And you have mastery of that huge number?"

"Whoever mastered a planet? Why, we haven't yet dug into the heart of our own, and I doubt that we ever shall." He shrugged, finished, "No, we just amble around and maul them a bit. Same as you do."

"You mean you exploit them?"

"Put it that way if it makes you happy."

"Have you encountered no opposition at any time?"

"Feeble, friend, feeble," said Hillder.

"What did you do about it?"

"That depended upon circumstances. Some folk we ignored, some we smacked, some we led toward the light."

"What light?" asked the other, baffled.

"That of seeing things our way."

It was too much for a paunchy specimen in the third row. Coming to his feet he spoke in acidulated tones. "Do you expect *us* to see things your way?"

"Not immediately," Hillder said.

"Perhaps you consider us incapable of—"

The oldster who had first spoken now arose and interjected, "We must proceed with this inquisition logically or not at all. That means one line of questioning at a time and one questioner at a time." He gestured authoritatively toward the Vard with the charts. "Carry on, Thormin."

Thormin carried on for two solid hours. Apparently he was an astonomical expert, because all his questions bore more or less on that subject. He wanted details of distances, velocities, solar classifications, planetary conditions, and a host of similar items. Willingly, Hillder answered all that he could, pleaded ignorance with regard to the rest.

Eventually Thormin sat down and concentrated on his notes in the manner of one absorbed in fundamental truth. He was succeeded by a hard-eyed individual named Grasud, who for the last half-hour had been fidgeting with impatience.

"Is your vessel the most recent example of its type?"

"No."

"There are better models?"

"Yes," agreed Hillder.

"Very much better?"

"I wouldn't know, not having been assigned one yet."

"Strange, is it not," said Grasud pointedly, "that an old-type ship should discover us while superior ones have failed to do so?"

"Not at all. It was sheer luck. I happened to head this way. Other scouts, in old or new ships, boosted other ways. How many directions are there in deep space? How many radii can be extended from a sphere?"

"Not being a mathematician, I—"

"If you *were* a mathematician," Hillder interrupted, "you would know that the number works out at $2n$." He glanced over the audience, added in tutorial manner, "The factor of two being determined by the demonstrable fact that a radius is half a diameter and 2n being defined as the smallest number that makes one boggle.''

Grasud boggled as he tried to conceive it, gave it up, said, ''Therefore, the total number of your exploring vessels is of equal magnitude?''

''No. We don't have to probe in every direction. It is necessary only to make for visible stars.''

''Well, aren't there stars in every direction?''

''If distance is disregarded, yes. But one does not disregard distance. One makes for the nearest yet-unexplored solar systems and thus cuts down repeated jaunts to a reasonable number.''

''You are evading the issue,'' said Grasud. ''How many ships of your type are in actual operation?''

''Twenty.''

''Twenty?'' He made it sound anticlimactic. ''Is that all?''

''It's enough, isn't it? How long do you expect us to keep antiquated models in service?''

''I am not asking about out-of-date vessels. How many scout-ships of all types are functioning?''

''I don't really know. I doubt whether anyone knows. In addition to Earth's fleets, some of the most advanced colonies are running expeditions of their own. What's more, a couple of allied lifeforms have learned things from us, caught the fever and started poking around. We can no more take a complete census of ships than we can of people.''

Accepting that without argument, Grasud went on, ''Your vessel is not large by our standards. Doubtless you have others of greater mass.'' He leaned forward, gazed fixedly. ''What is the comparative size of your biggest ship?''

''The largest I've seen was the battleship *Lance*. Forty times the mass of my boat.''

''How many people does it carry?''

''It has a crew numbering more than six hundred but in a pinch it can transport three times that.''

''So you know of at least one ship with an emergency capacity of about two thousands?''

''Yes.''

More murmurings and fidgetings among the audience. Disregarding them, Grasud carried on with the air of one determined to learn the worst.

''You have other battleships of equal size?''

"Yes."

"How many?"

"I don't know. If I did, I'd tell you. Sorry."

"You may have some even bigger?"

"That is quite possible," Hillder conceded. "If so, I haven't seen one yet. But that means nothing. One can go through a lifetime and not see everything. If you calculate the number of seeable things in existence, deduct the number already viewed, the remainder represents the number yet to be seen. And if you study them at the rate of one per second it would require—"

"I am not interested," snapped Grasud, refusing to be bollixed by alien argument.

"You should be," said Hillder. "Because infinity minus umpteen millions leaves infinity. Which means that you can take the part from the whole and leave the whole still intact. You can eat your cake and have it. Can't you?"

Grasud flopped into his seat, spoke moodily to the oldster, "I seek information, not a blatant denial of logic. His talk confuses me. Let Shahding have him."

Coming up warily, Shahding started on the subject of weapons, their design, mode of operation, range and effectiveness. He stuck with determination to this single line of inquiry and avoided all temptations to be sidetracked. His questions were astute and penetrating. Hillder answered all he could, freely, without hesitation.

"So," commented Shahding, toward the finish, "it seems that you put your trust in force-fields, certain rays that paralyze the nervous system, bacteriological techniques, demonstrations of number and strength, and a good deal of persuasiveness. Your science of ballistics cannot be advanced after so much neglect."

"It could never advance," said Hillder. "That's why we abandoned it. We dropped fiddling around with bows and arrows for the same reason. No intitial thrust can outpace a continuous and prolonged one. Thus far and no farther shalt thou go." Then he added by way of speculative afterthought, "Anyway, it can be shown that no bullet can overtake a running man."

"Nonsense!" exclaimed Shahding, having once ducked a couple of slugs himself.

"By the time the bullet has reached the man's point of departure, the man has retreated," said Hillder. "The bullet then has to cover that extra distance but finds the man has retreated farther.

It covers that, too, only to find that again the man is not there. And so on and so on."

"The lead is reduced each successive time until it ceases to exist," Shahding scoffed.

"Each successive advance occupies a finite length of time, no matter how small," Hillder pointed out. "You cannot divide and subdivide a fraction to produce zero. The series is infinite. An infinite series of finite time-periods totals an infinite time. Work it out for yourself. The bullet does not hit the man because it cannot get to him."

The reaction showed that the audience had never encountered this argument before or concocted anything like it of their own accord. None were stupid enough to accept it as serious assertion of fact. All were sufficiently intelligent to recognize it as logical or pseudo-logical denial of something self-evident and demonstrably true.

Forthwith they started hunting for the flaw in this alien reasoning, discussing it between themselves so noisily that Shahding stood in silence waiting for a break. He posed like a dummy for ten minutes while the clamor rose to a crescendo. A group in the front semicircle left their seats, knelt and commenced drawing diagrams on the floor while arguing vociferously and with some heat. A couple of Vards in the back tier showed signs of coming to blows.

Finally the oldster, Shahding and two others bellowed a united, "Quiet!"

The investigatory commission settled down with reluctance, still muttering, gesturing, showing each other sketches on pieces of paper. Shahding fixed ireful attention on Hillder, opened his mouth in readiness to resume.

Beating him to it, Hillder said casually, "It sounds silly, doesn't it? But anything is possible, anything at all. A man can marry his widow's sister."

"Impossible," declared Shahding, able to dispose of that without abstruse calculations. "He must be dead for her to have the status of a widow."

"A man married a woman who died. He then married her sister. He died. Wasn't his first wife his widow's sister?"

Shahding shouted, "I am not here to be tricked by the tortuous squirmings of an alien mind." He sat down hard, fumed a bit, said to his neighbor, "All right, Kadina, you can have him and welcome."

Confident and self-assured, Kadina stood up, gazed authoritatively around. He was tall for a Vard, and wore a well-cut
uniform with crimson epaulettes and crimson-banded sleeves.
For the first time in a while there was silence. Satisfied with the
effect he had produced, he faced Hillder, spoke in tones deeper,
less squeaky than any heard so far.

"Apart from the petty problems with which it has amused you
to baffle my compatriots," he began in an oily manner, "you
have given candid, unhesitating answers to our questions. You
have provided much information that is useful from the military
viewpoint."

"I am glad you appreciate it," said Hillder.

"We do. Very much so," Kadina bestowed a craggy smile
that looked sinister. "However, there is one matter that needs
clarifying."

"What is that?"

"If the present situation were reversed, if a lone Vard-scout
was subject to intensive cross-examination by an assembly of
your lifeform, and if he surrendered information as willingly as
you have done . . ." He let it die while his eyes hardened, then
growled, "We would consider him a traitor to his kind! The
penalty would be death."

"How fortunate I am not to be a Vard," said Hillder.

"Do not congratulate yourself too early," Kadina retorted. "A
death sentence is meaningless only to those already under such
a sentence."

"What are you getting at?"

"I am wondering whether you are a major criminal seeking
sanctuary among us. There may be some other reason. Whatever
it is, you do not hesitate to betray your own kind." He put on
the same smile again. "It would be nice to know *why* you have
been so cooperative."

"That's an easy one," Hillder said, smiling back in a way that
Kadina did not like. "I am a consistent liar."

With that, he left his seat and walked boldly to the exit. The
guards led him to his cell.

He was there three days, eating regular meals and enjoying
them with irritating gusto, amusing himself writing figures in a
little notebook, as happy as a legendary space-scout named
Larry. At the end of that time a ruminative Vard paid a visit.

"I am Bulak. Perhaps you remember me. I was seated at the end of the second row when you were before the commission."

"Four hundred were there," Hillder reminded. "I cannot recall all of them. Only the ones who suffered." He pushed forward a chair. "But never mind. Sit down and put your feet up—if you do have feet inside those funny-looking boots. What can I do for you?"

"I don't know."

"You must have come for some reason, surely?"

Bulak looked mournful. "I'm a refugee from the fog."

"What fog?"

"The one you've spread all over the place." He rubbed a fur-coated ear, examined his fingers, stared at the wall. "The commission's main purpose was to determine relative standards of intelligence, to settle the prime question of whether your kind's cleverness is less than, greater than, or equal to our own. Upon that and that alone depends our reaction to contact with another space-conqueror."

"I did my best to help, didn't I?"

"Help?" echoed Bulak as if it were a new and strange word. "Help? Do you call it that? The true test should be that of whether your logic has been extended farther than has ours, whether your premises have been developed to more advanced conclusions."

"Well?"

"You ended up by trampling all over the laws of logic. A bullet cannot kill anybody. After three days fifty of them are still arguing about it, and this morning one of them proved that a person cannot climb a ladder. Friends have fallen out, relatives are starting to hate the sight of each other. The remaining three hundred fifty are in little better state."

"What's troubling them?" inquired Hillder with interest.

"They are debating veracity with everything but brickbats," Bulak informed, somewhat as if compelled to mention an obscene subject. "You are a consistent liar. Therefore the statement itself must be a lie. Therefore you are not a consistent liar. The conclusion is that you can be a consistent liar only by not being a consistent liar. Yet you cannot be a consistent liar without being consistent."

"That's bad," Hillder sympathized.

"It's worse," Bulak gave back. "Because if you really are a consistent liar—which logically is a self-contradiction—none of your evidence is worth a sack of rotten *muna*-seeds. If you have told us the truth all the way through, then your final claim to be a liar must also be true. But if you are a consistent liar then none of it is true.''

"Take a deep breath," advised Hillder.

"But," continued Bulak, taking a deep breath, "since that final statement must be untrue, all the rest may be true." A wild look came into his eyes and he started waving his arms around. "But the claim to consistency makes it impossible for any statement to be assessed as either true or untrue because, on analysis, there is an unresolvable contradiction that—"

"Now, now," said Hillder, patting his shoulder. "It is only natural that the lower should be confused by the higher. The trouble is that you've not yet advanced far enough. Your thinking remains a little primitive." He hesitated, added with the air of making a daring guess, "In fact it wouldn't surprise me if you still think *logically*."

"In the name of the Big Sun," exclaimed Bulak, "how *else* can we think?"

"Like us," said Hillder. "But only when you're mentally developed." He strolled twice around the cell, said by way of musing afterthought, "Right now you couldn't cope with the problem of why a mouse when it spins."

"Why a mouse when it spins?" parroted Bulak, letting his jaw hang down.

"Or let's try an easier one, a problem any Earth-child could tackle."

"Such as what?"

"By definition an island is a body of land entirely surrounded by water?"

"Yes, that is correct."

"Then let us suppose that the whole of this planet's northern hemisphere is land and all the southern hemisphere is water. Is the northern half an island? Or is the southern half a lake?"

Bulak gave it five minutes' thought. Then he drew a circle on a sheet of paper, divided it, shaded the top half and contemplated the result. In the end he pocketed the paper and got to his feet.

"Some of them would gladly cut your throat but for the possibility that your kind may have a shrewd idea where you are and be capable of retribution. Others would send you home with honors but for the risk of bowing to inferiors."

"They'll have to make up their minds someday," Hillder commented, refusing to show concern about which way it went.

"Meanwhile," Bulak continued morbidly, "we've had a look over your ship, which may be old or new according to whether or not you have lied about it. We can see everything but the engines and remote controls, everything but the things that matter. To determine whether they're superior to ours we'd have to pull the vessel apart, ruining it and making you a prisoner."

"Well, what's stopping you?"

"The fact that you may be bait. If your kind has great power and is looking for trouble, they'll need a pretext. Our victimization of you would provide it. The spark that fires the powder-barrel." He made a gesture of futility. "What can one do when working utterly in the dark?"

"One could try settling the question of whether a green leaf remains a green leaf in complete absence of light."

"I have had enough," declared Bulak, making for the door. "I have had more than enough. An island or a lake? Who cares? I am going to see Mordafa."

With that he departed, working his fingers around while the fur quivered on his face. A couple of guards peered through the bars in the uneasy manner of those assigned to keep watch upon a dangerous maniac.

Mordafa turned up next day in the mid-afternoon. He was a thin, elderly, and somewhat wizened specimen with incongruously youthful eyes. Accepting a seat, he studied Hillder, spoke with smooth deliberation.

"From what I have heard, from all that I have been told, I deduce a basic rule applying to lifeforms deemed intelligent."

"You deduce it?"

"I have to. There is no choice about the matter. All the lifeforms we have discovered so far have not been truly intelligent. Some have been superficially so, but not genuinely so. It is obvious that you have had experiences that may come to us sooner or later but have not arrived yet. In that respect we may have been fortunate, seeing that the results of such contact are highly speculative. There's just no way of telling."

"And what is this rule?"

"That the governing body of any lifeform such as ours will be composed of power-lovers rather than of specialists."

"Well, isn't it?"

"Unfortunately, it is. Government falls into the hands of those who desire authority and escapes those with other interests." He paused, went on, "That is not to say that those who govern us are stupid. They are quite clever in their own particular field of mass-organization. But by the same token they are pathetically ignorant of other fields. Knowing this, your tactic is to take advantage of their ignorance. The weakness of authority is that it cannot be diminished and retain strength. To play upon ignorance is to dull the voice of command."

"Hm!" Hillder surveyed him with mounting respect. "You're the first one I've encountered who can see beyond the end of his nose."

"Thank you," said Mordafa. "Now the very fact that you have taken the risk of landing here alone, and followed it up by confusing our leaders, proves that your kind has developed a technique for a given set of conditions and, in all probability, a series of techniques for various conditions."

"Go on," urged Hillder.

"Such techniques must be created empirically rather than theoretically," Mordafa continued. "In other words, they result from many experiences, the correcting of many errors, the search for workability, the effort to gain maximum results from minimum output." He glanced at the other. "Am I correct so far?"

"You're doing fine."

"To date we have established foothold on forty-two planets without ever having to combat other than primitive life. We may find foes worthy of our strength on the forty-third world, whenever that is discovered. Who knows? Let us assume for the sake of argument that intelligent life exists on one in every forty-three inhabitable planets."

"Where does that get us?" Hillder prompted.

"I would imagine," said Mordafa thoughtfully, "that the experience of making contact with at least six intelligent lifeforms would be necessary to enable you to evolve techniques for dealing with their like elsewhere. Therefore your kind must have discovered and explored not less than two hundred fifty worlds. That is an estimate in minimum terms. The correct figure may well be that stated by you."

"And I am not a consistent liar?" asked Hillder, grinning.

"That is beside the point, if only our leaders would hold on to their sanity long enough to see it. You may have distorted or exaggerated for purposes of your own. If so, there is nothing we can do about it. The prime fact holds fast, namely, that your space-venturings must be far more extensive than ours. Hence you must be older, more advanced, and numerically stronger."

"That's logical enough," conceded Hillder, broadening his grin.

"Now don't start on me," pleaded Mordafa. "If you fool me with an intriguing fallacy I won't rest until I get it straight. And that will do neither of us any good."

"Ah, so your intention is to do me good?"

"Somebody has to make a decision, seeing that the top brass is no longer capable of it. I am going to suggest that they set you free with our best wishes and assurances of friendship."

"Think they'll take any notice?"

"You know quite well they will. You've been counting on it all along." Mordafa eyed him shrewdly. "They'll grab at the advice to restore their self-esteem. If it works, they'll take the credit. If it doesn't, I'll get the blame." He brooded a few seconds, asked with open curiosity, "Do you find it the same elsewhere, among other peoples?"

"Exactly the same," Hillder assured him. "And there is always a Mordafa to settle the issue in the same way. Power and scapegoats go together like husband and wife."

"I'd like to meet my alien counterparts someday." Getting up, he moved to the door. "If I had not come along, how long would you have waited for your psychological mixture to congeal?"

"Until another of your type chipped in. If one doesn't arrive of his own accord, the powers-that-be lose patience and drag one in. The catalyst mined from its own kind. Authority lives by eating its vitals."

"That is putting it paradoxically," Mordafa observed, making it sound like a mild reproof. He went away.

Hillder stood behind the door and gazed through the bars in its top half. The pair of guards leaned against the opposite wall and stared back.

With amiable pleasantness, he said to them, "No cat has eight tails. Every cat has one tail more than no cat. Therefore every cat has nine tails."

They screwed up their eyes and scowled.

Quite an impressive deputation took him back to the ship. All the four hundred were there, about a quarter of them resplendent in uniforms, the rest in their Sunday best. An armed guard juggled guns at barked command. Kadina made an unctuous speech full of brotherly love and the glorious shape of things to come. Somebody presented a bouquet of evil-smelling weeds and Hillder made mental note of the difference in olfactory senses.

. Climbing eighty yards to the lock, Hillder looked down. Kadina waved an officious farewell. The crowd chanted, "Hurrah!" in conducted rhythm. He blew his nose on a handkerchief, that being deflatory gesture number nine, closed the lock, sat at the control board.

The tubes fired into a low roar. A cloud of vapor climbed around and sprinkled ground-dirt over the mob. That touch was involuntary and not recorded in the book. A pity, he thought. Everything ought to be listed. We should be systematic about such things. The showering of dirt should be duly noted under the heading of the spaceman's farewell.

The ship snored into the sky, left the Vard-world far behind. Hillder remained at the controls until free of the entire system's gravitational field. Then he headed for the beacon-area and locked the auto-pilot on that course.

For a while he sat gazing meditatively into star-spangled darkness. After a while he sighed, made notes in his log-book.

Cube K49, Sector 10, solar-grade D7, third planet. Name: Vard. Lifeform named Vards, cosmic intelligence rating BB, space-going, forty-two colonies. Comment: softened up.

He glanced over his tiny library fastened to a steel bulkhead. Two tomes were missing. They had swiped the two that were replete with diagrams and illustrations. They had left the rest, having no Rosetta Stone with which to translate cold print. They hadn't touched the nearest volume titled: *Diabologic, the Science of Driving People Nuts.*

Sighing again, he took paper from a drawer, commenced his hundredth, two hundredth or maybe three-hundredth try at concocting an Aleph number higher than A, but lower than C. He mauled his hair until it stuck out in spikes, and although he didn't know it, he did not look especially well-balanced himself.

Fighting Philosopher

by *E. B. Cole*

". . . And this, gentlemen, is what we saw from the *Rilno*."

The three-dimensional screen glowed as a dozen suns sprang into being within it. Light glanced fitfully from a multitude of spheres grouped about their primaries. These were the suns and planets of the Empire of Findur. Near the center of the screen, a number of small sparks dodged swiftly about in the emptiness of interstellar space. One of these seemed to be surrounded. Tiny lines of light swept from the others, causing the central spark to pulsate with a vivid glow.

"Captain Tero called me at this time," announced the voice from the darkness beside the screen. "He requested permission to cut a ten-degree, four-microsecond void, since he was englobed and his screens were in danger of overloading under the Finduran fire." The speaker paused, then continued. "I granted permission, since I could see no other feasible means of pulling him out of the globe. We could have opened fleet fire, but Tero's screens might have gone down before we could control the situation. The *Kleeros* acknowledged, then Tero cut in his space warp."

On the screen, a narrow fan of darkness spread from the englobed spark. The attacking sparks vanished before it. Suddenly, the dark fan widened, vibrated, then swung over a wide angle. As it swung, the brilliant suns went out like candles in a high wind. A black, impenetrable curtain spread over most of the scene. Abruptly, the spark at the origin of the darkness faded and was gone. The scene remained, showing an irregularly shaped, black pocket amongst the stars. It hung there, an empty, opaque, black spot in space, where a few moments before had been suns and planets and embattled ships.

"As you gentlemen know," the voice added tiredly, "before a space warp can be cut in, all screens must be lowered to prevent random secondary effects and permanent damage to the ship. The cut is so phased as to make it virtually impossible for a shear beam or any other force beam to penetrate, but there is one chance in several million of shear-beam penetration while the warp is being set up. The only assumption we could make aboard the *Rilno* was that a beam must have struck Tero's controls while his screens were being phased. He apparently swung out of control for a moment, then disrupted his ship to prevent total destruction of the Sector. Before he could act, however, he had destroyed his attackers and virtually all of the Finduran Empire. Of course, the warp remained on long enough to allow permanent establishment. We have nothing further to base opinions on, since Tero did not take the time to report before disrupting." The scene on the viewer faded and the room lights went on.

The speaker stood revealed as a slender, tall humanoid. His narrow face with its high brows and sharply outlined features gave the impression of continual amusement with the universe and all that was in it, but the slight narrowing of the eyes—the barely perceptible tightening of the mouth—evidenced a certain anxiety. Fine lines on his face indicated that this man had known cares and serious thoughts in the past. Now, he stood at attention, his hands aligned at the sides of his light-gray trousers. Fleet Commander Dalthos A-Riman, of the Seventeenth Border Sector, awaited the pleasure of the Board.

In front of him, the being at the desk nodded at the other members of the Board. "Are there any questions, gentlemen?"

A small, lithe member raised a hand slightly. A-Riman looked toward him. He had met Sector Chief Sesnir before, and knew his sharp, incisive questions.

"You said that Captain Tero was at point, commander," stated Sesnir. "How did he happen to get so far in advance of the rest of the fleet that he could be englobed?"

"You remember, sir," replied A-Riman, "the Findurans had developed a form of polyphase screen which made their ships nearly undetectable when at rest. We could only detect them when they were in action, or when they were within a half parsec. This encounter took place several parsecs outside their normal area of operation." The fleet commander brought a hand to his face, then dropped it. "I was just about to call Tero in to form a slightly more compact grouping when he ran into the middle of their formation."

"You mean they had maneuvered a fleet well inside Federation borders, and had it resting in ambush?" persisted the questioner. "What was wrong with your light scouts?"

"That, sir," A-Riman told him, "was the reason I approached in fleet strength. I had received no scout reports for three days. I knew there was enemy action in the region, but had no intelligence reports."

"You mean," another Board member broke in, "you went charging into an unknown situation in open fleet formation?"

"I felt I had to, sir. I regarded open formation as precautionary, since damage to one ship would be far less serious than involvement of the entire fleet in an ambush. I was sure I had lost several scouts, and was not inclined to lose more. Tero volunteered to draw fire, then planned to take evasive action while the rest of the fleet moved in." A-Riman paused. "Except for superb planning by the Finduran admiral and a million-to-one accident, Tero would have extricated himself easily, and we could have moved in to take police action in accordance with the council's orders."

"I see," commented the questioning member. "Probably would've done the same thing myself."

"Why," demanded Sesnir impatiently, "didn't you simply open up from a safe distance with a ten-microsecond, forty-degree space warp? You'd still have been within your orders, we'd have saved a ship, the Findurans would've given us no more trouble—ever—and we wouldn't have a permanent space fold to worry about in Sector Seventeen."

A-Riman looked at the sector chief. "That, sir," he announced firmly, "is just what I wanted to avoid doing. I felt, and still feel, that complete destruction of suns, planets and youthful cultures, however inimical they may seem to be at the time, is wasteful, dangerous, and in direct violation of the first law of Galactic Ethics."

The president of the Board looked up. "The Ethic refers to Federation members, commander," he said. "Remember?"

"I believe it should be extended to include all intelligent life, sir," A-Riman answered.

"You will find 'Treat all others as you would wish yourself to be treated in like circumstances' a very poor defense against a well-directed shear beam," commented Sesnir.

A-Riman smiled. "True," he admitted, "but there are possibilities. Why—"

Vandor ka Bensir, Chief of Stellar Guard Operations, rapped on his desk. "Gentlemen," he said dryly, "a discussion of the Galactic Ethics is always very interesting, but I believe it is out of order here. Unless there are more questions or comments pertinent to this inquiry, I will close the Board." He looked about the room. "No comments? Then, as president of this Board of Inquiry, I order the Board closed for deliberation." Again, he rapped on the desk. "Will you please retire, Commander A-Riman? We will notify you when we have reached our findings and recommendations."

As the door closed, Bensir turned to the other Board members. "The floor is open for discussion," he said. "You're the junior member, Commander Dal Klar. Do you have any comments?"

"Admiral, I have what almost amounts to a short speech." Dal Klar glanced at the chief of operations, then looked slowly about at the rest of his colleagues. "But I hesitate to take up too much of the Board's time."

Ka Bensir smiled gently. "You mean that juniors should be seen and not heard?" he queried.

"Something like that, sir."

"This Board," ruled its president, "has all the time in the Universe. You can think out loud; you can bring up any points you wish; you can come to whatever conclusions you want to. The floor is yours."

Dal Klar took a deep breath. "Well, in that case, here I go: In the first place, I feel that A-Riman acted properly and in accordance with his ethics and those of his civilization. If you gentlemen will remember, A-Riman is from the Celstor Republic, which is one of the older members of the Federation. The Celstorians have been responsible for many of the scientific advances and for a large share of the philosophy of our civilization. A-Riman, himself, has written two notable commentaries on philosophy and ethics, both of which have been well received in the Federation."

Dal Klar glanced toward Sector Chief Sesnir, then continued. "Had the commander destroyed without warning, inflicting utter and complete destruction upon a young and comparatively helpless civilization, he would have been acting in direct contravention to his own stated ethical code. In that case, he would have been deserving of all the censure we could give. As it is, I feel that he acted in accordance with the best traditions of the Guard, and simply met with an unforseen and unfortunate accident which could have happened to any fleet commander who went on that mission.''

Dal Klar paused, cleared his throat, then concluded. "We have heard definite testimony that there was no laxity in drill or maintenance in A-Riman's fleet. On the contrary, some of his officers feel that he is extremely strict about both action drill and maintenance. Certainly, then, we can't say he was negligent.''

As Dal Klar stopped, Ka Bensir looked at another Board member, who shook his head.

"I might have phrased it a little differently, sir,'' he commented, "but the commander expressed my views quite well. I have nothing to add.''

Two more members declined to comment, then Sector Chief Sesnir wagged his head.

"I seem to be in the minority,'' he remarked, "but I feel that the coddling of these young, semibarbaric and aggressive cultures is suicidal. Before we could teach them our ways of thinking, they would inflict tremendous damage upon us. They might even subvert some of our own younger members, and set up a rival Federation. Then, we would have real trouble. I have read A-Riman's commentaries on ethics, and I know the history of the 'Fighting Philosopher.' Frankly, I feel that a man with his views should not be in the Combat Arm of the Guard. He is simply too soft.''

The Board president nodded. "I'll reserve comment,'' he decided. "Will you gentlemen please record your findings?''

A few minutes later, the clerk inserted a small file of recordings into the machine in front of him. The viewscreen lit up.

Findings: The Kleeros, *a Class A Guard ship, was lost, and a permanent space-fold was set up in Sector Seventeen due to the ill-advised tactics of Fleet Commander Dalthos A-Riman, who risked his fleet against an unscouted force rather than destroy a criminal civilization by means of his hand.*

Ka Bensir pointed at Dal Klar, who shook his head. "No,'' he said decisively. The pointing finger moved to the next member. Again, the answer was a definite "No.'' Only one member assented to the proposed finding. Ka Bensir nodded to the clerk. "Next recording," he said.

Findings: The Class A Guard ship, Kleeros, was destroyed by its captain to avert major disaster. The cause of failure of the space-warp controls aboard the Kleeros *cannot be accurately determined due to the destruction of the ship with all on board and to the lack of communication prior to that destruction. Fleet Commander Dalthos A-Riman was acting within his orders and was using reasonable caution prior to the incident. The failure of the space-warp controls and the permanent space-fold resulting therefrom could not have been foreseen by the fleet commander or by Captain Nalver Tero. Since the use of the space-warp is recognized as a legitimate defensive tactic by single ships of the Federation, no censure will be brought against Captain Tero for requesting permission to use the warp, nor against Commander A-Riman for granting that permission. The disaster was due to circumstances beyond the control of any of its participants.*

Again, Ka Bensir pointed at Dal Klar, who nodded. "I agree," he said. The next member assented. So did the next, and the next. Finally, Ka Bensir rapped on his desk. "The findings are complete, then," he said. "Since we find that no censure will be brought against Commander A-Riman, we need not go into that phase of the matter. Do I hear a verbal motion on a citation for Captain Tero and his crew?"

"Federation Cluster for Tero; Heroic Citations for his crew," rumbled a deep voice. "Second," came a sharp reply.

"All in favor?" An assenting murmur arose. "Unanimous," commented Bensir. "Record it."

Vandor ka Bensir drew his side arm. "Have Fleet Commander Dalthos A-Riman come in," he ordered. He laid the weapon on his desk, its needlelike nose pointing away from the door and toward the screen which still bore the accepted findings of the Board and the posthumous citation for the captain and crew of the *Kleeros*.

A-Riman stepped in. Glancing at the weapon on the desk, he nodded slightly, then looked at the viewscreen. "Thank you, gentlemen," he acknowledged. "Now that the inquiry is over, I wish to request reassignment to the Criminal Apprehension Corps. I feel that I may be more useful there than in the Combat Arm." He nodded at the screen. "In spite of the recorded findings, it is possible that some of you agree. My real reason, however, for requesting reassignment, is my feeling that I may be able to offer some constructive recommendations which should result in fewer problems for the Combat Arm in the future, and I wish to be in Criminal Apprehension where I can furnish practical proof of the feasibility of those recommendations.''

The Tenth Sector Officers' Club wasn't particularly crowded. Commander A-Riman walked into the Senior Officers' dining room. At one of the tables, he saw two old acquaintances. He went toward them.

"Mind if I join you?"

They looked up. "Dalthos," exclaimed one, "where'd you come from? Thought you were over in Seventeen."

A-Riman grabbed a chair, pulling it out. "Just reported for duty, Veldon," he remarked as he sat down. "I'm the new CAC Group Commander."

Veldon Bolsein looked at him quizzically. "Heard you had a little trouble with a runaway warp," he remarked. "What'd they do, damp your beams?"

"No, they decided I wasn't at fault," grinned A-Riman. "I requested transfer to CAC."

Bolsein cocked one eyebrow up and the other down. Then, tilting his head to one side, he looked hard at A-Riman. "My hearing must be going bad," he decided. "I was sure you said you requested transfer."

"I did."

"How barbarous," murmured Fleet Commander Plios Knolu, as he placed his elbows on the table. He leaned forward, cupped his face in his hands, and fixed A-Riman with a pitying stare. "Tell me," he asked, "did they beat your brains out with clubs, or did they use surgery?"

A-Riman leaned back and laughed. "Thought you'd have lost your touch by now," he remarked. "No, I'm still sane as ever, but—"

"Jets ahead," warned Bolsein softly. He started to rise. A-Riman glanced around to see the sector chief walking into the room. He and Knolu got to their feet.

Sector Chief Dal-Kun took his seat at the head of the table. "Your health, gentlemen," he greeted them. "I see you have already met." He looked over the menu card and dialed a selection. "I've been checking over your records, A-Riman," he continued. "Look good, all of them, up to that space-fold. Board didn't hold you responsible for that, either." He paused as his dishes rose to the table top. Lifting a cover, he examined the contents of a platter. "Food Service is in good condition, I see," he remarked. He transferred a helping to his plate. "Can't understand how you happened to go into Criminal Apprehension, though. No promotion there."

A-Riman smiled. "I was just about to explain to Bolsein and Knolu when you came in, sir." He paused, collecting his thoughts. "I've been doing some thinking on criminology for quite a while, and I've a few theories on preventative work in the new civilizations I'd like to try out. There are several systems in this sector that would stand some investigation, and—"

Dal-Kun laid his utensils down. "Let's not get in too much of a hurry, commander. Suppose you turn in some good, routine work for a couple of cycles or so, then we'll talk about new theories." He picked up his fork again. "We've got a lot of these young, do-nothing Drones roaming about in this sector, getting into scrapes, violating quarantines, creating space hazards. They'll keep you busy for a while." He grunted angrily. "'Why, right now, you've got five pickup orders on file, and those people of yours can't seem to get anywhere with them."

"In that case, I'll get to work immediately," said A-Riman. "Can I have Fleet Support where necessary?"

The sector chief grunted again. "Don't see why not. Commander Knolu hasn't done anything but routine patrol for two cycles. Do him good to run around a bit and work off some of his fat." He continued with his meal.

Finally, the chief left the table. Bolsein dialed another glass of *Telon* and leaned back. "Don't worry too much about the boss," he remarked. "He snarls like mad, but he'll back you up all the way, long's you're somewhere near the center of the screen."

"Just what's this big, new idea of yours, A-Riman?" inquired Knolu.

"Either of you ever get a 'cut back, or destroy' order?"

Knolu nodded. "Sure—several of them. Last one was in this sector, not more than ten cycles ago."

"How did you feel about it?"

Knolu shook his head. "How does anyone feel about destruction? I hated it, but the council doesn't put out an order like that unless it has been proven necessary. They hate destruction and waste, too."

"Suppose we could figure out a method of eliminating most of this type of destruction?"

Bolsein narrowed his eyes. "It would take a terrible load off the mind of every combat commander." He sighed, "But what can be done? We contact new civilizations as soon as they achieve space travel, and the negotiators fail with a good share of them. Pretty soon, they're too big for their system. They try to take over the Federation, or part of it, and we're ordered into action."

"Suppose we contacted them long before they came out into space?"

"Unethical. You know that."

"Is guidance and instruction unethical?"

Knolu sat up sharply. "I think I see what you're driving at," he said, "but who's going to spend his time and effort on a primitive planet, living with primitive people, just so he can teach them? What guarantee has he of success?"

A-Riman smiled. "You heard the chief. I've got five pickups in the files. I'll bet, without looking, that three of them at least are for quarantine violations on primitive planets. Now—"

Bolsein interrupted. "All five of 'em are," he grumbled. "We have more trouble in this sector with these foolish Drones violating quarantine than we do with anything else. I even had a minor engagement with a bunch of them last cycle. They'd organized some sort of an eight-way chess game, with the planetary population as pieces." He hesitated. "What a nasty mess that was," he added. "My captains were so disgusted, they didn't pick them up for rehabilitation; they just blasted them out of space. I lost a ship, too, over the deal."

"There," announced A-Riman, "you had quite a few people who were willing to live with primitives on a primitive planet."

"Sure," grunted Bolsein. "Drones, though."

"What is a Drone?"

Knolu leaned back, smiling. "I read the manual once, too, remember?" He folded his arms. " 'A Drone,' " he quoted in a singsong voice, " 'is an entity who prefers not to do anything productive. Having acquired the necessary equipment for subsistence, he devotes his time to the pursuit of pleasure, to the exclusion of all other activity.' " He sat forward again. "I've gotten a few more thoughts on the subject, though. In my opinion, a Drone is an entity which should be picked up for rehabilitation as soon as he shows his characteristics."

He held up a hand as Bolsein started to speak. "Oh, I know,

E. B. Cole

the Ethic says we should not interfere with the chosen course of any citizen so long as he does no harm, commits no unethical act, or interferes with the legitimate good of no other citizen, but this should be an exception. Most Drones tire of normal pleasures in a few cycles. Within a hundred cycles, they turn to exotic pleasures. Finally, they tire even of these, and get into some form of unethical, immoral, or downright criminal activity. Eventually, we have to pick most of them up anyway, so why not pick them up right away?"

"More than a thousand periods ago," commented A-Riman, "long before the Celstorians burst out into space, my planet had a problem like this. To be sure, it was on a much smaller scale, but there were similarities. The governors set up a sort of 'Thought Police,' to combat the evil at its roots. It led to a dictatorship, and the civilization of Celstor was set back a thousand planetary cycles. We almost reverted to barbarism, and the matter wasn't corrected until a planet-wide uprising overthrew the Board of Governors and destroyed the Police State. Finally, the Republic was founded, but not until many sterile reversions had been set up and overthrown. No, we don't want to amend or correct the Ethic. We merely need to extend it."

He looked at Knolu. "But to get back to my original query. In my opinion, a Drone is an entity whose original training was somehow less than completely successful. He is an entity who wishes excitement—action, if you will—but is unable to accept the discipline which goes with productive work. At the present civilization level, subsistence is easy to get, on almost any desired scale. Matter converters allow us to live wherever we are, and live well. Subsistence and property then are no incentives. Most of us, who are well oriented, get our pleasure and our reward from a feeling of accomplishment. The Drone, however, has not yet reached that stage of development. It is only when his pursuit of pleasure has led him far out of the normal paths of pleasure that he is a fit subject for rehabilitation. After rehabilitation, he can be a very useful citizen. Many of them are, you know."

"Thus speaks the 'Fighting Philosopher,' " laughed Knolu. "A-Riman ever since you published 'Galactic Ethics, an Extension,' you've been living in a world of your own."

"No," denied A-Riman, "I've been trying to investigate the entire Galactic civilization. I've been trying to solve the problem of these new civilizations, many of which have risen from the ashes of former civilizations which either destroyed themselves or were destroyed by Interstellar conflict anywhere from twenty to several hundred periods ago.'' He hesitated, then continued. "It takes a long time for a burned-out planet to produce a new civilization. It takes even longer for a damped sun to return to life and to liven its planets. Why, the Finduran Empire, which one of my captains took with him into final oblivion, had its beginnings when my father was a very young schoolboy, still learning primitive manual writing and the basic principles of life. These periods of progress, of learning, of life, should not be merely thrown away. They should be conserved."

"How?" Bolsein leaned forward.

"For short times, say ten cycles or so, I can order my CAC agents in to work on primitive worlds. Of course, I must then grant them long leaves, but during those small spaces of time, I plan to prove that an impetus can be given to a primitive civilization, which will cause it to conform to the Galactic Ethic, and will predispose it to desire membership in the Galactic Federation when it becomes aware of the existence of such a body. If this works out, I feel sure that we can find recruits who will be willing to spend even longer stretches of time as educators and guides.

"I may even be able to train certain primitives and enlist their aid on their native planets. If a group of Drones can find amusement on a primitive world, surely productive personnel can stand considerable tours of duty, and can so guide primitive civilizations from their infant, barbaric beginnings that very few if any new civilizations, upon bursting into space, will have a desire to form great empires of their own. They will be willing and even glad to exchange technologies and ideas with the rest of the galaxy, and will become useful and honored members of the Federation."

"So, what do we do?" queried Knolu.

"Easy. I've got five pickups on file. The chief wants 'em cleared immediately if not sooner. I gather he expects me to take a couple of cycles to clean up things. Let me have full co-operation, and then we can go to work."

Bolsein shook his head. "I never thought I'd see the day I'd be following CAC orders," he complained. "What do you want? Do you need both fleets, or will a few hundred scouts satisfy you?"

*   *   *

Unquestionably, Besiro was the most beautiful capital on all the planet. Here was gathered all the talent, all the beauty, all the wit, and most of the wealth of the civilized world. Here, also, were gathered the most clever, the most experienced, the most depraved thieves and criminals of the planet. After dark, the Elegants of the Court, the wealthy idlers, and the solid merchants of the city took care to have a trusted bodyguard when they ventured abroad. It was strange, then, that on this night, there was a lone pedestrian in the narrow side street which led to the Guest House of the Three Kings.

The man was dressed expensively and well. His ornate, feathered hat was cocked at exactly the fashionable angle, the foam of lace at his shoulders jutted up and out precisely the correct distance, and the jeweled buckles of his shoes and his coat buttons reflected the glow of the occasional street taper like miniature suns. He strode casually along the street, glancing incuriously at the shuttered windows of the houses along the way. Finally, he approached the entrance to an alley. Momentarily, he paused, tilting his head in a listening attitude, then he smiled to himself and continued. He brushed a hand lightly against his belt, then took the hilt of his sword in a firm grasp.

In the alley, "Sailor" Klur was giving his last-minute instructions in a low tone.

"Now, One-eye," he said, "soon's he heaves into sight, you dive for his feet. Me'n Slogger'll finish him off before he gets up." As the footsteps approached, Klur gave One-eye a slight shove.

"Now," he whispered. One-eye dove for the glittering shoe buckles.

At the slight commotion, the pedestrian stopped abruptly, then danced back half a pace. One-eye never realized he had failed in his assignment, for the long, sharp sword in the elegantly ringed hand severed his head before he had time to hit the stones of the street. Klur's intended victim turned smoothly, meeting the sailor's rush with a well-directed point. Klur dropped his long knife, looked for a moment at the foppish figure before him, then collapsed silently to the pavement. The victor advanced, forcing "Slogger" Marl against the wall, the point of his sword making a dent in the man's clothing. Marl sobbed in terror.

"Please, my master, please, they made me do it. I'm a peace-loving man. I wouldn't do nothing. On my honor, I wouldn't."

The man with the sword smiled engagingly. "I can see that," he agreed. "Drop your club, my man."

The club clattered to the alley.

"Now," said the Elegant, "I'm minded to let you go, for you're such a poor thing beside those two valiants who lie there." He dropped the sword point slightly. "Be off," he ordered. With a gasp of surprised relief, Marl turned to make his way to safer parts.

The sword licked out suddenly, and Marl's sudden protesting cry of surprise and pain became a mere gurgle as the flowing blood stopped his voice.

The killer stepped toward the body, glanced disdainfully at its clothing, and shook his head.

"Filthy," he murmured. He walked out to the street, examining the other two. Finally, he decided that Klur's coat was comparatively clean. Leaning down, he carefully wiped his sword blade on the skirt of the coat, then restored the weapon to its sheath, carefully adjusted his hat, and sauntered on his way. Manir Kal, master swordsman, had proved his ability again, and to his own critical satisfaction.

The reports were long and detailed. A-Riman checked them over, rapidly at first, then more slowly, gathering each detail. Occasionally, he nodded his head. Some of these agents were good. Others were very good. He touched a button on his desk. Nothing happened. He frowned and touched another button. Still, nothing happened.

Indignantly, A-Riman glanced down at the call-board and punched two more buttons in quick succession. His viewscreen remained dark, and he punched the button marked "Conference," then sat back to await developments. A minute passed, then a light blinked on the desk. As A-Riman pressed the button below the light, the door opened to admit a captain, who took two paces forward, halted, came to rigid attention, saluted, and announced himself. "Captain Poltar reporting, sir." He remained at attention.

"Relax, captain," ordered A-Riman. "Why didn't you answer my screen?"

The captain was still at attention. "The previous commander wanted personal contact, sir," he said, then, as the order to relax penetrated, he quickly took a more comfortable pose.

"Open the door again, then take a chair. I think we're going to have company," smiled his superior.

A voice drifted through the open door. "Oh, I suppose he wants someone to check the guards on that suspect planet. As though we haven't—" The voice trailed off, as the speaker realized the group commander's door was open. Two highly embarrassed officers entered, announced themselves, stood at attention, and waited for the thunders of wrath to descend about their ears.

"Sit down, gentlemen," ordered A-Riman mildly. "We'll have more company in a minute."

Three more officers filed into the room, took two paces, saluted, and announced themselves. A-Riman waved a hand. "Relax, gentlemen," he told them. He turned to Captain Poltar. "Are there any more officers present?" he inquired.

Poltar glanced at the others present in the room, then shook his head. "No, sir. The rest are off the base, checking or investigating."

"Good." A-Riman nodded. "When they come in, have them report to me one at a time." He turned to face the entire group. "Gentlemen," he began, "this is my first, and very probably my last, staff meeting." He raised a hand. "No, I don't mean it that way. I plan to be here for a good many cycles, but I'm going to see to it that the 'conference' button gets good and corroded." He turned to Captain Poltar again. "What were you doing when I buzzed you?"

"Working out the deci-cyclic report, sir."

"It took you over a minute to get here," stated the commander.

"Yes, sir."

"It'll take you ten or fifteen minutes to get back on your train of thought and start over where you left off?"

"About that, sir."

"So, you will lose at least a quarter of an hour from your work, plus the time we take in this discussion. How long is that?"

"I expect to lose about an hour and a half, sir."

A-Riman glanced about the group. "Anyone here think he'll lose any less than that?" There was silence.

"So," decided the commander, "I push a few buttons and lose nine man-hours of work—more than one day for an officer." He frowned at the row of buttons on his desk. "Mr. Kelnar, you're engineering, I believe. Have these things rewired right away so that when I call someone I am cut into his viewscreen. There'll be no more of this."

An older man, one of the last to report, rose to his feet. "I'm on my way, sir," he announced, and turned to go out the door.

"Just a minute," ordered A-Riman. "You were in the Combat Arm once. How did you happen to transfer out?"

"Crash-landed in a repair ship on a primitive planet, sir. When they got me patched up, a Board decided I was unfit for further combat duty."

"Why didn't you retire?"

"I like it here."

A-Riman waved a dismissal. The senior technician saluted, swung through the door, and was gone. The group commander gazed after him thoughtfully, then returned his attention to the five remaining officers.

"Maybe, gentlemen, we're not wasting so much time, at that," he remarked softly. "Maybe I'd better go into my philosophy of operation. I just came from the Combat Arm, gentlemen. No one forced me into this job. I came here because I was something like Mr. Kelnar. I like it here. From now on, we're going to work. There'll be very little time for two-stepping, reporting, and so on. We've got a job to do, and we're going to concentrate on it. When I call one of you, I expect an immediate answer by viviscreen, or I expect someone in your office to locate you within a very short time. Then, you will call me. If you have any problems, I expect a prompt call. I'll probably be out of my office. I may be at the other end of the sector, but there'll be someone here that'll know how to get in touch with me."

He picked up the tiny recordings of the pickup data. "We have five pickups of Drones who have violated quarantine of Planet Five, Sun Gorgon Three, number four five seven six, Sector Ten. They are still at large and presumably still on the planet. What's wrong?"

"We have guards staked out all around the Sun's system, waiting for them to move, sir. So far, they haven't attempted to leave." Captain Poltar looked a little surprised.

"You're sure they are on the planet?"

"Yes, sir, definitely. We tracked them in shortly after they made planetfall. Since then, not a dust mote could've gotten out. Our people are keeping constant watch on their actions.''

"What's your disposition?''

"It's in the report, sir," said another officer. "We have ten two-man scouts englobing the planet, at close range, with detectors full out. If they even move, we know it.''

"That's twenty men on full-time duty, just watching a mouse hole," commented A-Riman. "Why not simply send in five of the scouts, hunt up your people on the planet, and bring them back here?''

Captain Poltar looked shocked. "Regulations, sir," he exclaimed.

"Which regulations?''

"Why, I believe it's SGR 344–53–4, sir. I'll have it checked if you wish.''

"Don't bother." A-Riman smiled at him wryly. "I checked it. It says, 'Excepting in cases of extreme emergency, no Guard Unit will make planetfall on any primitive world without prior clearance from higher authority.' Have you checked with the sector chief for permission to make planetfall?''

"I haven't, sir. Commander Redendale said 'Higher Authority' in this case meant the council, and he wasn't about to contact the council to cover my people's incompetence. He said they should certainly be able to do a simple thing like bringing the quarry into the open.''

The commander grinned. "He told you, of course, how that was to be done?''

"No, sir.''

"And they sent that guy to Combat," mused A-Riman silently, shaking his head. He punched a sequence of buttons on his desk.

The viewscreen lit up, showing a blue haze, then cleared as an alert face appeared, and a voice said crisply, "Admiral's office, Orderly here.''

"CAC group commander here," he was told. "Let me talk to the admiral.''

"Yes, sir.'' The orderly reached forward and his image was abruptly blanked out. A few seconds later, Sector Chief Dal-Kun's heavy face appeared. "Yes, commander, what is it?''

"Sir, I would like permission to land ten of my people on a primitive planet.''

"Why?''

"I have five pickup orders, sir. The subjects have been located, and I'd like to land agents to bring them in."

"When were they located?"

"Half a cycle ago, sir."

The sector commander's face whitened slightly, then its normal silvery gray became suffused with a pale bluish tint. "Why," he demanded angrily, "wasn't I contacted for this permission half a cycle ago?"

"I don't know of my own knowledge, admiral," replied A-Riman softly.

"Find out, commander. Call me back with the answer within an hour." The sector chief leaned forward. "Go in and get those Drones—now. I want a report on their apprehension within ten days." The screen became blank.

A-Riman looked up. "Gentlemen, you heard the conversation, so now you know where 'Higher Authority' may be found. The admiral said ten days. I know that doesn't leave much time to comb an entire planet and locate five men." He paused, looking about the group. "But I'm going to make it stiffer. If our people are any good at all, they'll have kept some track of our subjects. I want to see those Drones tomorrow, right after lunch—alive."

The five officers looked at each other. Then, they looked at their new group commander. "Tomorrow, sir?" said one, "Right after lunch?"

A-Riman nodded. "Alive," he emphasized. "I don't care how you do it. If you wish, and if ten men can, you may turn the planet inside out, but bring them in. We'll pick up the pieces and clean up the mess later. Now, let's get at it. You go to work while I explain to the admiral why this wasn't reported to him long ago." He touched the buttons again. "This meeting's adjourned."

Master Search Technician Kembar looked sourly at the communicator.

"Half a cycle, I'm hanging around this planet, watching a bunch of monkeys swagger around. They won't let me touch 'em. I can't just go in, fiddle around for a couple of days, then pick them up. No—I sit here, rigging gadgets to let me watch 'em." He turned to his companion, who merely grinned.

"Go ahead. Grin, you prehistoric Dawn-man. It ain't funny."

Scout Pilot First Class Dayne stretched his long arms. "So, now they tell you to go in. What's wrong with that?"

Kembar wagged his head. "Half a cycle, that's what's wrong. Then, they tell me to bring 'em in for lunch tomorrow." He glanced over the pilot's shoulder at the clock. "Well, set her down just outside of the city, and we'll get on with it. Tell the rest of the section to meet us in that park just outside of town."

Dayne nodded and turned to his controls. "They've got the old-style Mohrkan body shields, haven't they?" he asked, over his shoulder.

"Yeah," replied Kembar. He opened a locker, pulling out equipment and clothing. "Set up your hideaway projector now."

The Guest House of the Three Kings wasn't a very elaborate place, nor was it in the best section of Besiro. It had become the haunt of some of the capital's Elegants due to some chance whim of one of the leaders of fashion, and an astute proprietor had held this favor by quickly hiring excellent help, and stocking the best wines, while still retaining the casual atmosphere of a small, slightly down-at-the-heels public drinking place.

In the guest room, long wooden benches lined the walls. Before these were the scrubbed wooden tables. The center of the room was normally kept clear, so that the waiters could move more quickly to their customers. Sometimes, the customers used this open area for swordplay, but this was discouraged. Master Korno didn't like bloodstains marring the scrubbed whiteness of his floors.

Outside the Guest Room, in the large hall, Manir Kal met his friends. Balc was teasing one of the waitresses, while Kem-dor looked on with mild amusement.

"Where's Bintar?" queried Kal.

Kem-dor gestured. "Kitchen," he said. "He wanted the roast done just so."

Balc gave the waitress a slight shove. "I'm getting tired of this place," he remarked. "Getting to be a routine. How about finding something else?"

Kal shook his head. "Have to wait awhile," he explained. "Malon says they're still watching. Better not move till they give up." He frowned a little, looking at the bare hallway.

Kem-dor nodded. "I suppose you're right," he agreed, "but there must be something better than these silly gambling games. I'm just turning into a money-making machine, and it's beginning to bore me."

"Try their business houses," suggested Balc. "Might be some interest there."

Kem-dor snorted. "Tried that long ago," he complained. "At first, their elementary tricks were amusing, but—" He waved a jeweled hand.

"I know what you mean," said Kal. "The bravos don't put up much of a fight, either." He started for a door. "Well, let's go in and get a drink, anyway."

As he entered the Guest Room, Manir Kal started for the usual table over in the far corner. There was a large man sitting on the bench. Kal looked him over casually. He was a tall, lean individual—well enough dressed, but not in the precise height of style. Probably some rustic landowner in for the carnival, decided Kal. He walked over.

"Sorry, fellow," he remarked. "You're in my place."

The man looked up, but made no effort to move. "Plenty more tables," he remarked. "I've been here for quite a while." He gestured at the table next to his. "Here, try this spot."

Kal smiled inwardly. Perhaps this one would provide some sport. "Possibly you didn't understand me," he said evenly. "You are sitting in the place I am accustomed to occupy. I'll thank you to move immediately."

The other picked up his glass and took a casual drink. "As I said," he remarked, setting the glass down again, "I've been here quite a while. I like it here." He looked Manir Kal over carefully. "Surely, you can get used to another table."

Someone at another table laughed.

Manir Kal's face flushed. He swept a hand past his belt, then picked up the stranger's glass and dashed it at the man's face.

The rustic vaulted over the table so rapidly he seemed to float. A hard fist struck Manir Kal in the nose, then, as he staggered back, a backhanded cuff sent him reeling against a table. For an instant, rage flooded through him. He snatched his sword out.

"I'll cut you to ribbons for this," he snarled.

The stranger had a sword, too. "Come and try," he invited.

Korno interposed his fat body between the two disputants. "Now, gentlemen," he protested, "there's a—"

Impatiently, Kal poked him with his sword. "Out of the way, fool," he growled, "before we use your body for a fencing mat."

With a shriek, Korno leaped out of the center of the room,

then stood and rubbed his injured posterior as he watched the fight.

The blades slithered against each other as the duelists felt each other out, then Kal tried a quick thrust. It was parried, and the riposte nearly threw Kal out of balance. He felt a surge of enthusiasm. At least, this one could fight. He wove a bewildering net of thrusts and counterthrusts, then moved in with his favorite trick, a disarm he had learned long ago.

Somehow, it didn't work. He found his blade borne down to the floor. Quickly, he swung it up again, closing in to avoid a thrust.

"Have to do better than that," laughed the stranger in Kal's native language. "Much better."

Manir Kal started to answer, then the significance of the sudden language change struck him. "You're—"

With an easy shove, the stranger pushed Kal back, then, beating his blade aside, pierced the swordman's shoulder with a straight thrust.

"That's right," he admitted, "I am."

"Hey," protested someone. "The Old Man said to bring 'em in alive."

"I know," replied Kal's assailant, sheathing his sword, "but he didn't say anything about cuts and bruises."

For a moment, Manir Kal stood, looking at this man who had so easily brushed aside his swordsmanship, then a haze closed in on him and he slipped to the floor. His three companions started for the door, but were met by several grim looking individuals with small objects in their hands—familiar objects.

"Screens down," ordered one of these. As the three hesitated in bewilderment, he added, "Don't tempt us, children."

The large duelist hoisted Manir Kal to his shoulder and started for the door.

"All right, fellows," he said, "let's go." Then, he caught sight of Korno. "Oh, yes," he remarked. "We're taking this man to a doctor. His friends are going along with us."

A-Riman sat back in his chair. For the moment, his work was done and nothing remained outside of purely routine matters, which he had no intention of considering. He yawned, then glanced at his watch. It was just about time for someone to come up with a report on those five Drones. He smiled to himself.

"Wonder what action they've taken so far?" he asked himself.

He leaned forward and touched a button. An enlisted man's face showed in the screen for an instant, then blanked out, and Captain Poltar appeared.

"Yes, sir."

"How about those five pickups?"

The captain glanced down at his desk. "They're being interrogated right now, sir," he explained. "We planned to bring them to you after lunch as you ordered."

A-Riman raised his eyebrows. "Who brought them in, and when?"

"Lieutenant Norkal's patrol was on duty, sir. Sergeant Kembar took his section in and made the pickup. He came in early this morning."

"Very good," nodded the commander. "I like operations that come off ahead of schedule." He glanced at his watch again. "I think I can wait a little before lunch. Have the sergeant bring them here." He shut off the screen and sat back, waiting.

The door light flashed, and as A-Riman touched the button, Sergeant Kembar walked in and saluted. He was in a fresh uniform, his insignia gleaming like a new rainbow against the blackness of his clothing. He stepped to the side of the door and drew his sidearm.

"Send 'em in, corporal," he instructed.

Five slightly disheveled individuals filed in, followed by a pair of neatly uniformed guards, who quickly herded them into a line facing the group commander.

A-Riman looked over the tableau, then laughed. "Fine, useful bunch of citizens," he remarked amusedly. "We have here a real credit to the Galactic Civilization."

Sergeant Kembar looked over the prisoners. "Things like these will happen, sir," he commented expressionlessly.

The group commander's amusement evaporated. "Unfortunately, sergeant," he replied, "they do." He pointed at Manir Kal, who stood facing him defiantly. The former swordsman of Besiro had a fresh bandage on his shoulder. His arm was carried in a sling, but he attempted to carry himself with something of his former swagger.

"What's this one good for?"

Sergeant Kembar smiled slightly. "It picks fights," he stated.

"Has it found anyone it can lick yet?"

The sergeant's smile broadened. "With the help of a body shield, it can conquer almost any primitive swordsman," he answered. "Of course, its knowledge of fighting arts is limited, but it knows which end of the sword is sharp—now." The sergeant glanced pointedly at the bandage.

Manir Kal looked angrily over at the sergeant, started to speak, then looked at his feet.

"Well," prompted A-Riman.

"He had a body shield, too," stated Kal.

A-Riman looked at the sergeant, who grinned. "Naturally, sir. Mine wasn't neutralized, either, but the subject found that out after it got pinked, fainted, and came to on the scout ship. It couldn't direct its blade close enough to me to find my shield during the little tussle." He examined his knuckles reflectively. "It leads with its nose, too," he added.

Manir Kal was stung. "I'm a Galactic Citizen," he stated angrily. "I object to being referred to as an 'it'!"

Dalhos A-Riman looked at him sternly. "You gave up your citizenship when you made planetfall on a primitive world," he commented coldly. "Now, you're simply a subject for rehabilitation. You are regarded as being of insufficient competence to speak for yourself." He waved a hand at Balc. "This one?"

The sergeant made a grimace of disgust. "It runs after females," he growled. He looked down the line of prisoners. "This one eats," he added, pointing. "This one, with the aid of a calculator, can solve elementary permutations and possibilities. It fancies itself as a gambler." The sergeant paused, then pointed again. "Here is the talented one. It can actually land a pleasure cruiser without having a wreck."

Malon looked at him sneeringly. "I managed to evade you," he pointed out.

The sergeant was unperturbed. "The subject ship headed in for planetfall after giving a false course plan," he said. "We could have blasted, but we were ordered not to destroy unless necessary. We have had all five of these subjects under close observation ever since their landing."

A-Riman nodded. "These are typical Drones?" he asked.

"Yes, sir. Some of them engage in other forms of amusement, some show a little more imagination, but these five are typical."

"I see." A-Riman stood up. "Take these things out, tag them, and ship them to Rehabilitation. In the future, simply pick up any criminal Drones, ship them to Aldebaran Base with suitable tags, and make out a report. I've seen enough of them."

He started for the door. "I'm going to lunch now, sergeant," he added. "Be ready to report to me with your section when I return."

The sector chief was halfway through his lunch when A-Riman walked into the dining room. With a quick "By your leave, sir," the group commander slid into a chair and consulted the menu. As he dialed his choice, Dal-Kun cleared his throat.

"Hate to spoil your appetite, commander," he said, "but what's being done about those five Drones?"

A-Riman glanced at his watch. "They should be about ready for shipment to Aldebaran by now, sir," he reported. "The reports are being prepared for submission to your office."

Dal-Kun speared a morsel of food. "Very good, commander," he started. "I'm—" Then, he looked up. "You picked 'em up in less than one day?" he roared. "What's been happening for the last half cycle?"

A-Riman shook his head. "I reported the situation to you, sir. The scouts were forbidden to make planetfall until yesterday afternoon. They had their subjects under extremely close observation and were able to bring them immediately they were granted permission to act."

"I suppose they made a mess on the planet. How long will it take you to clean up and prevent a stir for the planetary historians to pick over?"

"The pickup created very little disturbance." A-Riman frowned thoughtfully. "But I'm not sure yet about the effects of the Drones' stay. It may take as much as two tenths of a cycle for complete cover-up."

Bolsein and Knolu looked up as the sector chief planted both hands on the table.

"Commander," he demanded, "are you giving me a story?" He looked at his subordinate sharply. "Commander Redendale always insisted that it frequently took cycles to cover up a planetary landing by Guard Units."

A-Riman nodded his head. "Sometimes it does," he admitted. "I'd rather not comment on the commander, sir. I inherited some very good people from him." He touched the side of his face. "So good," he added, "that they went into this planet without more than ten people seeing them. They staged a minor barroom brawl, picked up their subjects, and were gone without any contact with the planetary authorities.

"I have ordered the sergeant in charge of the section to report to me this afternoon," he added. "I believe he and his entire section are due for a commendation on the operation. When I get through congratulating them, I'm going to order them back to clear up the rather unsavory mess our subjects left for them."

Dal-Kun grunted. "You didn't inherit anything from Redendale but trouble," he announced. "Those people of yours either just came in from other sectors or were trained by previous commanders." The admiral glanced down at his plates distastefully, then punched a button for their removal.

"Redendale was here for less than a cycle," he continued. "I had him transferred because I wasn't sure he was the man for the job. Now, I'm almost sorry I didn't hold him for a Board." He leaned back, folding his arms.

"I believe, commander, that you said something about some experiments you wanted to make. As long as you can keep up with your routine like this, and you don't break any regulations, go ahead. Do you need any clearances?"

"Yes, sir," A-Riman told him. "I need planetfall clearance and at least a three-cycle occupation clearance for personnel on a primitive planet."

"For what reason?"

"General rehabilitation, sir. The civilization I have in mind is still in its infancy. Observer reports say that it is not a particularly desirable civilization, and I'd like to try a rehabilitation program.

"I feel that this civilization will either destroy itself in the near future, or force us to destroy it within five periods. I feel that, with proper supervision, it can be rebuilt into a useful, law-abiding culture, and one which will be a valuable addition to the Federation." He placed his hand on the table. "I feel we can do this without changing the basic characteristics of the civilization in question, and I feel that it is our Ethical duty to do so."

Dal-Kun looked at him thoughtfully. "I've read your 'Fighting Philosophy,' " he admitted, "but this is something new, isn't it?" He drummed on the table, then looked down the table. "Where are you going to get the personnel?"

"I can use existing CAC personnel for the first few cycles, sir, and possibly borrow a few men from the Fleets. After that, if the experiment shows promise, I will request additional agents."

"Do you think Operations will hold still for a further personnel requisition? You're a little fat right now."

"I know that, sir, but I hope to be able to show the desirability of my experiment before the ten-cycle survey. I should be able to establish a trend in eight cycles at the most."

"It'll be intensive work." The sector chief shook his head slowly, "About four thousand days to make noticeable changes in a planetary civilization which is at least that many cycles old." He looked at A-Riman searchingly. "Wonder if your people can swing it." Slowly, he nodded his head, then brought a hand down on the table. "Go ahead, commander. Try it. If you can show me convincing trends within six cycles, I'll keep the survey people off your back for another ten and let you build a case." He looked at the three officers for a moment, then abruptly got up and left the room.

Veldon Bolsein exhaled explosively. "Brother," he said, "what a bill of goods." He looked at A-Riman, smiling crookedly. "You better make good, Old Philosopher. If you muff this one, your name's not even 'Space Dust.' "

Knolu grinned. "The man's right," he announced. "Slip up, and the Old Man'll feed you to the matter converter in tiny chunks, then he'll resynthesize you to make a new pair of shoes."

A-Riman nodded. "I know," he told them. "I came here to try this, though, and I'm going to do it." He eyed the other two seriously for a moment. "If I mess this up," he added, "the Old Man'll have to do some delicate filtering to find enough of me to feed the converter with." He started for the door.

"See you," he called back. "I've got me a job of work to do."

Quel-tze, high priest of Gundar, Lord of the Sky, stood at the altar atop the temple of Dolezin. He looked skyward, estimating the time needed for Gundar to mount to his zenith, for it was nearly time for the sacrifice. The bright sun shone out of a cloudless sky on the spectacle. The large altar of white, polished stone reflected the light dazzlingly, causing the under-priests to avert their eyes from its surface. The shadow of the ring atop the pinnacle of the temple slowly approached the altar.

Quel-tze glanced about him at his priests, making a last-minute check to see that all was in order. The five were at their proper stations, their regalia in proper order, reflecting the light of Gundar with the proper glory. One of them held the large golden bowl, another, the long sacrificial knife. The others were properly placed to strap the sacrifice into position with a minimum of lost motion. The high priest looked out over the city, where a sea of upturned faces greeted him. Good enough—all the populace were present.

The shadow started to mount the altar and Quel-tze made a sign behind his back, reaching for the knife with his other hand. A sonorous chant started from the level below and before the altar. The walls of this level, cut into a reflector, projected the chant out over the waiting people, and prevented more than a low murmur to reach the priests of the altar. The hymn to the Sun flooded the city of Dolezin to the exclusion of other sounds.

From the shadowed doorway behind the altar, two powerfully built priests came, holding the arms of a feebly protesting girl. Two more priests followed them. As she looked at the waiting altar, the girl's eyes widened, and her mouth opened.

"Silence, my child," instructed Quel-tze. "You are being honored beyond all other women of the city."

"I don't want to be honored," sobbed the girl. "I want to go home."

The high priest smiled thinly. "That cannot be, my daughter," he said.

He nodded to two priests behind the girl, who quickly removed the ceremonial kilt and the heavy breastplates and collar which she wore. They laid these aside and, grasping her ankles, they assisted the two who held her arms as they laid her quickly on the altar. The priests waiting at the altar quickly adjusted the straps to wrists and ankles so that the girl lay helpless on the altar, facing the sky and Gundar. She closed her eyes against the glare and screamed.

Below, the chanting voices harmonized with the scream, the basses weaving a slow, rhythmic pattern with the high, terrorized ululations.

The shadow of the great ring crept slowly along the girl's body, the brilliant disk of light within it approaching the breast.

Quel-tze raised both hands and gazed upward in a gesture of supplication. Below, the chorus chanted, "Grant, O Great Gundar, that our crops be fertile, that our ventures be successful."

The disk of light crept to the breasts. Quel-tze brought the knife down in a swift arc, ending at the center of the disk. Then, he made a rapid incision, the blade making a tearing noise as it progressed. The body of the girl twitched, then lay quietly. Now, the chant softened, and was still.

Reaching down, Quel-tze grasped the still feebly pulsing heart of the Harvest Maiden, cut it free with a few skillful slashes of the knife, and held it aloft for a moment before he handed it to one of the attendant priests. He held his hands up once more.

"The Harvest Maiden has gone to the realm of the Lord of the Sky," he declaimed. "Her pure spirit will assure us of plenty in the year to come."

A sigh arose from the onlookers below. Slowly, they started to disperse to their homes. On the outskirts of the crowd, an elderly man slowly led his obviously heartbroken wife away.

Quel-tze turned and made his way down the stairs to his apartment. As usual, he felt tired—emotionally spent—after the exhilaration of the sacrificial moment. This girl had been of striking beauty, he realized, but there were plenty of these.

He made a gesture of dismissal to his attendant priests and entered his rooms. He closed the door and took a few steps toward his sleeping room.

"Well," commented a voice, "our boy's come to us, all in one piece."

Quel-tze turned to the door, but a man stood before it. He was a large man, dressed in unrelieved black, from which blazed small insignia. In his hand, he held a small instrument. Somehow, the manner in which he held this unfamiliar object made Quel-tze realize that here was a weapon which could easily prevent any effort of his to approach its holder. He turned again.

Now, where before there had been merely a vacant space, stood another man. This one was dressed in the ceremonial robes of the high priest of Gundar—Quel-tze's robes. He, also, held one of the small objects.

"They can't talk to you here," this man explained, "so I'm going to stand in for you while you become educated and instructed in your duties."

It seemed to Quel-tze that the object in the pseudo high priest's hand glowed for an instant. Then, all became dark.

Slowly, consciousness returned to Quel-tze. First, he was aware of the sounds of conversation about him, then of light, then of the straps which held him in his chair. Angrily, he strained at these bonds.

"You'll suffer for this," he threatened. "When I am missed—"

He was interrupted. A man in black uniform came into his field of vision. "Afraid you're wrong, baby," he said. "First, you won't be missed. Second, your world is far behind us." He stepped aside, waving to a screen, which lit up, showing small points of light in a black void. "That little one over there," he explained, pointing, "is your 'Lord of the Sky.' "

He turned again, smiling at Quel-tze. "Third," he added, "your re-education is about to begin." Again, he gestured to the screen.

"Many thousands of cycles ago," said a calm voice, "suns shone on their planets much as they do now. The planets were hardly more than cinders, but on scores of them were the faint stirrings of life."

Quel-tze felt a strong mental compulsion which forced him to look at the screen closely, to become part of it, to take up every bit of the offered information and absorb it into his awareness.

On the screen, the field of view narrowed, to show a single sun, with its planets, then one planet gradually filled the screen, its surface details becoming plain to see.

The lesson continued step by step. Quel-tze saw the beginnings of life. He saw the rising of life forms, then the beginnings of civilization. He was fed. He slept. The lessons continued.

Civilizations rose and flourished. Some declined and fell. The voice pointed out the reasons for their successes and their failures. As Quel-tze watched, a civilization reached peaks of technical and mechanical ability almost beyond his comprehension. The people of the planet traveled into space, reached for the stars, then, turning again to their old, internecine struggles, destroyed the results of centuries of slow development in a few short, blazing weeks. A few dazed survivors sadly picked over the wreckage of their once powerful, luxurious world. Their descendants reverted to savagery, then slowly began the laborious climb to civilization. Quel-tze shuddered—tried to shut the images from his mind—but always at the threshold of his consciousness was the almost inaudible, but powerful command: "Learn, for only by learning will you survive."

On the screen, the civilization was rebuilding, its development accelerating as it progressed. Again, this planet reached to space—successfully, this time. Other solar systems were reached. Interstellar conquest began, and Quel-tze watched the building of an interstellar empire. He also saw destruction, as civilizations crumbled to ruins, then to complete obliteration before the weapons of implacable conquerors.

The tone of the instruction changed. Before, the emphasis had been on the technologies of the subject civilizations. This second phase of his instruction was focused upon the growth of custom, of ethics, and of law. Again, the civilizations were on the march, their legal, ethical, and religious structures laid bare for observation. Cultures were traced, their oscillations—from high, super morality to definite immorality, to high morality again—becoming obvious under the quiet analysis of the teacher. Some of these systems of life led to decline and fall, others to sudden, blazing extinction. Several of them were successful, and were still extant in the galaxy. The basic framework of the Galactic Federation was exposed, and Quel-tze saw how multitudes of worlds, inhabited by varying peoples of widely varying origins, differing physical shapes, bodily chemistry, and mentalities, could live in harmony and complete tolerance.

On one world, he saw a quiet, pastoral people, tending to their own business. Here was civilization which was fully cognizant of the high technology surrounding it, but which preferred to pursue its own quiet ways of life. Quel-tze came to the realization that in the eyes of the rest of the Federation, this technically undeveloped civilization was recognized as an equal. In the council, delegates from this world were received with respect when they voiced their opinions. Further, it was pointed out, the people of this world were by no means all indigenous. Numbers of them were natives of worlds far removed in space, and of totally differing original cultural pattern. Quel-tze also noted that in several cases, the ships flitting about in space actually formed cultures of their own. There were Federation members who rarely set foot upon any planet, and then not for long. Yet, these wanderers, too, were regarded as equals. They had their voice in the council, and contributed to the welfare and development of the Galactic Civilization in their own way.

The screen cleared. Again, dead planets circled a brilliant sun. Life stirred. Life forms grew and developed. One of these became predominant and formed a civilization, which slowly grew, rose, and flourished in its way. Quel-tze stirred uneasily. This was a familiar pattern. He examined the ethical structure, realizing that it was very familiar indeed. A religion came into power, superseding the power of state and of the people. The Sun became the "Lord of all Creation." Ceremonies were instituted, and the priesthood of the Sun gradually took over the reins of actual power, though none outside the temple realized what was actually happening. Quel-tze shook his head. He had seen similar patterns in previously analyzed civilizations, and the result had been invariable—decline, failure, fall or destruction.

Quel-tze squirmed in his chair as the account went on. A minor government official was proving to be unexpectedly and annoyingly honest. Despite veiled warnings from visiting priests and from some of his own associates, he refused steadfastly to condone and allow certain lucrative practices. Finally, the Temple acted. The daughter of the annoying officer was chosen for the annual sacrifice.

As the ceremony went on, the analytic voice detailed motives, reasons, probable consequences. Other similar situations were recalled. Quel-tze shuddered, and as the climax of the ceremony occurred, he strained at his bonds for a moment, then collapsed in the chair.

Two men hurried to his side. One applied a small instrument to his throat, listened for a moment, then nodded.

"Close, sergeant," he remarked, "but he's still with us."

He made an injection in the high priest's arm and stood back.

Again, consciousness slowly returned to Quel-tze. This time, the room was silent. For a moment, madness crept into his eyes, then, he sat back quietly and waited for the screen to light up again. Nothing happened.

"You may continue with my education, gentlemen," remarked Quel-tze calmly. "I am ready again."

The black uniformed psychologist came into his field of vision. He looked closely at the captive, then smiled at him. Bending over him, he loosened the confining straps.

"I think you are, Quel-tze," he answered. "Would you like to meet your fellow students?"

Quel-tze nodded wordlessly, then stood, flexing his muscles. He looked about the room for a moment, then followed the two guardsmen into the next compartment, where several people waited. One man came forward as the priest entered.

"Quel-tze," he said, holding out his hand. "A few days ago I hated you, but now, I think I can work with you."

Quel-tze raised his own hand. For a moment, the two men stood, hands on each other's shoulders. "I'm sorry, Tal-Quor," said the priest.

"I was at fault, too," the other admitted. "Had it been someone else's daughter, I would have remained undisturbed."

A trill of silvery laughter sounded through the room. "It was all an illusion," announced a girlish voice. "This year, the Harvest Maiden was a large swamp lizard."

Somone called "Attention." Sector Chief Dal-Kun walked to the front of the room, looked at the twenty officers, then nodded.

"At ease, gentlemen," he ordered. "We seldom have a full staff meeting here, but Commander A-Riman has a report which should be of interest to all of us. I would like to have comments when it is completed. Commander A-Riman."

The CAC Commander faced the group. "As many of you gentlemen know," he began, "CAC has been engaged in an experiment for the past five cycles. The Criminal Apprehension personnel, as well as many of the Combat personnel, have become extremely interested in this experiment, and most of them have worked much more than normal time on it. With the co-operation of the sector comptroller"—A-Riman nodded to an elderly officer—"we have written off a good deal of our time to training. We think this time has not been wasted. I believe you gentlemen will agree after reviewing this report." A-Riman bowed slightly and took a seat.

The lights dimmed and the viewscreen lit up. A solar system appeared as seen from an approaching ship. One planet crept to the center of the screen and grew larger. The voice of an observer came from the speaker.

"This is the seventh planet of Sun Frank Three, number six two nine, Tenth Sector. Life has been in existence here for at least a thousand periods. The age of the present dominant civilization is estimated at seven periods."

The screen closed in, to show details of cities. Conversations between members of the populace were repeated. The thoughts and actions of officials were shown. The growth of cruelty in government, in private life, in the temple, was shown, as was the appearance of immorality and of human sacrifice. Finally, detailed scenes of the Harvest Maiden sacrifice appeared. The voice broke in again.

"As can be seen, this civilization has a high probability of failure. It will stagnate and eventually be eliminated, either by another civilization not yet formed, or by Federation Council orders, if it progresses far enough to warrant that attention." There was a pause. The screen showed an overall view of a large city, its buildings gleaming in the sun. "This is the civilization picked for initial experiment," added the voice.

The abduction of Quel-tze and his companions was shown.

Scenes of their training appeared in brief flashes, then their return to their own world was shown. The reforms instituted by these people began to appear, one scene showing Quel-tze as he faced six councilors of the Kelmiran Empire. One of them was speaking.

"This tampering with the time-honored ceremonies of our religion will not be tolerated," he announced.

"I thought I was the high priest," objected Quel-tze mildly.

The councilor looked at him scornfully. "You should know, priest, that your temple has always been the creature of the state. We give the orders—you merely furnish the cloak of sanctity."

"This borders upon sacrilege," remarked the priest.

"This is merely practical government," snorted the councilor. "Now, for the last time, will you accept our nomination for the Harvest Maiden?"

Quel-tze smiled gently. "As I said before," he insisted, "the Harvest Ceremony is being changed to conform with the ceremony of many years ago, before the age of cruelty and immorality. The altar has been removed."

The councilor's mouth tightened. "Then, you force us to act," he growled with a gesture of finality. For a moment, he stood looking at the high priest, then he turned. "Guards," he called, "arrest this man for treason."

A group of armed priests stepped into the room. The councilors looked at them in puzzlement.

"These," explained Quel-tze calmly, "are my guards. Yours are in the temple dungeons, where you will soon join them." He looked at the leader of the priestly warriors. "Take them below, Qual-mar. They will await a Temple Trial for Sacrilege."

The six councilors blanched. "The emperor—" one of them quavered.

Again, Quel-tze smiled. "The emperor," he told them, "is receiving a priestly delegation. I might add that it is a much more effective delegation than yours. No threats will be made, no violence will be offered, but tomorrow, the emperor will find it expedient to appoint new councilors."

Further scenes showed the operations of the new Imperial Council. The final scene showed the Harvest Maiden, standing proudly atop the temple at Dolezin. She had reason to be proud, for she had been chosen from all the young girls of the city as the most beautiful, the most talented, of all. By her side stood a prize draft animal, which would be later used in the Imperial stables. In her hands, she held the best of the year's crop. Below her, the priests chanted. It was the same hymn to the Sun, but now it was slightly muted, and the clear, high voice of the Harvest Maiden could be plainly heard, leading the melody. The voice broke in again.

"Probable success is now indicated for this culture. Considerable supervision must be given for at least a period, but it is believed that the civilization will now progress to become a valued member of the Federation."

The lights brightened. Commander A-Riman stood again. "Gentlemen," he said, "this is the report on the first five cycles of this experiment. You have seen most of the steps taken. Of course, we forced this process somewhat to prove our point in a short space of time. I believe further activity of this type should take place at a more leisurely pace, but we think we have shown a desirable result. Are there any comments?"

Geronor Keldon, the sector comptroller, stood. "Gentlemen," he said, "I will admit that I authorized the utilization of Commander A-Riman's personnel on this experiment with some misgivings. Now that I've seen the results, I have no further objections to continuation."

Several other officers added their remarks. Most of them were laudatory. A few expressed regret that they had not been involved in the operation. Finally, Dal-Kun got to his feet.

"Well," he remarked, looking about the room, "it seems that the report has met with general favor. I would like formal reports of your reactions, and any suggestions as to improvement. I feel that this report, with recommendations should be presented to the Federation Council for consideration." Again, he looked about the room. "This meeting is adjourned."

A-Riman switched off the report as the buzzer sounded. The screen lit up and his secretary's face appeared.

"Who is it?" queried the commander.

"Captain Poltar, sir."

"Put him on."

The captain's face was slightly amused as he appeared on the screen. "The new personnel just came in, sir," he announced. "Do you want to see them now?"

A-Riman dropped the report recordings into their cases. "Send them in," he instructed. "How do they look to you?"

"Pretty good, sir." Again, the expression of secret amusement crossed the captain's face. It annoyed A-Riman slightly.

"What's so funny, captain?" he demanded.

"Nothing important, sir. I'll send in the first one now."

"Bring him in personally," growled his superior. "Then, we'll both be able to enjoy the joke." He switched off and waited. There must be something very strange about this new batch of personnel to make Poltar laugh. A-Riman couldn't remember too many times that officer had even smiled.

He pressed the admittance button at the signal, and the captain walked in. "Here's the first one, sir," he said, stepping aside.

A guardsman entered. He held his head directly to the front, paying no attention to the furnishings of the office. Pacing off the prescribed two paces with mathematical precision, he halted and came to a rigid salute. A-Riman's practiced eyes took in the man's entire appearance at a glance. He was freshly uniformed. No spot of light reflected from the absolute, dead blackness of his clothing, excepting where the iridescent glow of the torches at his collar picked up the light and broke it into a blazing spectrum.

"Junior Search Technician Manir Kal reporting for duty, sir," the man reported. He dropped his hand sharply, standing at perfect attention.

"At ease, guardsman," said A-Riman. "Haven't I seen you before?"

"Yes, sir," the man replied. "I've been here before."

"I remember," commented the group commander dryly. He fixed Captain Poltar with a mildly scornful look. "It's happened before," he remarked. "What's funny?"

"There's more to it, sir," grinned Poltar. He moved to the door and beckoned. Another guardsman entered and stood at salute.

"Junior Psychologist Barc Kor Delthos reporting for duty, sir."

"Well, well," commented A-Riman. "Any more?"

"Three more, sir," said Poltar. "A physicist, a trend analyst, and a pilot."

A-Riman's face broke into a grin, then he sat back and laughed. "All right," he admitted. "You've scored. Bring 'em in and send for Sergeant Kembar."

Three more men filed in, reported, and stepped to the side. A-Riman looked at them severely. "Now," he inquired, "just who dreamed up this idea?"

Manir Kal raised a hand. "I'm afraid I did, sir," he admitted. "Of course, Senior Rehabilitation Technician Kwybold had something to do with it, too."

A-Riman nodded. "I thought I recognized his delicate touch," he commented. "How was rehabilitation?"

Manir Kal grimaced. "I spent a good share of it in the hospital, sir." He rubbed his chest reflectively. "I can name at least twenty guardsmen who can beat me at swordplay. They all tried it." He paused for a moment. "I learned plenty, though," he added. "I've an idea I could give Sergeant Kembar a hard time now."

"Want the opportunity?" A-Riman smiled at him.

Manir Kal shook his head. "Thank you, sir, no," he said decidedly. "Next time I unsheath a sword, it'll be in line of duty. It's part of my business now, and I'm not giving out any free samples of my swordsmanship."

Sergeant Kembar came into the office. A-Riman caught him on the first pace. "At ease, sergeant." He waved a hand. "Here are five more men for you."

"Thank you, sir. I'm a little short-handed right now." Kembar looked toward the five guardsmen. "I'll get their—" he looked again, then stared directly at Manir Kal. "I've met you before," he stated positively. Then, he looked at the others.

"This one picks fights," stated Manir Kal expressionlessly.

"It runs after females," announced Barc.

"I'm the talented one," boasted Malon.

Kembar placed his hands on his hips, and shook his head helplessly. "All right," he chuckled, "so I know Rehabilitation, too. How do you think a lot of us got into this business?"

A-Riman coughed. "I've got news for you, sergeant," he said.

Master Search Technician Kembar snapped to attention. "Yes, sir."

"I know Mr. Kwybold, too." A-Riman told him. "A few thousand cycles ago, I led a revolution against the Federation Council."

Kilar Mar-Li arose slowly from his chair. As the senior delegate from Celstor, he realized that his word carried weight. He also realized that this report and proposal was from a compatriot and protégé of his. He thought, however, that the report still warranted comment.

"Fellow members," he began, "we have just seen an interim report, and heard a proposal." He noticed smiles on the faces of several members and decided against too dignified an approach. He smiled, too. "Terrible introduction, I'll admit," he added, "but the fact remains that for the past four Galactic Standard Hours, we've been watching a report from Sector Ten. A new experiment has been tried, and I think it's worth following up. I would like to move that the council issue special authorization to Commander A-Riman to continue his operations."

A delegate from the comparatively new Paldorian Empire arose. "I would like to propose an amendment," he said, "to the effect that a motion be entered for the consideration of the delegate from the seventh planet, Sun Frank Three, number six two nine, Tenth Sector, for the establishment of a new corps in the Stellar Guard, this corps to be devoted to the education and, where necessary, the rehabilitation of new cultures over the entire galaxy."

The chairman laughed. "I might remind the delegate," he commented, "that it may be a couple of thousand Standard Cycles before that still unborn gentleman takes his seat."

Mar-Li arose again. "I accept the amendment," he remarked. "The Federation has waited for more than a thousand periods for this experiment to begin. We can wait for two or three more periods to see its results. I predict that many of us here will be present to welcome the new delegate to his seat."

Marzold Quonzar, first delegate to the Federation Council from the newly admitted Gundarian Association, blinked his eyes as the lights came on.

"So that's the true story," he mused. For a few minutes he sat thinking, then he called his secretary.

"Write a motion for consideration of the Federation Council. Title it 'A proposal for the formation of a new corps in the Stellar Guard.' You can word most of it, of course." He paused. "Let me see," he reflected. "That Commander was nicknamed 'The Fighting Philosopher.'" He nodded his head. "We will recommend as a name for this new organization 'The Philosophical Corps.'"

Honorable Enemies

by *Poul Anderson*

1

The door swung open behind him and a voice murmured gently, "Good evening, Captain Flandry."

He spun around, grabbing for his stun pistol in a wild reflex, and found himself looking down the muzzle of a blaster. Slowly, then, he let his hands fall and stood taut, his eyes searching beyond the weapon, and the slender six-fingered hand that held it, to the tall gaunt body and the sardonically smiling face behind.

The face was humanoid—lean, hawk-nosed, golden-skinned, with brilliant amber eyes under feathery blue brows, and a high crest of shining blue feathers rising from the narrow hairless skull. The being was dressed in the simple white tunic of his people, leaving his clawed avian feet bare, but there were insignia of rank bejeweled around his neck and a cloak like a gush of blood from his wide shoulders. A Merseian.

But they'd all been occupied elsewhere—Flandry had seen to that. What had slipped up—?

With an effort, Flandry relaxed and let a wry smile cross his face. Never mind who was to blame; he was trapped in the Merseian chambers and had to think of a way to escape with a whole skin. His mind whirred with thought. Memory came—this was Aycharaych of Chereion, who had come to join the Merseian embassy only a few days before, presumably on some mission corresponding to Flandry's.

"Pardon the intrusion," he said; "it was purely professional. No offense meant."

"And none taken," said Aycharaych politely. He spoke fault-less Anglic, only the faintest hint of his race's harsh accent in the syllables. But courtesy between spies was meaningless. It would be too easy to blast down the intruder and later express his immense regret that he had shot down the ace intelligence officer of the Terrestrial Empire under the mistaken impression that it was a burglar.

Somehow, though, Flandry didn't think that the Chereionite would be guilty of such crudeness. His mysterious people were too old, too coldly civilized, and Aycharaych himself had too great a reputation for subtlety. Flandry had heard of him before; he would be planning something worse.

"That is quite correct," nodded Aycharaych. Flandry started—could the being guess his exact thoughts? "But if you will pardon my saying so, you yourself have committed a bit of clumsiness in trying to search our quarters. There are better ways of getting information."

Flandry gauged distances and angles. There was a vase on a table close to hand. If he could grab it up and throw it at Aycharaych's gun hand—

The blaster waved negligently. "I would advise against the attempt," said the Chereionite.

He stood aside. "Good evening, Captain Flandry," he said.

The Terran moved toward the door. He couldn't let himself be thrown out this way, not when his whole mission depended on finding out what the Merseians were up to. If he could make a sudden lunge as he passed close—

He threw himself sideways with a twisting motion that brought him under the blaster muzzle. Hampered by a greater gravity than the folk of his small planet were used to, Aycharaych couldn't dodge quickly enough. But he swung the blaster with a vicious precision across Flandry's jaw. The Terran stumbled, clasping the Chereionite's narrow waist. Aycharaych slugged him at the base of the skull and he fell to the floor.

He lay there a moment, gasping, blood running from his face. Aycharaych's voice jeered at him from a roaring darkness: "Really, Captain Flandry, I had thought better of you. Now please leave."

Sickly, the Terran crawled to his feet and went out the door. Aycharaych stood in the entrance watching him go, a faint smile on his hard, gaunt visage.

Flandry went down endless corridors of polished stone to the suite given the Terrestrial mission. Most of them were at the feast; the ornate rooms stood almost empty. He threw himself into a chair and signaled his personal slave for a drink. A stiff one.

There was a light step and the suggestive whisper of a long silkite skirt behind him. He looked around and saw Aline Chang-Lei, the Lady Marr of Syrtis, his partner on the mission and one of Sol's loveliest women—as well as one of its top field agents for intelligence.

She was tall and slender, dark of hair and eye, with the high cheekbones and ivory skin of a mixed heritage such as most Terrans showed these days; her sea-blue gown did little more than emphasize the appropriate features. Flandry liked to look at her, though he was pretty well immune to beautiful women by now.

"What was the trouble?" she asked at once.

"What brings you here?" he responded. "I thought you'd be at the party, helping distract everyone."

"I just wanted to rest for a while," she said. "Official functions at Sol get awfully dull and stuffy, but they go to the other extreme at Betelgeuse. I wanted to hear silence for a while." And then, with grave concern: "But you ran into trouble."

"How the hell it happened, I can't imagine," said Flandry. "Look—we prevailed on the Sartaz to throw a brawl with everybody invited. We made double sure that every Merseian on the planet would be there. They'd trust to their robolocks to keep their quarters safe—they have absolutely no way of knowing that I've found a way to nullify a robolock. So what happens? I no sooner get inside than Aycharaych of Chereion walks in with a blaster in his hot little hand. He anticipates everything I try and finally shows me the door. Finish."

"Aycharaych—I've heard the name somewhere. But it doesn't sound Merseian."

"It isn't. Chereion is an obscure but very old planet in the Merseian Empire. Its people have full citizenship with the dominant race, just as our empire grants Terrestrial citizenship to many nonhumans. Aycharaych is one of Merseia's leading intelligence agents. Few people have heard of him, precisely because he is so good. I've never clashed with him before, though."

"I know whom you mean now," she nodded. "If he's as you say, and he's here on Alfzar, it isn't good news."

Flandry shrugged. "We'll just have to take him into account, then. As if this mission weren't tough enough!"

He got up and walked to the balcony window. The two moons of Alfzar were up, pouring coppery light on the broad reach of the palace gardens. The warm wind blew in with scent of strange flowers that had never bloomed under Sol and they caught the faint sound of the weird, tuneless music which the monarch of Betelgeuse favored.

For a moment, as he looked at the ruddy moonlight and the thronging stars, Flandry felt a wave of discouragement. The Galaxy was too big. Even the four million stars of the Terrestrial Empire were too many for one man ever to know in a lifetime. And there were the rival imperia out in the darkness of space, Gorrazan and Ythri and Merseia, like a hungry beast of prey—

Too much, too much. The individual counted for too little in the enormous chaos which was modern civilization. He thought of Aline—it was her business to know who such beings as Aycharaych were, but one human skull couldn't hold a universe; knowledge and power were lacking.

Too many mutually alien races; too many forces clashing in space, and so desperately few who comprehended the situation and tried their feeble best to help—naked hands battering at an avalanche as it ground down on them.

Aline came over and took his arm. Her white lovely face turned up to his, vague in the moonlight, with a look he knew too well. He'd have to avoid her, when or if they got back to Terra; he didn't want to hurt her, but neither could he be tied to any single human.

"You're discouraged with one failure?" she asked lightly. "Dominic Flandry, the single-handed conqueror of Scothania, worried by one skinny bird-being?"

"I just don't see how he knew I was going to search his place," muttered Flandry. "I've never been caught that way before, not even when I was the worst cub in the Service. Some of our best men have gone down before Aycharaych. I'm convinced MacMurtrie's disappearance at Polaris was his work. Maybe it's our turn now."

"Oh, come off it," she laughed. "You must have been drinking *sorgan* when they told you about him."

"*Sorgan?*" His brows lifted.

"Ah, now I can tell you something you don't know." She was trying desperately hard to be gay. "Not that it's very important; I only happened to hear of it while talking with one of the Alfzarian narcotics detail. It's just a drug produced on one of the planets here—Cingetor, I think—with the curious property of depressing certain brain centers such that the victim loses all critical sense. He has absolute faith in whatever he's told.''

"Hm. Could be useful in our line of work."

"Not very. Hypnoprobes are better for interrogation, and there are more reliable ways of producing fanatics. The drug has an antidote which also confers permanent immunity. So it's not much use, really, and the Sartaz has suppressed its manufacture."

"I should think our Intelligence would like to keep a little on hand, just in case," he said thoughtfully. "And of course certain nobles in all the empires, our included, would find it handy for purposes of seduction."

"What *are* you thinking of?" she teased him.

"Nothing; I don't need it," he said smugly.

The digression had shaken him out of his dark mood. "Come on," he said. "Let's go join the party."

She went along at his side. There was a speculative look about her.

2

Usually the giant stars have many planets, and Betelgeuse, with forty-seven, is no exception. Of these, six have intelligent native races, and the combined resources of the whole system are considerable, even in a civilization used to thinking in terms of thousands of stars.

When the first Terrestrial explorers arrived, almost a thousand years previously, they found that the people of Alfzar had already mastered interplanetary travel and were in the process of conquering the other worlds—a process speeded up by their rapid adoption of the more advanced human technology. However, they had not attempted to establish an empire on the scale of Sol or Merseia, contenting themselves with maintaining hegemony over enough neighbor suns to protect themselves. There had been clashes with the expanding powers around them, but generations of wily Sartazes had found it profitable to play their potential enemies off against each other; and the great states had, in turn, found it expedient to maintain Betelgeuse as a buffer against their rivals and against the peripheral barbarians.

But the gathering tension between Terra and Merseia had raised Betelgeuse to a position of critical importance. Lying squarely between the two great empires, she was in a position

with her powerful fleet to command the most direct route between them and, if allied with either one, to strike at the heart of
the other. If Merseia could get the alliance, it would very
probably be the last preparation she considered necessary for war
with Terra. If Terra could get it, Merseia would suddenly be in a
deteriorated position and would almost have to make concessions.

So both empires had missions on Alfzar trying to persuade the
Sartaz of the rightness of their respective causes and the immense profits to be had by joining. Pressure was being applied
wherever possible; officials were lavishly bribed; spies were
swarming through the system getting whatever information they
could and—of course—being immediately disowned by their
governments if they were caught.

It was normal diplomatic procedure, but its critical importance
had made the Service send two of its best agents, Flandry and
Aline, to Betelgeuse to do what they could in persuading the
Sartaz, finding out his weaknesses, and throwing as many mon-
key wrenches as possible into the Merseian activities. Aline was
especially useful in working on the many humans who had
settled in the system long before and become citizens of the
kingdom—quite a few of them held important positions in the
government and the military. Flandry—

And now, it seemed, Merseia had called in *her* top spy, and
the subtle, polite, and utterly deadly battle was on.

The Sartaz gave a hunting party for his distinguished guests. It
pleased his sardonic temperament to bring enemies together under conditions where they had to be friendly to each other. Most
of the Merseians must have been pleased, too; hunting was their
favorite sport. The more citified Terrestrials were not at all
happy about it, but they could hardly refuse.

Flandry was especially disgruntled at the prospect. He had
never cared for physical exertion, though he kept his wiry body
in trim as a matter of necessity. And he had too much else to do.

Too many things were going disastrously wrong. The network
of agents, both Imperial and bribed Betelgeusean—who ultimately were under his command—were finding the going suddenly rugged. One after another, they disappeared; they walked
into Merseian or Betelgeusean traps; they found their best ap-
proaches blocked by unexpected watchfulness. Flandry couldn't
locate the source of the difficulty, but since it had begun with
Aycharaych's arrival, he could guess. The Chereionite was too

damned smart to be true. Sunblaze, it just wasn't possible that anyone could have known about those Jurovian projects, or that Yamatsu's hiding place should have been discovered, or— And now this damned hunting party! Flandry groaned.

His slave roused him in the dawn. Mist, tinged with blood by the red sun, drifted through the high windows of his suite. Someone was blowing a horn somewhere, a wild call in the vague mysterious light, and he heard the growl of engines warming up.

"Sometimes," he muttered sourly, "I feel like going to the Emperor and telling him where to put our beloved Empire."

Breakfast made the universe slightly more tolerable. Flandry dressed with his usual finicky care; an ornate suit of skin-tight green and a golden cloak with hood and goggles, hung a needle gun and dueling sword at his waist, and let the slave trim his reddish-brown mustache to the micrometric precision he demanded. Then he went down long flights of marble stairs, past royal guards in helmet and corselet, to the courtyard.

The hunting party was gathering. The Sartaz himself was present, a typical Alfzarian humanoid—short, stocky, hairless, blue-skinned, with huge yellow eyes in the round, blunt-faced head. There were other nobles of Alfzar and its fellow planets, more guardsmen, a riot of color in the brightening dawn. There were the other members of the regular Terrestrial embassy and the special mission, a harried and unhappy-looking crew. And there were the Merseians.

Flandry gave them all formal greetings—after all, Terra and Merseia were nominally at peace, however many men were being shot and cities burned on the marches. His gray eyes looked sleepy and indifferent, but they missed no detail of the enemy's appearance.

The Merseian nobles glanced at him with the thinly covered contempt they had for all humans. They were mammals, but with more traces of reptilian ancestry in them than Terrans showed. A huge-thewed two meters they stood, with a spiny ridge running from forehead to the end of the long, thick tail which they could use to such terrible effect in hand-to-hand battle. Their hairless skins were pale green, faintly scaled, but their massive faces were practically human. Arrogant black eyes under heavy brow ridges met Flandry's gaze with a challenge.

I can understand that they despise us, he thought. *Their civilization is young and vigorous, its energies turned ruthlessly*

*outward; Terra is old, satiated—decadent. Our whole policy is
directed toward maintaining the Galactic status quo, not because
we love peace but because we're comfortable the way things are.
We stand in the way of Merseia's dream of an all-embracing
Galactic empire. We're the first ones they have to smash.*

*I wonder—historically, they may be on the right side. But
Terra has seen too much bloodshed in her history, has too wise
and weary a view of life. We've given up seeking perfection and
glory; we've learned that they're chimerical—but that knowledge
is a kind of death within us.*

*Still—I certainly don't want to see planets aflame and humans
enslaved and an alien culture taking up the future. Terra is
willing to compromise; but the only compromise Merseia will
ever make is with overwhelming force. Which is why I'm here.*

There was a stir in the streaming red mist, and Aycharaych's
tall form was beside him. The Chereionite's lean face smiled
amiably at him. "Good morning, Captain Flandry," he said.

"Oh—good morning," said Flandry, starting. The avian un-
nerved him. For the first time, he had met his professional
superior, and he didn't like it.

But he couldn't help liking Aycharaych personally. As they
stood waiting, they fell to talking of Polaris and its strange
worlds, from which the conversation drifted to the comparative
"Anthropology" of intelligent primitives throughout the Galaxy.
Aycharaych had a vast fund of knowledge and a wry humor
matching Flandry's. When the horn blew for assembly, they
exchanged the regretful glance of brave enemies. *It's too bad we
have to be on opposite sides. If things had been different—*

But they weren't.

The hunters strapped themselves into their tiny one-man airjets.
There was a needle-beam projector in the nose of each one, not
too much armament when you hunted the Borthudian dragons.
Flandry thought that the Sartaz would be more than pleased if the
game disposed of one or more of his guests.

The squadron lifted into the sky and streaked northward for
the mountains. Fields and forests lay in dissolving fog below
them, and the enormous red disc of Betelgeuse was rising into a
purplish sky. Despite himself, Flandry enjoyed the reckless speed
and the roar of cloven air around him. It was godlike, this
rushing over the world to fight the monsters at its edge.

In a couple of hours, they raised the Borthudian mountains,
gaunt windy peaks rearing into the upper sky, the snow on their

flanks like blood in the ominous light. Signals began coming over the radio; scouts had spotted dragons here and there, and jet after jet broke away to pursue them. Presently Flandry found himself alone with one other vessel.

As they hummed over fanged crags and swooping canyons, he saw two shadows rise from the ground and his belly muscles tightened. Dragons!

The monsters were a good ten meters of scaled, snakelike length, with jaws and talons to rend steel. Huge leathery wings bore them aloft, riding the wind with lordly arrogance as they hunted the great beasts that terrorized villagers but were their prey.

Flandry kicked over his jet and swooped for one of them. It grew monstrously in his sights; he caught the red glare of its eyes as it banked to meet him. No running away here; the dragons had never learned to be afraid. It rose against him.

He squeezed his trigger and a thin sword of energy leaped out to burn past the creature's scales into its belly. The dragon held to its collision course. Flandry rolled out of its way; the mighty wings clashed meters from him.

He had not allowed for the tail. It swung savagely, and the blow shivered the teeth in his skull. The airjet reeled and went into a spin. The dragon swooped down on it, and the terrible claws ripped through the thin hull.

Wildly, Flandry slammed over his controls, tearing himself loose. He barrel-rolled, metal screaming as he swung about to meet the charge. His needle beam lashed into the open jaws and the dragon stumbled in midflight. Flandry pulled away and shot again, flaying one of the wings.

He could hear the dragon's scream. It rushed straight at him, swinging with fantastic speed and precision as he sought to dodge. The jaws snapped together and a section of hull skin was torn from the framework. Wind came in to sear the man with numbing cold.

Recklessly, he dove to meet the plunging monster, his beam before him like a lance. The dragon recoiled. With a savage grin, Flandry pursued, slashing and tearing.

The torn airjet handled clumsily. In midflight, it lurched and the dragon was out of his sights. Its wings buffeted him and he went spinning aside with the dragon after him.

The damned thing was forcing him toward the cragged mountainside. Its peaks reached hungrily after him, and the wind seemed to be a demon harrying him closer to disaster. He swung desperately, aware with sudden grimness that it had become a struggle for life with the odds on the dragon's side.

If this was the end, to be shattered against a mountain and eaten by his own quarry— He fought for control.

The dragon was almost on him, rushing down like a thunderbolt. It could survive a collision, but the jet would be knocked to earth. Flandry fired again, struggling to pull free. The dragon swerved and came on in the very teeth of his beam.

Suddenly it reeled and fell aside. The other jet was on it from behind, searing it with deadly precision. Flandry thought briefly that the remaining dragon must be dead or escaped and now its hunter had come to his aid—all the gods bless him, whoever he was!

Even as he watched, the dragon fell to death, writhing and snapping as it died. It crashed onto a ledge and lay still.

Flandry brought his jet to a landing nearby. He was shaking with reaction, but his chief emotion was a sudden overwhelming sadness. There went another brave creature down into darkness, wiped out by a senseless history that seemed only to have the objective of destroying. He raised a hand in salute as he grounded.

The other jet had already landed a few meters off. As Flandry opened his cockpit canopy, its pilot stepped out.

Aycharaych.

The man's reaction was almost instantaneous. Gratitude and honor had no part in the grim code of Service—here was his greatest enemy, all unsuspecting, and it would be the simplest thing in the world to shoot him down. Aycharaych of Chereion, lost in a hunt for dangerous game, too bad—and remorse could come later, when there was time—

His needle pistol was halfway from the holster when Aycharaych's weapon was drawn. Through the booming wind, he heard the alien's quiet voice: "No."

He raised his own hands, and his smile was bitter. "Go ahead," he invited. "You've got the drop on me."

"Not at all," said Aycharaych. "Believe me, Captain Flandry, I will never kill you except in self-defense. But since I will always be forewarned of your plans, you may as well abandon them."

Flandry nodded, too weary to feel the shock of the tremendous revelation which was there. "Thanks," he said. "For saving my life, that is."

"You're too useful to die," replied Aycharaych candidly; "but I'm glad of it."

They took the dragon's head and flew slowly back toward the palace. Flandry's mind whirled with a gathering dismay.

There was only one way in which Aycharaych could have known of the murder plan, when it had sprung into instantaneous being. And that same fact explained how he knew of every activity and scheme the Terrestrials tried, and how he could frustrate every one of them while his own work went on unhampered.

Aycharaych could read minds.

3

Aline's face was white and tense in the red light that streamed into the room. "No," she whispered.

"Yes," said Flandry grimly. "It's the only answer."

"But telepathy—everyone knows its limitations—"

Flandry nodded. "The mental patterns of different races are so alien that a telepath who can sense them has to learn a different 'language' for every species—in fact, for every individual among nontelepathic peoples, whose minds, lacking mutual contact, develop purely personal thought-types. Even then it's irregular and unreliable. I've never let myself be studied by any telepath not on our side, so I'd always considered myself safe.

"But Chereion is a very old planet. Its people have the reputation among the more superstitious Merseians of being sorcerers. Actually, of course, it's simply that they've discovered certain things about the nervous system which nobody else suspects yet. Somehow, Aycharaych must be able to detect some underlying resonance-pattern common to all intelligent beings.

"I'm sure he can only read surface thoughts, those in the immediate consciousness. Otherwise he'd have found out so much from all the Terrans with whom he must have had contact that Merseia would be ruling Sol by now. But that's bad enough!"

Aline said drearily, "No wonder he spared your life; you've become the most valuable man on his side!"

"And not a thing I can do about it," said Flandry dully. "He sees me every day. I don't know what the range of his mind is—probably only a few meters; it's known that all mental pulses are weak and fade rapidly with distance. But in any case, every time he meets me he skims my mind, reads all my plans—I just can't help thinking about them all the time—and takes action to forestall them.''

"We'll have to get the Imperial scientists to work on a thought screen.''

"Of course. But that doesn't help us now.''

"Couldn't you just avoid him, stay in your rooms—''

"Sure. And become a complete cipher. I have to get around, see my agents and the rulers of Betelgeuse, learn facts and keep my network operating. And every single thing I learn is just so much work done for Aycharaych—with no effort on his part.'' Flandry puffed a cigarette into lighting and blew nervous clouds of smoke. "What to do, what to do?''

"Whatever we do,'' said Aline, "it has to be done fast. The Sartaz is getting more and more cool toward our people. While we blunder and fail, Aycharaych is working—bribing, blackmailing, influencing one key official after another. We'll wake up some fine morning to find ourselves under arrest and Betelgeuse the loyal ally of Merseia.''

"Fine prospect,'' said Flandry bitterly.

The waning red sunlight streamed through his windows, throwing pools of dried blood on the floor. The palace was quiet, the nobles resting after the hunt, the servants scurrying about preparing the night's feast. Flandry looked around at the weird decorations, at the unearthly light and the distorted landscape beyond the windows. Strange world under a strange sun, and himself the virtual prisoner of its alien and increasingly hostile people. He had a sudden wild feeling of being trapped.

"I suppose I should be spinning some elaborate counterplot,'' he said hopelessly. "And then, of course, I'll have to go down to the banquet and let Aycharaych read every detail of it—every little thing I know, laid open to his eyes because I just can't suppress my own thoughts—''

Aline's eyes widened, and her slim hand tightened over his. "What is it?'' he asked. "What's your idea?''

"Oh—nothing, Dominic, nothing.'' She smiled wearily. "I have some direct contact with Sol and—''

"You never told me that.''

"No reason for you to know it. I was just wondering if I should report this new trouble or not. Galaxy knows how those muddleheaded bureaucrats back home will react to the news. Probably yank us back and cashier us for incompetence.''

She leaned closer and her words came low and urgent. "Go find Aycharaych, Dominic. Talk to him, keep him busy, don't let him come near me to interfere. He'll know what you're doing, naturally, but he won't be able to do much about it if you're as clever a talker as they say. Make some excuse for me tonight, too, so I don't have to attend the banquet—tell them I'm sick or something. Keep *him* away from me!"

"Sure," he said with a little of his old spirit. "But whatever you're hatching in that lovely head, be quick about it. He'll get at you mighty soon, you know."

He got up and left. She watched him go and there was a dawning smile on her lips.

Flandry was more than a little drunk when the party ended. Wine flowed freely at a Betelgeusean banquet, together with music, food, and dancing girls of every race present. He had enjoyed himself—in spite of everything—most of all, he admitted, he'd enjoyed talking to Aycharaych. The being was a genius of the first order in almost every field, and it had been pleasant to forget the dreadfully imminent catastrophe for a while.

He entered his chambers. Aline stood by a little table, and the muted light streamed off her unbound hair and the shimmering robe she wore. Impulsively, he kissed her.

"Goodnight, honey," he said. "It was nice of you to wait for me."

She didn't leave for her own quarters. Instead, she held out one of the ornate goblets on the table. "Have a nightcap, Dominic," she invited.

"No, thanks. I've had entirely too much."

"For me." She smiled irresistibly. He clinked glasses with her and let the dark wine go down his throat.

It had a peculiar taste, and suddenly he felt dizzy, the room wavered and tilted under him. He sat down on his bed until it had passed, but there was an—oddness—in his head that wouldn't go away.

"Potent stuff," he muttered.

"We don't have the easiest job in the world," said Aline softly. "We deserve a little relaxation." She sat down beside him. "Just tonight, that's all we have. Tomorrow is another day, and a worse day."

He would never have agreed before, his nature was too cool

and self-contained, but now it was all at once utterly reasonable. He nodded.

"And you love me, you know," said Aline.

And he did.

Much later, she leaned close against him in the dark, her hair brushing his cheek, and whispered urgently: "Listen, Dominic, I have to tell you this regardless of the consequences; you have to be prepared for it."

He stiffened with a return of the old tension. Her voice went on, a muted whisper in the night: "I've called Sol on the secret beam and gotten in touch with Fenross. He has brains, and he saw at once what must be done. It's a poor way, but the only way.

"The fleet is already bound for Betelgeuse. The Merseians think most of our strength is concentrated near Llynathawr, but that's just a brilliant piece of deception—Fenross' work. Actually, the main body is quite near, and they've got a new energy screen that'll let them slip past the Betelgeusean cordon without being detected. The night after tomorrow, a strong squadron will land in Gunazar Valley, in the Borthudians, and establish a beachhead. A detachment will immediately move to occupy the capital and capture the Sartaz and his court."

Flandry lay rigid with the shock of it. "But this means war!" he gasped. "Merseia will strike at once, and we'll have to fight Betelgeuse too."

"I know. But the Imperium has decided we'll have a better chance this way. Otherwise, it looks as if Betelgeuse will go to the enemy by default.

"It's up to us to keep the Sartaz and his court from suspecting the truth till too late. We have to keep them here at the palace. The capture of the leaders of an absolute monarchy is always a disastrous blow—Fenross and Walton think Betelgeuse will surrender before Merseia can get here.

"By hook or crook, Dominic, you've got to keep them unaware. That's your job; at the same time, keep on distracting Aycharaych, keep him off my neck."

She yawned and kissed him. "Better go to sleep now," she said. "We've got a tough couple of days ahead of us."

He couldn't sleep. He got up when she was breathing quietly and walked over to the balcony. The knowledge was staggering. That the Empire, the bungling decadent Empire, could pull such a stroke and hope to get away with it!

Something stirred in the garden below. The moonlight was like clotted blood on the figure that paced between two Merseian bodyguards. Aycharaych!

Flandry stiffened in dismay. The Chereionite looked up and he saw the wise smile on the telepath's face. *He knew.*

In the following two days, Flandry worked as he had rarely worked before. There wasn't much physical labor involved, but he had to maintain a web of complications such that the Sartaz would have no chance for a private audience with Merseian and would not leave the capital on one of his capricious journeys. There was also the matter of informing such Betelgeusean traitors as were on his side to be ready, and—

It was nerve-shattering. To make matters worse, something was wrong with him; clear thought was an effort; he had a new and disastrous tendency to take everything at face value. What had happened to him?

Aycharaych excused himself on the morning after Aline's revelation and disappeared. He was out arranging something hellish for the Terrans when they arrived, and there was nothing Flandry could do about it. But at least it left him and Aline free to carry on their own work.

He knew the Merseian fleet could not get near Betelgeuse before the Terrans landed. It is simply not possible to conceal the approximate whereabouts of a large fighting force from the enemy. How it had been managed for Terra, Flandry couldn't imagine. He supposed that it would not be too large a task force which was to occupy Alfzar—but that made its mission all the more precarious.

The tension gathered, hour by slow hour. Aline went her own way, conferring with General Bronson—the human-Betelgeusean officer whom she had made her personal property. Perhaps he could disorganize the native fleet at the moment when Terra struck. The Merseian nobles plainly knew what Aycharaych had found out; they looked at the humans with frank hatred, but they made no overt attempt to warn the Sartaz. Maybe they didn't think they could work through the wall of suborned and confused officials which Flandry had built around him—more likely, Aycharaych had suggested a better plan for them. There was none of the sense of defeat in them which slowly gathered in the human.

It was like being caught in spiderwebs, fighting clinging gray stuff that blinded and choked and couldn't be pulled away.

Flandry grew haggard, he shook with nervousness, and the two days dragged on.

He looked up Gunazar Valley in the atlas. It was uninhabited and desolate, the home of winds and the lair of dragons, a good place for a secret landing—only how secret was a landing that Aycharaych knew all about and was obviously ready to meet?

"There isn't much chance, Aline," he said to her. "Not a prayer, really."

"We'll just have to keep going." She was more buoyant than he, seemed almost cheerful as time stumbled past. She stroked his hair tenderly. "Poor Dominic, it isn't easy for you—"

The huge sun sank below the horizon—the second day, and tonight was the hour of decision. Flandry came into the great conference hall to find it almost empty.

"Where are the Merseians, your majesty?" he asked the Sartaz.

"They all went off on a special mission," snapped the ruler. He was plainly ill-pleased with the intriguing around him, of which he would be well aware.

A special mission—O almighty gods!

Aline and Bronson came in and gave the monarch formal greeting. "With your permission, your majesty," said the general, "I would like to show you something of great importance in about two hours."

"Yes, yes," mumbled the Sartaz and stalked out.

Flandry sat down and rested his head on one hand. Aline touched his shoulder gently. "Tired, Dominic?" she asked.

"Yeah," he said. "I feel rotten. Just can't think these days."

She signaled to a slave, who brought a beaker forward. "This will help," she said. He noticed sudden tears in her eyes. What was the matter?

He drank it down without thought. It caught at him, he choked and grabbed the chair arms for support. "What the devil—" he gasped.

It spread through him with a sudden coolness that ran along his nerves toward his brain. It was like the hand that Aline had laid on his head, calming, soothing—

Clearing!

Suddenly he sprang to his feet. The whole preposterous thing stood forth in its raw grotesquerie—tissue of falsehoods, monstrosity of illogic!

The fleet *couldn't* have moved a whole task force this close without the Merseian intelligence knowing of it. There *couldn't* be a new energy screen that he hadn't heard of. Fenross would never try so fantastic a scheme as the occupation of Betelgeuse before all hope was gone.

He didn't love Aline. She was brave and lovely, but he didn't love her.

But he *had*. Three minutes ago, he had been desperately in love with her.

He looked at her through blurring eyes as the enormous truth grew on him. She nodded, gravely, not seeming to care that tears were running down her cheeks. Her lips whispered a word that he could barely catch.

"Goodbye. Goodbye, my dearest."

4

They had set up a giant televisor screen in the conference hall, with a row of seats for the great of Alfzar. Bronson had also taken the precaution of lining the walls with royal guardsmen whom he could trust—long rows of flashing steel and impassive blue faces, silent and moveless as the great pillars holding up the soaring roof.

The general paced nervously up and down before the screen, looking at his watch unnecessarily often. Sweat glistened on his forehead. Flandry sat relaxed; only one who knew him well could have read the tension that was like a coiled spring in him. Only Aline seemed remote from the scene, too wrapped in her own thoughts to care what went on.

"If this doesn't work, you know, we'll probably be hanged," said Bronson.

"It ought to," answered Flandry tonelessly. "If it doesn't, I won't give much of a damn whether we hang or not."

He was prevaricating there; Flandry was uncommonly fond of living, for all the wistful half-dreams that sometimes rose to torment him.

A trumpet shrilled, high brassy music between the walls and up to the ringing rafters. They rose and stood at attention as the Sartaz and his court swept in.

His yellow eyes were suspicious as they raked the three humans.

"You said that there was to be a showing of an important matter," he declared flatly. "I *hope* that is correct."

"It is, your majesty," said Flandry easily. He was back in his element, the fencing with words, the casting of nets to entrap minds. "It is a matter of such immense importance that it should have been revealed to you weeks ago. Unfortunately, circumstances did not permit that—as the court shall presently see—so that your majesty's loyal general was forced to act on his own discretion with what help we of Terra could give him. But if our work has gone well, the moment of revelation should also be that of salvation."

"It had better be," said the Sartaz ominously. "I warn you—all of you—that I am sick of the spying and corruption the empires have brought with them. It is about time to cut the evil growth from Betelgeuse."

"Terra has never wished Betelgeuse anything but good, your majesty," said Flandry, "and as it happens, we can now offer proof of that. If—"

Another trumpet cut off his voice, and the warder's shout rang and boomed down the hall: "Your majesty, the Ambassador of the Empire of Merseia asks audience."

The huge green form of Lord Korvash of Merseia filled the doorway with a flare of gold and jewelry. And beside him— Aycharaych!

Flandry was briefly rigid with shock. If his brilliant and deadly opponent came into the game now, the whole plan might crash to ruin. It was a daring, precarious structure which Aline had built; the faintest breath of argument could dissolve it—and then the lightning would strike!

It was not permitted to bear firearms within the palace, but the dueling sword was a part of full dress. Flandry drew his with a hiss of metal and shouted aloud: "Seize those beings! They mean to kill the Sartaz!"

Aycharaych's golden eyes widened as he saw what was in Flandry's mind. He opened his mouth to denounce the Terran— and leaped back just in time to avoid the man's murderous thrust.

His own rapier sprang into his hand. In a whirr of steel, the two spies met.

Korvash the Merseian drew his own great blade in sheer reflex. "Strike him down!" yelled Aline. Before the amazed Sartaz could act, she had pulled the stun pistol he carried from the holster and sent the Merseian toppling to the floor.

She bent over him, deftly removing a tiny needle gun from her bodice and palming it on the ambassador. "Look, your majesty," she said breathlessly, "he had a deadly weapon. We knew the Merseians planned no good, but we never thought they would dare—"

The Sartaz's gaze was shrewd on her. "Maybe we'd better wait to hear his side of it," he murmured.

Since Korvash would be in no position to explain his side for a good hour, Aline considered it a victory.

But Flandry—her eyes grew wide and she drew a hissing gasp as she saw him fighting Aycharaych. It was the swiftest, most vicious duel she had ever seen, leaping figures and blades that were a blur of speed, back and forth along the hall in a clamor of steel and blood.

"Stop them!" she cried, and raised the stunner.

The Sartaz laid a hand on hers and took the weapon away. "No," he said. "Let them have it out. I haven't seen such a show in years."

"Dominic—" she whispered.

Flandry had always thought himself a peerless fencer, but Aycharaych was his match. The Chereionite was hampered by gravity, but he had a speed and precision which no human could ever meet, his thin blade whistled in and out, around and under the man's guard to rake face and hands and breast, and he was smiling—smiling.

His telepathy did him little or no good. Fencing is a matter of conditioned reflex—at such speeds, there isn't time for conscious thought. But perhaps it gave him an extra edge, just compensating for the handicap of weight.

Leaping, slashing, thrusting, parrying, clang and clash of cold steel, no time to feel the biting edge or the growing weariness—dance of death while the court stood by and cheered.

Flandry's own blade was finding its mark; blood ran down Aycharaych's gaunt cheeks and his tunic was slashed to red ribbons. The Terran's plan was simple and the only one possible for him. Aycharaych would tire sooner, his reactions would slow—the thing to do was to stay alive that long!

He let the Chereionite drive him backward down the length of the hall, leap by leap, whirling around with sword shrieking in hand. Thrust, parry, riposte, recovery—*whirr, clang!* The rattle of steel filled the hall and the Sartaz watched with hungry eyes.

The end came as he was wondering if he would ever live to see Betelgeuse rise again. Aycharaych lunged and his blade pierced Flandry's left shoulder. Before he could disengage it, the earthman had knocked the weapon spinning from his hand and had his own point against the throat of the Chereionite.

The hall rang with the savage cheering of Betelgeuse's masters. "Disarm them!" shouted the Sartaz.

Flandry drew a sobbing breath. "Your majesty," he gasped, "let me guard this fellow while General Bronson goes on with our show."

The Sartaz nodded. It fitted his sense of things.

Flandry thought with a hard glee; *Aycharaych, if you open your mouth, so help me, I'll run you through.*

The Chereionite shrugged, but his smile was bitter.

"Dominic, Dominic!" cried Aline, between laughter and tears.

General Bronson turned to her. He was shaken by the near ruin. "Can you talk to them?" he whispered. "I'm no good at it."

Aline nodded and stood boldly forth. "Your majesty and nobles of the court," she said, "we shall now prove the statements we made about the treachery of Merseia.

"We of Terra found out that the Merseians were planning to seize Alfzar and hold it and yourselves until their own fleet could arrive to complete the occupation. To that end they are assembling this very night in Gunazar Valley of the Borthudian range. A flying squad will attack and capture the palace—"

She waited until the uproar had subsided. "We could not tell your majesty or any of the highest in the court," she resumed coolly, "for the Merseian spies were everywhere and we had reason to believe that one of them could read your minds. If they had known anyone knew of their plans, they would have acted at once. Instead we contacted General Bronson, who was not high enough to merit their attention, but who did have enough power to act as the situation required.

"We planned a trap for the enemy. For one thing, we mounted telescopic telecameras in the valley. With your permission, I will now show what is going on there this instant."

She turned a switch and the scene came to life—naked crags and cliffs reaching up toward the red moons, and a stir of activity in the shadows. Armored forms were moving about, setting up atomic guns, warming the engines of spaceships—and they were Merseians.

The Sartaz snarled. Someone asked, "How do we know this is not a falsified transmission?"

"You will be able to see their remains for yourself," said

Aline. "Our plan was very simple. We planted atomic land mines in the ground. They are radio-controlled." She held up a small switchbox wired to the televisor, and her smile was grim. "This is the control. Perhaps your majesty would like to press the button?"

"Give it to me," said the Sartaz thickly. He thumbed he switch.

A blue-white glare of hell-flame lit the screen. They had a vision of the ground fountaining upward, the cliffs toppling down, a cloud of radioactive dust boiling up toward the moons, and then the screen went dark.

"The cameras have been destroyed," said Aline quietly. "Now, your majesty, I suggest that you send scouts there immediately. They will find enough remains to verify what the televisor has shown. I would further suggest that a power which maintains armed forces within your own territory is not a friendly one!"

Korvash and Aycharaych were to be deported with whatever other Merseians were left in the system—once Betelgeuse had broken diplomatic relations with their state and begun negotiating an alliance with Terra. The evening before they left, Flandry gave a small party for them in his apartment. Only he and Aline were there to meet them when they entered.

"Congratulations," said Aycharaych wryly. "The Sartaz was so furious he wouldn't even listen to our protestations. I can't blame him—you certainly put us in a bad light."

"No worse than your own," grunted Korvash angrily. "Hell take you for a lying hypocrite, Flandry. You know that Terra has her own forces and agents in the Betelgeusean System, hidden on wild moons and asteroids. It's part of the game."

"Of course I know it," smiled the Terran. "But does the Sartaz? However, it's as you say—the game, the great game. You don't hate the one who beats you in chess. Why then hate us for winning this round?"

"Oh, I don't," said Aycharaych. "There will be other rounds."

"You've lost much less than we would have," said Flandry. "This alliance has strengthened Terra enough for her to halt your designs, at least temporarily. But we aren't going to use that strength to launch a war against you, though I admit that we should. The Empire wants only to keep the peace."

"Because it doesn't dare fight a war," snapped Korvash.

They didn't answer. Perhaps they were thinking of the cities that would not be bombed and the young men that would not have to go out to be killed. Perhaps they were simply enjoying a victory.

Flandry poured wine. "To our future amiable enmity," he toasted.

"I still don't see how you did it," said Korvash.

"Aline did it," said Flandry. "Tell them, Aline."

She shook her head. She had withdrawn into a quietness which was foreign to her. "Go ahead, Dominic," she murmured. "It was really your show."

"Well," said Flandry, not loath to expound, "when we realized that Aycharaych could read our minds, it looked pretty hopeless. How can you possibly lie to a telepath? Aline found the answer—by getting information which just isn't true.

"There's a drug in this system called *sorgan* which has the property of making its user believe anything he's told. Aline fed me some without my knowledge and then told me that fantastic lie about Terra coming in to occupy Alfzar. And, of course, I accepted it as absolute truth. Which you, Aycharaych, read in my mind."

"I was puzzled," admitted the Chereionite. "It just didn't look reasonable to me; but as you said, there didn't seem to be any way to lie to a telepath."

"Aline's main worry was then to keep out of mindreading range," said Flandry. "You helped us there by going off to prepare a warm reception for the Terrans. You gathered all your forces in the valley, ready to blast our ships out of the sky."

"Why didn't you go to the Sartaz with what you knew—or thought you knew?" asked Korvash accusingly.

Aycharaych shrugged. "I knew Captain Flandry would be doing his best to prevent me from doing that and to discredit any information I could get that high," he said. "You yourself agreed that our best opportunity lay in repulsing the initial attack ourselves. That would gain us far more favor with the Sartaz; moreover, since there would have been overt acts on both sides, war between Betelgeuse and Terra would then have been inevitable—whereas if the Sartaz had learned in time of the impending assault, he might have tried to negotiate."

"I suppose so," said Korvash glumly.

"Aline, of course, prevailed on Bronson to mine the valley," said Flandry. "The rest you know. When you yourselves showed up—"

"To tell the Sartaz, now that it was too late," said Aycharaych.

"—we were afraid that the ensuing argument would damage our own show. So we used violence to shut you up until it had been played out." Flandry spread his hands in a gesture of finality. "And that, gentlemen, is that."

"There will be other tomorrows," said Aycharaych gently. "But I am glad we can meet in peace tonight."

The party lasted well on toward dawn. When the aliens left, with many slightly tipsy expressions of goodwill and respect, Aycharaych took Aline's hand in his own bony fingers. His strange golden eyes searched hers, even as she knew his mind was looking into the depths of her own.

"Goodbye, my dear," he said, too softly for the others to hear. "As long as there are women like you, I think Terra will endure."

She watched his tall form go down the corridor and her vision blurred a little. It was strange to think that her enemy knew what the man beside her did not.

ABOUT THE EDITORS

Isaac Asimov has been called "one of America's treasures." Born in the Soviet Union, he was brought to the United States at the age of three (along with his family) by agents of the American government in a successful attempt to prevent him from working for the wrong side. He quickly established himself as one of this country's foremost science fiction writers and writer about everything, and although now approaching middle age, he is going stronger than ever. He long ago passed his age and weight in books, and with some 285 to his credit threatens to close in on his I.Q. His sequel to THE FOUNDATION TRILOGY—FOUNDATION'S EDGE —was one of the best-selling books of 1982 and 1983.

Martin H. Greenberg has been called (in THE SCIENCE FICTION AND FANTASY BOOK RE-VIEW) "The King of the Anthologists"; to which he replied—"It's good to be the King!" He has produced more than seventy of them, usually in collaboration with a multitude of co-conspirators, most frequently the two who have given you WIZARDS. A Professor of Regional Analysis and Political Science at the University of Wisconsin-Green Bay, he is still trying to publish his weight.

Charles G. Waugh is a Professor of Psychology and Communications at the University of Maine at Augusta who is still trying to figure out how he got himself into all this. He has also worked with many collaborators, since he is basically a very friendly fellow. He has done some fifty anthologies and single-author collections, and especially enjoys locating unjustly ignored stories. He also claims that he met his wife via computer dating—her choice was an entire fraternity or him, and she has only minor regrets.